BRIAN DRINKWATER

Book of
"THE GRAVE"

Twisted H2O Publishing

Book of
"The Grave"

For more information on this
and other titles, please visit:

AuthorBrianDrinkwater.com

Twisted H2O Publishing

ISBN: 0615995691
ISBN-13: 978-0615995694

DEDICATION

This book is dedicated to my wife for putting up with me for all these years, and for supporting my dream of breathing life into each of my characters...even William.

I love you.

.

"Death is but a tale we must all someday read"

William Grave, 1880

ONE

The scraping of steel links over coarse pavement, though muffled by distance, rattled the eardrums and mind of Geoffrey McDaniel. For nearly five minutes his sweat glands had been in full production, dowsing his body and clothing in a cool layer of perspiration.

He'd ducked into Mrs. Moore's side yard, as opposed to making a mad dash home, for one reason only. With his house still a good fifty yards away and his pursuer's four to two advantage in limbs, he knew that he had no chance of outrunning the vicious creature. At least huddled beneath Mrs. Moore's azalea bush he stood a chance of eluding the dog's elevated senses. The flowering bush was in full bloom and abundant with the sweet scent of spring but even with its dominating hold on the night air, he feared that it still wouldn't be enough to mask the seemingly appealing scent of the ten year old meal cowering beneath its branches.

The day had been relatively pleasant until his chance encounter with the neighborhood terror. He and his best friend Peter Madison had just concluded a lengthy Back to The Future marathon, capped off by the devouring of a massive Oreo ice cream cake, bought in celebration of

Peter's father's first published book. It had been a great night, full of fun and carefree laughs and with the promise of the soon ending school year rapidly approaching, the boys were looking forward to many similar evenings to come.

Mr. Madison had offered Geoffrey a ride home when the evening's festivities had ended and looking back on the offer, he now wished that he'd accepted. But his house was only a few streets over and having made the short journey on countless occasions, both day and night, he'd seen no harm in letting his legs play chauffeur for the evening.

He had nearly made it home, rounding the corner of McMulholland Boulevard onto Shady lane when he'd spotted the four legged member of the Weaver family. The dog had been standing motionless in the center of the dimly lit, two lane road, as if anticipating Geoffrey's arrival.

The dog had been tied up in the Weaver's back yard earlier that day. Geoffrey had seen it from his bedroom window, securely tethered to the corner of the neighbor's house. Though the dog's presence beyond the limiting confines of its fenced in yard had startled Geoffrey, it hadn't surprised him. The German Shepherd was a beast of an animal, in both size and demeanor. It had spent its first year of life training with the local police department before deemed UN-trainable by the K-9 unit and subsequently beginning its journey from one adoptive family to the next. Somewhere along the way it had acquired a taste for neighborhood pets, though the Weavers had done their best to conceal that fact. Now it seemed that the four legged monster was eager for an upgrade to its carnivorous diet and leg of boy was at the top of the menu.

Geoffrey, though struggling to remain motionless, could not control the nervous tremors continually plaguing his tension riddled body. A few of the bottom branches rattled with each quiver, forcing him to readjust beneath the bush until eventually lying flat on his stomach.

The intensity of the scraping chain increased, as did Geoffrey's fear. The dog was going to find him. He knew it. The damn thing had set its mind on the fifth grader as a meal and, based on its persistent pursuit, appeared to have no intention of forfeiting its hard sought after craving.

A cool breeze blew over the cowering boy, traveling up his sweat soaked back toward the street. Geoffrey's heartbeat quickened as he imagined the wind lifting his perspiring scent into the air and carrying it to the hungry beast's over active olfactory glands.

At times his imagination could be a blessing. It had always been a beloved tool of his when creating music on the piano or drawings in his overstuffed sketchpad. At times such as this however, it seemed more like a curse. All he could imagine was the ferocious dog plucking his scent from the air and using it like a map to locate the prize it thought it had lost. He imagined the four legged hunter tearing around the corner of the house and making a B-line for its cowering prey.

If his sense of sight and sound hadn't been present to overrule his brain's intensely realistic imagination, he would've sworn that the dog had already begun its determined gnawing; searching for the bone it would eventually take great pleasure in burying.

The very real pain inflicted by the imaginary attack grew so intense that he couldn't help but swat at its fictitious source, causing the bush to spring to life, its leaves rustling in the night.

Geoffrey froze as the bush settled and silence claimed the air. The dragging chain's familiar scraping no longer haunted the street. Scanning his surroundings he half expected to find that the evil mutt was standing beside him, having taken advantage of its prey's momentary distraction. The yard was deserted though. Other than the occasional ant or moth, it was all his. Comforted by his solitude and the animal's apparent loss of interest,

Geoffrey's heart rate slowed.

More at ease, he began to entertain the thought of emerging from his hideout of dirt and flowers and making a run for the far more assuring safety of his own home. It was only five houses away and if he was able to get to his feet without any noise, he could make a mad dash out of Mrs. Moore's side yard and down the street, taking the dog by surprise. That is if the animal was even still out there.

No that's ridiculous, he thought to himself, vetoing his own idiotic idea. Most likely the dog was still out there, somewhere and though he may hold the element of surprise over the K-9, the thought that he could outrun a physically dominant, police trained attack dog was retarded. Most likely he'd round the corner of the safe haven that Mrs. Moore's house had provided and run smack into the awaiting creature. Once the dog had him in his jaws, there'd be no escaping.

No, running from his current position provided no better odds than did playing Russian roulette with a fully loaded revolver. He had to stay where he was, all night if need be.

As he prepared for his night beneath the sheltering plant, a faint crack emanated from the front yard. Geoffrey again stared out at the street, scanning the surrounding area for any signs of movement. Maybe someone was taking a late night stroll, he hoped. Maybe he wouldn't have to spend the night in the neighbor's garden after all.

All hopes of a savior quickly vanished though, as a small shadow slowly appeared from around the front corner of the house, followed by the massive head of the surreptitious beast. Just as Geoffrey had used the bush to conceal his location, the dog had used the house to do the same. The dog knew where he was. It had known all along. It was hard to fathom that the intellectual abilities required to not only stage such a deceptive feat of trickery but to pull it off as well could be so deftly displayed by an animal so far down on the evolutionary ladder but the dog had done just that. For nearly five minutes it had dragged its chain around the street, continuing to announce its presence before relocating to the grass where its movements could go undetected, lulling its victim into a false sense of security by tricking Geoffrey into thinking it had finally given up and moved on to its next late night escapade. The whole time though, the animal had been concealing itself just around the corner, hoping that its sought after meal would be stupid enough to emerge from beneath the bush.

However, even though the dog displayed an exceptional ability in the art of logical reasoning, it did not appear to have much in the way of patience. More likely than not, it had grown weary of waiting. It wanted its meal. It wanted to see just what its prey was doing and in its impatient glance, had forfeited its hideout.

Geoffrey and the German Shepherd locked eyes, the two vigilantly studying one another in hopes of predicting the other's next move. Suddenly the dog sprang to its feet, tearing around the corner of the house at full stride. The chain around its neck leapt into the air, striking the corner of the house with a loud snap.

Geoffrey knew that he couldn't run. By the time he slid out from beneath the bush and got to his feet, the dog would be air born, teeth snapping with hungry anticipation. The time for hide and seek was over. A defensive stand was the only hope he had left. He frantically dragged himself even further beneath his inferior protector, pulling his knees to this chest in an attempt to entwine himself around the narrow trunk. At any moment the once imaginary burn of the dogs clenching jaws would become reality, their ferocious excitement fueled by the warm blood of their captured prey.

Terror once again washed over him, evident by the blizzard of leaves and flower pedals raining down around him.

Too much time had passed, he thought to himself. He should be dog food by now but no bites had come, at least not that he'd felt. He feared that maybe his adrenaline levels had spiked and were somehow acting as a form of Novocain, numbing his body to the excruciating pain of its own consumption. He wanted to look, to see if his fears were true but his mind wouldn't let him. If his leg was already half eaten he didn't want to see it. That would be like asking for the accompanying pain, which had so graciously remained at bay, to suddenly arrive in full force. He didn't want to see his own demise. He didn't want to see the dog feasting on chunks of his own flesh. No, he definitely did not want to see any of that...but he had to. Something in his mind was fascinated by the lack of pain. Maybe no pain meant no dog. Maybe he was safe. He had to look, just a quick peek to satisfy his curiosity.

Geoffrey opened his eyes and looked at his leg. All was intact, his bones safely concealed beneath muscle, skin and jeans. Relief washed over him. He turned toward the street once again, just in time to see a snarling set of drool coated fangs lunging toward him.

Geoffrey shot up, nearly casting the denim covers from his bed. Before sleep could fade and reality set in, he jerked his head from side to side, searching for the lunging creature. Instead, only the glow of his alarm clock caught his eye.

Five o'clock Thursday morning. The clock's alarm would not begin its rousing mantra of famous movie quotes for another hour yet but having managed to survive a dream of such intensity and realism, Geoffrey found little interest in tempting fate by returning to sleep. He'd heard of tales in which people had died in their dreams, only never to wake the next morning. Hollywood had even done an extensive series on such a topic; something to do with a guy named Freddie Grubber...or something like that. He couldn't be too sure since he never had cared much for films of such a grotesque nature. His interests had always lied more with science fiction and the mind bending plot twists of sophisticated dramas.

Blinking his eyes, in an attempt to bring his bedroom back into focus, Geoffrey recalled the image of the vicious dog from his past. This hadn't been the first time such a dream had startled him awake. He'd had the same one at least a dozen times before; the last one being on his twelfth birthday. Now, at age fifteen, he had hoped that the horrible memory had finally been laid to rest by his maturing mind but clearly the attack, which had left his body pocked with scars, still held a room at the cerebral inn.

A muffled series of deep barks echoed through the early morning air, just beyond his drawn blinds. Geoffrey jumped but quickly let out a quiet chuckle at his ridiculous reaction. The dog, which had caused his deep-seeded fear of "man's best friend", had long since been put down; sentenced to death for the brutal attack it had engaged in five years earlier. The dog's owners had also left the neighborhood since the incident, though their whereabouts were far less clear than that of their dog's. Most likely they'd chosen a new home far from the neighborhood which had lambasted them for their carelessness and the judge who had declared them, and their pet, a menace to society...just before awarding Geoffrey and his parents a large sum of money for their suffering.

Though scarred by the violent encounter, Geoffrey did not share the judge's harsh opinion. The Weavers had always been kind and caring people. Unfortunately, at the ages of seventy-two and seventy-seven, the dog's size and mentality was far beyond the control of the elderly couple and no matter what attempts they made to keep the dog safely contained within the confines of their property, it always seemed to break free and run amuck throughout town.

It had simply been a case of bad luck that he'd come across the dog that night when its craving for blood had outweighed that of its typical canned food.

Since the Weaver's departure, numerous other families had come and gone from the neighboring house, none staying longer than six month to a year at a time though. Some of the kids in the neighborhood believed that the house was haunted by the dead dog and that, each night, it frantically ran from room to room, searching for the owners it had once loved. They claimed that that was why no one could ever spend more than a year in the house. Eventually, the mysterious noises would make their way to the master bedroom, rousing the current owners from their sleep to the horrific sight of a blood soaked dog staring back at them from beside the bed.

While the thought of awakening to such a ghastly sight did frighten Geoffrey, he was intelligent enough to recognize the story's misplaced presence in a world governed by science and reality; not to mention the fact that the house was a rental, which was reason enough to explain its frequent turnover in occupants without having to resort to tales of ghosts and goblins.

No, the dog was dead and gone. This new bark could have only come from one place, the mouth of the new pet next-door. And, though Geoffrey wanted nothing to do with this new, four legged neighbor, he did recognized that his own fears were not the fault of the harmless animal.

Prince was a one year old yellow lab who, unlike its predecessor, didn't possess a mean bone in his body. He belonged to the McGregor family, a younger couple with two small children. Not once had Geoffrey seen Prince act in a hostile manor with his two younger family members. Most of the time it seemed that the dog should have been the one living in fear, seeing as the kids frequently chased him around the yard, playfully tackling him to the ground. Prince seemed to love it though, so Geoffrey felt at ease.

Shifting beneath what few lengths of fabric still remained on his bed after his startled awakening, Geoffrey's hand brushed against the fitted sheet on which he sat. It was soaked. He hadn't wet the bed since he was four and he doubted his encounter with the imaginary terror had regressed his mind and body all the way back to those toddler years. Curious though, he lifted his hand to his nose and took a deep breath.

Sweat.

The covers were wet, the sheets were wet but the wettest of all were the flannel pajama pants clinging to his legs. Though he had just showered the night before, this pungent cologne of human secretion suggested that, maybe another was in order. He swung his bare feet out from beneath their burrow of warmth and into the cool climate of an excessively air conditioned house.

If it weren't for the calendar by the door to remind him that it was only September, Geoffrey might have expected to find a snow covered landscape beyond the walls of his house but the likeliness of a winter wonderland so early in the year seemed nearly impossible. No, his mother just had a thing about heat...she hated it and as a result, always kept the thermostat hovering around sixty degrees. He would've turned it up and occasionally he had but the resulting warmth generated by a normally set thermostat was in no way incentive enough to choose heat over hard to come by peace between he and his mother, so he remained cold.

Having gone to bed shirtless, Geoffrey scurried to his dresser for a T-shirt to aid in his icy journey down the hall to the upstairs bathroom.

Again the neighboring dog declared its presence from beyond the blind covered windows. Geoffrey released his grip on the dresser drawer, puzzled by the typically quiet dog's uncharacteristic rant.

The barking increased as Geoffrey, driven by curiosity, grabbed hold of the blind's dangling cord and yanked down. In the side yard, of the neighboring house, stood Prince at full alert. Once staring at the outward facing surface of Geoffrey's blinds he now eyed Geoffrey himself, a steady stream of drool seeping from the corners of his snarling jowls. With a visual on his now obvious point of interest, the dog growled and gnashed his teeth between barks, all the while pulling at the long chain which bound him to his dog house nearly thirty feet away.

Geoffrey's heart began to race as his body froze. He wanted to shut the blinds but couldn't. The Weaver's dog had acted the same way on numerous occasions before the attack. Now, Prince was displaying the very same behavior.

Geoffrey couldn't help but think of the neighborhood kid's and their silly tales of a ghost dog. What if it was true? What if the spirit of the dead dog was in fact real? What if Prince had come across the wandering ex-pet and now, he himself housed the spirit of the evil creature?

Shuddering at the thought, he quickly lowered the blinds.

TWO

"Peter. Peter. Wake up Peter," the adorably soft voice of four year old Emily Madison beckoned from beside her older brother's bed. "It's time to get up. You have to go to school," the persistent toddler continued, giving her brother's shoulder a light shake.

Peter was awake. He had been for several minutes now, just lying in wait for his cue.

After several months of this routine, the morning awakening had become somewhat of a game. Each morning Emily would march into the room, making as much noise as she could with the door and then, by stomping across the room toward her sleeping sibling. With each "Peter", she would inch closer and closer until, standing beside him, she'd lay her head on the pillow and whisper from mere inches away. That was the signal for him to spring up and scare his playful participant. Emily would jump into the air and take off down the hall screaming, "Mommy!", the entire way.

Before Emily had been born, Peter had always thought that having a little sister wouldn't be all that fun, at least not until she was older and better able to communicate and interact on a more sophisticated level. He'd been wrong. Emily was one of the best things in his life and he loved every second he got to spend with the little angel.

"Peter, you have to get up sleepy head," Emily continued.

Peter could feel the pillow shift beneath him. In a moment the time for relaxation would be over and his day would jump to a start with a screaming four year old and a few laughs. Waiting, anticipating the whisper, it seemed as if Emily was taking a longer pause than usual before issuing the green light statement. She knew what was coming and though hesitant, he knew that she couldn't wait for her morning scare.

"Peter," Emily finally whispered.

"Roar!" Peter filled the room with an echoing cry as his eye's burst open and his head jumped from the pillow, only this time he was not met with the usual scream and quickly retreating toddler. Instead he was greeted by the smack of a tiny palm and five little digits across his cheek.

"It's not polite to scare people," Emily admonished her older brother, her face portraying a maturity far beyond that of any typical four-year-old.

Peter was taken aback. The unexpected change to their routine had caught him completely off guard and while the slap had not hurt, he didn't know how to react. He was supposed to posses the upper hand in this situation but suddenly their roles had been reversed. He wasn't sure whether he should laugh or act as though he'd just taken a punch from a heavyweight contender. For all he knew, he was the one now expected to run down the hall, screaming for mommy.

Emily continued to stare at her surprised big brother, her seriousness subsiding as a slight grin attempted to push past the playfully pouty lips of the little girl.

Peter grabbed his little sister and hoisted her into the air, bringing her crashing to the bed as his fingers went to work on her sides. The previously anticipated scream, which Emily had so well controlled, finally poured out of her as her arms and legs flailed wildly in a half hearted attempt to break free from her captor. After nearly thirty-seconds of good, hard tickling, Peter released the young girl and laughed as she hopped from the bed and took off down the hall, screaming for her mommy the entire way.

With his morning duty completed, it was time to get up and join the world in yet another day of what he liked to refer to as "the societal advancement toward world of peace, hope and harmonious cohabitation". It was a tall order, even for someone of his aspirations.

"If you dream small dreams, only small things happen," he always told himself.

Before the senate could make space for his idealistic views however, he had to take a whiz.

*****

The kitchen was filled with the consuming aroma of bacon, hissing and popping its way to crispness on top of the large, stainless steel griddle built directly into the counter beside the inset gas stove of the granite island. The griddle had been a Christmas gift for Peter's father a few years back and was just another extravagant upgrade to a house once considered ordinary and past its prime.

Though one of the largest houses in the neighborhood; Peter's parents had gotten an amazing deal on the partial fixer-upper. Its previous owners had been an elderly couple by the names of Mr. and Mrs. Webber. They'd loved the house and had done their best to maintain the large, four bedroom dwelling but both had been in their late eighties, making it nearly impossible for them to keep up with the needs of the aging structure.

When Mr. Webber had died, reality had set in and Mrs. Webber had decided that it was time to let the house go. There was no way that she could've handled such a large place on her own and with no family to help out, she'd decided that it was finally time to check herself into a retirement home, where she could wait out her final years before once again taking her place by her husband's side.

Mrs. Webber had not been looking to make a killing on the sale. She'd only wanted enough money to help pay for her new home and supply herself with enough yarn to continue a lifelong passion for knitting. So, as one would expect of a house of its size, priced so far below market value, there had been much competition to snatch up the amazing find. Peter's parents had been one such set of eager hunters.

In its first day on the market, Mrs. Webber had received eight offers. Some had been ridiculously low. Others had been a bit more than the asking price. Peter's parents had offered exactly what the kind old lady had asked. Later they had learned that it had actually been then nine year old Peter who had won the house for his family. Mrs. Webber loved children. In her earlier years she had run her own daycare from the house. She had always loved the sounds of little voices echoing throughout the halls and tiny feet stomping around the rooms. Unfortunately she had never been able to have children of her own and seeing Peter with his two parents had touched that emotional void.

"I don't care about the money," she had told James Madison, Peter's father. "This house has seen so many children grow up within its walls that I just couldn't bear the thought of knowing it might never hear a precious young voice again. It's been far too long already and I think it's about time for another family to bring joy to this lovely old place. Maybe someday you will even have more children," she had added with a sense of hope.

"We hope so," Peter's mother had responded.

Two years later, Mrs. Webber got her wish with the addition of Emily to the Madison family. Unfortunately, the kind old woman had never received the good news. Only six months after leaving her lifelong home for the cold white walls of The Meadow View Retirement Home,

Mrs. Webber had died of what most, including the doctors, had declared to be nothing more than natural old age. Peter's mother had a different opinion though.

"Mrs. Webber spent the majority of her life with her husband. Anyone who can stay together that long becomes more than just husband and wife. They become one. One soul, split between two bodies. When one of those bodies goes away, half of that soul moves on to a better place," Rebecca Madison had tried explaining to her son.

"You mean heaven?" Peter eagerly followed his mother's lesson.

"That's right baby. When that half of the soul goes to heaven, the remaining half feels lonely. It remains on earth, incomplete and wishing it could again be with its other half. Sure death is natural, all death, only its causes differ. Mrs. Webber died of a broken soul but now she is in heaven with her husband again, their soul complete and both happier than they could have ever dreamt, because heaven is a place of only happiness. There is no sadness in heaven."

"But what if you get hurt or cut yourself? I know that doesn't make me happy. What if it happens in heaven?" Peter attempted to understand.

"Pain is only a part of life in this world. You wouldn't get hurt or feel pain in heaven and if you did, someone would always be there to take care of you."

"You or dad?"

"Maybe, but you don't have to worry about that for a very long time. No one is going anywhere. The only thing you need to worry about now is having fun and being a kid. All I ask is that you always remember that your father and I love you very much and that no matter what may separate us in the future, we will always be with you in one form or another."

Looking back on the conversation he'd had with his mother so many years ago, it really was surprising that he hadn't spent the next few years worrying about either his parent's or his own mortality. Most young children couldn't handle such a mature concept but Peter trusted his mother. If she said that he would never be alone, then he believed her. She had always done right by her word and never given him any reason to believe otherwise. As far as he was concerned, Rebecca Madison could do no wrong.

"Shit," Mrs. Madison softly exclaimed as a drop of grease exploded into the air, landing on her exposed arm.

"That's one dollar mom," Peter playfully admonished his mother for her slip.

Tucked in the far back corner of the counter, between the refrigerator and the sink, stood a large flour jar filled just over half way with one dollar bills. The Madison family had made an agreement a few years back. Any swear uttered within earshot of another family member required the deposit of a single dollar into the jar. Peter had made the first contribution at age twelve with the regurgitation of a derogatory name he'd picked up at school. The F-word, followed by "nut" had cost him a dollar and had not been spoken since. It had also landed him his first taste of Irish Spring soap. Because of that slip, he now knew what morning sunrise tasted like and it wasn't nearly as pleasant as its name suggested. Since then very little of his own currency had come to reside within the glass container of sin. Most belonged to his father, the result of many long and frustrating sessions locked within the fourth bedroom of the house, which had been converted into a private office for his writing. Often, one could walk by the office and hear the vulgar words of frustration erupting from the old man's mouth. Peter liked to stand just outside the door while he worked, waiting for that sudden burst of expletive laden frustration to find its way out of the room and when it did, he would respond by shouting, "One dollar old man". Moments later a dollar bill would slide out from beneath the door and Peter would immediately snatch it up and deposit it into the awaiting flour jar.

For the moment Mr. Madison quietly sat at the kitchen table, flipping through the morning paper as he did every morning, while Emily sat beside him sipping a tall glass of orange juice. Upon seeing Peter enter the kitchen Emily released the glass and jumped down from her chair, screaming as she made her way around the island toward the perceived safety of her mother's leg.

"Mommy, mommy, he's gonna get me again!" Emily playfully cried.

"Sweetie, I don't want you standing here. The grease is hot and I don't want you to get burned," Mrs. Madison responded to her daughter's plea for help.

"But he's gonna tickle me again."

"Peter, are you going to tickle your sister again?"

"Of course not," Peter lied.

"See? He won't tickle you."

"He's lying!" Emily perceptively read her older brother.

"Sweetie, you need to go back to the table and drink your juice," Mrs. Madison urged, meanwhile attempting to free her leg from the surprisingly strong child's grasp.

Emily finally let go and returned to the table, eyeing her brother the entire way. Peter just stared back, smiling deviously as he tracked his sister's nervous migration across the kitchen.

Emily raised her hand and waved a fist. "You'd better watch it dude," she warned. "I know how to use this."

Peter laughed. She never ceased to amaze him. It seemed every day she had some new expression or mannerism that made him forget that she was only four. This had been a new one, most likely picked up from their limited time allowed in front of the television.

"You have time for some bacon and eggs this morning, sweetie?" Mrs. Madison addressed her eldest child as he lifted his backpack from its position on top of one of the island barstools.

"I don't think so. I have to get to school early today. I have a big test first period and I want as much time as possible to study so I don't fail."

"I highly doubt that you will ever fail at anything in your life, let alone a test," Mrs. Madison praised her son. "Why don't you study here while you eat?"

Peter glanced at the table and at Emily. Again she waived her fist and tightened her lips.

"I don't really feel safe here," Peter joked. "Besides, I study better when I'm at school."

"Well, you have to eat, so how about something for the road?" his mother insisted as she finished dabbing the grease from the freshly fried bacon.

Peter rounded the island and snatched a few pieces of the crispy flesh before heading for the door.

"Ah," Mrs. Madison stopped her retreating son as she pointed at her cheek.

Peter again rounded the island and planted a light kiss on his mother's cheek.

"Don't forget your father and sister as well."

Peter slowly passed by the tough little girl at the table and slipping around his father's engrossing paper, planted a kiss on the old man's stubbly cheek.

"What about me?" Emily complained.

"What about you?" Peter joked as he approached her. "Is it safe?"

"Only one way to find out."

Peter watched as Emily slowly formed a fist in her lap. Quickly he grabbed both of her arms and landed a long wet kiss on the middle of her forehead.

"Ewe!" Emily complained as she frantically wiped away the slobbery show of affection.

Peter laughed and jostled her hair before exiting the house through the kitchen door.

THREE

Steven Oliver Bishop. The name oozed of arrogance and while it was true that more often than not he did hold himself in the highest regard, he hated the term snob. Often the condescending term portrayed a man of not just refined taste and abundant wealth but also of overwhelmingly feminine mannerisms and traits. Steven was no such man. He enjoyed violent sports and in no way found half naked cheerleaders offensive or degrading. He preferred beer over any of its more exotic counterparts and when it came to steak, the bloodier the better.

The biggest dividing trait though, between he and his "snobby" brethren, was his utter hatred for loafers. Men who ran around in loafers were the queerest of the snob crowd. It was as though they'd just given up; relinquishing all prior claim to their God given manhood by diving head first into the alarmingly expanding pool of fagottry.

The only men worse than the loafer wearing fagots though, were the ones who attempted to conceal their homoerotic ways by stomping around in construction boots. The unblemished boots were often enough to indicated the owner's lack of masculinity. That combined with perfectly manicured finger nails and immaculately groomed facial hair was all that Steven needed to determine which team the pole smoker was on.

Sneakers were Steven's shoe of choice, always had been and always would be. They were the only truly masculine footwear and Steven was, what seemed to be a dying breed, one of the few, true men left in the world.

Michael Oliver Bishop had been the man responsible for burdening his son with the pretentious title, sighting that the name, Oliver Bishop, could be traced back hundreds of years to their eldest European ancestor, Sir. Oliver Bishop and that every man in the family since then had carried the distinguished title. Though always respectful, at least to his face, when receiving such a lesson from his father, Steven had every intention of bringing an end to the ridiculous tradition. He was only thankful Oliver had at some point been relegated to the middle name, allowing room for a more current and less embarrassing title to claim top billing. One of his ancestors had probably felt the same as he but had lacked the backbone to launch such a devastating assault on the family heritage. He lacked no such bone.

As much as he despised his father's ridiculous devotion to tradition, he did hold at least some respect for the sentimental bastard. The crazy bitch Steven called mother, had originally wanted to burden her son with the name Stefán. Thankfully his father's blatant hatred for queers had overruled that potentially stigmatizing decision. Steven was the compromise and he could live with that, keeping his more historical, middle name hidden from the world.

Apart from his politically incorrect, though beneficial, queer bashing mentality, Michael Oliver Bishop had been good for only one thing...money. The man was a business genius. The owner of the largest chain of car dealerships in all of Nevada, Mr. Bishop had been able to provide a life for his family commonly achieved only in books and movies. And even though the man had abandoned his wife and two children to run off with some nineteen-year-old hooker in Vegas three years ago, Steven couldn't hold a grudge. The man had built an empire from nothing. He'd established a fortune that would ensure his children comfortable, carefree lives and considering that his whore-bag mother had herself been less than faithful, he really couldn't blame the man for finding a younger, more taught piece of ass to fall asleep in at night.

The nasally whine of a revving engine quickly returned Steven from his trip into the Bishop family history. Looking to his left, a lowered, ridiculously accessorized Honda Civic stood beside his brand new Dodge Charger. The little car lurched forward with each rev, dying to release all four of its cylinders on the pavement ahead.

Steven knew what the import driving, speed demon wanted. He'd behaved in the same manor on numerous occasions, though looking much less retarded in doing so. The driver was all of sixteen years old, only a couple of years younger than Steven but seemingly many more with his blue hair and patchy goatee. The teenage circus freak stared at the American muscle car, ridicule and jest seeping from his disapproving glare.

Steven lowered the charger's window with the push of a button. Normally he wanted nothing to do with such a loser but it was as if a comic book had come to life beside him and he couldn't resist his nagging curiosity.

The Honda driver leaned over the passenger seat and slowly began cranking down his window. This drew a smile from Steven.

"What the fuck are you smiling at?"

Fighting back his laughter, "Maybe next time, if you spend a bit less on stickers, you might be able to afford power windows."

"I don't need no fucking power windows. It's what's under the hood that counts."

"So, how many lawn mower power is that thing anyway?"

"Fucking lawn mower, ha, ha. This baby has two hundred and twenty horses, with dual exhaust, air intake and a few extra tweaks."

Steven continued to battle his amusement.

"You think that's funny huh? Beats the shit out of that piece of crap you're driving."

He couldn't let an insult like that go, especially when directed at a living legend of American automotive engineering. "Do you know what this is?" Steven posed the question with no intention of allowing the obnoxious twerp to answer. "This is a 2012 Dodge Charger Daytona R/T with a 450 horsepower HEMI V8...no tweaks necessary."

A pause in the other driver's response confirmed to Steven that he'd already won this confrontation...as if there had even been a question in the matter.

"Oh, yeah, Well, it looks like an American piece of shit to me. You wanna go?"

If the naive kid had been in his face when issuing such a challenge, Steven would have just decked the misguided youth. On the road however, he let his vehicle do the decking.

The sixteen-year-old impatiently shifted in his seat, his vision sharing time with the red light before them and his opponent to his right. Steven remained calm. He had all the confidence in the world that his modern, American muscle car would easily stomp the tricked out rice burner. Glancing in the rear view mirror he smiled as he imagined the show that was about to go down for those behind them. Depressing the clutch he set the Dodge beast in gear. The cross traffic began to slow and with the last few cars slipping through the intersection, the green light flashed to life. The Japanese roller-skate peeled out on the pavement, burning away at the rubber surrounding the ridiculously oversized set of rims before darting across the intersection in a frantic race for the invisible finish line ahead.

Steven slowly accelerated, shifting gears as he made a right turn into Mills Lake Subdivision while glancing in his rearview mirror just in time to see the police cruiser he'd spotted behind them, quickly take pursuit of the law breaking delinquent.

"Kids."

Mills Lake was like many of the subdivisions boasting entrances on Whistler Avenue; middle to upper middle class and kept neat and tidy under the ever watchful eye of a tyrannical homeowner's association. Communities like these were what kept Mercedes and other foreign, luxury car companies in business. With homeowners ever intent on matching or one-upping their neighboring competition, it was no surprise that nearly every house boasted a shiny black toy in the driveway. Steven preferred his American dream car to those claiming overseas origins.

As he turned left onto Lake View Terrace one such competition driven homeowner slowly rolled through a stop sign, likely in route to begin yet another arduous day, confined to the stuffy, repressive walls of some downtown high rise.

Even though work was and would always be more an escape from boredom than a source of necessary income, Steven still wished to make something of himself and the more liked portions of his name. A powerfully confident personality and extensive knowledge of the athletic world made him already well equipped for a role in sports broadcasting and it was his goal to answer that calling. Only his senior year of high school and a neglectful, yet controlling mother stood in his way.

Arlene Bishop was, as far as society was concerned, the most loving mother a boy could hope to have. She did and had always done her best to shower her two sons with all of the love and attention she could...in public at least. When not attempting to win an Oscar for best performance in a mothering role, she hardly gave her sons a second thought. More often than not she passed the

23

time of her carefree life by fucking everything on two legs and once even a cripple with just one.

Steven's father had known about his wife's infidelities, hell at least once he'd even arranged such an encounter, egger to watch his then young bride fucked to within an inch of her life by another man.

The extreme differences between he and his brother, Paul Oliver Bishop, had Steven convinced that his younger sibling had been a direct result of one such voyeuristic encounter, though he'd never been able to prove such a claim.

Paul was seven years his younger and far more the nerd than was Steven. While Steven was involved in football, baseball and every other athletic endeavor his busy schedule allowed, Paul had his nose buried deep within the pages of literary masterpieces far beyond his peer's current reading levels.

Steven had no such interest or talent for the comprehension or creation of such art and therefore had relied on Cliff's notes to aid in his successful advancement through the grades. On the other hand, Paul seemed to know just about everything, possessing a greater than gifted intelligence, arguably superior to many twice or three times his age.

Surprisingly though, as different as they were from one another, neither had ever desired to emulate the other's personality or skills, leading to a fairly uneventful and smooth cohabitation. Steven did what he wanted and Paul the same, never threatening, ridiculing or belittling one another for their differences. Steven directed this negativity towards other targets.

Apart from sports, there was no other activity he enjoyed more than nerd bashing. They never stood their ground and always cowered beneath his dominant oppression. He liked the power he held over the weaker class and loved the status bestowed upon him by the socially elite faction of Eagle Roost High. He was a god among his peers, living in the now and enjoying every minute of it, dependent on his family's financial status to back him through whatever UN-pleasantries might arise as a result of such a carefree lifestyle.

Dessert Rose Court came into view as he rounded a tight turn towards the back of the subdivision. He turned left onto the short cul-de-sac. Only three houses occupied the oblong roadway; one to either side and one straight ahead. Each one boasting a sophisticated elegance common with the numerous surrounding subdivisions and though the two story miniature mansions were undeniably beautiful, Steven couldn't dream of passing life within the confining walls of such diminutive structures. Hell the first floor's minute eighteen hundred square feet was still a shade smaller than his entire wing of the Bishop family's hillside manor. But as much as he despised the idea of such confined living quarters, he understood, at least in part, the unfortunate restrictions a limited income could create. His best friend and inhabitant of the center house was one such unfortunate soul.

The Charger's engine growled as it passed over the curb and came to a rest at the center of Dexter Brice's brick paved driveway. Steven honked the horn, the deep blast reverberating off of the surrounding houses and their statuary decorations, acting as a final wake up call to those whose alarms had failed to rouse them from slumber. The side door, which commonly displayed the comic sight of his groggy eyed friend, remained closed with not so much as a signal to indicate his tardy pal's need for more time. Steven honked repeatedly. Still, there was no sign of Dexter.

"God damn it," he huffed as he jabbed at the ignition button and yanked up on the parking brake.

The heavy car door swung open, releasing its impatient driver onto the ornately paved driveway. Approaching the house he half expected a frantic Dexter to come darting from the doorway at any moment, but as he approached the door with still no sign of his tardy friend it was clear that his fist would have to accomplish the job that his car horn had not.

Four firm strikes seemed sufficient. No answer. A second, more forceful set struck the wooden surface, demanding Steven's presence be acknowledged. Still nothing.

Steven attempted to peer into the kitchen through the door's glass insert, however the frosted panes made it impossible to make out any real detail within the darkly lit room.

"Asshole," Steven muttered as he turn in frustration at his friend's lack of consideration. If he didn't need to be picked up he could have at least called, Steven thought to himself as he descended the short steps.

Finally the door swung open exposing a disheveled Dexter. "I'm here!"

Steven turned at the sound of Dexter's voice. The teen's untamed hair all but stood on end and his stained, white tee-shirt and cotton pajama pants confirmed to Steven that he'd still be making the short trip alone this morning.

"What the hell happened to you?"

"Good morning to you too," Dexter responded in a mildly hoarse voice as he waived his ride in.

"Never mind you. What the hell happened here?" Steven changed his line of questioning as he entered the Kitchen that had previously been concealed behind the sight impeding glass. Glasses and beer cans littered the counters and floor. Trash occupied the remaining spaces left void of discarded drinking containers. "Oh yeah, that was last night wasn't it? So, how does it feel to be a free man, liberated from the oppressive rules of parental intervention?"

"It hurts like hell," Dexter responded holding his head. "I have the headache to end all headaches right now."

"What happened to that chaser shit you were bragging

about? Drink all you want with no hangover or some shit like that."

"Yeah...it didn't work. After it caught up with the tequila, the two had one hell of a fiesta in my stomach...that is before relocating the party to the kitchen floor." Dexter pointed to the corner of the room, behind the breakfast nook. A pile of paper towels rested in a heap on the marble tile.

Steven groaned as he covered his nose, now aware of the stench wafting through the house. "Why didn't you clean that shit up?"

"I would have but it seemed insignificant when compared to the mess upstairs. I don't think I'm going today."

"I assumed as much. I thought this thing was supposed to be small, only a few people."

"So did I," Dexter responded as he began tossing the haphazardly discarded beer cans into a large trash bag.

"So?" Steven added, still looking for an explanation.

"You know, a few people asked if they could bring a friend or two and then their friends brought some of their own friends and so on until it seemed that half of the school was in my living room." Dexter paused in his cleaning. "There were so many people," he spoke, seemingly reliving the apparent nightmare.

"When do your parents get back?"

"Not until tomorrow night," Dexter responded, continuing his custodial duties.

"So we can do it again tonight, right?" Steven joked as he meandered toward the living room.

"No...I've grown quite fond of my legs these last eighteen years. It'd be ashamed for my dad to have to break them now. I still don't know how to handle the neighbors and the stories that are sure to find my parent's ears."

"Any stragglers?" Steven questioned as he approached the arched opening that connected the kitchen to the large, once formally decorated living room, now looking as if it had been redesigned by a college fraternity.

"Steve, wait!" Dexter suddenly called out, dropping his bag of aluminum remains.

"What the fuck is this!?" Seven exclaimed.

A young female awkwardly adorned the larger of two brown leather sofas, her face buried in the crease between the far seat cushion and arm rest. The remainder of her scantily clad body stretched the length of the three cushion sofa, her right leg threatening to fall from the edge to the beer soaked, hardwood floor below.

"What the fuck is Becky doing on your couch?" Steven questioned as Dexter hurried to his side.

"It's not like that," Dexter immediately went on the defensive. "She had a bit too much to drink. The next thing I knew she was passed out on the couch. I couldn't just send her home to her parents that way. You know how her father is. He'd have killed her."

"So instead you fucked her."

"What? No. I didn't even touch her. She's been lying that way since last night."

"You're telling me that Becky, one of the hottest pieces of ass in school, was passed out on your couch all night and you didn't fuck her? You fucking liar."

"She's your ex-girlfriend man. I wouldn't dream of doing something like that. Well, I might dream."

Steven's face reddened.

"A joke, just a joke," Dexter retracted his ill received attempt at humor, half expecting to become closely acquainted with Steven's fist. "Look nothing happened last night, with anybody and her. I kept an eye on her for you."

"What makes you think I give a shit what or who that bitch does?"

"You don't?"

Steven had no response. Dexter was right. Becky had dumped him just a week ago and as much as he attempted to mask his true emotions behind a tough exterior, he knew it would be some time before he'd get over the personal, not to mention social pain of such a loss. Afraid that his pause and moment of introspection would blow his masculine façade, he assaulted Dexter with another misguided accusation. "You were probably keeping an eye out for yourself."

Becky shifted on the couch, emitting a muffled groan before falling still again. Her position remained much the same as it had been, though now her leg hung from the sofa, her bare toes against the floor with her knee hovering inches from a Heineken puddle.

Both Steven and Dexter paused to admire the girl's new position. The slight shift had provided an almost unobstructed view of the girl's ass and the lacy white thong doing little to cover it.

For fear that his gawking would land him in even more trouble with his longtime friend, Dexter reluctantly broke his gaze and continued to defend his position. "Look Steve. I never have and would never even think of going after someone like Becky."

"What the hell is wrong with Becky?"

"Oh, fuck you. You know what I mean."

Steven was surprised and a bit impressed by his friend's sudden and gutsy outburst.

"All right, I can think of only one thing that can settle this for good," Steven spoke with a slight smile.

"Great, anything," Dexter responded, worn out from a night of unanticipated hell compounded by the current, uncomfortable situation.

"I've gotta fuck her."

"You two aren't even going out anymore."

"So."

Dexter looked at his tiresome friend. Steven returned his curious gaze with a smile.

"No. No, I can't let you."

"See, you do have feelings for her," Steven asserted.

"God damn it, no! I said I don't and that's it!"

"Then you won't be upset or jealous if I give her a little go."

Dexter couldn't believe what he was hearing. He knew Steven could be an asshole at times but this. There was no way. "Steve, no. You can't do that to her. She's not even awake for Christ sake."

"I guess she can't say no then, can she?" he responded as he approached his unconscious ex.

"What if she wakes up?"

Steven abruptly smacked Becky on the ass. The jolt slightly shifted the unconscious girl's body on the cushions however she remained asleep.

"This girl's a very deep sleeper and when she gets a bit of the happy juice in her system, she's near impossible to wake. You could pull out each of her toe nails one by one and she still wouldn't wake up."

Dexter cringed at the disturbing example.

"What about a condom then? I don't have any. Do you?"

"Who needs a condom? We never used them before. Besides she's been on birth control since her fourteenth birthday."

"Steve," Dexter resorted to begging.

Steven unzipped his pants. "Unless your fagotty ass wants a mental portrait of my hog to jerk off to, I think it's about time you went back to straightening up that mess in there."

Dexter continued to stare in disbelief as Steven's fingers parted the fly of his pants, then, doing as he was told he returned to the kitchen, hating himself for his weakness.

FOUR

Ashmont, Jordan M., 28, Reno, Nevada died September 5, 2012, at River of Mercy Hospital. Born and raised in Nevada, Jordan loved to hunt, fish and generally live life to the fullest. He is survived by his parents Joseph and Kitty Ashmont and older brother Jonathan Ashmont...

He was aware of how his morbid fascination with the local obituaries probably appeared to others however, since the age of fourteen, James Madison had made it a point to begin each day with a quick scan of the somber pages, picking out only the lengthier of the brief, life descriptions. The shorter listings possessed no heart...no soul. Typically they simply announced the subject's passing and informed every one of where to meet to pay their last respects but given the brevity of the listing and the lacking of any personal history, it seemed that announcing a funeral was kind of a waste of time and money. If no one had cared enough about the person to write even a few kind words, then how could anyone expect those same, non-caring acquaintances to take time out of their apparently busy lives just to drive down town and stare at a casket containing a dead guy they probably didn't even like to begin with? In fact, many were probably glad to see the son-of-bitch gone.

No, the short obituaries contained nothing of interest. The lengthier ones on the other hand, though in no way complete biographies, did contain much more information about the individual. They often listed the names of remaining relatives and the hobbies that the deceased had enjoyed in life. But, most of all, James liked to look at the subject's age. An eighty-six year old dying in the hospital from a long term decease or fatal heart attack was understandable and contained no real mystery. On the other hand, a twenty year old dropping dead with no mention of a prior medical condition, was something different all together. Though the exact cause of their demise was usually withheld from print, the age, combined with the history was often enough for James to construct his own version of the unfortunate deceased's life and death. It was from there that the characters for his books were often born. Though he never used the person's real name or life history, it was a jumping off point; a place at which to start when concocting new stories and plot twists.

"Mommy, mommy!" Emily screamed as she jumped from her chair to take a guarded position alongside her mother.

James didn't look up. One, because he was deep in thought about poor Jordan Ashmont and two, because he knew exactly what was going on. The same morning routine of screams and laughter had filled the Madison household for the past three months and, though havoc on a writer's concentration, he was glad to see his children engaged in typical, childlike behaviors. So often they displayed traits well beyond their years that, at times, he found himself forgetting just how young they really were.

"Sweetie, I don't want you standing here. The grease is hot and I don't want you to get burned," Rebecca redirected their daughter back to her chair.

His wife on the other hand, still saw them both as her little babies and would often address them as such. While fitting with four year old Emily, it could be a bit uncomfortable for Peter.

At age fifteen his son was a fine young man with great aspirations in life. He was, and had always been, well beyond the demeaning nature of baby talk but, demonstrating true diplomatic skill, he'd continued to allow his mother the hard to break habit and had accepted it as just another sign of love from what was probably the best mother any child could ever wish for.

Rebecca really was amazing. The knowledge and skill she exuded when it came to child rearing was astounding. James wasn't going to kid himself. He knew who was raising both children. Sure he had a part in their upbringing; with the obvious donation of genetic material and a life lesson here and there but it had been his wife who'd almost single handedly molded both kids into what they were today and for such devoted dedication he would always cherish her.

Still staring at his paper, James displayed a slight grin as Peter planted a quick kiss on his cheek before tormenting his sister one last time and ducking out the door to begin another day of school.

"Sweetie, I need you to go get your shoes on," Rebecca instructed their daughter as Emily finished the last of her breakfast.

"But I want another piece of bacon."

"After you come back down with your shoes on. Auntie Mary is going to be here soon and you need to be ready to go."

"OK, mommy," Emily accepted the terms of the brief negotiation and taking one last sip of orange juice, hopped down from her chair and dashed out of the room and up the stairs in search of her shoes.

With the children temporarily absent, the soft sizzle of bacon was the only noise left in the room but even that soothing backdrop slowly began to fade as Rebecca carefully removed each piece from the hot griddle.

"So who'd you fuck last night?" James questioned his wife without lifting his gaze from the page of recorded deaths.

"Excuse me?"

"Oh, I'm sorry. I forgot. You just lay there. What I meant to say was, so, who fucked you last night?" James rephrased the question, still refraining from glancing in his wife's direction.

"I don't know, you tell me yours first. Oh, that's right, you're a worthless sack of shit that no one wants, including me," Rebecca struck back.

"Not true. In-fact I had a hell of a night," James snidely rebutted.

"Oh yeah, with who?"

"Trusty old lefty," James held up his left hand while attempting, unsuccessfully, to balance the unfolded paper with his right. "You know, it's almost like there's another person right their tugging on your meat."

"You're disgusting," Rebecca disengaged herself from the childish conversation and returned to dabbing grease from the bacon.

"And you're a slut."

It wasn't that he didn't love his wife, just the opposite in-fact. James probably loved his wife as much now as he had when they'd first met, seventeen years ago. She had sworn to God to love and cherish him until the end of time and he'd done the same. So in the sense that it was a sworn obligation to his creator, yes he loved her but he did not like her. Lately, he couldn't stand the woman.

The rocky decline in their marriage had started nearly three years ago, November 20, 2009, to be exact. The exact date was easy to recall because it had been the first day of his first--and only--national book tour. Only two and a half years after the publication of his first novel James Madison was quickly becoming a household name among the publishing industry not to mention every horror junky in the country. One reviewer had even gone as far as to declared him the "sure fire successor to horror masters, Steven King and Dean Koontz", though he considered his work pitiful when compared to such literary geniuses of his genre. No, he hadn't set out to create a masterpiece or even a bestseller at that. It had just happened and as quiet and reclusive as he often boasted himself to be, he'd quickly found himself caught up in the sudden fame.

He could have refused to take the six week tour set up by his agent and publisher. He could have chosen to spend Thanksgiving and much of the weeks leading up to Christmas with his family. He could have also refrained from banging that twenty-one year old during a memorable stop in Tampa.

Though initially put off by the girl's somewhat juvenile and long winded expression of awe, James had managed to look past her star struck reaction. After the signing he'd taken her back to his hotel and in doing so had discovered what other, more pleasureful talents the blonde's delicate mouth possessed.

He'd never seen the girl again, at least not in person. At the time of their affair, he hadn't even bothered to memorize her name. As far as he'd been concerned, he never wanted to think about the encounter again. He'd shamed his family. He'd sinned against God but most of all he'd betrayed his marriage. There was no forgiving what he'd done and during the following month he'd made weekly visits to the confessional, expressing his sorrow and regret.

It wasn't until a week after the tour had ended that James had learned the girls name, Joey Fuller. The Enquire had informed him, along with the rest of the world, of such. Apparently, as he'd been battling his own demons, on whether to divulge his secret encounter to his wife, her demons had been holding meetings with publicists and cashing checks in exchange for every juicy detail about the brief encounter.

It was ridiculous. Never before had James ever seen such national attention bestowed upon an author but there he was, a humble writer caught up in an x-rated whirlwind that had probably been the tabloid journalist's most illustrious work to date.

Young Miss Fuller had left out no detail about the steamy night. Size, stamina, everything right down to the tiny birthmark on his left testicle had found its way into those trashy pages. She'd disclosed it all and the sordid writer had gleefully translated it to print.

That holiday season he'd watched as his career and life had crumbled around him. Rebecca had understandably been furious at the betrayal. His publisher had been infuriated by the negative publicity and just about every women's rights and faith based group wanted nothing less than to cut off his birth marked left nut and place it on display for the rest of the unfaithful men in the world to bear witness to.

As quickly as the story of James Madison's infidelity had blown up though, thankfully, it had quickly faded away; replaced by a dog that had supposedly, single handedly taken down a terrorist cell somewhere in Ohio.

The country forgot; his publisher recovered with some creative P.R. and his wife, though furious, had remained by his side. The only aspect of his life which had not returned to normal had been his book sales. He'd never again been able to match the level of success he'd experienced prior to that year and had all but disappeared from the public's easily distracted eye.

"All set mommy," Emily announced the successful completion of her mission as she tore around the corner and reentered the kitchen with shoes on her feet. "I even tied them myself," she stated proudly.

"That's very good sweetie," Rebecca praised her daughter.

"Now where's the bacon?" the young girl firmly expressed her desire to conclude their prior agreement.

"That's not very polite talk little miss," James lightly admonished his daughter's rudeness.

"Sorry daddy."

James just cleared his throat in Rebecca's direction.

"Sorry mommy."

"That's all right dear. Here you go." Rebecca handed her daughter another piece of bacon.

A knock at the kitchen door interrupted Emily's continued politeness just as she was about to issue a thank you for the food. Just beyond the sheer curtain, covering the kitchen door's glass insert, was the hazy outline of Rebecca's sister, come to take Emily for the day.

"Auntie Mary, Auntie Mary!" Emily excitedly cheered as she ran toward the door. As always Mary took it upon herself to let herself in, meeting the excited girl with an equally enthusiastic hug.

"Wow, I love your hair," Rebecca greeted her sister, who hoisted her excited niece into her arms.

"Do you? I just had it done yesterday. I'm still not sure whether I like it or not."

"No, I love it. What does Mike think?"

"You know Mike. He didn't even notice until after the game was over and even then it took me waiving it around in front of him for about an hour or so."

"What do you think honey?" Rebecca requested James's opinion.

"Wow," he responded never removing his eyes from the paper.

"Hey Jim," Mary greeted her brother-in-law with about as much enthusiasms as he'd offered to show her new do.

He hated the name Jim. His name was James. He didn't care if Jim was short for James. His parents had named him James. His birth certificate read James. His driver's license read James. His name was James. He'd never been a big hit with his wife's side of the family and his past indiscretion hadn't made matters any better.

"So, what would you like to do today?" Aunt Mary questioned Emily.

"Ride a kangaroo."

"A kangaroo, well, I don't think we have time to go all the way to Australia today but we could go to the park and ride the seesaw."

"The seesaw is for babies."

"Hey, you know, I happen to love the seesaw," Mary defended her recommendation.

"And?"

"Emily," Rebecca scolded her daughter.

"Sorry mommy. Sorry Aunt Mary."

"That's okay dear. You are an awfully big girl. Maybe the seesaw isn't such a good toy for someone your age." Mary played into the little girl's big persona before turning again to her father. "That's lovely Jim. She has your personality."

"Pool boy couldn't contribute it all," he rebutted the backhanded compliment, quickly wishing he hadn't made such a comment in front of his daughter. As much as he and Rebecca fought, they'd made an agreement to never degrade or insult one another in front of the children. He'd slipped and could feel the burning glare of female eyes on the back of his head.

Luckily Emily hadn't yet been exposed to the world of sex and promiscuity and hence, had not understood the attack on her mother's character.

"I'll drive aunt Mary," Emily announced, extending her hand for the keys.

"OK, but I don't think you can reach the pedals and see over the dash at the same time," Mary teased.

"Don't worry so much. We'll be fine," Emily responded to the joke in a very serious tone.

Mary handed her niece the keys to the Jeep and Emily darted out the door.

"I guess you should go," Rebecca bid farewell to her

sister. "I wouldn't put it past her to have the thing in gear and doing doughnuts on the front lawn in the next thirty-seconds."

"No, probably not," Mary agreed. "I'll see you later. See ya Jim."

"A pleasure as always," he responded as he continued to read his paper.

"I'll be by around three," Rebecca established a pick up time.

"Take your time. No hurry." Mary waved as she hurried toward the Jeep before Emily could get the key in the ignition.

"Nice. I thought we agreed, not in front of the children," Rebecca scolded, turning her focus toward her husband as she shut the door.

"I know. I forgot," he apologized, this time actually feeling bad about his behavior.

"I'm going to the gym for a couple of hours and then I'm meeting Caroline for lunch. You think you can handle sitting around the house and doing nothing for the next few hours?"

Rebecca grabbed her gym bag and stared at James.

"Yeah, I think I'll be fine. Maybe old lefty will stop by for another quick romp or two while you're gone."

"God you're disgusting. Why don't you turn to the arts section and see if there's another article on how pathetic you are?" Rebecca bid farewell as she disappeared out the door.

"Whore," he mumbled, unheard.

James flipped through the pages to the arts section as instructed. Nope, another day free from the disheartening words of the press. His last two books hadn't been received well by the media, not to mention the public. He hoped that his latest book, *The Doorway to My Own Hell*, would fare better, though initial sales were not looking promising. The true test wouldn't come until the Sunday paper.

The New York World Journal had chosen his book as its review of the month, an honor that could either make or break an author. This was his chance to get back on top and prove to the world that his long dormant career wasn't over; that he could still create material worth reading and that he truly was the successor to the aging greats of his time.

The Doorway to My Own Hell would receive a good review. It had to

FIVE

Peter's house was only a few streets over from Eagle Roost High and because of this, received no bus service. Though for much of the year Carson City saw warm to mild weather, there were those few months when the biting cold of winter did touch the high mountain valley, bringing in tow the occasional snow and ice storms to the elevated desert. Those days were the worst for a student without a bus to seek shelter in but year after year Peter had made the short, icy trek.

For years he'd looked forward to his freshman year of high school, not only for its symbolic indication of his advancement in life but because the high school had been on the other side of town and for the first time in his life, he'd be able to experience the door to door service that a school bus could provide. That hope had been destroyed a year ago though when the city had decided that, since it had the land and both the junior high and elementary school were already located together, why not erect a new high school alongside its sibling educational establishments.

For years, complaints of overcrowding had plagued the city school board meetings until finally the approval to build the new school had been given. Peter's hopes of sheltered transportation were destroyed and his sentence of an unassisted commute would continue for another four years.

Geoffrey McDaniel had been another such unfortunate soul forced to brave the cold of winter. Fortunately, it was early in the school year and though a cool breeze hinted at the season to come, the September air remained pleasantly warm. Geoffrey's house was a couple of streets over and lucky for him, much closer to the school than Peter's.

Geoffrey wasn't outside awaiting his friend's arrival as usual but given Peter's early departure this morning he wasn't surprised. Peter wasn't sure how ready Geoffrey would be or whether he'd even want to make the trek a half hour ahead of their scheduled time but seeing as they'd been the best of friends ever since Peter's family had moved into the neighborhood, he figured he should at least give his pal a chance to decide.

As he ascended the front steps toward the uniquely painted, purple door of the two story, brick dwelling, he wasn't surprised to hear a loud voice bellowing from within. Geoffrey's mother had given her life over to alcoholism ever since her second husband had died a little over three years ago; only six years after losing her first love, Geoffrey's father, to cancer. Since then she'd done nothing but suck down one bottle of wine after another in an attempt to mask the obvious pain of her tragic losses.

"Where the hell are you going?" Miss McDaniel's voice boomed from within the house.

Peter refrained from knocking as he sensed movement just beyond the door's elegantly etched, glass insert.

"I have to go to school mom!" Geoffrey yelled back in response to his mother's drunken questioning. "I'll be home this afternoon!"

"Bring back another bottle of Sutter Home for me, would ya?"

"I'll do that mom. Love you," Geoffrey agreed to the

task that he knew he would and could not perform. Besides, he knew by the time that he got home, she'd most likely be passed out on the couch and would never even remember the impossible request she'd made of her son that morning.

Peter stepped back as the knob began to turn and the door swung inward to reveal a surprisingly ready Geoffrey.

"Jesus Christ!" Geoffrey exclaimed in response to his friend's unexpected presence. "Sorry Pete."

"No problem. It's just a ticket to Hell that you're purchasing," Peter poked fun at his friend's non-religious ways. Though his family believed deeply in Christianity he understood that not all families shared the same spiritual dedication. Geoffrey's family had been through a lot and though he believed that a strong faith in a higher power could aid in their recovery, he knew that it wasn't his place to push his beliefs on others. He didn't need to recruit others to be favored kindly in God's eyes. As long as he lived a whole and decent life, he would always feel the love of his creator and be provided with all that he could ever need to make it through this life and into the next.

"What are you doing here so early?"

"Remember the big math test I was telling you about yesterday? That's today and I thought it best I get to school early so I can be ready."

"Doesn't it get old always being so dedicated and responsible?" Geoffrey questioned as he shut the door.

"I don't know. You tell me," Peter responded with a smile, knowing full and well that Geoffrey was just as much a geek as was he. He figured that was probably the reason the two had always gotten along so well. Not too many kids these days viewed school and the future as they did. They knew that they would need to make something of themselves in this ever complicating world. Success would surely be an invaluable future commodity. Kicking back and riding the wave of carelessness, as most teens commonly did, was just not an option.

"So, where were you off to at such an early hour?" Peter took his turn to show surprise at his friend's early preparedness.

"Your place. Couldn't sleep last night so I thought I'd get up and head over to your house for some of your mom's amazing breakfast but on top of no sleep, it looks like I get no food as well now."

"I did bring some bacon," Peter lifted his friend's hopes. "But it was such a long journey; halfway here I thought I wasn't going to make it, so I ate it all. There might be a few crumbs left in my teeth."

"Jerk," Geoffrey playfully slugged Peter's arm.

A loud bark abruptly ended the jovial banter though as both Peter and Geoffrey stopped in their tracks and spun to observe the neighbor's dog, Prince, standing on his hind legs behind the chain link fence of the McGregor's side yard. The dog's front paws aided the frantically barking animal in his erect pose while his back paws seemed to push against the ground as if attempting to generate enough leverage to topple the steel barrier.

"What's gotten into him?" Peter questioned, surprised by the normally calm animal's new found aggression.

"I don't know. That's why I woke up so early. He's been barking on and off like that all morning. It gets worse when he sees me, as if it's me that he has a problem with."

"That's strange," Peter spoke as he watch a long flow of drool escape the aggressive animal's snapping jowls.

Dismissing the animal's peculiar conduct the two turned again and continued on their way, the vicious barking persisting behind them until the line of sight between themselves and the dog was broken by the McGregor's sculpted hedge.

The dog's sudden silence again inciting a pause in the boys' short commute.

"See," Geoffrey confirmed his theory.

"Like I said, strange."

SIX

From what James Madison had seen in his limited travels of the United States, Highway Fifty had to be one the most unequivocally diverse stretches of road in the entire country. If one were to drive from the road's inception at the heart of Utah, all the way to the capital of California, they'd see not only the stereotypical desert landscapes of the west but vast stretches of salt flats and grand mountain ranges as well. The lengthy highway stretched three states but James's favorite portion of the extensive route was the relatively short length which ran along Lake Tahoe's south shore. Some of his best memories had occurred along that brief stretch of road, including the birth of his son at nearby St. David's Memorial Hospital.

The lake was also home to what had once been one of his worst memories...his father. The man had spent all his life working in the towering high-rises of Chicago, strategizing company expansion and workforce policies for H.P. Leverson, a conglomerate which owned numerous smaller companies such as Mrs. Annie's Cream Puffs and Shockwave Energy Drink. That was of course until, as a result of his tireless work concerning redundant infrastructure and excess staff, he'd managed to unintentionally prove that he himself was nothing more than dead weight and just like the men and women he'd been assigned to cut, he too had watched his career die.

Though the company had decided to release him of his services, at the time he'd commanded a fairly hefty salary and therefore had departed with a reasonably handsome severance package. So in no way had the family been hurting for money. That was of course until, because of what James could only assume to have been a midlife crisis, his father had up and left Chicago, leaving his wife of sixteen years and two children, ages twelve and nine, to fend for themselves.

"A selfish motherfucker." That was how James's mother had referred to her husband shortly after his departure, not to mention about a dozen other expletive laden terms.

James too had been devastated and hurt by his father's brief abandonment. Brief because, no more than a year later, a head on collision with a drunk driver had claimed the life of his mother and brother and again returned James to his father's custody. There he'd spent the next six years absorbing the beauty of nature's majestic, Sierra hideaway.

Once a puppet for corporate America, the urbanized man he'd come to know as his father had been suddenly transformed. Where he'd once seen land ripe for development, he suddenly saw vast stretches of forest in desperate need of preservation. The water and air he'd once helped to pollute had all of a sudden become treasures to be cherished and adored.

"Listen James," his father had said. "I know what I did was pretty shitty...leaving you guys like that."

James hadn't disagreed.

"But you have to understand. When I was fired I got to thinking. What am I doing with my life? All that time spent slaving behind a desk and for what? So a few people above me could get rich? It was then that I realized that the city just wasn't the place for me anymore. I needed to quit living the life that was expected of me and finally go in search of my dreams. That's why I moved up here to the lake. Deep down, I craved tranquility; far away from the noises of the city; far away from rush hour traffic and nightly news reports of violence and death. Far away from--"

"Far away from us," James had interrupted.

"That's fair. I deserved that," his father had accepted the criticism just before issuing a piece of advice that would stick with his son for the rest of his life. "Don't do what's expected of you. Chase after your dreams and when you find them, don't think about the consequences and the what-ifs. You grab hold and never let go. You hear me? Never let go."

James had never seen his father cry before but in that brief, emotional moment, the old man had been unable to fight back the single tear that had broken free and traversed his father's cheek.

At the time, James hadn't been entirely sure what exactly the escaped tear had meant and given his bitter hatred for the man, he couldn't say that he'd cared. Looking back though, on that important moment from his past, he liked to think that, in that single tear was the proof of his father's sorrow and regret for what he'd done with his life...for what he'd done to his family. He'd never gotten the chance to question the man's moment of vulnerability however. While James had been in only his second year at the University of Reno, Roger Madison had died in his sleep of a massive heart attack, leaving his last living son and the small cabin as the only remaining proof that he'd ever existed.

Turning left off of Fifty, James navigated his Toyota pickup along Pine View Terrace as the road bobbed and weaved among the tall, Tahoe pines. Steadily he ascended the mountainside to a point where the paved road gave way to dirt for the remaining hundred yards toward the old cabin.

The property wasn't really much to look at; never had been. It had always possessed more the feeling of a hideaway, rather than a retreat. The trees and vegetation surrounding the old place were overgrown. The dirt road was in desperate need of re-grading and the cabin itself could have used a fresh coat of paint and a bit of tender love 'n care. But, as much as the property itself looked in disarray, no one could argue with its breathtaking view of the majestic lake to its north.

In the summer, the plant life sprang back to its majestic green splendor, framing the crystal blue water at the base of the tall mountains. In the winter the snow frosted limbs captured the reflective light of the seemingly luminescent lake in a display of light and natural wonder unmatched anywhere else in the world.

As much as James told himself that what his father had done was wrong, deep down he also knew that, in some small way, he'd been right. A life of serene solitude had been his father's dream, just as writing had always been his. Largely, James had his father to thank for having had the courage and complete lack of moral judgment to set an example, however wrong, that had pushed his son to pursue nothing short of his passion.

James smiled at the thought of his long deceased father. It had been years since he'd found cause to smile at the memory of the man but in that brief moment of retrospection, something inside had finally managed to summon the necessary emotion needed to invoke the long dormant sign of forgiveness.

Cautiously making a sharp right around a huge oak, the old cabin came into view. It was a small structure, no more than eight hundred square feet and only contained two small bedrooms, a kitchen, a bathroom and a small gathering area most would consider to be the living room. Though, with barely enough room to house a small couch and at most a nineteen inch television, he hardly found the space large enough to justify any designation other than a large, open closet.

A black Mercedes was parked beside the cabin under the single vehicle carport to the west. Philip Prescott was early, though that wasn't at all surprising for a man who would, and had, chastised his own mother for being one second late to a pre-arranged engagement. Living by example was kind of a necessity when harboring such critical expectations of others.

James pulled in behind the black car just as the driver's side door swung open, revealing his friend. Killing the engine, James stepped out onto the pine needle ground.

"You styling son of a bitch!" James exclaimed, greeting his friend with a hug. "When the hell did you get this?" he spoke while eyeing Philip's new car.

"Just picked it up yesterday," Philip grinned widely.

"This is the SLK350 right?"

"Yep, three point five liters, two hundred sixty eight horses," Philip bragged.

"Hell my truck has that."

"Your truck is also double the size. Take away all that excess weight and imagine what you could do."

"Get myself killed probably," James joked.

"I don't know, with a road like this, it's a bit difficult to get it up to speed," Philip commented on the dirt trail leading up to the cabin. "You should really do something about that."

"No, you should do something about it. This place isn't my problem anymore," James said as he held out the keys to the cabin.

"Are you sure about this?" Philip questioned, hesitant in accepting the small metallic tools of entry. "I mean, I know this place must hold quite a bit of history for you, with your father and all."

"I'm not really sure I would consider that a history worth holding onto."

"Then, what about Peter? I know the two of you come up here occasionally. What does he think about you selling the place?"

"He...he's fine with it."

"You didn't tell him, did you? Don't you think you should at least give him the heads-up? I know memories of your father are a bit tough but I'm sure he's full of good ones about you."

"Do you want the place or not?" James snapped.

Philip took the keys.

"I'm sorry, you're right. I should have told him but what good would it do? One way or another I have to get rid of it. We need the money."

"I don't mean to pry but aren't you a pretty successful writer? I mean, I see your stuff on the shelves all the time."

"Yeah that's the problem. You see my stuff on the shelves. With the exception of my first couple of books I haven't sold crap. No one cares about the horror genera anymore. Everyone wants biographies and political dramas. Hell, that midget from that movie...you know which one."

Philip nodded.

"Even his book outsold mine last year and it was titled, 'Farts Smell Even Worse Down Here'. I have to face the facts here. My career is in the shitter and if I don't do something now my family's gonna to end up on the street."

"But, what about your new book? Didn't that just come out this week? What if it does well?"

"If that happens then maybe there's hope but I can't just sit around waiting for that slim possibility. The payment on my already double mortgaged house is due and I'm running out of sources to borrow against. This has to be done."

"What is Rebecca going to do? Is she gonna go back to work?"

"Mrs. Madison is currently attending her hundred and fifty dollar a week personal training session with Francesco Savaree," he pronounced the trainer's name with disgust.

"Maybe you should cut out the pricy expenses, don't you think?"

"Who else would she fuck then? Certainly not me. She's made that perfectly clear by taking over the bedroom and leaving me with the sofa in my office."

"Oh," Philip uncomfortably responded to the colorful bit of information, unsure of where next to take the conversation. "Well, if there's anything I can do, please let me know. I hate to see a friend in trouble."

"You're doing enough already by taking this dump off my hands. As long as your check clears, which I don't think will be a problem..." James spoke while eyeing the pricy car once again, "...I think we'll be fine. Shall we take a look around?" he returned his attention to his friend as he patted him on the back.

The muffled sounds of Who Let the Dogs Out suddenly began playing from James's left pocket.

"That's probably the year 2000 calling," Philip motioned toward the music's source. "I think it wants it's song back."

"Funny," James spoke with a grin as he freed the Baha Men from their denim prison. "Peter thinks it's funny to keep switching my ringtones on me. Last week it was the Macarenna. "Hello," he answered, indicating to Philip that he would only be a minute.

"Hey James. I'm glad you answered," the voice on the other end greeted him in an excited tone.

"Oh, hi Brandon."

Brandon was, and had been, his literary agent and publicist for the past three years; ever since the tabloid nightmare that had scared away his previous agent. Not only was Brandon his agent though, he'd also been a close friend of his during his childhood in Chicago. He'd always been the outgoing type, much more so than James, so when James had heard of his friend's involvement in the more social side of his similar field, he'd given his old acquaintance a call and from that point on had reinstated their friendship on both a personal and business level.

"Listen, James. I'm going to be in San Francisco tomorrow and I just received word that Westcroft and Heisner, your publisher--"

"Yeah, I think I know who my publisher is," James joked.

"Anyway, they want to meet with you about your latest book and I think it's good news."

"Meet about what?"

"I don't know. Westcroft's assistant wouldn't say. She just said that he was really eager to sit down with you and discuss your future. I think they might be looking to extend your contract and if we play our cards right, we could be looking at a fairly generous sum of money."

James could picture Brandon as he mentioned the money. The man may be a friend and a damn good agent but he was also a shark in a business where only the most vicious survive. James knew that whatever dollar figure the man was contemplating had already been broken down into its many parts, the most important being his fifteen percent fee for representation.

"There's a flight already set up for you on a seven am out of Reno. The meeting is at nine. I'll have my secretary email you the specifics. See you tomorrow." And with that flood of information the line went dead, leaving no time for questions or comment about the unexpected meeting.

"Good news?" Philip questioned as James returned the phone to his pocket.

"I hope so."

"Well, I know I questioned your interest in selling this place before but I really want it, so you're not getting the keys back."

"It's all yours," James patted his friend on the back

again. "Let's go take a look around."

SEVEN

Even with the opening of the new high school, it seemed that the ever present problem of overcrowding still had not been resolved.

Peter remained in close quarters to his open locker as the countless hordes of migrating bodies passed only inches from his back, occasionally bumping him on their way by. He didn't know who had designed the new building but it was clear that, whoever it was had had no idea what they were doing. The halls were too narrow and the number of routes used to access the different wings were too few.

"This place is a dysfunctional nightmare," Geoffrey nearly had to shout as he broke free from the flow of noisy traffic and squeezed in beside his friend.

"You read my mind," Peter responded, struggling to pull his algebra book free from his backpack without elbowing the girl who occupied the locker to his left.

"Good thing my locker is on the second floor. Things are a bit less crowded up there."

"Gee, thanks for rubbing it in," Peter spoke with playful disgust as the book finally slipped free from the bag and into his locker.

"So how'd it go?"

"What?"

"The math test...you know, the one you dragged me out of the house for this morning."

"I don't think I dragged you anywhere,"

"That's true. You're a bit on the scrawny side to be dragging people around, let alone big old me."

"Oh yeah, you're so huge. Look at that gut of yours. It must be all those beers."

"I wasn't talking about my stomach," Geoffrey, in jest, flexed his underdeveloped biceps."

"Ooh, tough guy!" a voice shouted at Geoffrey's back as a hand shoved him into Peter's locker, slamming the door shut with his face.

Holding his battered nose, Geoffrey turned just in time to see Mark Faulty retreating from the assault with a devious grin before joining up with fellow school bully, Steven Bishop. Both were on the high school football team and both had a reputation for mischief, especially when it came to underclass-men. For some reason the seniors had chosen Geoffrey and occasionally Peter, as their favored targets this year. Both had heard of Mark and Steven's antics while making their way up through junior high and both had agreed to do everything in their power to avoid contact with the tormenting duo. Only in the second week of the school year though, both had already had their fair share of unpleasant run-ins.

Though discouraged by this disheartening welcome to high school, it wasn't as if they'd never before experienced such negative favoritism. As far back as second grade, Geoffrey could remember being picked on by his fellow classmates. He'd always been small for his age and his, what some would refer to as nerdy appearance, had always made him a prime target for those students nearer the bottom of the grade point average.

"What a jerk," Peter vocalized his take on the obnoxious upper class-man as both he and Geoffrey observed Mark take his place alongside Steven and another student, whom they'd not yet become familiar with...and had no immediate interest in doing so.

"I know," Geoffrey agreed in a nasally tone before removing his hand from his throbbing nose. There was no blood or misaligned cartilage, only the residual pain generated by the vertical face plant.

"He could have broken my locker," Peter faked concern as he jiggled the lever on the closed metal door.

"Ha, ha, very funny."

Peter smiled. "What do you have next?"

"Surgery I think."

"You all right?" Peter asked sincerely.

"I'm fine. Just some damaged pride."

"Oh you don't need that anyway. I lost my pride years ago when Chad Minor pantsed me in the middle of gym class."

"That was pretty funny, T.W.," Geoffrey chuckled, reviving the nickname Peter had been burdened with ever since that day.

"Not that it's any of your business but I have since switched to boxers thank you very much, so I really don't think that T.W. is all that fitting anymore, Pug."

"Pug? What's that supposed to mean?"

"Well from this angle your nose does look a bit flatter."

"Really?"

Geoffrey ran his hand over his nose with a look of concern, as if he really could feel a difference in his features.

Both smiled.

"Really, what class do you have next?" Peter again posed the unanswered question.

"Architectural drafting," Geoffrey finally answered.

"Good. Maybe you can fix this disaster we're forced to call a high school."

"In my professional opinion, we need to knock it down and start fresh."

"Sounds about right to me," Peter agreed.

"Before I can order the demolition though, Mr. Monroe asked me to draw up a map of the library, you know, something that can be hung on the wall as a kind of reference tool to help students find their way around."

"That seems kind of pointless if you're just gonna knock it down anyway."

"Well, I was thinking that I might spare that portion of the building. As a well respected figure in my field of study, I believe that the designer of this architectural nightmare, which you so plainly refer to as a high school, must have been a big reader, because the library seems to be the only portion of the building that isn't completely screwed up."

"Then why do they need you to draw a map of it?"

"Good point."

"Anyway, I've gotta get going. See you at lunch?"

"If I can find my way there," Geoffrey book ended the joke as the two departed in opposite directions.

EIGHT

Eagle Roost was much like any other public high school; overcrowded, underfunded and intent on warping the blossoming minds of America's youth into the dysfunctional, self important members of the ever collapsing society of tomorrow.

Though financially capable of attending the most elite, private schools in the country, Steven's father had thought it best that his sons find their educations just as he had, within the public school system. He hadn't attended any fancy prep schools or Ivy League colleges. He'd graduated from Herbert Miller High in Salt Lake City and had then gone on to get his BS in Business from Utah State. State run institutions had done him just fine and he believed that they'd do the same for his boys.

Steven admired his father's faith in an educational program that, in his day, had indeed worked but remained shocked by the brilliant man's lack of insight into the fractured remains of his beloved system. How a man, who had built an empire from nothing, could be so blind to the obvious was baffling.

Even considering his father's misguided devotion; Steven didn't mind having to attend a school filled with the petty offspring of day laborers and blue collared men and women. The curriculum was far easier than its private counterparts and with a natural ability in the athletic arts, the substandard educational institution fit his mentality perfectly.

As if a minimal difficulty level weren't already enough of an incentive to keep his attendance, Eagle Roost somehow, in a city brimming with less than attractive residents, managed to contain a disproportionately large pool of big breasted, tight assed hotties for men such as he to exploit. It was an all you can eat smorgasbord of flesh taco and Steven's craving for the tasty, south of the border treat never seemed to wane.

"Hey Steven," Felicia Timmor flirted, brushing her hand across his chest as they passed in the hall.

She wanted it. Steven knew it. One would have to be a blind, deaf quadriplegic not to see the signs and possess the desire to act upon them. He had time though. She was only one in a long line of prospects he hoped...no planned to conquer before his impending graduation promised to yank him from the over stocked market of fresh, young meat. Young Felicia was only a sophomore and just naive enough to fall for every line known to the modern Homosapien male. She would be an effortless endeavor, easily squeezed in between more long term conquests.

"As I was saying, the only reason Coach Steiner keeps playing the little twerp is because of his family's name," Charlie Burbank continued his rant.

Steven hadn't heard a word of what his "friend" had been saying, nor did he care. Charlie Burbank's existence in this world was for one purpose, to play the social whipping boy to those smart enough to use him as such. If there was a mindless or dangerous task in need of performing, Charlie was the man for the job. With surprisingly little coaxing, he could be talked into doing just about anything that would provide some bit of entertainment to the more respectable members of their social click. Steven knew that his friend of convenience performed such feats of stupidity merely for the attention and status that they afforded him but he didn't care. As long as Charlie was doing stupid shit and somebody was finding amusement in it, he could tolerate the self allowed toy's mindless banter.

"Where the hell were you last night? That party was insane," Mark Faulty announced his presence as he swooped in on the two man, migrating group, flanking Steven's right as to avoid infection from the idiotic babble being spewed to Steven's left.

"Piano recital," Steven answered unenthused.

"I didn't know you played the piano. When did you turn queer?" Mark expressed his disapproval.

"Not me...my little brother. My mother dragged me to it."

"Oh, did you go on a date with mommy? How sweet," Mark childishly mocked.

Steven tattooed his shoulder with an imprint of his class ring, not so much for the comment but more so for just how close to the truth the remark had been. His mother wasn't a family woman. She didn't give a shit whether she saw her youngest son's performance and she especially couldn't have cared less that Steven be there to offer moral support to his younger sibling. The only reason Arlene Bishop did anything in her life was for Arlene Bishop and last night had been no exception. With her mind and her twat set on conquering a man more intellectually inclined, namely her youngest son's music instructor, Steven had been dragged along as nothing more than a mock, younger date who's only purpose was to show the barely post teen music man that, even at age thirty-five, his mother was still capable of landing a man much younger than she. Though disturbing, Steven's cooperation insured a peaceful home life and continued access to his financial resources. If successful, it also assured a parentless environment, sometimes for days at a time and see that he hadn't seen or heard from his mother since the previous night's escapade, he assumed the mission a success and looked forward to the next few days of peace.

"Ouch! Dick!" Mark yelped at the assault on his arm.

"That's what your mom said when I stuck it in last night," Steven, without hesitation, fired off the return insult.

Charlie snickered. Mark glared. Charlie stopped.

"Like I was saying, you missed one hell of party. I half expected the halls to be empty today. I bet the bed of choice last night was the bathroom floor."

Steven remained unimpressed. Though the mess left behind by the gathering at Dexter's place had been extensive, last night's social get together had likely paled in comparison to the parties he was oft to throw at his extravagant abode. Even if one were to remove the always important presence of alcohol, the pool alone was enough of an attraction to allure nearly every teenager in the city to his front door. His father had built it to mimic the Playboy Grotto and much like its inspirer, on nights of such social extravagance, the beautifully carved concrete hole probably contained many fluids other than just water.

"So when's the next ho down at your place?" Mark intuitively inquired.

"Ho down?" Steven questioned, amused by his friend's choice of words.

"Yeah, it's a southern thing."

"But you're from Oregon."

"Yeah so, the southern half."

The raucous crowd, impeding their travels, began to dissipate as anticipation of the second period bell herded the migrating cattle into their respective, educational pens. Steven wasn't worried about being late. His next class was computer lab and the teacher was the varsity football coach. Steven could do no wrong as long as his legs continued to carry the ball to a Talon's victory each Friday night. Charlie, on the other hand, had no such skills to fall back on and promptly dismissed himself from the group with a silent wave before darting into a nearby classroom.

"I should probably go too," Mark announced, leaving Steven to make his final hundred foot journey alone.

Maybe it was about time to throw another big bash at his place, Steven thought to himself but before his contemplative questioning could progress any further, a familiar voice interrupted.

"Steve!" the voice called out to his back.

Continuing to walk, he glanced over his shoulder to see Dexter hurrying toward him.

Confused by the party thrower's presence after the morning's frantic cleaning activities, Steven continued a few steps further before colliding head on with another student, emerging from an adjoining hallway. The collision did little to affect his impeccable balance. His blood pressure, on the other hand, immediately began a steady climb as he prepared to unleash his easily triggered rage upon the careless student. A split second of eye contact with the source of his anger however quickly altered his emotional state from rage to that of fear and confusion. Becky Alverez quickly diverted her attention away from her ex and fell to her knees, franticly eager to retrieve her dropped belongings before darting from the scene of the accident and into a nearby class.

Steven paused for a moment, taken aback by the very familiar girl's puzzling behavior.

"Steve," Dexter huffed, flanking his friend's right side.

Steven quickly turned to his out of breath company. "What the fuck is she doing here!?"

"That's why I was trying to catch you," Dexter spoke, breathing as if he'd just completed the Boston marathon in record time.

"You didn't fucking tell her, did you? Did you!? The empty halls amplified his voice, sending his words on a quest for the ears of the few carefree stragglers still roaming the halls. He was thankful Becky had closed the classroom door behind her. He didn't need to give her even the slightest suspicion to what he'd done just a couple of hours ago.

"I didn't say anything. She woke up shortly after you left and was all panicked about a test or something she had today. I told her to stay and rest but she wouldn't listen. When I came back from taking a shit she was gone."

The disturbing image of Dexter perched on top of the porcelain dumping station, straining to evacuate his bowels, almost caused Steven to forget his current, dubious situation.

Dexter said he hadn't told her. Her behavior seemed to indicate otherwise though. Maybe she'd been awake after all. Why wouldn't she have stopped him then? Unless...maybe she'd wanted it. No. She'd dumped him and had done so quite cruelly, declaring that she wanted to see other people. Of course what Steven had heard was... "I've been fucking this college guy named Brady". Probably some preppy, loafer wearing faggot. They all were.

"I have to go. I'll talk to you later," Dexter spoke, pulling Steven from his introspective questioning before retreating back in the direction from which he'd come.

Before Steven could respond to his friend's sudden departure, Dexter rounded a corner and was gone, leaving Steven alone with his thoughts.

The Bell rang.

NINE

Geoffrey's eyes bounced back and forth between the numbers on the extended tape measure and the library's architectural plans. The professionally produced floor plan's once sharp lines and detailed dimensions, were now masked beneath Geoffrey's own measurements and rough pencil sketches, creating a jumbled mess he would soon have to decipher to recreate the complex interior space.

Over the last couple of days he'd managed to take measurements of almost everything within the large, busy space, including the locations and dimensions of computer stations, tables, doorways, windows...everything. All that remained were the dozen or so enormous bookshelves packed into the Northwest corner of the educational environment.

Row after row of carefully organized literature filled the back quarter of the library. Geoffrey, being on the small side, dreaded the day he might need to actually find a particular selection in the towering maze of paper, not so much due to the complexity of its organization but more so because he highly doubted his short legs and arms would allow him to reach the numerous publications perched on the upper shelves.

Releasing the lock on the twenty-five foot tape,

Geoffrey watched as the long metal tongue swiftly returned to its body, coming to halt with a loud snap he hoped had not disturbed the few literary patrons *actually* making use of the less than popular place. Quickly, he knelt to the floor and added his most recent measurement to the crowded plans, before rising again with plans in hand and eager to move on to the next set of storage giants.

A student being asked to create detailed maps of his or her school was in no way a normal occurrence but since the beginning of the school year only two weeks earlier, Geoffrey had already proven himself far more advanced than the remainder of his drafting class and had therefore earned the right to bypass all fundamental teachings until the rest of his classmates had reached at least a somewhat functional skill level. And since that wouldn't be for at least another week, he'd enthusiastically accepted the proposed library assignment as a means to pass time.

Again Geoffrey extracted the long, metal tape from its housing, running it across the floor until its metal tip met flush with the nearby wall. He laid the other end of the tape measure beside the nearest shelving unit.

"Three feet, four inches," he read the measurement aloud before adding it to the plans.

"Geeooffrreey," a subtle rush of air seemed to whisper, shifting his hair as it passed and rustling the plans on the floor. Geoffrey shot to his feet, nervously scanning his surroundings for a potential assault from a certain group of upper class-men. No such attack came however and with no other students in sight, he took a deep sigh and smiled at his comically nervous reaction.

A ribbon dancing beneath the powerful air vent overhead even further aided in his relaxation, allowing his mind's uninhibited return to the task before him.

He wasn't usually so jumpy but given his recent introduction to the senior class, he understood the cause for his overreaction.

Dismissing the chatty vent, Geoffrey again withdrew the long tape, sliding it across the floor until its flanged end again met with the nearby wall.

"Three feet, four inches," the measurement was again read aloud, though this time in a voice other than Geoffrey's.

He again turned to locate the source of the mysterious voice but instead of sighting the vent overhead as the impish culprit, the true source presented itself in the form of Steven Bishop.

Startled by the unexpected presence of the upper class-man, Geoffrey stumbled backward, crashing into the shelving unit that he'd just finished measuring and falling to the floor with a quiet thud.

Laughing in an obnoxiously loud voice at the results of his prank, Steven stood over the toppled freshman.

"A bit jumpy are we?" Steven asked, continuing his audible amusement.

Geoffrey didn't answer. Instead he just stared up at his elder peer, perplexed by the senior's out of place presence in a place commonly deemed beneficial only by the more intellectually driven members of the student body.

"Let me guess what's going through your mind right now," Steven continued, standing over his cornered prey. "You're probably asking yourself what a person like me is doing in a place where only people like you hang out. Am I right?"

Geoffrey was surprised by the moron's unexpectedly perceptive deduction.

"I'll take your silence as a yes," Steven continued. "Listen, I didn't come here to pick on you."

Somehow Geoffrey found that statement hard to believe, since every day so far the jerk had found one way or another to make his tormenting presence felt.

"I saw what Mark did to you in the hall this morning and I just wanted to apologize personally for his behavior.

I know it's only been two weeks and we've put you through a lot already but I just wanted you to know that it's because we have a deep respect for you."

"Some way of showing it," Geoffrey mumbled.

"What was that?"

"Nothing."

"Like I was saying, you're probably one of the smartest kids in the school. Your grade point average is what, three point two, three point three?"

"Three point nine actually," Geoffrey answered, not sure exactly why he'd decided to join in on the conversation, or even why knowing that bit of information was all that important to the oversized jock.

"Three point nine? Wow. Now that's impressive. Your parents must be very proud of you."

Geoffrey opted to refrain from divulging any information about his dysfunctional home life.

"Let me get to the point. Like I was saying, I just wanted to apologize and make you an offer."

Geoffrey remained motionless against the book shelf.

"I'm prepared to offer you a truce. No one else will ever lay a hand on you again."

What was he up to? Geoffrey continued to wonder.

"All you have to do is promise to help me and a couple of my friends with our studies."

"I don't write other people's papers," Geoffrey smugly rejected what he thought the upper class-man was suggesting.

"I don't want you to write any papers. I just want some help understanding some of my classes."

"You're kidding right?" Geoffrey asked curiously. He had a hard time believing that the self proclaimed "king" of the school would ask anyone for help, especially him.

"Why would I be kidding?" Steven questioned. "I know. I don't exactly come across as the type that would go about asking for help, especially from a nerd such as yourself."

Was that supposed to be a compliment? Geoffrey wondered.

"But I do need help with my grades if I plan to remain on the team this year."

Maybe Steven was telling the truth. Maybe he really did need help. There was a GPA requirement that each player had to meet to remain an active member of any school team. It wasn't unheard of for players to be cut for letting their grades slip. It certainly wouldn't have been surprising to find out that Steven was one such player.

"What do you need help in?" Geoffrey hesitantly questioned, deciding to entertain the possibility that maybe the proposal was being presented with all sincerity.

"First off, I'm sorry for scaring you like that. Let me help you up."

Geoffrey eyed the helping hand with suspicion. He was fairly certain that the offered help was only part of a much larger joke about to be unveiled but if it was sincere, he couldn't afford to just let it slip away. Only two weeks into what had already promised to be a long first year of high school, Geoffrey had grown tired of the constant torment and wished for nothing more than a way to make it stop, even if it meant taking the risk. Maybe this was his chance. Maybe the muscle head before him was telling the truth. Maybe he could complete the rest of the year in relative peace. He had to take the chance.

Geoffrey accepted Steven's offered hand but, only halfway to his feet, regretted his gullibility as Steven's other hand suddenly appeared as a clenched fist, cutting through the air before making painful contact with his lower ribs. Geoffrey fell back again, this time striking the wooden shelves with much more force.

"Oh, did you fall down?" Steven mocked. "Here let me help you up." Steven offered his hand again.

Geoffrey wouldn't fall for the same trick twice. He ignored the offer.

"Well, you may be gullible but at least you learn

quickly," Steven responded to Geoffrey's refusal of assistance. "What's that?" Steven questioned as he took notice of the heavily marked sketch beside his fallen victim.

Geoffrey quickly slapped his hand over the paper but was unable to protect his hard work from being yanked away by his much stronger tormentor.

Steven looked at the paper for a moment and then turned it one hundred and eighty degrees in his hands before rotating it again. Geoffrey wasn't surprised by the idiot's apparent inability to read a map. It probably wasn't the only thing he couldn't read.

"I'll be honest. I don't know what the fuck I'm looking at here but I can safely say that it looks like shit," Steven shared his colorful opinion of the note covered map as he tore it in half and then tore those halves into quarters and then eighths.

Steven released the shredded page and Geoffrey watched as his hard work fluttered to the carpet, its tiny fragments twirling and dancing beneath the influence of the powerful vent overhead.

"Now that I understand," Steven pointed at the dropped tape measure. Before Geoffrey could grab the extended tape, Steven had it in his grasp.

"Give it back!" Geoffrey cried.

"Oh, a bit touchy about the tape are we?"

The tape measure had been his father's. Geoffrey had stumbled across it in the garage a few months ago and had ever since been eager to find a use for the tool from his past. His father had always been into carpentry and Geoffrey could remember countless weekends spent with his father building and refurbishing elaborate pieces of furniture he would then sell at the local flea market.

As his father's right hand man for such projects, Geoffrey had always been in charge of the tape measure. Whenever there had been a measurement in need of calculating, he had been expected to be there and ready.

Of course between needed measurements he'd often become easily distracted by other random tasks, such as the measuring of the lawn mower or the handle bars of his bike. He even remembered attempting to measure a wandering ant one time, which had proved nearly impossible since the darn thing had refused to hold still long enough to get an accurate reading.

He cherished the limited memories he possessed of his father; every one of them. So, when the opportunity to create the requested map had presented itself, he had immediately thought of the sentimental tool to aid in his task.

Steven stared at the tape for a moment, "Three feet, four inches," he announced for a second time before placing the tape behind him, positioning it between his legs as if a tool of phallic measurement. "Yep, that seems about right," he laughed, retracting the tape and walking away.

Geoffrey watched as the bully slowly strutted toward the front of the library. He wanted to jump to his feet and go after the tyrant. He wanted to jump on his back and bash the jerk's skull in with the stolen tape but instead he remained against the bookshelf, watching as Steven deposited his newly acquired toy into the book return before noisily whistling his way out into the quiet halls.

Holding his battered ribs, Geoffrey slowly picked himself up and began gathering the remains of his scattered plans. With any luck, he would be able to tape the pieces together and wouldn't have to start all over again on the project he thought had been nearly complete.

"Are you just going to let him get away with that?" a new voice unexpectedly spoke out.

Geoffrey, now with good reason to be startled, stumbled back against the bookshelf, half expecting Mark Faulty to now appear before him and continue where Steven had left off, but no one else was around.

He nervously searched his surroundings, glancing

around bookshelves and through the gaps, left above each book, to the neighboring isle. He was alone.

"How can you just sit there and let such reprehensible behavior go unrequited?" the voice continued.

"Who's there?" Geoffrey questioned as he took notice of a book, on a shelf about ten feet away, shift ever so slightly.

He stared at the book, straining to see beyond the densely packed shelf to the person who had caused its sudden movement but, given his awkward angle, no one was visible, leading him to doubt whether he'd even seen the book move at all.

"Get to you feet and go after the bloody prick," the mysterious voice spoke more assertively and in a heavy British accent.

Geoffrey couldn't think of one person he knew that spoke with the foreign dialect. It couldn't have been Steven. He'd seen him leave and, having spent the last couple of days examining every detail of the library, he knew for certain that there was only one way in and one way out of the large space.

Maybe it was one of his cronies, he thought to himself but quickly recanted the improbable theory. Though talented in the ways of sport and torment, that was the extent of Steven Bishop's and his friend's abilities.

"The yearning for revenge tugs at your soul, my boy," the unseen stranger continued. "I can feel it as can you. The pain he has wreaked upon you cannot be left unrequited. He must pay."

Geoffrey was intrigued. "Who are you?"

"Who I am is of no consequence. It is what I am able to offer you that is of far greater significance."

Geoffrey watched as the same book again began to shift, sliding itself out from between a collection of dated text books and into a situation which left it teetering half on and half off of the shelf. Slowly Geoffrey approached the balancing tome, finally able to see through the shelf

71

and into the adjoining isle...empty. Not one person wandered the maze of literature with him, meaning that there had been no one to propel the apparently self motivated novel.

Cautiously he took one final step, bringing himself to within mere feet of the animated hardback. Again the book shifted. No longer finding room on the shelf to support its sizable mass, it toppled to the floor face up.

Geoffrey had never before seen a book of such lavish, yet simple detail, especially in a school library. Its covers were wrapped entirely of leather, with two, three inch wide strips of additional leather stretched diagonally from all four corners to form an "X" across the books face.

In addition to the tightly sewn threading, which had been used in joining the strips to their base, five, large, steel buttons assisted in permanently fastening the leather "X" to the cover; one in each of the four corners with a fifth centered perfectly on the cover.

Geoffrey lifted the cumbersome book from the floor. A large, dark blemish discolored the lower right corner of the front cover and, at the top, burned haphazardly into the leather, was the title, *Tales from "The Grave"*.

What a strangely macabre title for a book located in today's politically scrutinized school libraries, he thought to himself as he flipped through the first few pages in search of a publisher, author or even a date that would indicate when the aged book had been printed. Instead, starting from the very first page, he found only the elegantly scribed words of what appeared to be the first in a collection of hand written stories.

Though intrigued by the story's content, Geoffrey's interest in the book's origin continued to captivate his attention as he flipped to the inside of the back cover. Where he expected to find the book's library card, neatly tucked within its protective sleeve, he found only an empty page glued to the backside of the old, tarnished leather.

"Is this yours Geoffrey?"

Geoffrey jumped, quickly closing the book and looking up to find Mrs. White, the librarian, standing before him with his tape measure in hand. His mind still engrossed with the book, he didn't respond but instead just stared at his new, unexpected company.

"Are you all right?" Mrs. White asked concerned.

"Sure," Geoffrey finally managed to speak. "I mean yeah of course, just a friend playing a prank," he attempted to explain away Steven's behavior. He couldn't tell the librarian of his bully troubles. It was one thing to tattle to the school principle or even a teacher but to run to the little old lady with the books for help would surely do nothing more than paint him as the school sissy and make him an even juicier target for the Bishop crew; not to mention any other tormenting groups on the prowl for new game.

"Ah," Mrs. White responded, suspicious of the explanation. "You know, if you're having any problems you can talk to me, right?"

"I know, like I said, just a harmless prank. I'm fine, really."

"Ok," Mrs. White reluctantly accepted his explanation and handed him the tape measure before returning to her desk.

Geoffrey watched the elderly librarian as she again retreated from sight. His hopes of isolating the book's source to a particular author, or even a relative period, had proved to be a task that would require much more time and attention than just a simple examination could provide. Maybe a hint to the books origins was contained within the graceful words printed within.

He again opened the book, but unlike before, was not greeted with the looping letters and meticulously straight lines of text from before. Instead, only the color white filled the vast first page...and the second...and the third, fourth, fifth, sixth... Confused, he flipped through nearly a quarter of the lengthy book; each page blank until...page two hundred and sixty-one contained what looked to be a message; a message which sent a cold shiver the length of Geoffrey's spine.

I can help you.

The bizarre sentence was the only line of text on the page and was written in the same extraordinarily elegant handwriting he'd seen before.

Geoffrey slammed the book shut and hastily gathered the remains of his map from its scattered locations before shoving the book and scraps into his backpack.

Without issuing even a farewell glance to the now seated and reading Mrs. White, Geoffrey scurried from the library.

TEN

A Strange sight caught Peter's eye as he slowly approached the cash-register and it wasn't the burnt hunk of vegetable laden beef that the lunch-ladies we attempting to pass off as meatloaf.

At a table, near the back corner of the cafeteria, Geoffrey McDaniel sat alone, awaiting the arrival of his best friend. However, it wasn't Geoffrey's isolated presence that caused Peter to raise a brow. Voluntary or not, isolation was fairly common place for them both. What struck him as odd was that, even though Geoffrey was alone at the table, it appeared that his friend was involved in what seemed to be a very intense conversation, waving his hands and shaking his head in response to his invisible companion.

"Four-fifty," the cashier requested with an outstretched hand after quickly examining the contents of Peter's tray.

"Oh, yeah," Peter acknowledged handing over a five dollar bill, all the while keeping his eyes intently focused on his seemingly delusional friend.

The cashier plucked the bill from his open palm and in its place deposited two quarters which, by their blackened appearance, were hardly recognizable as United States currency. His mind preoccupied with Geoffrey's peculiar behavior though, Peter shoved the two bits into his pocket without so much as a shudder at the unsanitary coins.

"No!" Geoffrey firmly rejected whatever his imaginary friend had proposed.

Peter watched from a distance as he slowly approached the table. Steven Bishop and his crew sat only three tables away but unlike most days, when girl's rear ends and profane jokes were the topic of discussion, all eyes were currently focused on the lone freshman's one sided conversation.

"I can't," Geoffrey continued to stand his ground.

"You can't what?" Peter questioned as he took a seat between Geoffrey and the table of amused eves droppers.

"Aw. Boo," a collective roar erupted behind him as what he could only assume to be a hunk of meatloaf or a rogue piece of broccoli, struck the back of his head. As always, he showed no reaction to the group of delinquents.

Geoffrey looked up from his backpack.

"Did you know that the term midget or little person, as politically correct society would have us say, is reserved for people possessing a vertical stature of no more than four-feet, ten-inches?"

Geoffrey just stared at Peter, expressionless.

"I would guess that your new friend there doesn't quite fit into that category though. I mean, to squeeze into a bag that small, we'd have to be dealing with a gnome or a fairy or something."

A look of mental cloudiness hung heavy in Geoffrey's eyes for a few moments longer before clarity returned and with it, his usual, upbeat self.

"Hey Pete," Geoffrey greeted his friend as if finally noticing his presence at the table.

"Never mind."

"What?"

"All that trouble to set up a joke and you didn't even hear it," Peter explained in a defeated tone. "Are you all right?"

"Yeah, why and what joke?"

"Forget the joke. You just spent the better part of five minutes locked in a heated debate with your backpack."

"I did?"

"You don't remember?" Peter traded concern for confusion.

"I think if I'd been talking to my backpack, I'd remember."

"If you don't believe me, maybe you should ask them." Peter motioned over his shoulder.

Mark Faulty had a backpack in his outstretched hands as he mimed a conversation before drawing the bag closer for an intense make out session to the approving cheers of his table-mates.

"That's great. That's all I need. As if being the school geek wasn't bad enough, now I'm the crazy kid as well."

"It could be worse," Peter asserted in a comforting tone.

"Really? How? How could this get any worse?" he retorted in a disgusted tone, directing Peter's attention back to the juvenile table of jocks.

Mark had laid the backpack across the table and was currently writhing on top of it in a sick display of sexual humor.

"Mr. Faulty!" the lunch monitor scolded from across the cafeteria.

Mark climbed down from his latest conquest to the applause of the cafeteria.

"All right, that is pretty bad," Peter agreed, "but think of it this way, you'll always have a friend to talk to."

"Thanks Pete. You are a good friend."

"I wasn't talking about me," Peter rejected the compliment as he peered in the direction of Geoffrey's backpack.

This time he was confident of the projectile's identity as a dry piece of hamburger struck him between the eyes.

77

ELEVEN

"All right, listen up!" Mr. Manning commanded the attention of the hundred plus students before him. Most did as they were told and quieted at the sound of his voice. The demanding gym teacher was not the type to cross. With a physique to rival that of Arnold Schwarzenaeggar, before the Governator years, and a bullish attitude to match, if one wasn't careful they could easily find themselves doing laps until the end of time...maybe even longer.

Steven had learned of Mr. Manning's strict guidelines the hard way. The hot headed gym teacher had been the head coach of varsity football when Steven first made the team. Before then, every coach he'd come across had been a push over, sensitive to the feelings of others and eager not to offend any players or their parents. Mr. Manning, however, seemed to have no feelings. If a player screwed up on his field, he first turned his verbal hostility on the boy's spectating parents before seeking vengeance on the fearful youth. Luckily, Steven had been an exceptional player, having never been so unfortunate as to place himself, or his parents, in the crosshairs of the raving lunatic.

As devastating as the verbal batteries doled out by Mr. Manning could be, his practice sessions were even worse. Steven had heard of coaches running their players to the point of vomiting and apparently so had Manning. However, after they threw up, Manning seemed to believed that they then should be capable of running much faster, no longer having to carry around the cumbersome weight of the day's meals. This belief had never proved true and by the end of Steven's sophomore year, Coach Manning had been faced with an ultimatum, step down as coach of all youth sports and keep his teaching position or face immediate termination from both. He stepped down.

Apparently some of the other players, along with their parents, had grown tired of the routine abuse and had rallied for the termination of Mr. Manning from Eagle Roost all together but the school board had felt that action too extreme and in turn had proposed the eventual outcome.

Steven missed his head coach's presence on the field. Since then the team had fallen into a slump, winning only forty percent of their games over the last two seasons and losing their once deserved status of most feared high school in Nevada.

"I said shut the hell up!" cried Manning again, displaying an uncharacteristic moment of kindness by offering his students a second chance to obey his first order. Unfortunately for one student, there would be no third.

"You, ten laps around the gym now. You've got five minutes." Manning set his watch.

The freshman girl stood stunned. It was early in the school year and apparently, being new to High School, she hadn't yet learned of the teacher's insanity driven personality.

"Tick, tock, tick tock, the sound of your feet should match the clock," Manning taunted the girl as she began to slowly move away from the group in her forced circular journey. "I'd pick it up if I were you. You don't make it in time it's ten more."

The girl began to run.

"Now that I have your full attention I'm going to explain why we're all gathered here at once today. Apparently, many of the teacher's, whom classes you would normally be sleeping in right now, are involved in that meeting we've all been hearing so much about lately. Instead of hiring that many substitutes to baby sit your asses, you have all been placed in the custody of myself and my fellow athletic counselors."

"Talk about a power trip," a freshman beside Steven whispered in his friend's ear.

Steven smiled in anticipation of what was coming.

"You two, join her," Manning pointed at the girl who had completed only half a lap.

Like their misbehaving predecessor, the boys stood stunned.

"Tick tock, tick tock. You know the fucking rhyme."

The boys began to run.

"Like I was saying," Mr. Manning continued. "You will all be broken into groups. Each group will participate in one of three activities. You will not choose the activity. It will be chosen for you by Mrs. Murphy, who will assign each of you a number of one, two or three. When you have received your number, gather into the appropriate groups and await further instruction." Manning turned to the teacher on his right. "Mrs. Murphy."

Mrs. Murphy approached the group and began assigning numbers, almost taking out lap girl as she narrowly avoided ending lap one with a time consuming collision.

"I do not want to hear any complaining about what group you're in," Manning continued. "If I hear a complaint, you too can join our circling friends here."

The boys quickly approached the last turn of their first lap.

"They will be running for as long as it takes them to accomplish the goal that I've set forth and so will you. And, since I have no life outside of this fine, athletic environment, that could be a very long time."

The boys accelerated their already frantic pace, quickly gaining on the slowing girl.

"One," Mrs. Murphy assigned Steven's number before moving on to the next student.

Steven glanced at his slowly forming group. "Freshmen."

Though annoyed by this turn of events, Steven did as he had been instructed and joined the forming group without even so much as a sigh to indicate his disapproval.

Though surrounded by the child like faces of his usual prey, he felt remarkably comfortable in the group. Each person there or at least the ones who knew of him, remained at a distance, fearful of the wolf amongst their flock. Maybe this unwanted placement wasn't such a bad turn of events after all. With a little creativity, he could unleash as much, if not more fury on the little twerps and this time the only teacher was Mr. Manning, a man who lived his life for moments of physical confrontation and aggression in the name of sport. There's no way the man could decipher between uncalled for brutality and a spirited player determined to do anything and everything to be the best. Steven could pummel his competition as long as he did so in the spirit of the game. He'd be creative in his attacks. He'd choose his targets carefully. But most of all, he'd have fun.

Steven's mood brightened at the thought of the abuse he was about to inflict but was almost instantly cut down as his wandering eyes spotted Becky at the back of the remaining, unnumbered crowd. She wasn't normally in his class. She must have been part of those other classes Manning had reference in his speech.

As Mrs. Murphy continued to dole out the numerical assignments, Steven found himself praying that his ex received anything but the number one. Though unsure whether she knew or not, he was in no way ready to learn of just how much of the morning's events she might recall. In fact, he couldn't think of any time in the future, near or far, when he would be ready to discover that potentially life altering news. If she was aware of what had been done to her, he hoped that she was either too frightened or too ashamed to tell anyone.

Though exhilaration had driven him to complete the heinous act, the feeling had passed and he now wished the despicable idea had never even entered his mind. Never had he truly believed that a loser such as Dexter could get a girl of Becky's caliber. The pain of his own recent rejection had clouded his judgment. Deep down he feared that maybe he too was not good enough for someone such as the teenage beauty-queen standing amongst the crowd before him. Maybe he too was nothing but a loser with little to offer other than overplayed masculinity and a false sense of security.

Steven watched as Mrs. Murphy made her way down the line, drawing ever closer to issuing Becky's numerical fate. He began counting ahead, trying to guess which number would befall his ex's precious ears. As far as he could guess she was destined to become a three. Good, safe for at least another period.

"Two," Mrs. Murphy assigned a number to the girl on Becky's left before skipping over the perplexed teen and continuing down the line.

Steven stood puzzled, the tension in his stomach stirring up feelings similar to those once caused by Manning's brutal workouts.

"Mrs. Murphy," Becky, after a confused pause, spoke up. "I think you forgot me."

Mrs. Murphy turned to the forgotten student. "I did...oh...umm...why don't you go over to group number one dear."

"Shit!" Steven quietly exclaimed.

The freshmen, who had chosen to brave close quarters with their elder classmate, finally saw fit to seek potentially less threatening locations within the group.

Becky glanced toward the group that she'd been instructed to join, her eyes immediately locking with Steven's. He wasn't surprised by her suddenly uncomfortable expression. He'd seen the same look earlier in the hall. Apparently Becky too hadn't been aware of her ex's proximity but now, with a shared numerical identity, it was as if all the other students ceased to exist.

"Mrs. Murphy, I don't think--"

Becky was unable to complete her protest before Mr. Manning was in her face ready to draw blood for her blatant disregard for his clearly stated directions.

"Miss Alverez, was that a complaint I was about to hear escape your trap!?" the mentally unbalanced teacher questioned as he drew closer to his defiant student.

Becky thought a moment, staring back at the intense set of eyes glaring at her from only a few feet away.

"Do you wish to run laps for the rest of the period? Because if you do, by all means, finish whatever it was you were about to share with us."

Again Becky thought. Mr. Manning continued to burn a hole through the girl's skull.

"Yes," Becky nervously responded.

"Yes, what?" Manning sought clarification, salivating at the chance to dispense yet another punishment.

Steven was stunned. Becky was a straight "A" student, the class president and the most popular girl in school. She'd proven that she was capable of doing and being just about anything she wanted...anything but defiant. In all the years Steven had spent climbing the educational ladder with Becky, he'd never once seen her flout an authority figure, especially one as hardnosed as Manning. This obvious attempt to avoid her ex was all he needed. Steven was convinced. She must know.

"Yes that was a complaint. I do not want to be a part

of group one," the newly rebellious girl announced, this time with much more confidence.

"Well, Miss Class President," Manning punctuated his words with a mist of spittle. "That doesn't seem like good politics to me. Those poor pathetic souls you just rejected are your voters. Without them you'd be nothing; just another pretty little girl on the road to becoming nothing more than a live in housekeeper for whatever poor soul you deceive into marriage."

This time Manning had gone too far. Who the hell did he think he was to say such things to one of his own students and one of his normally best students at that? Steven was going to say something. He had to say something, even if it meant bringing his unspeakable actions to light. No one could belittle his girlfriend and get away with it. An angry, curse laden rant sped through Steven's mind. The endless flow of insults gathering in his throat, dying for the chance to be set free but his lips remained silent and Manning, unchallenged, drew a single tear from his victim.

"So you don't like group one, huh?" Manning continued. "Well, maybe you'd prefer group four then. They should be passing by any minute now. You can join them. Get running," Manning ended his attack in a threatening whisper.

Becky did as she was told.

Steven watched as the torn down girl slowly walked by, somehow still possessing the nerve to continually defy an already irate lunatic. Not once did Becky lift her gaze from the floor in front of her, utilizing her other senses to navigate a continually shape shifting group number two, which acted as an obstacle to the small group of disciplined runners.

Dexter stood at the edge of that wandering mass. Apparently he too had witness the peculiar exchange. How could he not? A shrug and look of perplexity was all he had to offer a stunned and now fearful Steven.

She definitely knew. There was no other explanation for her actions. The only thing he didn't know, was how she had found out and just what she intended to do.

*****

Though new to the school, Geoffrey and Peter both understood the rules of etiquette which dictated one's behavior in Mr. Manning's gym class.

During the first day of class Mr. Manning had, from what they could tell, shown an uncharacteristic soft spot in his heart, demanding that each student only try his or her hardest to reach a ribbon which had been tied to the top of one of several ropes, dangling from the gym's high, steel rafters. Having gotten to know the eccentric teacher's personality a bit better over the last couple of weeks, they now suspected the phrase, "try your hardest" had only been a onetime deal. For the remainder of the year, and most likely every year to follow, Manning's choice phrase would likely be "just do it", as if under contract with Nike.

Francis Philmore, another candidate for Eagle Roost's geek coalition, which Geoffrey had apparently and unwillingly beaten for the presidential title, had a slight fear of heights. Unfortunately, he'd opted to share this fear with Manning. The next thing he knew, he'd been clinging to the rope only inches from the thirty foot high ceiling, screaming for someone to help him down.

Quite frankly, Geoffrey had been surprised that Francis had even had the arm strength to reach such a height but with Manning screaming threats and obscenities the entire time, maybe it hadn't been so astounding that the kid had been able to muster the strength needed to flee from the aggressive pit-bull barking up at him from below.

Apparently, Manning too had been surprised, not to mention impressed by Francis's speedy accent. His insults had quickly turned to praise as the kid screamed for help. But when it became clear that his newly created, gym class monkey would be unable to return to the safety of solid ground, those praises had returned to a tone of mockery and insult.

Neither Geoffrey nor Peter had ever heard such profane language uttered by any person in their lives, let alone a school teacher. Manning attacked Francis. He lambasted Frances's mother. At one point Geoffrey could have sworn that he'd even heard the madman go after the poor kid's family dog. The whole time Francis had remained at the top of the rope, whimpering over his perceived, perilous predicament, until Robert Shear, a member of the school's wrestling team and a kid whose kind heart so drastically contradicted his massive physique, climbed the rope beside Francis and coached the boy through a slow and safe decent. When both had returned safely to earth, Manning yelled, Robert ran laps and Francis spent the remainder of the class crying, alone in the corner.

Bearing witness to Mr. Manning's sadistic form of education, Geoffrey and Peter knew good and well never to cross the likely steroid ingesting lunatic. Others, however, hadn't so easily picked up on the harsh lesson and currently found themselves lapping the basketball court which, for the time being, had become the field of play for one of Manning's favorite activities, Ultimate Frisbee.

Somehow Geoffrey, a self-proclaimed, coordination-deficient human being, had found himself tattooed with the unlucky number of one in Mr. Manning's random numbering system. He could have been a two and currently been playing Badminton in the other gym or even a three and found himself on a nice little power walk around the school campus but no, he had to be involved in a game that required both skill and coordination. The only plus in the situation was that miraculously, Peter too had been placed in the same group. On the other hand, so had Steven Bishop.

"Come on, ya little shit, throw it," Steven barked at Geoffrey from only three feet way.

"Mr. Bishop! Language!" Manning lightly scolded Steven for his profanity.

Geoffrey didn't know what to do. Sweat began beading on his forehead as a realization came to mind. He'd never in his life even held a Frisbee, let alone thrown one. This thought surprised him. How could he have made it to the ripe old age of fifteen and never used a Frisbee?

"Throw it!" Steven screamed, breaking Geoffrey of his introspective wondering.

"Over here Geoff," Peter cried for the disk.

Steven towered over him. There was no way he could get the disk around the pumped up beast and since he'd already taken his three allowed steps toward the other team's end zone he found himself frozen in place. Steven however, free of the burdening rules dictated by the small plastic toy, bounced back and forth, ready to snatch the saucer out of the air at first flight.

"Geoff, I'm open," Peter cried out again.

Geoffrey wound and threw, shocked as the disk took flight with an upward path as opposed to diving straight into the gymnasium floor. He wasn't surprised however that, as anticipated, Steven's massive paw quickly reacted, snatching the disk out of the air and immediately taking his three long strides toward the opposite end zone. Unable to sidestep the oncoming train, Geoffrey was met with the lowered shoulder of the charging senior and knocked to the ground with a mind jarring crash.

Steven released the Frisbee to another teammate who, possessing either a strong determination to win or simply an understandable interest in self-preservation, quickly returned the disk to Steven who was already waiting in the end zone.

It was five to one already, Steven having scored all five points for his team. The one point earned by Geoffrey and Peter's team had amazingly been scored by Peter himself but only due to his constant presence in Steven's end zone, far away from the carnage ensuing in the center of the court. Someone had thrown the disk and more in self-defense than actual effort, he'd caught it. Steven had been more than furious by the loss of his potential shutout and had expressed himself as such on the next possession by hurling the disk directly at Peter's head. Steven had claimed it to be an accident and Manning had allowed it as such but both Geoffrey and Peter, as well as everyone else in the game, had known the true nature of the "accidental" attack.

"That's five baby. Woo!" Steven celebrated in the end zone as he began riding the disk like a bull.

"Get up," a soft voice ordered Geoffrey.

He looked around but failed to see anyone nearby or even gazing in his general direction.

"He mustn't go unpunished. Now get up!" the voice spoke again.

The phantom voice was back and though he didn't fully understand its origins, Geoffrey knew it was right. He had to get up. He had to make a stand. If he continued to go about each day in this submissive manor, he wasn't going to live to see the end of high school. Hell, he'd only just begun the year and already a handful of bruises adorned his body. He must get up. He must make a stand.

"Are you all right?" Peter grabbed hold of Geoffrey's arm, helping him to his feet.

Geoffrey yanked his arm away and glared at his assisting friend.

"Whoa, sorry," Peter spoke surprised as he backed away.

"Sorry," Geoffrey responded, his angry expression softening but still intact.

"You're all right though, right?" Peter again asked, more hesitantly this time.

"Yeah, I'm fine. Just my pride, right?"

"Who needs that anyway?" Peter joked. He got no response.

"All right. Winners disk," Manning announced as he tossed the Frisbee to Steven at the far end of the court.

Geoffrey left Peter's side as Steven took three steps out of his own end zone before tossing the disk to a nearby teammate who, once again, immediately returned it to its previous owner. Three more steps placed Steven at center court where a fuming Geoffrey stood in his way.

"What, you want more?" Steven responded to the freshman's hostile expression.

Geoffrey just glared.

"Look, I'm gonna give you one chance to get out of my way before I run your ass over...again."

Geoffrey stood his ground as he balled his right hand into a fist.

"What, you think you're gonna kick my ass?"

"Just shut up and throw it asshole," Geoffrey mumbled.

"What did you just call me?" Steven responded, shock by the unexpected insult.

"You heard me dick-wad, I said throw it. I dare you."

Steven let out a small chuckle. "Hey kid, say hi to your backpack for me."

Almost before Steven could finish his sentence a small fist collided with his right eye.

Geoffrey snatched the disk from his stunned opponent and ran toward the opposite end zone. Three steps, four steps, five. For the first time in his life he didn't care that he was breaking the rules. The pain in his fist felt great and the nearer to the end zone he drew, the more his excitement grew.

Peter, along with the rest of the class, watched in awe as Geoffrey strutted into the end zone, dancing with the Frisbee raised high overhead before smashing it to the ground in victory, causing the flat, plastic object to split down the middle.

"Mr. McDaniel!" Manning exploded. "What in fuck's name is wrong with you!?"

Suddenly, excited Geoffrey vanished and timid, shy Geoffrey returned, seeming to cower at the very thought of Manning's wrath.

"I cannot believe what I just saw on my playing field! What the fuck makes you think you can just go around taking swings at people, huh!?" Manning laid into his frightened victim.

Geoffrey's legs began to weaken as he slowly sank into the floor beneath the towering teacher.

"I should allow Mr. Bishop over there a free shot at your sorry ass, just to teach you what an unsportsmanlike act that was."

Peter looked at Steven who seemed overjoyed with the proposal Manning had just made.

"But, seeing that Mr. Bishop might kill you in the process, maybe you should just start running!"

Geoffrey was thrilled with the punishment. He'd expected Manning himself to send a blow his way. Instead, he just had to run some laps for the remainder of the period. That was just fine with him.

"By the way, nice swing kid," Manning whispered as Geoffrey took his first departing step.

Geoffrey smiled at the unexpected praise. As he took his first few strides along the outer perimeter of the gym, he glanced over at Steven, whose eye was already reddening from the blow.

Steven just glared, tracking his attacker around the gym.

"Try not to be such a sissy next time," Manning told Steven as he slapped a new Frisbee against his student's chest before blowing the whistle for the game to resume.

TWELVE

"That was awesome," Peter expressed his shocked approval over Geoffrey's sudden attack on Steven.

Geoffrey, seeming on the verge of vomiting or passing out...probably both...just looked over at his friend who stood changing only a few lockers from his. He was glad to see his friend so overjoyed by the action even he himself had never dreamt possible but he wasn't so sure it had been the wisest of moves.

Something had overcome him. Helplessly staring into that cretin's eyes as he taunted and pushed, had caused something to snap within. It had been as if he'd had no control over his own fist, almost like a puppet under the guiding motions of a malicious puppeteer. All he could do was sit back and watch as his fist had cut through the air, connecting with the senior's face. The whole experience had seemed somewhat surreal, the veil of cloudiness not lifting until Manning had gotten in his face.

"Maybe being known as the crazy kid isn't so bad after all," Peter continued to take delight in what he'd witnessed. "You never know when the crazy ones might snap." He playfully punched the air.

Again, Geoffrey glanced over at his ecstatic friend.

Peter could tell that he'd crossed the line. "Sorry."

"He's right," Ernesto Ganado, as if his position between the two automatically made him a part of the conversation, chose to join in. "You must be crazy. Only a crazy person would paint that big a target on his back."

"What?" Geoffrey looked over at the new addition to their semi private discussion.

"You really think taking a swing at that...," he paused to look around before continuing in a softer voice, "...prick is really going to keep him off of you? All I know is that, if I were you, I'd grow another set of eyes in the back my head, because now there's no telling where the next assault might come from." Ernesto slammed his locker door shut as he departed with a muffled, "crazy son of a bitch."

"He's right," Geoffrey muttered, staring into his locker.

"What? Don't listen to him," Peter attempted to comfort his increasingly panicked friend.

"No, he's right. What have I done? It was bad enough when Steven and his gang were picking on me simply for the fun of it but now, now they have a score to settle. I'm as good as dead, aren't I?"

"You're listening to a kid who lit his own hair on fire in the seventh grade because he wanted to see if the smell was really as bad as everyone said it would be," Peter attempted to nullify Ernesto's prodding words of wisdom, even though he believed there was some truth in what had been said.

"Maybe I can change schools," Geoffrey grasped for an answer to his dilemma while continuing to dress.

"And go where, Sierra High in the next valley over? I'm sure your mom would have no problem driving you over there, especially in her condition."

Peter cringed as soon as the words escaped his mouth. For the first time he'd let his true opinion of Geoffrey's mother and his friend's home life, slip into the open.

Instead of reacting with the same anger he'd displayed only a half hour ago, Geoffrey remained silent, staring at his locker as he withdrew his shirt.

"I'm sorry, I--"

"No, you're right. I can't run away from this situation. It's been done and I can't change it. Now I either fix it or hope that I can survive the rest of the year."

"What do you mean fix it?" Peter asked perplexed.

"I just need to go over there and apologize for my actions and hope that he can be a man about this whole thing."

Steven's angry voice suddenly echoed through the locker room, catching Peter's attention but apparently slipping right past Geoffrey's.

"I'm sure he'd understand. I know he's not happy but I'm sure he understands why I did it," Geoffrey continued to convince himself of his plan.

"You didn't just hear that?"

"He's a reasonable guy. I just need to be upfront and apologize for what I did."

"We're talking about the same Steven Bishop, right? Since when did he become such a reasonable, standup guy," Peter questioned, worried that Geoffrey might actually go through with his apologetic plan. "If you go over there, you won't have to worry about surviving another year, because you'll be lucky to survive another fifteen minutes. Don't go over there," Peter pleaded as he watched several curious students migrating in Steven's direction. Whatever was going on over there was unpleasant already and now his apparently crazy friend was set on just march over and offering his apologies? Peter frantically slipped his right leg into his jeans.

"That's what I'll do. I just need to apologize," Geoffrey continued to ignore Peter's reasoning as he fastened the last button on his shirt and, picking up his back pack, closed his locker.

Peter buttoned his pants, but seeing Geoffrey departing on what was sure to be a disastrous mission for peace, opted to remain shoeless as he chased after his friend.

*****

The unpleasant wall of stink struck Steven the moment he passed through the doorway. The stench of armpit scented T-shirts and sweat drenched gym shorts permeated the locker room air in conjunction with its arch nemesis, excessively applied cologne.

The more conscientious and courteous students usually made it a point to swap out their gland soaked gym clothes at least once a week. Steven was one such student, though more so for his own comfort than those around him. The majority of his sanitarily challenged classmates however often failed to display such a simple portrayal of good hygiene and manors, leaving their soiled apparel to fester within the one foot metal cubes for weeks, sometimes months at a time. Only two weeks into the school year and it was already apparent who these disgustingly inconsiderate students would be.

Luckily, having spent much of his adolescent life surrounded by the aromatic results of a sports filled life, he was more than accustom to the familiar male odor and therefore remained stone faced as he maneuvered his way through the larger than usual crowd of boys. He was on a mission. He was determined to find out just how much Becky knew and since he couldn't risk going directly to the source, there was only one other person who could possess such knowledge.

As he approached the row of lockers that would lead him to his informant, Steven again rubbed at his left eye. A small welt had already begun forming, announcing the impending arrival of the bruise that would soon follow.

That little shit had shown balls. Never before had the twerp fought back. Hell, he'd never even put up a struggle when receiving the punishment his kind often accepted as just a fact of life.

Though his face temporarily displayed potentially

damaging proof of his minor loss, Steven still found reason to smile. He knew the runt's swing, though impressive, lacked the brute force needed to do any real damage. It sure as hell wasn't about to deter him from unleashing his hostilities on the little fuck the next time he laid eyes upon him. The underclassman had sent an invitation and he couldn't wait to RSVP.

As he rounded the last row of lockers, Dexter came into view, standing at his locker in only a pair of tighty-whities and quickly shoving his odor harboring garments back into their hole for another week of growth. He hadn't even seen Steven coming but was quickly made aware of his presence by the hand around his throat and his body's involuntary migration backwards.

Steven slammed his unsuspecting victim's body against the concrete wall. Though unable to lift his equally sized foe, he was able to prevent his escape. Dexter, however, apparently possessed no desire to incite a struggle and as a result, remained motionless, trapped between Steven's grasp and the cold wall.

"What the hell?" Dexter mumbled, his voice impeded by the clenching grasp of Steven's fingers.

Only a few students possessed lockers in close proximity to the unfolding assault. All knew, either from experience or word of mouth, to keep their distance and focus only on what mattered to them or face the same display of hostility currently befalling their ill-fated neighbor.

"You're a lying sack of shit!" Steven exclaimed before realizing just how well his voice would travel within the room of steel and concrete.

"What are you talking about?" Dexter questioned, dumbfounded by the sudden assault on his body and character.

"Becky!" he answered in a slightly adjusted volume.

"I already told you," Dexter continued in his restricted voice.

Steven lessened his grasp, aware that such a tight hold would do little to help in obtaining his sought after information.

"I didn't say anything to her."

"That's bullshit. You saw the way she acted out there. She knows something. Only two people could have told her and I sure as hell didn't, so that leaves you."

"I swear I didn't say a thing. Why would I lie?"

"Why the fuck do you think?"

"Are we going to go through that again?" Dexter questioned, his voice changing from that of fear to annoyance. "I already told you, I have no interest in Becky. If I had any intentions of pursuing her, do you really think that I would have let you do what you did? How do you think she would react if she found out that I just let it happen? Hell, I'm in as much shit as you are on this one, so I can't think of any reason why I would even consider telling anyone about this. As far as I'm concerned, nothing happened and that's that."

Steven thought for a moment. Dexter was right. He was just as involved in this mess. It would be pretty stupid on his part to place himself in the line of fire, just for the chance to add one more conquest to his belt. "Well, if you didn't, then who did?" Steven questioned, releasing his reinstated friend.

"I don't know."

As the two continued their speculation, Steven caught a glimpse of Geoffrey McDaniel rounding the last row of lockers. Dexter would have to contemplate the Becky mystery on his own for the next few minutes as Steven locked eyes with the pint sized nerd.

"What happened to your face?" Dexter questioned his distracted friend, finally noticing the newly forming bruise.

Steven ignored the question and started toward Geoffrey. The weakling froze like a deer in headlights, his eyes locked with Steven's as his impending fate approached at an alarming pace. Steven sneered as he retracted his fist before delivering a vicious blow to the underclassman's upper intestines.

Geoffrey dropped, quickly taking hold of his injured abdomen. Even before the fallen twerp's mind had time to register the severity of the inflicted pain, Steven was in the face of Peter Madison.

"You so much as move and even your mother won't recognize the body," Steven threatened the stunned and fearful boy.

What had started as only a handful of nervous onlookers, had quickly grown to a mass of curious bodies, eager to witness the wrath of the clearly vexed upperclassman.

Steven knelt beside his gasping victim. "Next time you send a fist my way, you'd better hope it kills me," he whispered into Geoffrey's ear before applying two quick, firm slaps to the boy's face.

"Mr. Bishop!" a voice boomed from above.

Steven peered over his shoulder at the sight of Mr. Manning, looming over him. The man had approached under an almost mystical veil of silence, strategically positioning himself over the source of his evident rage.

Before Steven could do anything, he was lifted to his feet and sent stumbling across the dull linoleum floor, coming to a booming halt against a row of metal lockers. Though the crash and rumble of the now dented lockers sounded much like a cannon being fired off within the confined space, Steven quickly recovered, clenching his fists in preparation for the next phase of this unexpected attack.

"What, you're gonna kick my ass?" Manning taunted his enraged student.

Steven stood on guard, ready to deliver whatever damage he could before facing the unavoidable pummeling that would surely follow such an assault on the behemoth of a man. He knew the teacher hadn't even considered yet what battery on one of his own student would do to his career. That thought would likely not pass through the emotionally driven man's mind until long after the ambulance had left with the body and questions began arising as to what had actually occurred. Like Steven though, Manning showed restraint, refraining from immediately pouncing upon his lesser opponent.

"Get your ass to the office. I'll deal with you later and if you even think of making up some flagrant lie about me to Principle Sanchez, I'll run you so hard that only nubs will be left at the ends of those pathetic limbs you call legs."

Steven thought about the threat. He wanted to charge the lunatic educator; show him who the real boss was but he knew better. He couldn't survive such an encounter, so, reluctantly he let down his guard and retreated from the locker room as instructed.

"Are you alright son?" Manning turned to the fallen student but Geoffrey McDaniel and Peter Madison were gone, leaving in their place a crowd of curious and fearful students; students who were guaranteed never to disturb or disobey their hotheaded teacher from that point on.

"Get to class!" Manning shouted.

They too did as they were told.

THIRTEEN

"What was I thinking?" Geoffrey mumbled in a barely audible voice as he and Peter rounded the corner onto Shady Lane, bringing Geoffrey's house into view only fifty yards away.

It had been an hour and a half since the confrontation in the locker room and though they shared the same Spanish class the last period of the day, Geoffrey had remained stubbornly silent at his desk the entire time. Peter understood the embarrassment stemming from the encounter, he too had been left shaken by the incident but as much as he wanted to comfort his friend's damaged self esteem, he couldn't. He knew that anything he said, any words of encouragement he spoke, would be a waste of breath until Geoffrey himself was ready to receive them. So, when Geoffrey had finally chosen to break the long silence, Peter was more than happy to lend his encouraging words.

"Don't worry about it. Look at it this way, you were afraid of Steven killing you over the punch, which I still have to say, was pretty great."

Geoffrey shot Peter a look, disputing the greatness of his actions.

"Well, great or not, the problem's been settled. He got it out of his system and you're still alive, no need to worry."

"Yeah, right, no need to worry...until tomorrow when he decides to get it out of his system again and then the day after that and the day after that." Geoffrey began to panic at the thought of his ill fated future.

"Well, tomorrow being Friday, I think you can rest easy the following two days, unless of course you two have a play date this weekend."

"You know what I mean," Geoffrey rebuked the attempted joke. "Things were bad enough when they used to pick on me just because. Now they have a reason."

Geoffrey was overwhelmed by the thought of what the malicious crew might do to him next. Before, it had been just a simple case of practical jokes or the occasional smacking around. Now he had to fear more serious injuries; ones potentially involving ambulances and doctors. The bad thing was, he fully believed not only in their unquestionable capacity to enact such violence but in their absolute ability to get away with it as well. They were the pride of Eagle Roost's athletic department, with plenty of friends to help cover for them, just in case some tragic fate did happen to befall their new whipping boy. They could certainly pull it off. There was no doubt about it.

"Watch out!" Peter suddenly cried.

By the time Geoffrey saw the tennis ball, lying in the center of the sidewalk, it was too late. His foot was already rolling across the top of it, his balance severely compromised.

Surprised by the sudden interruption to his introspective self-pity, the stumbling teen could do little to reestablish his balance and within seconds of feeling his foot come down upon the ball, he found himself lying on the McGregor's front lawn.

"Shit," He muttered in a defeated tone as he rolled onto his back and just stared up at the sky.

The use of profanity from his usually clean mouthed friend would have surprised Peter on any other day, but after bearing witness to the uncharacteristic display in gym class, it was clear that there was still another side of Geoffrey that he'd not yet gotten to know.

"Are you all right?" Peter asked, standing over his friend.

"I think I'll just stay right here from now on," Geoffrey spoke while watching a couple of birds perform an elegant ballet overhead.

"Might get a bit cold at night," Peter responded.

"Aw, couldn't be that bad. So I lose a few fingers and toes to frost bite, couldn't be any worse than what might happen to me in the next gym class."

"What about when it snows?"

"You're a good friend. I know you'll come dig me out."

"Thanks for the vote of confidence but you know how I feel about the cold. If it starts snowing, you're on your own."

"Thanks buddy."

"Just warning you ahead of time. Would you like a hand?"

Geoffrey, bored with the birds, turned his eyes upon the offered hand. "I thought you wouldn't help?"

"I don't see any snow, do you?" Peter spoke as he tugged on his friend's arm.

"Not since your switch to Head and Shoulders," Geoffrey capitalized on the unintentional set up.

Peter released his grip, returning the jokester to his grassy bed with a thud.

Geoffrey laughed. Peter, playing hurt, had already chosen and was prepared to offer his own witty comeback, when a chain of vicious barking interrupted the jovial moment.

Twenty feet away, Prince had finally noticed the boy's presence and, continuing his rant from that morning, again growling and snapping at his ground ridden neighbor.

"You know, dogs have a very astute sense of smell," Peter spoke as he watched Prince bound back and forth on his hind legs. "Maybe he smells something he doesn't like, you know, like rotten eggs or something."

Geoffrey helped himself to his feet, unsure exactly of what Peter was referring to.

"When was the last time you showered?"

Geoffrey took a jab at Peter's shoulder.

"Cause you know, I thought I smelled something earlier," Peter continued, regardless of yet another blow to his arm. "I didn't want to say anything."

Geoffrey laughed as he playfully struck his buddy for a third time.

Glad to see a smile on his friend's face Peter leaned over to retrieve Geoffrey's bag from the ground.

"No! Don't touch that!" Geoffrey's smile quickly gave way to anger.

Peter, already holding the bag in his hand, stood surprised as Geoffrey ripped the bag from his grasp and held it close to his chest. "Whoa! Sorry."

Geoffrey's sudden anger slowly faded but his death grip on the backpack did not.

"What do you have in there?"

"Home...homework," Geoffrey searched for an answer.

"We've had mostly the same classes today and I don't recall being given any assignment that exhilarating."

Geoffrey just stared at his inquisitive friend.

"That must be a lot of homework. You don't usually bring home a bag that heavy," Peter continued searching for the explanation behind his friend's bizarre behavior. "What do you have in there really?"

"I told you, homework," Geoffrey snapped.

Peter was stunned. He could tell that the only way he was going to see the inside of that bag was if he were to pry it from his friend's cold, dead fingers but with enough people already lining up to perform the murderous task, he didn't think it was necessary that he too be added to the list.

"I think I'm going to go lay down for a while," Geoffrey excused himself from the uncomfortable situation as he turned to walk away.

"Maybe I can come in and play some X-Box?," Peter attempted to both change the subject as well as keep himself in proximity to the fiercely guarded backpack.

"I'm really not feeling all that well right now. I need to lie down," Geoffrey continued the lie, picking up the pace in reaction to Peter's trailing footsteps.

Continuing his frantic barking, Prince followed the boy's movements along the front lawn to Geoffrey's front door.

"Well, maybe you could come over later tonight," Peter continued, following his friend up the first couple of steps as Geoffrey fumbled with the door knob.

Geoffrey didn't answer. He turned the knob and pushed open the door.

"My mom's making a roast for dinner and--"

The door slammed shut.

Stunned, not only by Geoffrey's unusual behavior but by his rudeness as well, Peter just stared at the closed door.

"I guess I'll see you in the morning then!" he shouted at the house, pausing to see if his friend would reemerge, before finally giving up and walking home.

FOURTEEN

"Dear Lord we thank you for the wonderful meal you have provided us and for the blessing you have granted by allowing our family to unite as one around this table, free of illness and full of love," Mrs. Madison issued the nightly grace as the rest of the family bowed their heads in respectful silence. "And for the chance to live a life full of opportunity and privilege that many in the world deserve so much more. And..."

She was really going to town with this one, James thought to himself as he stole a peak at his wife, her head bowed at the opposite end of the table. She must have really sinned it up with Mr. Fitness this morning and though possessing no desire or real reason to stop, was apparently feeling a bit guilty about soiling the sacred vows she'd made on their wedding day.

"Amen," Rebecca finished the long winded prayer.

A collective "Amen" rose from the remainder of the family as they all lifted their heads and began filling their plates with the tasty morsels of the night's offerings.

As many complaints as he did have about his wife, he had no reason to find fault with her cooking. The woman was a genius in the kitchen and he was fairly sure that, if given only a pinecone and a handful of sugar, in some sort of MacGyverish way, she would find a way to create the most elegant of meals.

"That was a long one tonight, mom," Peter commented on his mother's prayer.

"That's because we have so much to be thankful for, honey," Rebecca responded, eyeing her husband with a look as if to say, "you have no idea what I did today".

He knew. He'd followed her to the gym a little over a month ago and peeking through the heavily tinted windows of Francesco's private fitness center, had seen the hulk of a man hammering his naked wife on a weight bench, while pumping what appeared to be at least a fifty pound dumbbell in each of his hands.

He'd suspected her infidelity much longer than that though but had never had the balls to pursue the proof, probably because he'd still harbored some hope that they would someday reconcile their differences and once again live a life of love and marital bliss. Those hopes had long since been dashed across the jagged rocks of reality though, leaving only the promise of divorce in their future.

They both knew their split was inevitable. Yet an agreement, made about six months ago, had them remaining together for no other reason than the kids. They had chosen to bring these two innocent lives into the world. It was only fair that they preserve that innocence until they were both old enough and better equipped to deal with such a life changing alteration to their family dynamic. Besides, they both new how any custody battle would go and neither wanted to subject the children, if not themselves, to the ugly world of a divorce proceeding. In fourteen years, when Emily turned eighteen, they would proceed with the separation but until then they would continue to live their lives under the false pretense of happiness. Rebecca would probably continue to bang everything with three legs and James would continue to sulk in the hell that had become his existence.

"So, what did you do in school today Peter?" James chose to redirect his internal anguish toward what he hoped would be a more uplifting and positive topic.

"Oh, you should have seen it," Peter immediately jumped at the chance to speak, as if he'd spent the last ten years in solitude, isolated and unable to purge himself of the pent-up information racing through his mind. "You know Steven Bishop, right?"

"Wasn't he that kid who was bothering you?" Rebecca joined the conversation, showing nervous concern over the information she was about to receive.

"Yeah but--"

"Is he bothering you again?" James joined in his wife's concern.

"No--"

"Because if he is, I could talk to the principle or his parents you know."

"Yeah, dad...that didn't really work out all that well the last time, so I'd rather you not. Anyway..."

James was surprised and proud of his son's ability to shrug off whatever occurrence his apparently poor choice of talking to the principle had caused.

"...Like I was saying," Peter continued. "You know Steven right? Well, Geoffrey decked him in gym class today."

"What?" Mrs. Madison responded, concerned over her son's enthusiasm toward violence.

"Yeah, nearly broke his nose...but he didn't."

"Looks like everyone was getting pounded in gym class today," James mumbled under his breath.

Rebecca, hearing the comment, shot her husband a threatening glare.

"What dad?" Peter paused in his story, confused by his father's odd comment.

"Nothing. I don't like the idea of you fighting," James reclaimed his position as parent.

"I didn't do anything. Geoffrey just snapped and the

next thing I knew Steven's eye was swelling up like a balloon."

"I thought you said he hit him in the nose," James caught the exaggeration.

"Nose, eye, it was his face anyway."

"I agree with your father. I don't like the idea of you fighting."

"Mom, I told you. I didn't do anything," Peter defended himself in frustration.

"Well, I know but you seem very excited about it."

"Yeah, I'm excited. No one has ever stood up to that jerk before. It was amazing."

"It was wrong," James admonished his son's enthusiasm. "You can't just go around hitting people and I hope Geoffrey's mother is telling her son the same thing right now," he continued, well aware of Mrs. McDaniel's drinking problem and complete lack of parenting skills.

"If this is how Geoffrey is going to behave now then maybe you shouldn't hang out with him anymore," Rebecca addressed Peter.

"He was just standing up for himself for once. It's not like he'd attack me or anything."

"I'm not saying he'd hit you. All I'm saying is that you don't need to be associating yourself with someone who feels that the only way to solve his problems is with his fists," Rebecca explained.

"I think I'll be fine mom. It's not like he's transformed into the school bully and goes around stealing everyone's lunch money."

"Not yet," James added.

Peter smiled at what he thought had been a joke but seeing the old man's expressionless face, figured he'd heard wrong and erased his grin.

"Take that," Emily shouted as she struck her big brother's arm with a closed fist.

"Ouch," Peter reacted to the unexpected and surprisingly solid strike.

"Emily Summer Madison," James raised his voice. "We don't hit."

"Sorry daddy," Emily bowed her head, returning to her dinner.

"Yeah, you never know when the tickle monster might come looking for you," Peter attempted to raise his scolded sister's temporarily pummeled spirits.

"No!" Emily screamed as she hopped down from her chair and took off toward the den, followed closely by her big brother.

"You both need to finish your dinner!" Rebecca shouted to the departing children but figured her voice had gone unheard when laughter and playful roars were all that returned.

Before returning to her meal Rebecca glanced over at James, who had already returned his attention to the plate before him and was shoveling one bite after another into his mouth, all the while displaying an expression of somber discontentedness.

"You seem awfully glum tonight," she questioned her husband's sullen demeanor.

"Well, some of us don't have a hearty sex life to get us through the day," he mumbled without lifting his eyes from his meal.

"What is that supposed to mean?" Rebecca changed her tone from, what had been an attempt at a civil conversation, to that of the typical hostility often present during any shared, verbal interaction.

"I think you know what it meant."

"No, I don't. Please, enlighten me."

She knew what he was talking about. It just hadn't been until today that the topic had come to the forefront for open discussion. She wasn't quite sure how to handle the delicate topic and, needing another moment to consider her approach, placed a piece of chicken in her mouth.

"I know this little game might seem fun to you but

come on."

"Game, what game?"

"The game that involves you doing your damnedest to drive the knife as deep into my heart as possible."

Rebecca just stared.

"Three years. It's been three years since I cheated on you," he quieted his tone, as not to alert the nearby children to their ensuing problems.

"Has it been that long? Wow. It seems like it was just yesterday that you betrayed our marriage."

"Me? No that was you and it wasn't yesterday, it was this morning."

"I still don't know what you're talking about."

"Well then maybe you should go ask Francesco for a bit of a reminder and while you're at it, could you be a doll and ask him a question for me too? I was just wondering, how in the hell does he get all those husbands, because I'm sure I'm not the only one, to pay those ludicrous fees to pork their wives? You know, just in case this writing thing doesn't pan out."

"I guess he's just that good," Rebecca picked at her husband's emotional scab.

Even though he knew the truth and had known for quite some time, it hurt to hear her finally admit to her ongoing infidelity. She hadn't directly come out and announced it, but he knew what she meant.

"You know. I don't think this is or ever was about my cheating on you. I think you kind of like it."

"What?"

"Torturing me. I think you take some sort of sick pleasure in watching me suffer. I admit it. I screwed up one time...one time. I said I was sorry. I thought you'd forgiven me but you knew then and there that it was over. You just found it more fun to stick around and make me pay, didn't you?"

Rebecca said nothing.

"Or is it the money? Is it the money that keeps you

around? Because guess what babe, the money train has left the station and is barreling toward a track that isn't quite built yet."

"You know, for a writer, that was an awfully piss poor analogy," Rebecca continued to hold her sights fixed on James's heart. "You know why I stick around. This isn't the first time we've had this conversation. I'm here for the kids and that's it. Don't make me out to be some kind of monster, holding you captive and all. You're free to go. If you want to leave, then be my guest."

"You know I can't do that."

"Why? Why would you want to hang around here anyway? Obviously I'm some kind of heartless bitch who finds joy in stomping up and down on your sensitive feelings."

"I'm here for the same reason as you. You know that and by the way, yes you are."

"You're such an asshole."

"Nice, breaking out the colorful language now. You know, resorting to language of a more vivid and exclamatory nature is a sure sign of low level intelligence."

"Fuck you."

"Ah the sounds of an IQ slowly dwindling in the night," James mocked.

"You know what; maybe it's me who shouldn't stick around. Maybe I should just leave but you can rest assured that I will have no problem taking the kids with me."

"Oh yeah, on what grounds? Do you really think that a judge would award two children to a woman who doesn't have and hasn't held a job in the past five years? How exactly do you plan to pay for everything?"

"I'm a poor, neglected housewife whose husband cheated on her...and got national coverage doing so. I don't think I'll have any problem getting a fair share of everything you own."

"Ooh, that will be a lot."

"Don't play coy with me. I know things aren't as bad

as you like to make them seem. You just can't go through life without some sort of problem to mope about. Currently its money, when most likely you have a fairly hefty treasure chest tucked away that I'm not even aware of."

"Nope."

"That's bullshit and you know it," Rebecca laughed at her husband's dishonesty.

No longer hungry, but looking for an excuse to disengage himself from the hostile conversation, he shoveled a large piece of chicken into his mouth, thinking as he chewed about how right she really was. He knew that if she left she would get the kids. She would end up getting a good portion of whatever he had left and he would be limited to weekend visits and a handful of holidays with his children.

"I sold the cabin," he mumbled while chewing the meat.

"You what?" Peter exclaimed from the doorway.

Shit, James thought to himself. He hadn't wanted to break the news to Peter like this.

"Why? Why did you sell it? I thought we were going up there next month to go fishing," Peter whined in disbelief.

"Yeah honey, why did you sell it?" Rebecca deviously added fuel to the fire.

"I'll be upstairs," James quickly proclaimed before tossing his napkin onto his plate and dismissing himself from the table.

"I'll be upstairs too," Emily mimicked her father's actions and began walking away from the table.

"No, you will sit down and finish your dinner little miss," Rebecca sternly returned her daughter to the table with a look.

Dejected by the heated conversation, the unveiling of the surprise sale and being scolded, Rebecca, Peter and Emily returned their attention to the plates before them and, in a veil of uncomfortable silence, finished their meals.

FIFTEEN

Barker Price would have titty-fucked the lifeless woman, but given that she'd been dead for several hours already, it was only a matter of time before rigor mortis set in. And, no longer possessing the ability to offer her suitor the benefit of self-lubrication, it was a race against the clock if he was to get as much enjoyment as he could from this one.

It had been nearly an hour since a burst of creativity had produced the disturbing, opening paragraph to James's newest novel and just fifteen minutes longer since he'd childishly sulked away from the dinner table and from an opportunity to provide his son with the explanation he so deserved.

Though overwhelmingly thrilled with the macabre opening, he wasn't entirely sure where it had come from. Scenes of necrophilia and similar sexual content weren't exactly typical subject matter for him. And, though he had no idea where the rest of the story was heading, he was sure of one thing. This would be his most unsettling and controversial work to date.

"James," a voice spoke through the door, followed by a light knocking.

She had some nerve coming up here after what had taken place around the dinner table, he thought to himself. His office was his space. It was the only space in the house where he could retreat from the troubles of the world and his own dysfunctional marriage and now, now it seemed that even here he wasn't safe from the tormenting attacks of the heartless shrew on the other side of the door.

"James."

"Yeah," he reluctantly answered.

"May I come in?"

"Why?"

"Because we need to talk."

"I think we did enough talking downstairs, don't you?"

"Just open the door."

"It's unlocked."

He knew she wouldn't go away until she got what she wanted; in this case another fight.

The door slowly swung open, revealing Rebecca, standing in the doorway with an unfamiliarly peaceful expression on her face.

"Please, sit down. Make yourself comfortable," he motioned toward the couch opposite his desk. "Not like I was working or anything."

"I didn't come up here to fight with you," Rebecca, addressing the sarcastic greeting, calmly closed the door and took a seat on the indicated couch, positioning herself between a pillow and a disheveled blanket.

It had been almost a year since the two had shared the same bed. Since the incident with loose lipped Joey Fuller, his and Rebecca's sex life had gone substantially down hill...well, his anyway. Over time they'd enjoyed fewer and fewer intimate moments until, one day, he'd chosen to sleep on the office couch and had never gone back.

"If you're not here to rip my balls off again, then what do you want?" he bluntly confronted his wife's intruding presence.

"I'll pretend that I don't hear the hostility in your voice."

He too chose to ignore her sarcasm.

"I just wanted to say that I'm sorry about what happened downstairs. I know how much that cabin meant to you."

"That cabin was a piece of shit."

"That cabin was your father's."

"My father was a piece of shit too."

"Whether you want to admit it or not, I know how you truly feel. We've been together for a long time. I think I can tell when you're trying to conceal your true emotions."

"Really, then what emotion am I concealing right now? Huh?"

"Honey, I didn't mean to come up here and--"

"Don't honey me. What emotion am I hiding?" he grilled his wife. "Pain. Pain is the mystery emotion of the day...every day in fact. I have a career that's beginning to reek somewhere on the level of...oh...let's say, a city landfill or an unattended septic system and pages upon pages of writing that the public seems to have deemed unworthy to even wipe their own asses with. I have nearly no money to my name and a son who hates me for ripping away his dreams of father-son-days up at the old cabin."

"Peter doesn't hate you he just--"

"And, to top it all off, I have a wife who'd rather fuck some walking, talking bicep than even look at her own husband."

"Look, about Francesco--"

"No, you know what? I don't even care anymore. You go ahead and do whatever it is you think you need to do."

"I--"

"You know what hurts the most though?" he again, refused to let her speak. "That you can't even be honest with me. That's what hurts the most."

"Honest? What the hell was I supposed to do?" Rebecca finally decided to abandon her peaceful approach, tossing the white flag aside. "What did you want me to say? Oh yeah honey, I think I'll go to the store and...well...you know how excited I get shopping, so after that I might swing by the gym and get my brains fucked out by that, as you call him, walking, talking bicep."

"Yeah, that's exactly how it should have gone. At least then I could have had the satisfaction of knowing exactly where I stood, instead of beating myself up in here every night, trying to figure out a way to salvage my marriage and resurrect my life."

"Right, I--"

"Hell, I bet that weight bench gets awfully uncomfortable at times though."

Rebecca didn't realize that he'd witnessed one of her "workout sessions".

"Why don't you just bring the big oaf back to our house some time. At least give the man a chance to put down his weights and fuck you in a real bed. I believe there's one across the hall in need of some attention."

"Fuck you!"

"Ooh, here we go again with the expletives. 89, 88, 87," he began rattling off IQ scores.

"You know, I came up here in hopes of having a peaceful conversation with you about our lives and our futures but you just can't stop being an asshole for one minute. Well fine. I'll just get to the point then. I want a divorce. So you'd better start looking for a damn good lawyer, because I've already found mine. And if it is true that you have no money, then I sure hope you find one willing to work for autographed copies of those shitty books of yours."

"And how exactly do you expect to pay for yours? Since when did they start accepting twat tours as tender?"

"Disgusting pig," Rebecca grumbled as she stormed from the room.

"You forgot to close the door sweetie. Twat tours. I like that," James took a moment to reflect on his new phrase as he scribbled the term in the upper right corner of his journal.

SIXTEEN

"Boo!"

Peter's eyes bust open.

Emily quickly removed herself from beside her brother's bed and hastily retreated down the hall, screaming for her mother the entire way.

Peter chuckled as he threw back the covers and, swinging his legs outward, hopped from the bed, ready to begin yet another glorious day.

*****

The morning air was cooler than usual for early September, tempting Peter to reach for his jacket just before leaving the house. But, unable to bring himself to break out the winter wear so early in the season, he'd opted for only a long sleeved shirt to shield him from the unusual weather.

A morning mist hung over the valley, its thick presence blocking his view of the majestic Sierras to the West. Nestled high in the towering, rocky slopes was a vacationer's delight. Lake Tahoe was one of the most beautiful pieces of nature he'd ever laid eyes on, quiet and secluded, yet brimming with activities from boating and jet-skiing in the summer, to some of the best snow skiing in the world during the winter months.

Peter missed the secluded getaway. They hadn't been up to the cabin in over six month and with news of the surprise sale, he wondered if yet another father son bond had faded away forever.

Without a doubt he knew that he loved his father; always had and always would but lately he seemed to be moving farther and farther away from the family, spending more time locked in his office writing than anywhere else in the house. He knew there had to be a reason for the old man's shift in sociality and though details of the situation hadn't yet been shared with he or his little sister, Peter was pretty confident that he knew the cause.

Six months ago he'd stumbled upon a shredded page from one of his father's literary magazines. After nearly an hour of puzzle work he'd managed to piece the destroyed page back together and had read the horrible review the sheet had contained. Through various sources he'd been made aware of how well or how poorly his father's books had performed but this writer had made it sound as if his father was the worst thing to ever hit the publishing world. The reviewer had lambasted his father. Paragraph after paragraph, not only his father's work but his character as well had been dragged through the mud.

Prior to that article he'd seen other such pages torn to shreds and discarded in the kitchen trash but had never possessed the reason or the curiosity to piece the torn papers back together again. Looking back on their destroyed state though, he was pretty sure what they'd said.

Knowing his father's personality he was sure that the gradual seclusion from the family was nothing more than the old man attempting to place all his focus on his next masterpiece. He probably wanted nothing more than to prove those writers wrong and had been hard at work doing just that. That had to be the reason for the peculiar behavior lately, what else did the man have to be concerned with?

Rounding the street corner onto McMulholand Boulevard, a brisk wind elicited a cold shiver up Peter's spine as a police cruiser blew by, lights twirling and sirens blaring. Being a reasonably uneventful neighborhood, it wasn't often that the excitement of police presence presented itself so nearby. Peter watched as human curiosity took control of his eyes, leading them down McMulholand Boulevard and onto Shady Lane.

Peter began walking faster. A second set of sirens raced at his back, stirring up yet another frigid gust, followed by another as an ambulance and fire truck also made the turn onto Geoffrey's street. What had started as a rubbernecker's curiosity was rapidly becoming genuine concern, as again his pace quickened to that of a light jog.

As he rounded the corner onto Shady Lane he found himself whispering a prayer for those in need. "Jesus Christ our lord and savior please grant unto those in need the strength to make it through whatever tragedy has befallen them and protect all those involved from harm." He would have finished with the typical "Amen" but "oh God" was the only additional phrase to slip passed his lips before all his breath became required for the all out sprint he suddenly found himself in.

The police cruiser had stopped in front of Geoffrey's house, joining the two additional cop cars which had already arrived on scene. The fire truck and ambulance had awkwardly positioned themselves alongside the cruisers, blocking the street in both directions. A group of nosy onlookers stood outside the McDaniel's and McGregor's residences, some already dressed for work while others looked as if they'd only just recently awoken from their nighttime slumber, probably by the commotion taking place outside.

Geoffrey's mother was one such bed dressed bystander

and one of the few people not gabbing on a cell phone or recording the activity for a later upload to Youtube. Mrs. McDaniel held only a wine glass in her hand and, with how frequently she was placing it to her lips, Peter figured it would probably be in need of a refill fairly soon.

Winded from his mad dash through the neighborhood, Peter took up a position alongside his best friend's mother, who just stared in the general direction of the curious group. Though glad to see Mrs. McDaniel unharmed, he was worried by the lacking presence of Geoffrey at her side.

Out of breath and almost unable to speak from the cold air in his lungs, Peter tapped Mrs. McDaniel on the shoulder.

"Oh, hey Peter," Mrs. McDaniel slurred her words as she greeted the familiar boy with a raise of her glass.

The upbeat woman's impaired speech was all Peter needed to verify how wrong his prior assumption had been. Mrs. McDaniel hadn't just risen from bed. Most likely she'd been up for hours already, probably well into her first bottle of the day if not her second. Thankfully though, she seemed in good spirits, which told Peter that whatever was going on either didn't involve her family or that she was too sloshed to realize it if it did. He prayed for the first of the two.

"Where's Geoff, Mrs. McDaniel?"

The impaired and distracted woman just ignored Peter's inquiry.

"What's going on here?" Peter decided to try his luck with a different question.

This time he got a response but instead of answering in words, the inebriated woman only lifted her glass in the general direction of interest before again placing it to her lips and emptying its contents down her gullet.

Curiosity finally getting the best of him, Peter turned to the apparent point of significance.

"Oh my God," he uttered for a second time that

morning.

*****

Growing up, Geoffrey's mother had always teased him about his ability to nearly sleep an entire day away, no matter what noise or commotion might be taking place around him. "Dead to the world," had been her phrase of choice. For the most part, she'd been correct. Neither noisy family members stomping up and down the halls, nor the loud beeps and bangs of nearby construction equipment had ever been able to wake him from the slumber of his childhood years, but in the last couple of years something had changed. Whether it had been just another curious side effect of puberty or merely a natural change in his internal clock, now, even the slightest noise could draw him from bed, alert and focused on locating the source of the offending commotion.

Along with noise, morning light had also recently proven itself a nuisance, which was the only explanation for the pitch black blinds hanging in his bedroom windows. He'd never been partial to black and nothing else in the room, other than a few electronic devices and a couple of pairs of shoes bore the hideously dark color. But when it came to blocking out light, it was the only color worthy of consideration.

Given his body's recent one eighty in sleep capabilities, he found it surprising that he'd managed to sleep through the annoyingly repetitive Jedi banter and light saber sound effects of his Star Wars alarm clock. The damn thing usually came on at six o'clock sharp and droned on forever with phrases like "use the force Luke" and "Luke, I am your father" spoken by a voice that resembled James Earl Jones's but was clearly some impressionist rip-off. The most annoying sound and the one which usually, finally caused him to leap from the comfort of his covers in a mad dash for the off button, was the sound of Jar-Jar

Binks's high pitched, whiny voice followed by Chewbacca's wookie rebuttal.

Neither of those noises had done their job that morning though and Geoffrey began to wonder what indeed had been the cause of his awakening. As he opened his eyes the ceiling slowly came into focus. The morning light, which had managed to penetrate the small gaps in the blinds, drew lines across his bedcovers and walls. And, although the light had managed to violate his dark space, it hadn't been allowed to intrude in a large enough quantity to have made itself the illusive cause of his awakening.

"I'm late!" he suddenly realized.

Geoffrey shot up in bed, turning his still focusing eyes on the Darth Vader clock across the room. Six-forty-five. He was late. Homeroom started in less than half an hour and he hadn't even showered yet. Maybe I can skip the shower this morning, he thought to himself, his mind already hard at work on devising a plan that would resolve his tardy awakening. No, I have to take a shower. He'd only held the title of the crazy kid in school for one day. He didn't need to add the label of smelly kid as well in such a short time.

Bang. Bang. Bang. Three loud knocks shook his bedroom door and suddenly, Geoffrey became aware of the sleep ending sound.

Bang. Bang. Bang. "Geoffrey wake up!" a voice now joined the pounding from the other side of the door.

"Peter?"

"Yeah, wake up already!"

Geoffrey was surprised and pleased to hear his friend's familiar voice. His mother had obviously not cared about her son's school attendance or had already spent enough time that morning with a box of Almaden to render the time management portion of her brain completely useless. Thankfully, he had a friend like Peter looking out for his wellbeing.

"Open the door, quick!" Peter continued from the hall in a frantic voice as he jiggled the locked door knob.

Geoffrey threw back the covers and hurried to the door, worried by Peter's frenzied voice. It was true he was late but it wasn't that big a deal. He could pull it off, even if he did have to suffer the title of smelly kid.

"Come on man."

"Ok, ok," Geoffrey attempted to calm his frenetic friend as he unlocked the knob and pulled open the door. Peter was standing only inches from the doorway. His eyes were wide with worry and his body's fidgety movements and bobbing excitement resembled that of a five year old on Christmas morning as he attempted to wake his parents for the scheduled shredding of decorative paper.

"Nice. Are those fire engines?" Peter paused in his excitement to question his friend's choice of bedtime apparel.

Geoffrey looked down. In his hasty dash for the door he'd forgotten to grab his pants, a robe or even a sheet to cover himself with, which wouldn't normally have been a necessity considering he always wore pajama pants to bed.

"How did I go to bed like this?" he questioned his own attire. Nonetheless, he had and now he found himself standing before his friend, door wide open and in nothing but a pair of fire engine covered underwear. "The nerd, the crazy kid, the smelly kid and now the sissy," he spoke aloud.

"What?" Peter questioned, confused by the random statement. "Never-mind. What are you still doing asleep?"

"Darth over there forgot to use the force this morning," Geoffrey motioned to the clock, for the first time noticing that the light saber in the ten inch tall figurine's hand failed to glow its typical red. "Crap."

Peter looked confused.

"I forgot to set it last night," Geoffrey acknowledged

his mistake, wondering how he could have forgotten the simple task, which had become habit during his nightly, bedtime ritual. Brush teeth, lock door, close blinds, set clock, he recited the routine in his head. "I'm not even sure I brushed my teeth last night."

"Gross," Peter responded to the unsolicited information. "But that's not why I'm here."

"I know. I'm late. Thanks for waking me. I'll be as quick as I can."

"No...I--"

"You can go if you want to," Geoffrey continued as he made his way over to his dresser and withdrew a freshly washed pair of jeans, hoping that the fabric softener he had thrown in with them would mask his potential odor.

"Shut up!" Peter demanded his friend's silence, bringing Geoffrey's dressing progress to a halt.

Geoffrey stood stunned. He couldn't remember the last time Peter had told him to shut up. In fact, he couldn't even recall a time when the impolite command had ever been uttered by his usually hospitable companion.

"I'm sorry," Peter apologized.

Geoffrey slipped one leg into the jeans.

"Have you been sleeping all night?"

"Well, typically that is what one does during the nocturnal hours," Geoffrey responded sarcastically.

"I mean after you went to bed last night. You didn't wake up to any noises or commotion outside?"

"To be honest, I don't even remember going to bed last night." Geoffrey again glanced at the silent alarm clock before pulling a fresh Polo shirt over his head. "Why?"

Geoffrey could hear Peter fumbling with the blinds, pulling the chord and lifting the slatted light barrier just as his head reemerged from within the collared shirt.

Light from the rising sun poured through the suddenly unfortified opening, temporarily blinding the still groggy teen but as his eyes regained their focus, Geoffrey couldn't believe what he was seeing outside his window.

Police and fire rescue lights flashed like strobes in the side yards of his and the McGregor's house. Several police officers also occupied each yard, separated by the six foot tall, wooden fence dividing the two properties. Each one of the uniformed men stood aghast, their collective attention focused on the lofty power line running between the two houses.

Hanging high overhead, attached to the chain that had once bound him to his doghouse, was Prince's lifeless body, swaying ever so gently in the morning breeze.

SEVENTEEN

A night spent analyzing the intricate swirls of the plaster ceiling above his bed had left Steven's eyes and his demeanor less than alert. He felt run down, even more so than on the days following a big game.

He was used to staying up late. Hell, he'd pulled all-nighters before, though they were usually spent mindlessly staring at the television or surfing the web for the latest pair of knockers to grace the digital world. Last night however, not even those two deliverers of entertainment and pornography could slow the frantic pace of Steven's worrisome mind.

It was only a matter of time before Becky would break her silence. Eventually, the shameful details of what had happened to her would come pouring out, bombarding the medaling ears of some do-gooder with likely exaggerated details of Steven's disgraceful actions.

She knew. She had to know. No other explanation could justify her behavior, which is why he'd spent the night sweating through two sets of clothes, awaiting the arrival of Carson City's finest, come calling for their suspect.

Besides extreme exhaustion, he struggled with the

effects brought on from a lack of food. His stomach turned. His head pounded, attempting through pain to persuade its host to bring an end to the abdominal organ's incessant nagging.

Steven was aware of his body's plea for nutrients but he didn't care. How could he eat when constant worry would only cause such consumables to return, almost instantly, from their southerly journey? He had to know. He had to find out just what Becky knew and what her intentions might be.

"You look like shit," Mark Faulty announced as he joined the early morning heard, migrating from the senior parking lot to the East entrance of Eagle Roost.

Steven shot Dexter a look, for he too had issued the same greeting only fifteen minutes earlier outside his house.

Though he'd offered Dexter the true explanation for his haggard appearance, he wasn't about to share such potentially damaging information with one of the biggest mouths in the school. Instead, he chose to slug the new arrival's shoulder, probably leaving a twin to the ring imprint that he'd tattooed upon him the day before.

"Ouch," Mark exclaimed, rubbing his battered shoulder. "You may look like shit but you defiantly seem yourself this morning."

"Hey, did you guys see Raw last night?" Charlie, who'd pulled in just after Steven and Dexter but had remained remarkably quiet since issuing a friendly hello, finally broke his silence.

"You do know that shit's fake, right?" Dexter turned to question the included outcast.

"Yeah I know."

Steven didn't believe him. Charlie's voice rang of uncertainty, its wavering tone suggesting that the three word response had been issued more in search of approval than agreement.

"Sure you do," Mark mocked, obviously sharing

Steven's opinion.

"Well anyway..." Charlie continued with his apparently preplanned rant.

It was now clear that the childlike teenager's earlier silence had only existed due to the simple fact that, at the time, he'd lacked a sufficient number of ears to victimize with his bothersome chatter.

"What the fuck is that!?" Mark exclaimed disapprovingly.

Charlie ceased his diatribe, obeying his place within the group by immediately relinquishing his self-perceived role of focal point for the time being.

Mark stopped. The group followed suit.

"What?" Steven questioned confused.

Mark just stared at a pickup truck as it pulled into a space one row over.

"That's a truck," Dexter mocked.

The driver's side door of the F-150 swung open. Steven didn't recognize the girl who hopped down from the elevated cab, probably since she lacked the necessary attractiveness usually needed to draw his scrutinizing gaze.

"And that's a girl," Dexter continued.

"Fuck you!" exclaimed Mark, his face showing anger but he knew full and well that he too would have issued the same playful taunts if roles had been reversed.

"What's what?" Steven repeated his apparently unheard question, eager for a response so that they could continue on their way.

"Who the hell still has one of those Calvin pissing on a logo stickers?" Mark finally indicated the source of his disapproval.

"Apparently she does," Dexter again showed excitement for the opportunity to throw in yet another taunting remark.

"Didn't that trend die off years ago?"

"You're just upset because it seems Calvin doesn't share the same hard-on for Chevy that you do," Steven joined in the tormenting.

"Charlie!" Mark shouted, apparently unaware that Charlie was standing only three feet behind him.

Excited, if for nothing other than the inclusion, Charlie quickly took his place beside his beckoner.

"I'll give you ten dead presidents if you go over there and take a piss on Calvin," Mark proposed as he withdrew the cash from his wallet.

Charlie didn't need the money. He'd have done it simply for the attention and approval it was sure to garner. The money was an added bonus though and without a word he snatched the bill from Mark's hand and stealthily, darted toward the target, though his motions resembled more those of an exaggerated cartoon character than of an actual, undercover agent.

"I knew we kept him around for a reason," Mark smiled.

They watched as Charlie scanned his surroundings. The majority of students had already arrived and made their way inside, so the parking lot contained limited witnesses. Charlie hoisted himself into the truck's exposed bed, using the oversized tire to aid in his accent.

"Steven," a soft voice spoke as a fingertip gently tapped at his back.

Steven turned to find Becky's staring up at him, her typical shy smile radiating from her perfectly painted face. He turned to Dexter, who'd apparently spotted the approaching girl but, frozen by fear, had failed to alert his prison bound friend.

As Steven returned his attention to the unexpected company, her frighteningly out of place smile grew, the reddening of her cheeks competing with the foundation on her skin as her eyes fell to her feet and her fingertips began doing battle with the beaded tassels dangling from her imitation, designer purse.

"Becky?" Steven spoke with both fear and confusion.

"Holy shit man! I think he's actually gonna do it!"

Mark bellowed.

Their hired clown's comedic antics apparently proved more riveting to Dexter than did the conflict about to unfold between Steven and his ex as he returned his gaze to their monetarily coaxed friend, figuring that whatever went down with Becky would surely take some time. Witnessing your friend piss on the back window of some girl's truck had to be a once in a lifetime moment.

"I...I need to talk to you about something," Becky spoke softly, apparently unwilling to share the likely personal topic with their present company.

Steven's heart began to race and just as they had the night before, he could feel his cloths steadily growing moist as his glands kicked into high gear. He could only stare at the girl who, unknowingly, had held his mind captive for the past twenty-four hours. He didn't know what to say and sure as hell didn't want to hear what she was about to say. Though aware that he was standing in the school parking lot, visions of his dim future consumed his mind.

"Steven? Are you all right?"

"That crazy fuck!" Mark exclaimed.

Mark's explicit commentary being enough to break his catatonic stare, Steven removed his petrified gaze from an equally interested Becky as he spotted Charlie standing in the back of the white pickup. Apparently not shy about his most private of areas, he'd already retracted his zipper and loosely held the smaller of his brains for all to see as a steady stream escaped his body and ran down the window.

Steven returned his focus to Becky as Mark and Dexter began hooting and hollering their temporary respect for the insane daredevil, who'd earned his place for yet another day.

"I need to talk to you," Becky repeated, this time in a more serious tone.

Her smile had faded slightly, causing Steven's nerves to twist even tighter.

"Alone."

He felt as though he was about to pass out.

"Steve, did you see that!?" Mark shouted as he turned from the action. "Oh, hi Becky."

"Hi Mark," she replied, gesturing for Steven's departure from the group.

"I...gotta go guys. I'll...catch up with you later," Steven hesitantly excused himself from the distracted remains of the group.

"Did you guys see that!?" Charlie shouted, returning to Mark's side, still on a high from the adrenaline generating stunt.

"Yeah, that was pretty good," Dexter responded, sounding less than enthusiastic, not wanting to elevate Charlie's status too high for fear of losing their toy of malicious intent.

Sufficiently entertained, Mark and Dexter continued on their temporarily delayed journey as Charlie returned to his role as submissive and fell in line behind his two departing friends.

"What's going on?" Steven, somehow managing to suppress his fears, finally gave Becky the attention she sought.

"Something happened."

Here we go, Steven thought. He'd never had a roommate before and wondered what it would be like to share an eight-by-ten cell with a man who would likely show more interested in his goods than all of his past sexual partners combined.

"There's this guy I like but I don't think he likes me very much right now."

What? This wasn't about yesterday's life altering mistake? Relief washed over him, calming his racing heart, not to mention excessive perspiration. On the other hand, what the hell was she talking about? What did he have to do with another guy, other than suddenly possessing the desire to kick his ass?

"You already did this to me last week Becky," Steven respond, half mad and half hurt.

"No, I don't think you understand. I broke up with him last week."

"So you dumped him less than a week after me? You're on a roll."

"No...well...yes...but...," she stumbled over her words. "I'm talking about you stupid."

If she'd possessed balls, he'd have decked her for such an insult, but since it was Becky, he'd let it go.

"Are you saying?"

Becky smiled and nodded. "What do ya say? You think we can give it another shot. It would be a shame to have to attend homecoming alone this year."

"Hey wait. It's my job to ask the girl to homecoming."

"Well?"

"My lady, could you find it in your heart to accompany me to our fine, educational establishment's, annual soiree of dance, school pride and the occasional alcoholic beverage?"

"Don't forget about the sex," Becky added with a smile.

The out of character comment shocked Steven but based on the growing discomfort in this Levis, he didn't mind.

"Never."

He wanted to kiss her; to take her in his arms and to again feel the warmth of her soft lips against his. He didn't have to.

With a squeal of joy, Becky jumped into his arms and taking the initiative, reintroduced their mouths to the passionate gesture handed down by the beret wearing nation of the world.

EIGHTEEN

In short, do not buy this book. Don't borrow it from a misguided friend or from one of those now illusive palaces of culture my generation once called a library. In fact, if you are out, in search of that ever elusive masterpiece, and you happen to come upon this pile of...well...you know, stop where you are, slowly turn and run as fast as you can in the opposite direction. The effects of this travesty aren't yet fully understood; though a one sitting read of the lengthy masterpiece "War and Peace" has been found to slow the devastating repercussions caused by such contamination...who has time for that?

Well, I guess that wasn't "in short" but neither was this book. One bookmark out of five.

Parker struck the final period of his first review with a sense of accomplishment and satisfaction he hadn't felt in his nearly three month leave from work. He'd always enjoyed his work. The Ability to express himself in a public forum and to vent his frustrations over society was an exhilarating release that most people would never experience. His favorite task, apart from composing lengthy rants for his readers, was his once a month chance to review some of the most anticipated literary works from some of the country's most renowned authors. Over the years, his straight forward approach and harsh views about modern literature had become a trademark of sorts; a calling card which publishers either loved or loathed.

On many occasions he'd handed out rave reviews, filled with praise and admiration. Those positive reviews were like gold to both authors and their publishers because more often than not, Parker found a way to tear at the literary fabric of even the most skillfully crafted stories. If there was a flaw he would find, identify and exploit it.

This month's review had been one such massacre. While he knew his reader's appetites for the fresh blood of yet another literary slaughter would be more than satisfied, for the first time in his fifteen year career, Parker feared it had been written from an unfairly negative mindset. No other review to date had contained such directly negative attacks on both the author and his work. The events of the last three month, while devastating to his own life, seemed to be reaching out through him in an attempt to squeeze the happiness from anything and anyone within reach.

"Parker," a voice squawked from the phone's intercom.

Yanked free of his recently familiar decent down the steep slope of depression, Parker responded to the intruding voice. "Yeah, Mike. What's going on?"

Michael Bestrone was more than just Parker's boss. He was one of his closest friends and mentors. Eighteen years his elder, Michael had taken the chance and hired the eager and somewhat over enthusiastic twenty-three year old Parker fifteen years earlier, helping to tame and mold the fervent youth's unpolished talents into the quality work that it was today.

"I don't mean to sound like the typical pain in the ass boss but are you finished with that review yet?"

"One can only sound as one is," parker answered, the corny wisdom escaping his lips before he could mentally edit himself.

"If that was an insult, your fired," Michael responded.

"Five-hundred-sixty-three," Parker answered back without pause, this time satisfied with the quality of his response.

Michael began laughing. Over the years he'd fired Parker five-hundred-sixty-three times, mostly in jest.

"I just hit save," Parker added as he saved the brutal review.

There was no time to soften his sharp tongued opinions now. Besides, he figured that since he'd already angered so many people in his industry, what could be the harm of adding one more to the list?

"Would you like that printed on lovely, pastel pink stationary to match that fabulous shirt of yours today?"

"Hey, men can wear pink nowadays and still be men."

"Is that what you're calling yourselves these days?"

"You'd better be careful what you say around here. You know how sensitive Simon is about his lifestyle."

"Hey," a second voice cried out through the speaker.

"Hello, Simon," Parker greeted the exposed eavesdropper.

Simon Miller's stunning wife and three children seemingly indicated a strictly heterosexual existence. On the other hand, his keen eye for the latest fashions and impeccable grooming habits left him vulnerable to the laid back humor of the twenty-third floor.

Apparently, in Parker's extended absence, it seemed that Simon's metro sexual ways had managed to rub off on Michael as well, leaving Parker to question when the anti-masculine disease would attempt an assault on his conservative wardrobe.

"I already turned in my article," Simon playfully jabbed at Parker.

Simon's humor infused, political columns were equally as popular as Parker's more serious and analytically opinionated ones, often resulting in a lighthearted interoffice competition.

"I too could just wipe my ass with a piece of paper and

hand it in but I prefer to take my time...you know...prepare multiple drafts until the stain comes out just right."

"Eloquent as always," Michael responded.

"No, just honest. I'll have a copy for you in a couple of minutes."

"All right," Michael's voice answered, followed by a click as the speaker fell silent.

With a click of the mouse, the printer on the far end of the desk sprang to life, promptly spitting out the two page butchery.

Parker stared at the freshly printed pages lying in the tray. Given the time, any good writer could find something about his work in need of repair. As he stared at the flowing lines of cleverly crafted insults, he wished that he not only had the time to re-craft his words but also to reread the book which he believed had not been the vile refuse his fragile emotional state had convinced him of. Unfortunately, the impending deadline would not allow for such drastic revisions.

Snatching the pages from the machine's tray, Parker spun his chair in the direction of the door. Turning the knob, the solid oak door swung inward, immersing his peaceful office in a flood of office chatter. Out of habit, he applied a gentle kiss to his right index finger before pressing it to the glass of a silver frame which housed the angelic face of a beautiful, brunette woman.

NINETEEN

James never had cared much for planes. Even the thought of being thirty feet above the ground was cause for alarm, let alone thirty-thousand.

He had, over the years, overheard many people describe their fear of flying as not actually having much to do with the plane or even the high altitude. Overwhelmingly it seemed to be the idea of an unscheduled return to earth which fueled their phobia. This, together with an actual fear of heights, was also the case for James. But his biggest fear, more so than an unnaturally high position above the earth or the possibility of a fiery death, was his fear of helplessness. He had no control over anything up there. He didn't know how to fly a plane and without the plane he obviously couldn't fly himself. He was completely dependent on the man up front to determine his fate.

What if the pilot was having a bad day? What if the man's life was in just as much disarray as his? Maybe Captain Bob had just walked in on his wife porking a fellow pilot the night before and that man was now his copilot. If pushed far enough, he might just decide to take the man out, along with himself and the rest of the passengers and crew, by nose diving straight into a mountain. Or better yet, maybe he'd make it a two for one job by turning the plane around and aiming for the house containing his whoring wife as well.

James had no control so high above the planet that he had, for some reason, chosen to temporarily abandon. Hell he couldn't even get up from his seat to take a piss unless the little light above his head told him so and that too was controlled by Bob.

Whether it had been the two shots of bourbon before takeoff or simply the thought of using the bathroom, his bladder was suddenly awakened. Bob however, like a sadistic school teacher refusing to grant bathroom brakes, continued to let the fasten seatbelt sign burn bright.

"Sir. Sir, are you all right?" a flight attendant questioned, noting James' sweat soaked forehead and clutching grasp of the arm rests beside him.

"Yeah, I'm good," he answered nervously.

Though his ticket had called for a window seat, he'd been glad to learn of the flight's nearly half empty status and had chosen to move himself from his assign location to a seat on the isle instead, far away from the tormenting view of the world below.

"First time on a plane?" she asked as she took a seat on the opposite side of the isle beside him.

"Believe it or not, no."

"Second then."

"More like twenty."

"Twenty times?" she gasped surprised.

"I know. The other flight attendants used to tell me it would get better each time; that I would get less and less nervous the more that I flew and that eventually, I would actually enjoy the idea of air travel."

"I would have to agree with that."

"Then you'd be a liar too."

The woman didn't know whether to take offense or be amused by the nervous man's insult.

"I'm sorry. I..."

"That's all right. It would seem in your case that maybe we are a bunch of liars. To tell you the truth, some people never get over their fear of planes."

It was refreshing to hear someone actually give what sounded like an honest answer for once, even though it did nothing to help him in his current situation.

"Do you want to know something else?" the truthful woman leaned across the isle.

James was intrigued, expecting to be told some long hidden airline secret that might aid him in his uneasy travels.

"You know that little speech we give every time before takeoff?"

James nodded, listening intently.

"You know how we mention that your seat cushion 'may' be used as a floatation devise?"

What did this have to do with his nerves? James thought to himself.

"Well, do you know why we say 'may'? It's because, in nearly all of the domestic flights in this country, how often do we really fly over water as compared to land? Also, if we were to crash land in the ocean or a lake, do you really think that there would be enough time for all of these people to remember, between screams, to strap themselves to their seat cushions and squeeze through those six little doors before this giant metal bird sank straight to the bottom?"

Who the hell was this lady and who in the hell was the irresponsible idiot who'd hired her? James thought to himself, now more worried than ever.

"Miss. Miss, I'm going to have to ask you to return to your seat. The captain has not yet extinguished the fasten seatbelt sign," a man wearing a similar, yet different colored sweater as the nut job beside him, politely addressed the woman.

"Oh, ok. I'm sorry. It was very nice to meet you and I

hope you feel better," the woman addressed James before returning to her seat toward the back of the plane.

What the hell? James thought to himself.

"Sir, are you all right?" the real flight attendant questioned James's now terrified appearance.

"Who was that lady?" James questioned, trying to figure out why a perfect stranger would even think that such a disturbing conversation was amusing, if in fact she was trying to be funny and wasn't just out of her mind. "You know what, forget about her. Are we gonna die?"

*****

The flight attendant hadn't cared much for James's rather morbid question half way into the forty-five minute jump over the Sierras. Neither had the few passengers who'd also shared the misfortune of overhearing a question that nowadays was likely to land you in some small holding room with an FBI agent named Bubba eager to perform his very first cavity search. Luckily, no one had over reacted, Captain Bob had landed the plane on the runway and James had arrived with his dignity still intact.

With his feet safely planted on the ground, James now had a new fear to face. He'd only been to his publisher's headquarters once before and that had been to sign his very first contract into the literary world. He could only hope that this second visit would be as lucrative as the last.

Brandon had made the news sound good on the phone and he doubted that a company, in the business of making money, would go through the trouble and expense of flying in one of their authors only to tell him that he was no longer a viable commodity. This had to be good news. Maybe things weren't so bad after all. Money had been tight but with all the confidence in the world in his agent and having learned his lesson from an irresponsible financial past, maybe life could finally return to the way it used to be.

"Your floor sir," the elevator operator announced as the gold plated doors slid aside to reveal a marble floor leading up to a large granite desk behind which sat Mr. Westcroft's personal assistant.

Randolph Westcroft was one of the country's most powerful businessmen, at least in the publishing world. If he liked your work, you were set for life. Unfortunately, it had been Michael Heisner who had originally penned James's deal and with Heisner's recent passing, Westcroft had taken over majority control of the company; a turn of events that even further concerned James.

Sure, Westcroft had said that he liked James's work, though he'd only done so after the contract had been signed and James had become a company asset. The man was interested in only one thing, money. He knew nothing about the literary world. That had been Heisner's field. Westcroft was a businessman, plain and simple. The man based his daily mood on the company's stock performance and nothing else. If shares were up, then so was his mood. If they were down...well...James prayed they were up.

"James!" a voice cried out to his right as he approached the woman behind the desk.

James turned to find Brandon leaping to his feet as he strutted across the polished stone floor and grabbed hold of his client's hand with a grip far stronger than his petite physique would suggest possible.

"It's been a hell of a long time. How you been?" Brandon traded the hand for a hug.

Though James hadn't physically met with Brandon face to face in over a year, he knew what to expect. Brandon was the touchy-feely type. He greeted with hugs. He held your shoulder while he talked and occasionally, pushing the envelope, he insisted on whispering little secrets in your ear from an uncomfortably close distance.

James never had understood the gay lifestyle but he did respect the man and respect was all that was needed when it came to business, so he tolerated his agent's occasionally intrusive mannerisms.

"How long's it been?" Brandon questioned, looking up at the ceiling as if the answer were painted on the gold leaf molding overhead.

"A bit less than twenty-four hours I believe," James sarcastically answered, knowing full and well what the man had meant.

"Oh, always the funny one," Brandon playfully swatted.

"I hope you haven't been waiting long."

"All my life darling. I was wondering when you would come around," Brandon took his turn to make a joke.

James just smiled uncomfortably.

"I'm just kidding."

"Mrs. Ramsler, would you send Mr. Madison and Mr. Richards in now," Mr. Westcroft's stern voice interrupted through the intercom.

"Mr. Westcroft will see you now."

"Thanks sweetie," Brandon responded, patting James on the back. "Let's go get you some money, all right?"

Mr. Westcroft's personal assistant blushed at the agent's sugar coated gratitude, bowing her eyes and probably contemplating what it would take to return the attractive, yet effeminate man, back to his genetically assigned team.

Brandon had always had a way with the ladies. At every school dance, up until his grand sexual unveiling at senior prom, Brandon had never gone without one or sometime even two luscious hotties nestled up beside him on the dance floor. The man just had a air about him. It was a quality that made everyone want to be around him, men and women. He just had this overwhelming life force that could convince even the most hardened criminal to rethink his chosen path, and in his line of work a persuasive personality was far from a hindrance.

As the tall, frosted glass doors to Mr. Westcroft's twentieth floor office slowly swung open under the influence of invisible hands, James could see the business

143

mogul sitting behind his desk, his back turned to his requested company. He stared out through the ten foot tall wall of glass at the San Francisco Bay and the Golden Gate Bridge in the distance.

"Mr. Westcroft, it's a pleasure to--," Brandon attempted to take early control of the conversation.

"Please, sit down," Westcroft immediately interrupted as if anticipating the agent's initial move for dominance.

James and Brandon did as they were told and took a seat in the oversized leather chairs positioned submissively in the shadows of the man's immense stone desk. Between the chairs stood a small, oval end table with two fresh glasses of ice water.

Water wasn't a good sign, James thought to himself. Water was cheap. Water indicated a man concerned about his money.

"Let me just say that this office is absolutely fantastic, Mr. Westcroft sir," Brandon attempted to reestablish his active position as the leader of the conversation.

"I don't like you very much," Westcroft responded while keeping his back to his two visitors.

"Excuse me sir. I don't believe we've ever met," Brandon took offense to the uncalled for and unfair judgment.

"Not you," Westcroft correct as he turn in his chair. "Him."

"Me sir?"

"Yeah, you."

"Mr. Westcroft sir, I don't believe that you and my client have ever met before either. I believe it was Mr. Heisner who initially established Mr. Madison's contract."

"Heisner was a jack off; a fagotty little prick with not one bit of money sense in his bones, no offense."

"Of course not," Brandon lied.

"This man here costs me money," Westcroft continued as if James weren't even in the room, but given the man's apparently shrewd personality, James didn't mind if he wasn't called upon to speak.

"Sir, I know that my client's recent publications have generated a bit less than initially hoped for but I bet if you take a look at the overall performance of Mr. Madison's work, you will find--"

"One-hundred-eighty-two-thousand dollars," Westcroft again interrupted.

"Excuse me?" Brandon was confused by the sudden numerical outburst.

"That's what this guy has cost me over the last five years."

"Well, one-hundred-thousand dollars to a company of this size is a drop in the bucket if you ask me."

"Not one-hundred-thousand, one-hundred-eighty-two-thousand and thirty-two cents, and, if you ask me, one-hundred-eighty-two-thousand and thirty-two cents too much," Mr. Westcroft reiterated.

"Still--"

"No, not still. That's unacceptable. This isn't some nonprofit organization dedicated to making shitty authors feel good about themselves. We're all here to make money and all I see when I look at this guy is red. That's why I'm opting to terminate the remainder of your contract," Westcroft finally spoke directly to James.

"Terminate?"

"Now I don't think any irrational moves should be made until--" Brandon continued, unable to get a word in.

"Irrational? Did you just refer to me as irrational?" Westcroft, if not already upset, now clearly was.

"No sir, I--"

"Listen here you little, fudge packing, butt pirate...-"

The prejudiced slander spewing from the CEO's mouth was unbelievable. For a moment, James actually thought that he was at home creating the animated hothead in the pages of his journal, though he highly doubted that even he would have had the nerve to push the bigot envelope so far.

"As I told you before, I don't like your client. Never have and probably never will. I think his books are crap and every time I look his track record, I get a strong urge to go across the hall and blow that prick Heisner's head clean off, but seeing as the poor bastard's heart did the job for me, I'm now free and clear to do with the company as I please and that involves canning your sorry asses."

"Well, what about my client's latest book?" Brandon switched gears from the hunt for a new deal, to squeezing as much money from the stingy old bastard as possible. "I believe Mr. Madison is still under contract to create one more book for your company and seeing as that book is almost complete, I believe that my client is entitled to the fulfillment of his original deal as penned by Mr. Heisner."

The book wasn't almost done. In fact, other necrophilia filled paragraph from the night before, James hadn't even started it, but sensing where his agent was going, he remained silent.

"I'm willing to fulfill this company's end of the initial agreement on a financial level only. We're not interested in sending Mr. Madison's latest rubbish to print, for fear of greater loss to this establishment. My secretary will get you a final check for the remainder of the balance owed under Heisner's deal."

"And the rights to my client's work?"

"We would be willing to work a deal for Mr. Madison to buy back all rights to previously published work, let's say...for the remainder owed to him under his contract," Westcroft proposed with an evil grin.

"Deal," Brandon quickly answered, knowing that what James would get in future marketability was far greater than the lump sum amount Westcroft was initially willing to pay.

"Wait," James chimed in.

"James. Take the deal," Brandon whispered to his client.

"But."

"Listen to me, not only as your agent but as your friend. The money owed to you is piddly compared to what we could get shopping it elsewhere. It's a deal," Brandon returned his attention to Westcroft.

"Good luck finding anyone willing to kill even one tree to print that worthless shit," Westcroft took one last jab at the newly independent author.

"And what about the nearly finished book?" Brandon continued tying up all loose ends.

"It's yours. Take it," Westcroft answered uninterested

"Mr. Westcroft," James finally decided to speak for himself.

"Listen kid."

At forty-two, James was hardly a kid but when compared to the seventy-six year old man sitting before him he could understand the man's point of view.

"You've had a good run; made some good money but this gravy train's pulling out of the station and you're not on it. You're through here, so why don't you just take my more than generous offer, run along with your boyfriend here and go enjoy a parade or whatever it is that you people do?"

Though offended by Westcroft's persistent gay bashing Brandon continued to smile. James wasn't his only client with Westcroft and Heisner Publishing.

"Thank you very much for your time sir and I hope we get a chance to sit down again in the near future," Brandon kissed the man's ass in an attempt to salvage his connection.

"Yeah, yeah. Get out," Westcroft dismissively waved as he returned to his godlike view of the world below.

Again playing the role of submissive, James and Brandon did as they were instructed and exited the CEO's office.

*****

Though he'd been there for the entire exchange between Brandon and Westcroft, it had taken a few minutes to process everything that had just occurred. The career, which he'd once aspired to attain at any cost, was now officially dead. He was without a deal and with his current track record, finding another company willing to invest in a washed up writer wasn't just going to be difficult...it was going to be damn near impossible.

"What just happened up there?" James questioned Brandon as the elevator doors slid open to reveal the lobby. It had been the first words spoken by either man since the less than productive meeting with Mr. Westcroft.

"Well, I believe that, if we were involved in what most would consider a normal line of work, you could say that we just got fired," Brandon answered James in a ho-hum tone.

"We!? What the hell do you mean we!?" James blurted loudly, drawing the attention of the security guard behind the lobby desk and the few other suits, there on business.

"James, calm down," Brandon tried to control his client as he guided him through the door and onto the sidewalk out front.

"Calm down! Sure, you can be calm. You still have a job! You have other clients! What do I have!? Let's see; one, a wife who hates my guts, who by the way, just a little over twelve hours ago, asked for a divorce; two, two children that I will probably never see again because the cheating whore will probably run off with them now to some foreign country with her boyfriend Francesco and why...oh wait, let's think about it...oh yeah, because you just flushed my entire career down the shitter!" James yelled, turning heads and drawing dirty looks from passersby.

"I flushed it!? I'm not the one who fired you!"

"Oh yeah, because you did so much to prevent it from happening."

"He was going to fire you no matter what I said. Can't

you see that?"

"Well you sure as hell didn't try to put up a fight. You just rolled over and took the first deal the man offered."

"I got you back the rights to all of your past work. Most writers would put that far above any dollar amount offered. And, by the way, who was the dip-shit who signed over his rights in the first place!?"

"Well, a bunch of words on paper don't pay the bills."

"Well, maybe if someone hadn't been so irresponsible with the deal they'd gotten in the first place, then someone wouldn't be in such dire straits financially...as he currently claims to be."

"What, you think I'm lying now? You think I'm just fabricating my problems for sympathy?"

"I didn't say that."

"Then what did you say?"

"All I'm saying is that we got the best deal there was to get. The remaining amount owed under contract was minuscule compared to the value of your rights. I was looking out for your best interests here. I don't get a cut from your stories. I only make money when you do and let's face it James, that hasn't been a whole hell of a lot lately."

"Funny. You think now that I'm no longer an asset to you, you can just throw little jabs and wise cracks at me?"

"What are you going to do James? Do you want to hit me? Would that make you feel better; bash on the little gay man's skull for a while, while continuing to ignore what you should have done a long time ago?"

"And what's that?" James asked curiously.

"Get your life back together. Salvage your marriage. Spend time with your kids. You know, the important things in life. There will always be money out there for a guy of your talent. Take a few weeks to relax, no writing, no worrying, just time with your family, and while you do that, I'll start working on finding you another publisher. Trust me. This whole thing is a blessing in disguise. I'm going to find you a better deal with a more writer friendly company and things will be back where they were when you started your dream."

"You know what? Don't bother."

"What?"

"Don't bother trying to help me. I don't need it. I saw how your loyalties work. At the first sign of conflict between you and your precious business contact, you folded on me."

"James I told you--"

"You're fired."

"What?" Brandon questioned, hearing what James had said but unable to believe what he had just heard.

"You heard me. YOU-ARE-FIRED! I don't want your help anymore."

"James, this is a mistake. I--"

"Forget it. It's over."

Brandon couldn't believe what he was hearing. He knew the meeting had gone unexpectedly bad but he truly believed this unfortunate turn of events could actually turn out to be a good thing. No longer under contract, James was free to shop himself to any publisher in the country and potentially make twice the amount he'd originally signed on for but if the man was going to be this unreasonable, he didn't need the trouble. He had dozens of other clients requiring much less attention and bringing in much more revenue.

"So that's it?" Brandon questioned.

"That's it."

"All right. Well, I'll have my office finish the paperwork on today's deal and send everything over to you just as soon as it's ready," Brandon accepted the end to their business dealings and lowered himself into the black Lincoln which had pulled up to the curb beside them. "Good luck James. Let's go," he instructed the driver as he closed the door on James Madison.

TWENTY

The silver Mercedes quietly glided along the sparsely populated lanes of the sun baked highway. It being early Friday afternoon, Parker had escaped the city before its million plus, workforce captives had managed to break free of their employment chains in a frantic race to begin the weekend.

His Manhattan apartment lay fifty miles behind him. Since May, it remained home only to an extensive collection of designer furniture and the amenities of the modern world. Its only visitor was Miss. Rosa; a forty-three year old woman Parker had met ten years and three apartments ago.

Miss Rosa had come to Parker's attention in the same manner as she had the rest of the country, through the tragedy that had been her then current employer.

Ashton Baker had been the latest, baby faced star to capture the hearts of America with a string of romantic comedies, which Parker found to be nothing more than the same tired stories Hollywood had been pumping out for as long as he could remember. Mr. Baker had jumped aboard this train of mediocrity and gotten rich and famous in doing so. Unfortunately, the same fame which had brought the twenty-three year old star the wealth and ability to pay for such employees as Miss Rosa and others, had been the very same fame which had placed him on the receiving end of a fully loaded nine millimeter.

"Now there's nothing to stand in the way of our love," a crazed fan, turned stalker, had declared to the young star outside his Manhattan residence just before she'd discharged nine bullets into the object of her obsession, saving the final bullet for herself. At least that was how it had been reported on all the tabloid shows and in Parker's very own newspaper the next morning.

The world being the giant tabloid magazine that it is, it was inevitable that this horrific act would be splashed across every television set in the country. And with the general population's attention span being equal to that of a three year old, it had been only a matter of time before some young and ambitious reporter had dug deeper into the life of the struck down star to find the country's next, big story.

Miss Rosa had been that story. An illegal alien, in New York City, trying to make a living, Rosa had been unwillingly catapulted into the national spotlight as the poster child of an ongoing debate over illegal immigrants and the security of the country.

Headlines such as Alien Invasion, Will work for...Nothing?, and Jobs, Americans Need Not Apply, began popping up all across the country, stirring up a political battle which had placed the defenseless woman in the crosshairs of two political parties, eager to prove their firm stance on the delicate issue.

Parker had felt for the woman. She'd come to the U.S. yearning for the type of life that her country couldn't offer; to pursue the dreams and desires Americans often took for granted and commonly used as tools of manipulation and control over one-another.

After three weeks of intense and sometimes idiotic debate the country had decided, Miss Rosa had no place in this free nation.

He wasn't sure why he'd felt an obligation to help the poor woman, whom he'd never even met. He liked to think of it as his personal, one finger salute to the political, hate mongers and authority in general and often spoke of it as such when sharing the story with others. He knew though, that the true reason was that sometimes illusive soft spot for humanity, which his wife often said lived in the deepest recesses of his guarded heart.

After a few phone calls and a couple of political favors, Parker had watched, along with millions of television viewers, as Miss Rosa's plane pulled away from the gate at JFK, destined for Mexico City, where she had a prearranged seat on American Airlines flight 859, which would return her to the very same New York runway from which she'd departed only fifteen hours earlier.

America's interest in the story had departed along with the plane that had carried the unwanted woman across its borders, leaving only Parker to greet her at the gate with a job and a visa, which would insure her ability to stay in the United States until he could help her to attain the citizenship she'd for so long dreamt about.

After ten years, Miss Rosa was more than an employee. She was a trusted friend, a friend whom he'd seen very little of in the past three months since the accident, which had left him emotionally shattered and widowed.

A set of three, rapid beeps interrupted the narrative genius of Billy Joel's Piano Man, accompanied by a phone number and the words incoming call on the car's navigational display. This number had appeared frequently on Parker's car phone, along with just about every other phone that had some consistent relation to him.

The series of beeps pulsed through the car's audio system again, followed by a third set. "Answer phone", Parker reluctantly ordered the car. In an instant, the piano man's melodic voice was all but reduced to an enchanting whisper as a new voice filled the Bose controlled cabin.

"Oh my Lord! He's alive," an older woman's voice filled the car. "And he still knows how to use a phone. Thank God."

"Hello mother."

"If you didn't have a track record of being such an insensitive, selfish son, half of the New York City police department would already be out looking for you."

"What a pleasant way to greet your only son," Parker playfully jested.

"That's right, my only son. The only son that doesn't return phone calls and avoids his only mother."

"I wasn't avoiding you."

"Oh yeah, what's that noise in the background and why are you answering this phone? You typically hold meetings in your car?"

Shit, Parker thought to himself. He'd forgotten that he had asked Michael to inform his mother of his unavailability, due to an important meeting.

"Yeah, the open road really gets everyone's creative juices flowing, right guys?" he questioned his imaginary associates.

"So, when do you think I'll get a chance to meet him?"

"Meet who?" Parker questioned, confused by the random inquiry.

"Billy Joel, of course. I hear him singing in the back seat. When did he start writing for the Paper? I really think he should have stuck with music though. Singing sports columns doesn't really play well to the ears."

"Funny mom."

"Where are you going anyway?"

"You're really on a role today. Six questions in under a minute."

"And, not one answer yet."

Quick wit had always been Parker's favorite of his mother's many, quirky traits. "If you must know, I'm on my way to Cannon," he provided the first answer.

"Again? Honey, you can't hide out up there forever,"

Miss. Veracini's condescending tone changed to that of a concerned mother.

"I'm not hiding from anything, I find it relaxing. Besides, we've been through this before. I'm really not in the mood to go through it again."

"I know dear, it's just that...that...I don't think it's healthy for you to do this to yourself."

Parker was sure that his mother could hear his sigh, but escalating aggravation inhibited him from caring. "I'm not doing anything to myself other than being by myself, mother."

"By yourself. By yourself. That's the problem. Outside the three days a week you make that long trek into the city, you have no contact with anyone, including your own family."

"I'm sorry my depression is an inconvenience to you. There, I said it. I am mildly depressed. I think I have a pretty good reason to be. Don't you?" he snapped.

His outburst was followed by a brief moment of silence. The only noise to indicate his mother's silence and not a sudden case of deafness, was the low hum of the road and the inappropriate, upbeat tempo of Uptown Girl playing at a hushed volume.

"I'm sorry," his mother broke the silence. "It's just that I love you very much and I don't like seeing you this way. You need to be around family. You need to be back at home and back in your normal life again. It's been three months."

"I don't have a normal life anymore. Everything I knew to be normal was taken from me. This is my life. Normal or not, this is what's left. Now I am going to visit my wife and I do not want to have this conversation again. Good-bye mother."

Miss. Veracini began to speak but was promptly cut off as Parker touched the end call portion of the LCD. With the call ended, the music gradually returned to its previous volume.

Parker remained silent for a long moment before addressing his singing companion. "Sorry Billy."

With the push of a button, the radio fell silent and Parker Veracini drove the rest of the way in silence.

TWENTY-ONE

Mr. Monroe was a pain in the ass when it came to just about everything. Having served as Eagle Roost's "Technical Trades Advisor" for the past twenty years, the man had witnessed the birth of countless, student created abortions. During that time however, from the same lumber filled womb, had also been born several masterpieces. It was these magnificent creations that has elevated his expectations and turned him into the detail oriented, nit picking asshole he'd become.

A cumbersome hall pass had been one such creation. He loved that burdensome piece of shit. Apparently, three years ago, his best student had taken it upon himself to create the pass for his most beloved teacher. It hadn't been an assignment, just a severe case of ass kissing that had inspired the task. The result was an intricately carved hunk of wood, made to resemble a bald eagle perched upon a branch. The thing stood nearly a foot tall and with no portion of its body shaped conveniently enough for the grasp of any normal, human hand, the heavy wooden bird required two hands when being lugged around.

Steven hated the useless thing, though he did respect the detail and craftsmanship that had drawn his teacher's pathetic admiration. This minuscule respect, however, was still not enough to thwart Steven's nagging desire to one day wrap the thing in M-80s and watch as the beloved sculpture took on a new form with each violent explosion.

The eagle peered down at Steven from atop his locker, it's permanently vexed eyes sizing up its future executioner.

"Eighteen," Steven whispered aloud as the combination lock relinquished its guard and permitted the wobbly door to swing freely.

The inside of his locker was packed tight with books and school supplies; tools of education whose entombing layer of dust would continue to thicken as the school year progressed. Steven had no intention of disrupting the paper tower of knowledge however. What he sought lied just beyond.

Feeling around, his fingertips brushed a small, furry object. Anyone with the urge to snoop, based upon the overall appearance of the confined space, would probably think that they had just discovered the expired body of a pet hamster or some other tiny rodent. Steven grabbed hold of the furry object, carefully withdrawing a small, plastic Pez dispenser from the back of the unlit hole. The candy dispenser's head was one of those once trendy troll dolls, its orange, nylon hair protruding in all directions from its tiny plastic skull. The doll wore a look of confusion; this, combined with its tie-dye body, comically hinting at the troll's favorite, herbal past time.

He'd received the toy from his mother over ten years ago, before it had been deemed offensive and yanked from store shelves; one of the first victims of an already forming, politically correct society. Though he found the troll mildly amusing, it wasn't the image it portrayed or its sentimental origins that had persuaded Steven to keep it around. The treasure hidden within was what gave the tiny doll its true value.

Steven shoved the Pez in his pocket and resealed the

cavern of dust. He knew he had plenty of time. Mr. Monroe was most likely kicked back in his chair, feet up on his desk and engrossed in the newspaper as always. He didn't live his life by the clock but by the bell that would dictate throughout the day who he saw and when he could go home. He wasn't keeping track of Steven's absents and would likely have little knowledge of just how much time his student had spent away from class.

As he navigated the poorly lit hall, he glanced in at each passing classroom, confirming the much shared opinion that school sucks. The tired eyes of his peers told all that was needed to signify their boredom and hidden desire for God, or whomever, to strike down the over enthusiastic educator standing before them.

A skirt-less body, on a door hung placard, informed Steven of his arrival at the only place of solitude within the entire building. The heavy door swung inward, welcoming its new guest with an invisible cloud of bleach and berries. Five urinals lined the wall ahead, their shiny, porcelain surfaces glimmering under the influence of the light pouring through two large windows above.

He'd always found it puzzling that the architect had integrated two of the largest windows in the entire school, into a room with no need for a view of the busy world beyond its walls. And, to make their placement even stranger, the expansive sheets of glass stood free of tint or any other privacy lending enhancement. If it hadn't been for the windows' elevated positions and the school's lack of eight foot tall students, it would have seemed as though their sole purpose had been to place as many peckers on display as possible for all to see. Steven had no intention of becoming such a display piece this visit however, as he quickly searched the four stalls along the adjoining right wall before ending his bathroom analysis at a sink.

A half consumed cigarette rested over the drain, its paper and blackened, chemical contents swelling under the influence of numerous baths.

What a disgusting habit, Steven thought to himself, as he stared at the cancer causing demon while removing the troll from his pocket. Its squinting eyes stared at the windows, its permanent look of confusion seeming to also question their peculiar placement.

A soft creak arose from the troll's spring loaded neck as Steven thumbed at the tiny doll, enticing it to fulfill the purpose for which it had been created. Instead of dispensing a small, rectangular morsel of sugar though, an equally sized, oblong pill was propelled forward and into Steven's hand. Its smooth, white surface resembled that of any other prescription pill used to treat pain or discomfort, only Steven was not in any pain and he certainly had not received the cherished pill from the family doctor. Other than his body's nagging desire for the substance contained within the wild haired troll, he'd never felt better in his life. He was no longer only a guilty verdict away from becoming someone's bitch and he'd regained the love of the girl that he thought he'd lost. All he required now, to officially declare this day the best in recent memory, was the anticipated energy boost his tiny chemical friend promised to lend.

The troll stood and watched from the front corner of the sink as Steven turned the knob and, leaning forward, cupped a handful of water into his mouth. The tiny pill grew buoyant within its new environment, eager to release its chemically engineered magic as it began its journey toward digestion.

TWENTY-TWO

"Now, can anyone remember what rain symbolized in Hemingway's 'A Farewell to Arms'?" Mr. Macky questioned his quickly fading class. "Yes, Mr. Perez," he opted to forgo calling upon his usual three student panel of volunteers, instead summoning the Sleepy boy in the back row, who's inability to remain awake had been a source of amusement to those around him for the last twenty minutes.

Manny Perez's eyes burst open at the sound of his name. "Bad stuff," he answered, attempting to straighten his posture and conceal his temporary visit to la-la-land.

"Though vague, remarkably, you are correct. It would seem Mr. Perez, that you pay closer attention to me in your sleep than you do when you're awake. Could I get you a pillow, maybe even a cot so that you might join us more often and possibly, even one day, manage to receive a grade somewhere above the "D" range?"

Embarrassed but intent on maintaining his "tough guy" image, Manny remained stoned faced at the defamatory remark, while numerous other students delivered the laughter Mr. Macky had hardly sought but couldn't reject.

Dexter's laugh, however, was not solely the result of his

teacher's humorous attack. Instead, his jovial response stemmed more from the look on Manny's face. The kid was ridiculous. He wanted to be tough. He talked the bad boy talk and walked the bad boy walk but anyone could see in his eyes that he was just another scared teen, unsure of his place in life and doing what he could to find his illusive role.

Dexter hated Manny Perez. The guy was a constant source of trouble. He and Steven had had run-ins with the problematic nuisance on numerous occasions and though things had never turned physical, plenty of derogatory statements had been exchanged between all involved. It was only a matter of time before somebody overstepped their boundaries and fist would be called upon to settle the long time rivalry. Until then, Dexter just sat back and took pleasure in watching the pathetic turd take his deserved abuse from a source of authority he was either too cowardly to defy or too stupid to understand.

Two desks up from Dexter, Becky also took the opportunity to relieve a bit of pent up laughter, though most likely due to a genuine appreciation for the insulting joke and less at the person to whom it had been directed.

He couldn't believe that she'd just approached Steven like that this morning. She had seemed so happy and upbeat. How could she not know what had been done to her and what the hell could the two have discussed after he, Mark and Charlie had left? Whatever it was, she seemed far too chipper for a person about to file criminal charges.

"So, are you?" Stephanie Ranston questioned in a hushed tone, leaning towards Becky from the desk to her right.

Becky just nodded yes.

The secret conversation intrigued Dexter, though it remained at a volume which allowed only the occasional fragment to be heard. Eager to learn more about the apparently exciting topic, he placed all of his attention on the two chatty girls.

Apparently Dexter was not the only one interested in what the girls had to say as Mr. Macky, for a second time, ceased his rant on the genius behind his favorite dead author.

"Either my speech is that boring or you two have found it so compelling that you just can't wait to share your opinions. Since I like to think of myself as an extraordinarily interesting person, I can only assume that it's the latter. Maybe, Miss Ranston, you would like to come up here and continue the topic while I take your seat and continue your discussion about boys, hair, nails and whatever else it is that you self-proclaimed princesses discuss.

"No sir. Sorry," Stephanie lowered her eyes embarrassed but not surprised by the teacher's unorthodox admonishment.

"As I was saying," Macky continued.

Dexter's attention remained with Stephanie. He knew she'd talk again. Her proudly held title of school gossip was widely known around school. If you had a secret and someone else knew about it, it was only a matter of time before the forbidden topic reached Stephanie's ears and through her, every soul on the planet.

Though reprimanded by Macky, whatever tidbit of information she'd just received was far too juicy to keep pent up for the seemingly endless, final thirty minutes of the period. Either Chatterbox Ranston would continue the conversation which had drawn his attention or she'd explode under the mounting pressure. Either way Dexter was sure to be entertained.

"I can't believe you two got back together," she, as predicted, failed to remain quiet.

Mr. Macky cleared his throat.

"Sorry," Stephanie again ceded to the growingly frustrated man.

What? That's why Becky had approached Steven this

morning? It wasn't to confront her attacker about what he'd done?

Sometimes Steven's luck was sickening. No matter what went awry in his life, he always seemed to come out on top and usually better off than how he'd started.

Even with as much jealousy as Dexter often harbored for Steven Bishop, he also admired the guy. The man was a God. He'd challenged fate, potentially gambling away his entire life by taking that which was clearly not his and in the end, had been rewarded for doing so. He had to talk with Steven. He had to know if the news was true.

Glancing at his watch, Dexter smiled. Somehow, defying the laws of chatty Stephanie, he was the only other person aware of the god's little Speed habit. He also possessed the secret knowledge that this was the period in which his friend often escaped to the restroom for a quick refill of his dwindling tanks. He had to talk with Steven and, if he was lucky, maybe even obtain some of those magic little pills which seemed to supply his idol with not only seemingly endless energy but remarkably good fortune as well.

"Mr. Macky, may I use the restroom please?" he raised his hand as he spoke, stopping the teacher in mid-sentence.

"Thank you for raising your hand and not interrupting, Mr. Brice," Mr. Macky sarcastically acknowledge Dexter.

"Sorry sir, but I would really appreciate it if I could use the restroom please...sir," he laid on an unusually thick layer of politeness.

"Well, since I don't have time to explain to your parents why it is that their kid came home with wet trouser, I'll let you go. Come get the pass."

Dexter jumped from his seat and rushed to the desk to collect his pass before bursting through the door and disappearing into the quiet hall.

"Geish, I sure hope he makes it," Macky reacted to Dexter's quick exit, his comment drawing several more quiet chuckles.

TWENTY-THREE

S.S.R. or Silent Sustained Reading had been touted by the school board as one of the greatest additions to the educational process since federally mandated testing.

Peter had always thought that to be not only a highly overblown comparison but not even a very good one at that. All S.S.R. did was fill the remaining half of the lunch hour, typically held by recess in the earlier grades, with what board members had envisioned would be a "time of introspective self-teaching by way of literature and uninterrupted silence", as the superintendent had described the program. It had been a good theory, self-education through the written words of the world's verbal artists, both past and present, but as with so many other well intentioned ideas, it had proven a dismal failure, at least in Peter's opinion.

The teachers, who had been entrusted with the unwanted task of policing the brief periods, couldn't have cared less about what the students actually used the time for. All they cared about was that they not be bothered during the twenty minute moment of silence that had once been a part of their very own lunch breaks.

The students weren't much better when it came to

aiding in the success of the program's initial goal to help raise federally mandated test scores. While some students did utilize the time as intended, most just used it as a chance to get a jump on homework or to hone their artistic abilities with the creation of x-rated caricatures on the surfaces of their desks.

In junior high, Peter had discovered one such animation, involving himself and what appeared to be a goat, engaged in an act far beyond the intended definition of bestiality. Geoffrey claimed to have found three of himself, though had never opted to share their perverted content.

No such slanderous content had been found in the high school to date, though it was early in the year and with Peter and Geoffrey's rapidly growing popularity amongst their peers, Peter figured it was only a matter of time before he, the goat and all of the other barn yard animals got together once again for a new portrait in black and blue ink.

Peter was one of the few readers, as was Geoffrey, though on this day neither could pay much attention to their novels of choice; Peter reading the latest politically driven drama by Tom Clancy and Geoffrey more than halfway through the second of three books in Dean Koontz's modern take on the Frankenstein tales.

"How was he just hanging there?" Peter whispered to Geoffrey in the desk beside him as both continued to stare at their open books. "I mean, I know how, but how did he get up there?"

"Shh," the teacher, whose name Peter had not yet learned since she seldom spoke other than to utter an admonishing "shh" or "be quiet", finally broke what had been a three class silent streak.

"You're sure you didn't hear anything?" Peter continued to ponder the physical impossibilities of the hanging dog.

Geoffrey didn't respond but continued to stare forward

at his open book.

Maybe he really is reading, Peter thought to himself, though doubted the likeliness of that explanation given that, in the entire first five minutes of class, he hadn't once seen Geoffrey turn a page.

"It worked," Geoffrey muttered under his breath.

"What?" Peter questioned, intrigued. "What worked?"

"I didn't believe it but it really worked. You were right."

"What? Who are you talking to?" Peter asked, confused by his friend's one sided conversation. "Geoff, are you alright?"

Geoffrey gave no response. He didn't even show an acknowledgment that he'd heard Peter's concerned questioning.

"Geoffrey?" Peter spoke again as he leaned toward his friend's desk.

"Mr. Madison. How about you move to a desk in the back where you won't be able to bother anyone with you incessant rudeness," the no-name teacher constructed the longest sentence that anyone in the room had yet heard her speak to date.

"But...," Peter began to protest but, realizing the futility in such a stand, instead chose to do as he was told.

Geoffrey didn't even blink at the unfair castigation. He didn't follow his friend's movements to the back of the room. He didn't even offer a sympathetic gesture to indicate his firm stance on Peter's side. He didn't do anything that a best friend was expected to do in such an unfair situation. Instead, he remained in his seat, his head hovering low over his desk as he continued his pretend engrossment in the four hundred page prop before his eyes.

"Now?" Geoffrey seemed to question the same invisible party he'd recently been apt to engage in conversation.

Peter stared curiously from his location of banishment,

constantly adjusting his position to see around the continually shifting heads that blocked his view.

Geoffrey closed the novel and returned it to his backpack on the floor beside him. Free of the paperback, his left hand joined the right already inside the bag, where together they hoisted a much larger, hardcover book from within. The backpack slumped as the book, which had apparently been acting as the bags spine, was lifted into the air and place upon the desk.

A glimmer of light caught the curved edges of five silver buttons that adorned the book's front cover. Peter had never seen a book like it before. It was massive, at least a foot in height and ten inches in width with probably close to a thousand pages filling its dark brown, leather covers. From what Peter could tell, from his distant vantage point, the book appeared old...extremely old. It had to be. He couldn't think of even one time in his life that he'd seen its equal and though it appeared historic, with its yellow edged pages and carefully crafted construction, its leather looked almost new. Not one crack or dry spot. The binding appeared in perfect condition as well and was apparently functional as Geoffrey grabbed hold of the top cover and opened the book to a point approximately half way through the mountain of pages.

Peter was shocked, no yellowing. Sure, the outer edges had appeared worn as expected but inside there was not one bit of the decaying, brittle paper one would expect to find associated with an antique. The pages were bright white, almost blinding, causing Peter to shift his focus away from the book and back to his friend whom had already withdrawn a pen from his pocket and began positioning himself over the literary behemoth.

With no thought at all Geoffrey began scribbling his words across the blank pages. He wrote at such a furious pace that Peter was amazed his pen didn't tear right through to the pages beneath. A small grin began forming on the frantic author's face as his Bic continued to accelerate across the paper, its speed increasing with each new line of text.

Peter leaned forward, lifting his body out of his chair until he was practically hanging over the student seated in front of him. He had to see what was so captivating as to draw such a peculiarly, disturbing grin. He had to know what Geoffrey was writing.

Though impossible, he could have sworn that the already penned writing was growing smaller with every inch he drew nearer. Aiding in the concealment of the mysterious collection of words was the ever increasing luminosity of the paper itself. Peter looked around the room. No one else in the class seemed bothered by the bright paper. Not one person made comment or even turned in curiosity of the oddity taking place among them.

"Mr. Madison!" the teacher once again scolded.

The student, whose head space was being violated, lifted his gaze, catching a glimpse of Peter's face hovering uncomfortably close.

"Dude!" the student exclaimed, straightening his posture in his seat and returning Peter to his.

"Mr. Madison, if you are unable to sit still in my classroom without disturbing me or anyone else here, then I suggest that you find an alternative place to rest your overly active body for the next fifteen minutes. Might I suggest the office?"

"I'm fine, Miss…" Peter paused, remembering that he still did not know her name. "I'm sorry. I won't bother you again. Sorry," Peter then addressed the student in front of him, who just returned his gaze to his newest desk etching, while issuing an annoyed, "asshole".

Geoffrey again refrained from showing interest in the commotion. He continued to almost lie across the book, the words flowing from the pen and onto the mysterious paper as his once, happy grin took on a more devious and sinister nature.

TWENTY-FOUR

Steven shoveled another handful of water into his mouth, ensuring the small pill's quick and uninhibited descent. He'd consumed so many of the little miracle pills over the years that they had little, obvious effect on him at this point. They were more of a boost than anything else; his equivalent to the poor man's morning coffee.

Reaching for a paper towel, Steven wiped away the residual moisture gathered around his mouth and chin before returning to an upright posture. "Jesus!" he proclaimed, surprised by a second reflection in the mirror before him.

He hadn't heard the bathroom door open or the shuffling of footsteps but there she was, standing only three feet from him with a blank look upon her face. Either she'd been extraordinarily quiet or he'd been so consumed by his body's pleas that the world around him had momentarily ceased to exist.

Steven spun around, forgetting about the evidence housed within the tiny doll upon the sink. "Becky," his voice announced with both shock and intrigue.

Becky's cold, blank stare melted as a warm smile took its place.

The presence of the troll and his secret addiction suddenly returning to the forefront of his mind, he shifted slightly to the left, concealing the drug dealing doll. Though it was unclear just how long Becky had been standing behind him or how much she might have seen, he saw no reason to provide her with any more insight into his illegal habit. She'd never known about his chemical cravings and with the prospects of a reconciliation, he saw no good in her discovering them now.

"What are you doing here?" he asked, still confused and a bit nervous.

"Shh," Becky instructed as she placed her left index finger to his lips and her other hand on his chest. She took one step toward him, bringing their bodies to within inches of one another as she slid her quieting finger over his chin, down his neck and onto his chest beside her other appendage of seductive digits.

Becky had never been the forward type before. Steven had always played the antagonist but here she was, taking charge of a situation in which she, more often than not, had played the submissive. He couldn't complain. Even if he'd wanted to, his lower half would have overruled the thought and allowed the aggressive girl's actions to continue.

With a slight shove, Becky repositioned her boyfriend against the sink. She took another small step toward him, again positioning herself so that her right thigh ever so slightly pressed against his.

In a remarkable display of balance, Steven felt and watched as Becky ran her left foot up his leg, her toes rubbing and caressing the muscular limb beneath his jeans before placing her elevated foot upon the sink behind him. Her silky dress retreated from its loose hanging position, sliding into the crease now formed between the girl's hip and elevated leg.

His eyes traced the seductive outline of the perfect thigh. Even given Becky's newly contorted posture and her exposed left leg, she remain, for the most part, tastefully concealed beneath the pink, summer dress.

He returned his gaze to the still smiling aggressor. Continuing her penetrating stare, Becky slowly slid two fingers into the valley formed by her perky, teenage breasts and with the graceful touch of a magician, withdrew a pair of lacy, white panties.

She'd been planning this, he thought to himself. There's no way she could've snuck in here and partially stripped without him noticing. Hell it was hard enough to fathom just how she'd managed to slip thought the door undetected in the first place.

He wondered just how far she was willing to take this little game. Maybe that's all it was, just a game. Maybe she'd had no intention of ever getting back together again. Maybe she'd just wanted to get his hopes up; to get him more worked up than he'd ever been before, just so she could bring him crashing back to earth with the worst case of blue balls in history. Maybe this was all a punishment of some sort. The nausea of the previous night's sleepless hours suddenly returned. Maybe she did know after all.

Becky grabbed the back of his head, pulling his lips toward hers. Steven's worries quickly faded as her free hand, once positioned on his chest slowly began its descent toward the buckle of his belt.

All worries currently overridden by the girl's sudden aggression, Steven ran his hand up Becky's thigh. Her soft skin felt almost hot to the touch, as if she were on fire within, the burning flames of lust licking at his fingertips, eager for a taste of his masculine fuel. Rounding her hip, his aggressive digits pushed beneath her dress, their bold endeavor rewarded with a firm squeeze of bare ass-cheek.

As if the engine of her loins wasn't already racing at dangerously high rpm's, Steven's return of aggressive lust quickly accelerated its pace. With an impressive display of finger dexterity, she broke through the barrier put up by Levi Strauss, taking hold of the craved kindling that she required to keep her inner fire burning.

Only momentarily overwhelmed by the sudden and firm attention to his partner, Steven continued his journey, leaning slightly, preparing for a rear attack on her undoubtedly pre-lubed gates.

As his fingers detected the transition from the tight skin of her extended lower limb to the moist, silky entrance he sought, Becky dropped her leg from the sink, knocking his wandering hand away before it could complete its mission. Shocked by the sudden rejection, Steven returned his gaze northward. Becky's smile remained, her pleasant expression slowly joined by a look of contemplation. Before he had time to consider what might be running through the horny girl's mind, she grabbed his arm and, spinning counter clockwise, flung his body toward the stalls along the opposite wall.

Steven stumbled backward, crashing through the half open, center stall door, coming to a momentarily painful rest upon the lowered seat of the porcelain throne. The pain of the crash landing would've probably far exceeded its resulting intensity if it hadn't been for the adrenaline and testosterone fueled anesthetics pulsing through his veins.

He remained seated as Becky teasingly took her time to follow. She stared at her discarded toy, her smile never wavering as she started toward him, slowly lifting off her dress and unfastening her bra.

Having had plenty of experience with the opposite sex's physiologically altering effects on his manhood, he was well aware of the varying degrees of an erection. This was by far the most ridged his copilot had ever been, feeling as if at any moment the seemingly insufficient lack of skin would tear open, leaving him unable to accomplish the task Becky was obviously craving him to perform.

Entering the stall she swung the door shut and engaged the lock without ever lifting her eyes from her prey. This was not his usual choice of atmosphere for such an encounter but on the other hand, this was not the usual Becky.

She leaned over and, continuing her aggressive attack, yanked the unfastened jeans from Steven's body, leaving them in a crumpled heap around his ankles. Fearing his member removed in the next violent de-clothing, Steven chose to assist in the act and slid his boxers off his waist to join the discarded pants.

Becky's once broad smile faded and in its absence grew lust. She was eyeing his lower half as if it were a five star meal and she just couldn't wait to get a taste but instead of sampling the appetizer, she positioned herself over him and dove right in on the main course.

The feel of her soft, moist femininity sliding down upon him, instantly overwhelmed Steven's entire body as he closed his eyes and tilted his head back, allowing his sense of touch to remain uninhibited by sight.

As many times as they'd engaged in that exact position it had never felt so good. He wasn't sure if it was the aggressive foreplay or simply the erotically dirty nature of their environment but no matter what it was, he was sure of one thing, he would never again view a bathroom stall in the same way.

Becky glided up and down on her sought after probe, moaning and gasping with obviously no fear of discovery.

Quickly approaching climax Steven did all he could to distract his overly stimulated body, attempting to replace the thoughts of his current situation with those of a less sexual nature. Even before he could approve the seemingly silly methods of his mind, he found himself reciting the alphabet within his head, picturing each letter as it flashed across his mind's canvas.

A, B, C, D, he thought to himself, surprised to find the ridiculous method working as his rushing army of DNA slowed their advance. *E, F, G,* he continued.

The increased volume of Becky's erotic moans launched a counter attack, poking a hole in Steven's alphabetic distraction. Attempting to patch the hole, Steven imagined himself suddenly yelling the letters as they passed before him at a now accelerated rate.

H, I, J, K, L, M, N, O, P, he continued to hold on, feeling the army again increasing the pace of its march.

Q, R.

His recital was suddenly interrupted by a flash of pain. Forgetting the alphabet, the fear of his bursting foreskin again took control of his mind but faded as the sensation of his platoon, nearing the end of the tunnel, erased the pain.

Becky continued her ride, placing her hands upon his chest and arching her back.

As his wave of enlisted soldiers flooded the battlefield, the pain returned, unable to be concealed by the pleasureful sensation of the climactic moment. This time it was a fire in his lap. With each undulation the fire grew in intensity, searing his most delicate of flesh.

His eyes burst open. Becky's remained closed, her amazing breasts bouncing before him as her mouth hung open, still occupied with the production of the pornographic soundtrack. As his eyes traveled south along the girl's firm body he noticed a bit of color upon his lap. Looking closer the color began to spread, its wet crimson source glistening under the florescent lights overhead.

Blood! It had happened. His penis had ruptured under the excessive pressure. No, that can't happen...can it? He thought to himself as another flame licked at his masculinity.

Steven returned his gaze to his rider. Becky's body was no longer arched in a display of pleasure. Her eyes were wide open and her previously audible mouth fell silent as her lips slowly parted, displaying a terrifying set of razor like fangs.

Panic filled Steven's body but before he could dispense of the hideous rider, she lunged forward, sinking her snarling daggers deep within his throat.

TWENTY-FIVE

Since the South wing of the school housed only the auditorium, cafeteria, gym and a few language and shop classes, its construction remained that of only one story while the remainder of the building stood as two. Dexter knew this would make locating his troll keeping friend much easier. Only two bathrooms resided in the South wing, one of which was just down the hall from Steven's locker. He figured he'd try that one first, since Steven would probably wish to travel as short a distance as possible with the illegal toy in his possession.

Though he didn't customarily engage in the consumption of such narcotics, he had, on occasion, been lucky enough to catch Steven on a good day when his friend had been willing to share his pricy treasure. If the news about Steven and Becky was true, Dexter felt pretty safe in assuming that this would be one of those "good days".

He quickly rounded the corner, bringing the library into view just down the hall to his left. He'd started his journey with a frantic burst of speed, out of Mr. Mackey's class and down the second floor hallway but had quickly slowed to a brisk walk, not wishing to draw any more unnecessary attention. Though a swift travel time was necessary, given his classroom's location on the opposite side of the school, he couldn't afford to be stopped by a curious teacher or nosy, school police officer. They would surely begin asking him questions like, "Where are you going in such a hurry?" and, Officer Salinger's apparent favorite, "Whoa, where's the fire, chief?" Dexter couldn't lie, at least not convincingly and with the reputation he and his group had acquired over the years, he knew that any excuse he gave would be instantly deemed a lie, therefore initiating an interrogation process he neither had the patience nor the intelligence to withstand.

As he approached the library entrance he slowed even more, not in fear of the librarian but of the staff located directly across the hall in the main office. He needed to slip by without anyone of authority seeing him. Principal Sanchez and Vice Principle Browne were also well aware of Dexter and his friend's antics, probably more so than anyone else. Luckily Mr. Browne was out for the next two weeks learning how to be a dad with his recently ruined wife. Miss. Sanchez however, never missed a day. She had no family and her womb was most likely as barren as her personality.

Dexter slowly approached the large glass wall which made the office look more like an aquarium than an administrative headquarters. The secretary busily punched at her keyboard, her eyes focused on the screen before her. The remainder of the staff was nowhere in sight, probably occupied with a quick trip to the cafeteria, before another onslaught of students flooded the halls, on their way to another mid-day refueling on the tasteless, low fat slop society had deemed worthy of consumption by today's obesity plagued youth.

Dexter maintained his casual pace, continuing to keep watch for any unexpected witnesses to his travels. The last door of the office belonged to Miss. Sanchez. Her desk faced the hall and more often than not she could be seen just staring out at passersby, looking for one reason or another to pry her gargantuan ass from her squeaky, overstressed chair just to administer some obscure punishment kept on the books solely for the teacher's continued ability to harass what the school board liked referred to as "problem students".

As if someone was keeping watch over him, eager to see him succeed in his current mission, Miss. Sanchez's door was closed. Dexter quickly slipped by, still fearing that the dreaded doorway would burst open at any moment and the sound of Miss. Sanchez's nasally voice would assault his eardrums with the very sound of his own name. The door however remained closed as Dexter, relieved, slid by but not without sympathy for the poor schmuck currently trapped within that tiny office, probably wishing death upon either himself or the dictator-like sow before him. For all he knew, it could be Charlie in there, facing a brutal punishment for the publicly indecent stunt performed earlier that morning. Whoever it was, Dexter was just thankful for his unknowing assistance as he again quickened his pace and entered the South wing.

Steven's locker stood in line with the rest of the metallic vaults along the left-hand side of the hall. Other than the tiny metal tags which bore the locker's numbers, each was identical to the next.

Apparently it was against school policy to decorate the outside of the storage units. Dexter and Steven learned of this rule, like so many, the hard way. Though, since such an offense only drew a punishment of one day of detention, the two had been known to hold decorating contest, each decorating the other's locker with the most offensive material they could find in an attempt to see who could get whom in the most trouble. It had been a year since the last round of "Locker Tattoos" and unfortunately, it had probably been the last.

"I have never seen so many boobies in my life," Miss. Sanchez had exclaimed in response to Steven's artistic collage of breasts while scolding both he and Dexter for their X-rated hijinks. Steven had clearly won that round but an uncontrollable urge to laugh at the educational dictator's ridiculous comment had landed them both a one week suspension with the added threat of expulsion if it were to ever happen again.

As Dexter approached the undecorated, metallic vault, he suddenly had the urge to start another round of the prohibited game but given the severity of the threat, which he fully believed would be enforced, he refrained from etching the curse words that his mind had already placed upon the smooth red surface. Besides, someone had apparently already added a touch of décor to the boring structure.

Staring down at him from on top of its metallic perch was the eagle hall pass that he'd carved three years ago in Mr. Monroe's shop class. Having never had another class with his favorite teacher, he hadn't seen the sculpture since its completion but was shocked, as well as pleased to see the eagle still in use after all this time.

In addition to the long overdue reunion with his beloved creation, the familiar carving brought with it an added pleasure. It had come from Steven's current class. He must be in the bathroom just down the hall, Dexter though excitedly. This revelation brought a smile to his face as he continued on his way, again at the hurried pace with which he'd started.

As he blew by the few classrooms sharing the South wing with the larger, more craft oriented spaces, he ignored his inner voice, warning him to slow down or risk being caught. The bathroom was just ahead and the forgotten pass was proof that Steven and his troll were inside.

Dexter burst through the door expecting to find Steven at the sink, his troll doll relinquishing its hidden contents with only the faintest squeak of its tiny springs.

The anticipated dispenser stood patiently on the sink as

expected but Steven was nowhere to be seen.

What would cause him to leave such a treasured and illegal toy standing in the open for anyone to find? he thought.

His question was quickly answered by the soft giggle of a female voice emanating from the center stall to his right. The cute giggle was followed by a brief moment of sucking and what sounded like an overly enthusiastic lick.

No fucking way, Dexter thought to himself as he quietly approached the neighboring stall, eager to view the explicit activity taking place next door. Apparently the erotic couple had failed to hear his obnoxiously noisy entrance, which only excited him more. They were most likely in the middle of their encounter and completely oblivious to the world around them.

Even given the entertainers' most likely distracted mindsets, Dexter used as much caution as possible to not make a sound as he entered the stall and slowly stepped up, onto the toilet seat.

The stall walls were unusually tall in this bathroom, as if the builders were afraid that the confined spaces would likely be frequented by giants of some sort. In order to circumvent the visual impairment created by the inconvenient barrier, Dexter grabbed hold of the top edge and slowly lifted himself onto his tip toes, lifting his gaze just high enough to see the other side.

As the opposite wall of the adjoining space came into view he could feel his heart racing with excitement and his pants growing gradually tighter.

He lifted himself a bit higher, determined to see even lower into the adjoining stall, though quickly wished that he'd chosen to mind his own business, as the sight of his partially devoured friend came into view. A look of twisted horror plagued the uneaten remains of his friend's face while a naked, blood soaked Becky sat atop him, her tongue protruding an impossible distance from her mouth as it diligently excavated the deep recesses of Steven's right eye socket.

Dexter's stomach turned, threatening to return all it had recently been given and though he successfully fought back the mounting urge to hurl, he quickly regretted his impressive display of willpower. The waterfall of regurgitation might have temporarily blinded the ravenous female as she, sensing his presence, turned her animalistic gaze upon him with a vicious hiss.

Never before so eager to return to class, Dexter stumbled and fell from his voyeuristic perch, landing face first on the tile floor, half in and half out of the stall. The blow to his forehead had been painful and a burning sensation quickly enveloped his left wrist but the fear of being consumed alive instantly brought him to his feet. As he stood, he was shocked to find Becky standing before him, blocking his exit and prolonging his unanticipated visit to hell.

The Cannibalistic girl was completely naked from head to toe but wore a thick layer of blood and gore which oozed from her mouth and slowly traveled southward over her body. And though the thought of sex was the last thing on his mind, something inside had already instructed his eyes to check out the merchandise of the murderous savage. Before he knew it he was staring at the bloody pubes of the typically desirable plaything.

One glance would have been sufficient for his mind to gather all that it was seeking but his vision remained locked on the anything but erotic orifice, his continued attention compelled by an unusual chunk of shredded flesh protruding from the grotesque opening.

Becky must have noticed the source of his attention as she slowly slid her hand over her body, seductively smearing her runny outfit before grabbing hold of the unusual object.

Dexter looked up in fear and disgust at the girls sadistic smile, then back down at the source of intrigue. With a firm grip, Becky slowly slid the ravaged object out from between her legs.

For a second time, Dexter, who prided himself on his strong stomach, felt his morning breakfast threatening to return for a second tasting.

The familiar piece of meat between Becky's bloodied, manicured fingers wasn't as foreign as Dexter had thought. He had one just like it, only his had never looked as though it had just clogged up a meat grinder.

He wasn't going to escape. There was no way out of this room except inside the belly of the creature standing before him. He was going to die a horrible death, ironically, finally accomplishing his unspoken goal of being just like Steven.

As if reading her prospective victim's realization of mortality and wishing nothing more than to bring his fears to fruition, Becky dropped the once useful appendage of pleasure and grabbed hold of her new prey with both hands.

Dexter would have fought back but fear had rendered his muscles useless. All he could do was close his eyes and wait for the anticipated sensation of teeth as they tore into his flesh, devouring him alive.

She pulled Dexter close and, as if now desiring to engage in similar relations with this new toy, she assaulted his lips with the wettest of passionate kisses.

Dexter was surprised by the unexpected embrace but found no joy or erotic pleasure in it. Only fear and gut churning disgust occupied his mind as tiny bits of his friend's lifeless flesh were forced into his mouth, their numbers growing with each insertion of the psychotic female's lizard like tongue.

Unable to repress his body's regurgitative urges any longer, the morning's English muffin and eggs rose from their digestive grave. The liquefied breakfast erupted into the beast's mouth and splashed against her face, covering them both in the vile fluid.

Becky roared at the rejection and shoved her unwilling

suitor away, causing Dexter to strike the bank of sinks with such force that he would have swore that his spine had been severed if it weren't for the throbbing pain consuming his body from head to toe.

Though spared permanent paralysis, fear continued its hold over him, rendering him motionless on the floor and leaving his mind to contemplate the forthcoming, added pain of his own consumption.

What seemed like an eternity passed as his eyes remained closed, his body lying in wait to experience its own death. Everything he'd always heard about a person's life flashing before their eyes had been bullshit. The only image burned into his mind was that of the horrid beast, likely prepping itself for the second course of it conquered meal.

A remaining bit of flesh rolled across Dexter's tongue, replacing his fear of consumption with a conscious return to the vile taste still plaguing his mouth. A second onslaught of bile rushed passed his lips, coating the floor beside him and inadvertently drawing his eyes open to find the room abandoned.

Becky was gone.

She hadn't made a sound exiting and as strange as the entire encounter had been, Dexter wouldn't have been surprised at all if she'd just vanished into thin air. Either way, the room was deserted, its only inhabitants being himself and the remains of his ravaged friend, staring out at him from the blood spattered display case.

TWENTY-SIX

The bell rang almost simultaneously with Geoffrey's closing of the bizarre book, as if timed perfectly by the newly inspired author or as a direct result.

That's ridiculous, Peter thought to himself as he plucked his bag up from the floor and got to his feet.

Still consumed by the same, dazed state, Geoffrey quickly lifted the book from atop his desk and shoved it back into his bag, pulling the zipper shut before Peter could manage his way through the sea of evacuating bodies for a closer look.

"What in the world were you writing?" Peter questioned as he came along side Geoffrey's desk.

"What?"

"In the book. What were you writing?"

"What are you talking about?" Geoffrey questioned confused.

Peter didn't know what to say. For nearly twenty minutes he'd watched Geoffrey scribble line after line of text onto the luminescent paper and now, when faced with a simple question as to his undeniably odd behavior, he had the audacity to act as if nothing out of the ordinary had occurred?

"Are you feeling all right?" Geoffrey questioned his anxious friend.

"Am I all right?" Peter responded, wanting to laugh at the outlandish question. "I think I'm just fine. It's you I'm concerned about."

"Why? I'm fine."

"You just spent the last fifteen minutes of class franticly scribbling something in that massive book of yours."

"No I didn't."

"Yes, you did."

"You're sure you're all right?" Geoffrey again questioned, this time with more concern.

"Wait." Peter grabbed the shoulder of the student who's head space he'd earlier intruded upon. "You saw the book right? You saw him writing."

"Fuck off," the still annoyed, desktop artist shoved Peter aside before exiting the classroom.

"You were writing. I swear."

"Maybe I'm not the crazy kid after all," Geoffrey poked fun at his increasingly uneasy friend.

His friend's remark drawing a smile, Peter playfully shoved Geoffrey's chest, though almost instantly wished he hadn't as Geoffrey snatched the four fingers of his right hand out of the air and twisted Peter's arm to its near breaking point.

"Ah! What are you doing!?" Peter cried in pain as his knees began to buckle under the strain of his body's painfully contorted position.

Geoffrey just stood over his friend, gently increasing the pressure on Peter's fingers and arm as the same sinister smirk, from only minutes ago, once again commandeered his face.

"Let go," Peter pleaded.

Geoffrey released his grip, though more so in response to a blood curdling scream down the hall than his friend's pain filled plea.

Peter fell to one knee, bringing his twisted, pulsating digits close to his chest.

Repositioning his heavy backpack on his shoulder, Geoffrey ducked out of the room and into the hall.

"What was that?" Peter questioned aloud as he tested each finger for functionality. That wasn't the first time he'd responded to one of Geoffrey's mock insults in a playfully physical manner. What had set him off like that? He could understand Steven and the gym incident but he was Geoffrey's best friend.

Peter's internal questioning would have to wait as a growing commotion drew his attention to the hall. A fight was his first thought but most fights don't usually begin with a scream. Normally it's a barrage of insults followed by the chanting of "fight" or "kick his ass" that trigger the aggressive confrontations. Curious, just as his departed "friend" had been, Peter plucked his bag from the floor and slung it over his shoulder, continuing to nurse his wounded limb with a sequence of short testing movements.

Entering the hall he was nearly trampled by the rapidly converging horde of students, which by choice or not, hurriedly pushed him along toward the source of unknown intrigue.

Approaching the front of the compiling crowd, Peter noticed a gap in the sea of bodies, with the boy's bathroom at its center. The door remained peacefully still for a moment before, under the influence of an unseen party, beginning a slow swing inward, persuading the intrigued crowed to take one simultaneous step back.

"What's going on?" Peter asked a nearby student but received no response from the anticipation fixated boy.

Bobby Miller emerged from the bathroom, whiter than it seemed his dark skin could allow and holding his hand to his mouth as if the five digit barrier were enough to hold back his reaction to whatever he'd just encountered.

It wasn't.

Bobby bent forward, coating the floor in a chunky combination of stomach acids and what appeared to be a poorly chewed peanut butter and jelly sandwich. The crowd leapt back with a mass, vocal reaction of disgust as a second person appeared in the doorway.

"Holy shit," a member of the crowed exclaimed in a disturbingly calm tone, followed by a more appropriate second scream from a nearby girl.

Peter looked up from Bobby, who quickly scampered to the edge of the crowd. Standing in the doorway was Dexter Brice. His cloths were soaked with blood as was the lower half of his face, a small fleshy chunk clinging to the corner of the senior's mouth.

The crowd again took a collective step back, their looks of excitement and curiosity fading as disgust and horror took their place. No expression spoke truer to the disturbing nature of the moment though than did the one worn by Dexter himself as he stumbled from the bathroom and fainted at the feet of the screaming crowd.

TWENTY-SEVEN

If it was ever possible to be both lavish, yet modest at the same time, that would be how one would describe Veracini Two. Parker and Amanda had in no official way actually named their western Massachusetts hideaway but over the years Veracini Two was how they'd come to refer to their beloved palace of seclusion.

Veracini One was their uptown apartment in the heart of civilization, where sirens and the noises of city life filled the world with seemingly controlled chaos. While Veracini One had been constructed from steel and concrete to block all noises and disturbances from entering its walls, Veracini Two had been constructed with the exact opposite intent. Designed by one of Amanda's oldest friends and one of New York's most renowned architects, Patrick Henstridge, Veracini Two welcomed the outside world.

*****

"People hang pictures and paintings on their walls in an attempt to beautify their homes," Mr. Henstridge stated, as if only he were privy to the tidbit of obvious information.

189

Parker and Amanda listened quietly as Patrick explained his preliminary vision for Veracini Two.

"Much of this artwork displays or illustrates the natural beauty given to the earth and its inhabitants by their creator but the trends of modern design lead us to shun this gift, to block it from view with walls of concrete and wood or even destroy it altogether with the paving of our once, pristine forests, so that we may have a place to drive and park our gas guzzling SUV's."

Though a close friend to Amanda, Parker found it difficult to refer to the eccentric architect as anything more than a business acquaintance. It wasn't that he minded the exceedingly outgoing personality and confidence Patrick Henstridge displayed. In fact, Parker admired such qualities in a person living in a time when self-superiority was frowned upon by a society that had replaced the term loser with the idea that everyone could be a winner. It was the man's contradictory behavior, however, that gave Parker reason to remain distant. Though outwardly confident, Parker got the impression that, inside, Patrick was unsure about who he was and that his outwardly upbeat persona was nothing more than the first line of defense against a world which had most likely played the antagonist in the early chapters of his life.

"A tree hugging, SUV driving, fanatically religious, gay republican," was how Parker had once described his impression of Patrick.

Amanda had laughed at the colorfully contradictory description. "Well, whatever he is, he's an architectural genius."

Parker could not disagree with his wife's generous praise. Patrick Henstridge was a genius, which is why they'd fallen in love with the very first design that he'd pitched.

"Here it is," Patrick proudly announced as he unveiled his artistic rendition of Veracini Two.

Parker could see the excitement building on Patrick's

face. He had obviously led with his best work and eagerly anticipated there excited approval.

"That's a lot of Windex," were the first words to escape Parker's mouth; a phrase he regretted instantly as he watched the architect's excitement and confident façade, shatter before them.

"I love it," Amanda quickly proclaimed, attempting to reverse the affects left by her husband's smart ass response.

"You don't like it, Mr. Veracini?" Patrick hesitantly asked.

"No, I love it too."

Parker's answer was followed by an uncomfortable moment of silence.

"The Windex thing was a joke."

More silence.

"But...apparently I'm not that funny," he sheepishly added.

A cricket serenaded the room.

"Really, I'm serious."

"About what, loving the design or not being funny?" Amanda broke the awkward moment.

"Ha, ha," Parker responded, thankful for her intervention but confident that she'd enjoyed every awkward moment prior. "I really do love it. Honestly. It's breathtaking."

*****

Parker found himself muttering the word "breathtaking" as Veracini Two appeared from around the last bend of the long, gravel driveway.

Constructed of nearly seventy-five percent glass, the late afternoon sun gleamed from every surface. Patrick Henstridge had set out to design a house that utilized the beauty of nature in the décor of its walls. With its transparent construction, Veracini Two did so much more, ultimately allowing nature to pass right through, permitting the modestly sized, glass cube, while uniquely modern in appearance, to blend effortlessly with its rustic surroundings.

"What if I don't see the house and drive right through the living room?" Parker, in an attempt to redeem himself comically, had questioned at the conclusion of their meeting with Patrick.

"Then we'll be saving a hell of a lot of money on Windex," Amanda had responded with a grin.

Parker smiled at the memory of his late wife as he pulled the Mercedes into the carport, which protruded from the south side of the glass domicile. Like the rest of the house, the carport too had been constructed largely of glass. A set of three steps, leading to the glass door entrance of the first floor, lay before the idling vehicle. Though unable to clearly make it out, Parker read the familiar greeting etched into the door.

Relax

The elegantly scribed word had been added to the door upon the home's completion, not as a welcome to those who might come knocking but as a reminder to both Amanda and himself that the outside world, with all of its stresses and troubles, had no place within those walls.

A narrow crack meandered its way through the door, striking a line through the peaceful word. Parker rubbed his right hand at the memory of the news he had received in that doorway.

Though the glass hadn't shattered that night, two of his knuckles had.

TWENTY-EIGHT

With a handful of teachers already on scene and the
arrival of Officer Salinger, Peter could predict the scenario
that would soon unfold. In no time the school would be
flooded with cops, locked down for questioning and
inundated with grief counselors.

He read the paper and followed the news. There had
been enough school shootings and deaths in recent years
to make him all too familiar with just how the process
worked. He also knew that he wanted no part in any of it
so, in an effort to avoid the undesirable situation, he'd
ducked out of the nearest exit before a strong police
presence could establish a perimeter around the school.

He had nothing to hide. Other than witnessing a
murderous Dexter Brice emerge from the boy's bathroom,
covered in the proof of his heinous act, he knew nothing
and possessed no additional information for authorities
that couldn't easily be obtained from one of at least a
hundred other stunned students. And, while he possessed
no answers for the questions bound to be asked by
authorities, he did have some questions of his own and
Geoffrey, he felt, was the only one who knew the answers.

Leaping up the front steps to his friend's front door,

Peter thought about just bursting in, dashing upstairs and confronting Geoffrey about his recent behavior, about nearly breaking his fingers and most of all about the mysterious book he kept secretly tucked away within his bag. He had a feeling that the incident back at school and Geoffrey's recent fascination with the new found literature was in no way a coincidence. Unfortunately the door was locked and he was forced to ring the bell.

As he waited for someone to answer, he backed away from the door, making his way back down the short flight of steps and onto the front walkway.

Geoffrey's bedroom was located on the second floor, in the front left corner of the house. The blinds were drawn.

His hopes dashed by yet another barrier into the quiet home, he turned his attention to the power line, which just that morning, had played such a vital role in Prince's peculiar execution.

Peter shuddered at the memory of the dead dog, dangling from the high electrical line. There was no physical way anyone could have lifted the large animal to such a height, at least not without drawing someone's attention while doing so but from what he'd overheard during the morning's conversations between curious neighbors and stunned cops, no one had seen or heard a thing. Prince's owner had even seen the dog, alive, just fifteen minutes prior to finding his pet hanged in the side yard. None of it made sense and suddenly Peter found himself with yet another set of questions for his friend, who still had not answered the door.

Peter again climbed the steps, this time opting for the pounding of his fist, as opposed to the apparently un-received or ignored calling of the bell. Again he stepped back and waited and again got no response.

He knew Geoffrey was in there. Shortly after Dexter had made his bloody curtain call, Peter had unsuccessfully searched the stunned crowd for him.

He must've come home, he thought to himself as he again looked up at the bedroom window.

His presence obviously not welcome, he chose to pursue a less direct approach at gaining entry.

There was hardly ever a time when Mrs. McDaniel was sober. He also knew how much the woman loved the feeling of the cool, outside air blowing in through the windows. In her typically disoriented state, it was very possible that she could've forgotten to lock one such window. That was his ticket in.

Peter leapt from the front steps and began checking each of the ground floor windows to either side of the front door. Since it was the middle of the day, most of the neighbors were probably still at work, so he felt fairly confident that his intruding actions would go unnoticed but just to be safe he performed his task with the utmost caution. Instead of dashing from one window to the next, frantically tugging on each pane of glass to see which one would burst open first, he very calmly walked along the front of the house, quickly applying only the necessary pressure to determine if the chosen casement offered any room for play. The third did just that.

The living room, he thought to himself as he pictured the floor plan. It was risky. By late morning the living room was usually the pass out location of choice for Mrs. McDaniel. Many a weekends Peter and Geoffrey had found the sleeping woman passed out on the couch in front of the television, occasionally with her wine glass still, tightly clenched between her fingertips, though most of the time it lie either broken or toppled on the floor, its contents, if any, pooled in a colorful puddle on the laminate surface.

Peter pressed his face to the glass, attempting to get a glimpse of the room's interior but like Geoffrey's opaque blinds, the curtains had no trouble preventing unwanted eyes from violating the private space. He would have to risk it.

Peter gently pressed his palms to the glass and slowly lifted the window just enough to get his fingers under the pane before cautiously raising it the rest of the way. The gentle, westerly breeze rushed in, slightly rustling the curtains. Peter paused for a moment. He hoped that Geoffrey's mom, if in the room, was passed out as anticipated. If not, her head might pop through the closed curtains at any moment, curious as to what had caused the window dressing's sudden animation.

Nearly a minute passed and no head appeared. Feeling that it was safe and eager to depart from the front lawn before someone did take notice of his trespassing, Peter hesitantly parted the curtains just enough to peek inside.

His assumption had been correct. Mrs. McDaniel lay across the couch as expected but surprisingly her glass had not befallen the same, shattered fate as its brethren. This time the cheap stemware stood perfectly upright on the coffee table between her and the television. Suddenly, the fear that Mrs. McDaniel might awaken as he clung to the window sill, half in and half out, passed through his mind. If she'd been awake enough to carefully place the glass on the table this time, then maybe the depth of her slumber wasn't as deep as he'd hoped. It was even possible that she'd just closed her eyes and hadn't yet been fully welcomed into the land of dreams. His concern was quickly put to rest however as Mrs. McDaniel let out a steady chain of wall rattling snores.

Peter hoisted himself through the opening, pushing his head and upper torso through first, before bringing his legs in one at a time after. Apart from Mrs. McDaniel's rhythmic dream state, the house was silent. The television was off and the gaudy time piece on the wall had fifteen more minutes before its annoying coo-coo would be called upon to usher in the new hour.

Careful not to push his luck, Peter left the window open behind him. It had been kind to him the first time around, not making even the slightest squeak or creak as it slid freely in its track but fearing its benevolence temporary, he didn't see fit to tempt fate a second time. Besides, if Mrs. McDaniel did awaken to find an open window, her first though would most likely be that she herself had opened it, having just forgotten to close it before succumbing to her daily blackout.

A faint voice and the soft thud of footsteps in the room overhead took Peter's mind off of the window and the sleeping woman.

Geoffrey.

Now he could find out what was really going on. He headed for the stairs.

*****

"How is that even possible?" Geoffrey questioned aloud as he paced back and forth before the open book.

"Trust me my boy. It is quite possible," the phantom voice encouraged its new author's curiosity.

"Anything? You're telling me that I can have or do anything I want?"

"Anything," the voice answered. "Just as long as you keep this our little secret."

"But what about--" A knock at his bedroom door ended the conversation.

"Geoff, I know you're in there," Peter's voice called from the upstairs hall.

"Peter?"

"Yes, its--" Peter paused as the door swung open. "Yes, it's me."

"What are you doing here?" Geoffrey questioned nervously.

"I'm breaking and entering. I've come for the televisions and jewelry. What do you think I'm doing here?" he questioned as he pushed his way into the room. "Who were you talking to?"

"No one," Geoffrey lied, poorly.

197

"I heard you talking to someone."

Geoffrey quickly glanced toward the book before returning his gaze to his inquisitive friend.

"What is that?" Peter asked as he took a step toward the dresser, never lifting his eyes from the source of his question.

Geoffrey quickly jumped in his way. "No, I can't let you look at it."

"What, does it have some dirty pictures in it or something," he joked, all the while looking for his chance to slip around his impeding friend.

"No. It's just that, no one else can look at it. I promised."

Peter halted his attempted advance. "Promised who?"

Geoffrey stumbled over the answer in his mind.

"What's going on with you lately? First, I find you deep in conversation with your backpack and then you're trying to kill Steven with a vicious right hook and what about that little incident back in class?"

"What do you mean?"

"You know, the whole kung-fu, ninja grip you laid on me."

"The what?"

"You know, the whole trying to break my fingers thing...me yelling ouch."

Geoffrey just stared blankly, struggling to recall the supposed event.

"Don't tell me you don't remember. It was all of...," glancing at his watch, "...twenty minutes ago. You nearly broke my darn fingers."

"I did not," Geoffrey responded with a dismissive wave, positive now that Peter was making the whole thing up. He would never dream of hurting Peter and if he had, he surely would have remembered it.

"You honestly don't remember? Then what about Steven?"

"I know. I shouldn't have hit him."

"Hit him? I'm not talking about that."

"Then what are you talking about? Peter I don't know what you're trying--"

"You don't know?" Peter interrupted in shock. "Steven Bishop is dead."

"What?"

"They found him in the bathroom. They said it looked as though he'd been eaten or something."

"Eaten? By what?"

"Not by what, by whom," Peter continued. "Shortly after making your mad dash from class, Dexter Brice stumbled out of the men's bathroom, covered in blood and spitting up what I can only assume was...Steven." He shuddered at the recalled image of the cannibalistic teen. Maybe one of those grief counselors was in order after all or a well-trained psychiatrist.

"Didn't you hear the scream? Isn't that why you let me go, to find out what was going on?"

"What scream?"

Now Peter was worried. "If you weren't in the hall with everyone else, then where did you go?"

"I...I don't know. All I remember was you saying something about me writing and the next thing I knew, I was here with you pounding on my door."

"Geoff, that was twenty minutes. You're telling me that, for twenty minutes, you can't remember one thing you did?

Geoffrey now shared Peter's concern.

"You don't remember how you got home?" Peter attempted to probe Geoffrey's memory for the missing time.

Geoffrey shook his head no.

"And you still don't remember writing in that book?" Peter motioned toward the open book on the dresser.

"I found that in the library. Thought it would be a good read so I took it home." Geoffrey spoke the words as if reciting them from memory.

"You hate old books. Nothing from over two decades ago you once told me, remember? That thing must be going on what, eighty, ninety, a hundred years old. And you expect me to believe that you just stumbled upon that ancient thing in the library and, for the heck of it, decided to give it a read?"

Geoffrey had no scripted dialogue for this rebuttal.

"If you were so interested in reading it, then why did you spend nearly fifteen minutes writing all over it?" Peter posed another stumping question.

"I already told you, I don't remember writing anything in it."

"Yeah I know, you don't remember but you did. I watched you and the funny thing is, no matter how hard I tried to read what it was that you were writing, I couldn't. It was as if the book itself was stopping me."

"Now *you're* talking crazy."

"OK, so you're saying that you haven't written anything in it...ever?"

"I told you, no!"

"I'll prove it then," Peter stated assertively as he pushed his friend aside and swiped the book from the dresser, underestimating its weight and nearly dropping it to the floor.

Nestling the behemoth novel in the crook of his arm, he took his first close look at the mysterious pages. Blank. The crisp white coloring of the paper, which had earlier prevented his intruding gaze, was gone. The book now looked as old as its style suggested, with dry, yellowing pages and a worn binding that had seen better days. He turned the page. Again, nothing but blank, dated paper. He thumbed through more of the book. Blank. Page after page the book overflowed with nothingness. Not one word. Not even a scribble or a picture to fill the void. But most puzzling of all was the lack of Geoffrey's frantic writing. He *had* seen Geoffrey writing in the book. He'd seen the ink left behind by the wandering pen before being discouraged by the strange light. But now there was no sign of his friend's strange burst of creativity.

"Satisfied?" Geoffrey asked in an *I told you so* tone.

Peter ignored the condescending question and again thumbed through the book, only this time he was more interested in the possibility of missing pages than missing words. He must have torn the page out, he thought to himself as he quickly scanned the book. Though in rough shape, the binding was in tack and so were all of its pages.

"See?" Geoffrey lifted his nose at Peter.

"No. I saw you writing in it. I saw the words on the page before the glare got too bright."

"Glare? What are you talking about? Peter, I know that you think there's reason to be concerned over my mental well-being but have you even stopped to consider that maybe it's you who needs the help?"

Peter hadn't considered that possibility yet. He was confident in what he'd seen...wasn't he? Maybe he'd been seeing things. Maybe the recently added pressures of high school had gotten to him. Maybe Geoffrey was perfectly fine after all.

"Maybe you should go home and lie down for a while. You know, get some rest," Geoffrey encouraged his friend's departure as he inched closer.

"No," Peter announced firmly. "I know what I saw. Something's wrong with you. You haven't been acting yourself and it all started when you began carrying this...thing around," he gestured with the book. "Maybe if I take it away, you'll go back to normal; back to the friend I thought I knew. I'm taking it with me," Peter asserted as he took a step toward the door. It would be his only step though as a blunt pain, to the back of his right knee, sent him and the book crashing to the floor.

Geoffrey stomped his leg crippling foot down upon the closed book as Peter stared up at him in complete shock. "Go home I said," he spoke down to Peter in the same forceful tone that he'd used with Steven just before testing his right hook.

Peter stared into his friend's typically warm eyes but staring back at him was nothing but darkness.

His religion had warned him about the many tools of Satan, possession being one of them and though he'd never placed all that much faith in the made for TV condition, he was quickly reconsidering.

Sensing ensuing danger if he continued to stand his ground, Peter slowly got to his feet, leaving the book on the floor beneath Geoffrey's foot.

Geoffrey watched as Peter nervously backed himself against the wall and, feeling his way with his hands behind him, located the knob and excused himself from the room, closing the door behind him.

The anger in Geoffrey's face melted as he looked around the room confused. "Peter?"

"We have to get rid of him," the voice again filled the room.

"What?" Geoffrey questioned confused by the alarming statement as he removed his foot from the book.

"He is too close to the truth and could spoil everything. He must be dealt with," the voice continued.

"He's my friend. I don't know what you want me to do."

"Write it my boy. Scribe the gruesome details of his death."

"What are you talking about? What do you mean write it?"

"Don't you remember? Don't you remember the fun we had last night lynching that miserable nuisance of a mutt? Don't you remember the words you used to describe it? As each eternal second ticked by, the collar cut deeper and deeper into Prince's throat?" William recited a passage from the tale of execution. "Don't you remember the eyes...those big, brown, puppy dog eyes turned blood red as each delicate vessel succumbed to the mounting pressure."

Geoffrey didn't know what the voice was talking about. He didn't do anything to Prince. As much as he feared dogs, he could never imagine hurting one.

"Oh, how little old Prince loved his family," the voice went on. "How he loved those kids, Sarah and Michael. Oh how they used to wrestle in the back yard with their beloved pet but the four legged fuck just wouldn't shut up. Would he? He just wouldn't shut up, so you shut him up. Didn't you?"

A vague memory began to surface. Maybe he had written something but what? He struggled to remember.

"And what about Steven?" the voice continued. "Oh we had some real fun with him. Didn't we?"

"No," Geoffrey responded. "I had nothing to do with Steven. I wasn't even there when Dexter killed him."

"Dexter?" the voice laughed. "Dexter was just a pawn, a diversion from the true homicidal beast."

Geoffrey shook at what the book implied.

"That's right my boy. As much as you want to deny it now, you loved it. You loved every gruesome moment of it."

"No, that wasn't me. That was you. You killed Steven. You hung Prince."

"No, I only gave you the means. You created the tale."

The book flopped open, Its pages rapidly turning to the evidence which Peter had so desperately sought. Previously blank, they were now covered with ink. Lines of text wandered the pages showing no regard for the left to right rules of western literature.

Geoffrey cautiously knelt beside the open book. It was his handwriting.

Becky ferociously tugged at the loose strip of flesh dangling from Steven's partially exposed cheekbone as her victim gasped for his last dying breath.

"Oh my God," he spoke aloud as his eyes wandered to

the bottom of the page. At the end of the disgusting story was his name. Not just his name...his signature.

"God? No. But with my help, you could be."

"Fuck you!" Geoffrey shouted at the book.

"Ooh, how forceful for a twerp who couldn't even stand up for himself until I showed up."

"I can stand up for myself. I'm not afraid of you," Geoffrey lied to the voice as well as himself. "Besides, without me to write your sick stories you can't do a thing."

"Now, now, when did I give you that impression? My boy, I only said that I had provided you the means. I never said anything about being incapable of creating the tales on my own."

The page containing Steven's gruesome demise gently turned, exposing a new, fresh set of pages. Slowly a letter took form at the top of the fresh sheet, its ghost writer remaining hidden by the shrouds of invisibility.

Geoffrey leaned closer to the book as the first word appeared, followed by a second and then a third, each successive word materializing faster than the one before it.

The door locked with a loud click.

A sudden click jerked Geoffrey's attention to the bedroom door. It was locked.

As did the windows.

The windows locked as well and Geoffrey could feel the sweat already gathering across his brow. His analytical mind struggled with the impossible reality of the situation, while deep down, the dire truth behind his predicament was all too clear. There was no way out of this room, the book had seen to it. All he could do was watch as his impending fate materialized on the page before him.

The bed shuddered and thumped with the creation of the new life beneath it.

Geoffrey turned to the bed but saw nothing. Using his hands to support himself, he lowered his head to the floor, examining the underside of the mattress covered cross beams. Nothing.

As his gaze fell back upon each forming word, a single bead of sweat rolled down his brow.

Geoffrey wiped his forehead.

That was the scent; the scent craved by the beast; the scent that justified its ravenous hunger. The more Geoffrey read the more sweat his glands produced and the more impatient the thing beneath the bed grew. It wanted that scent. It needed it.

Geoffrey again turned to the bed and again, finding nothing, immediately returned to the book.

Unable to wait any longer, the creature thrust its dagger tipped tentacle, out from beneath the bed, to within mere inches of its meal's back.

He was terrified. He could sense something behind him. No matter how much Geoffrey's mind attempted to convince him of the impossibility of the situation, reality continued to defy logic.

Before he even realized it, his body began to turn, his mind eager to face its thought to be imaginary stalker and prove conclusively that its claims of an impossible reality were in fact that, impossible, but unfortunately, they were not. Reality had taken a break or at least the reality he'd grown to know. In that room, at that very moment, reality had taken on a whole new meaning. It was no longer just a concept of space and time. It was a living, breathing thing.

Geoffrey would've run if he'd though that it would have done him any good but he knew better. The book was in control now. Unless the words, Geoffrey runs for his life, appeared on the pages behind him, there was nothing he could do.

The scales of the long, snake like appendage glistened under the light of the ceiling fan over head as its reptilian form slowly undulated from side to side. Protruding from the end of the tentacle was a single, razor sharp claw, much like the ones made famous by the raptors of Jurassic Park, its pointed tip bobbing and weaving mere inches from Geoffrey's face before lifting high into the air.

Geoffrey turned back to the book in hopes of seeing those life sparing words.

Poised to strike, the beast dropped is lethal dagger down upon the boy.

Geoffrey felt a sudden pressure on the top of his head but surprisingly felt no pain. Probing around his now wet hair, his fingertips glided across the leathery tentacle, its claw buried deep within his head. Then, the pressure shifted as if the claw was searching for something specific within his brain.

Geoffrey glanced down at the floor, surprised to see a book before him. Straining, he attempted to make out what was written on its pages. Though faintly aware of his once taken for granted ability to read, what had been elegantly scribed on the page no longer made sense and with yet another violent change in pressure, what had once been known as words, instantly became nothing more than a collection of wavy lines.

As Geoffrey remained intrigued by the presence of the ink drawn squiggles, a new series of elegant letters slowly took form in the lower, right hand corner of the page.

William Grave

Geoffrey smiled at the new addition to the page. He liked how the lines traveled up and then down and then back up again with each looping letter and with that final thought, the world went dark.

*****

As Peter re-climbed each step with renewed determination to help his troubled friend, the faint click of a lock emanated from the hall above.

How'd he know I was coming back?, he wondered. He'd attempted to remain as silent as possible while retracing his retreating foot steps back toward the bedroom. That's fine. If he wants to lock me out I'll just kick the door in, he attempted to psych himself up for the difficult task ahead.

Testing his luck he reached for the knob. Locked as expected but before he could muster the will, not to mention the strength needed to kick in the impeding barrier, a small thump and clatter came from within the forbidden room. Peter pressed his ear to the door.

Silence. No movement. No talking. Just silence.

He pressed closer, knowing that by assuming such a position he was completely reliant on the wooden door to maintain his balance. If Geoffrey were to suddenly open the supporting barrier, he would most likely fall face first into the room from which he had only minutes ago been banished.

Accepting the risk, he continued to monitor the room's activities or lack thereof, until a soft crunch caught his ear, almost like that of a potato chip succumbing to the first destructive bite of a hungry set of jaws.

What? Did he work up such an appetite being a jerk that now it was time for a snack? Peter thought to himself. His determination to decipher the strange noise quickly faded though as a new noise took its place.

Peter jumped back, startled by the unlocking of the load bearing door. He half expected it to fly open and a rouge fist to come barreling toward his face but the door remained shut.

Maybe it's a trap, Peter thought to himself. Maybe Geoffrey wanted him to open the door so that he could inflict whatever new form of pain he'd devised since Peter's brief departure. No, he dismissed that line of thinking. Geoffrey was his friend and though he was not himself at the moment, he had not turned evil as Peter had previously suspected. He was just in need of help and, "When someone is in need, he deserves the caring heart of a close friend to guide him through his troubled times," he recalled the words from one of Father Lester Childs' Sunday masses.

Downstairs he'd come to the conclusion that, his being there for this difficult moment was God's will. Geoffrey was going through a troubling time for whatever reason and God had chosen him to help him through it.

Peter reached for the knob and pushed the door open. Geoffrey was gone. Cautiously, he entered the room, quickly scanning his surroundings. The closet door stood wide open, displaying no sign of his friend and with a twin size bed that possessed no skirting, it would have been nearly impossible for Geoffrey to completely conceal himself beneath its limited mass.

"Geoffrey?" Peter reluctantly called out but got no response.

Carefully he made his way to each window.

Locked.

"Geoffrey, if you're in here come out," his voice quivered. Again, he received no response.

Out of the corner of his eye he suddenly sensed movement at the bedroom door. Quickly he moved to the doorway, expecting to find his friend retreating into a nearby room or rounding the corner and heading down the stairs but the hall remained as still as he'd left it.

There was no sign of Geoffrey. The book however had somehow managed to find its way from the deserted bedroom, where Peter had last seen it, out onto the hallway floor, standing erect as if waiting to be noticed.

"That wasn't there before," Peter spoke softly as he again scanned the hall for movement and sound.

If Geoffrey was upstairs, he'd concealed himself well. Peter again turned for another look at the room to his back, afraid he might find Geoffrey standing behind him, ready to unload with a bat to the back of the head. The room remained still.

He must've slipped out. Probably ran downstairs or something, he attempted to comfort himself. Maybe even out of the house all together.

Eyes peeled the entire way, Peter slowly ventured out into the hall and lifted the abandoned book from the floor.

"Tales from "The Grave"", he read the title aloud while running his finger over the fire engraved lettering.

A creak resounded from a nearby room and before Peter even had a chance to process the direction from which the noise had come, he was halfway down the stairs and out the front door with the book in hand.

TWENTY-NINE

Returning home from what was already proving to be one of the worst days in recent memory, James was looking forward to plopping down on the couch and shutting down to the world around him as he slept away the remainder of the afternoon.

Swinging his truck into the driveway he was pleased to find the garage door open and his wife's car gone. Though he'd hoped for a chance to relax, he'd figured that that dream, like so many others lately, would be dashed by the incessantly nagging bitch he would soon no longer have the agony of calling his wife.

Placing the truck in park, James hopped from the cab, leaving the trash from his lunch scattered across the passenger seat and floor. He didn't care if the truck soon smelled like a fast food restaurant or if the wax coated, paper cup slowly deteriorated under the influence of its liquid contents. In a few months, when he could no longer afford to make the payments anymore, it would be the bank's problem to remove the pungent aroma and sticky residue. All he cared about at that moment was the promise of peace offered by the empty house.

Unlocking the garage door entrance to the house,

James entered the laundry room, through which a second door led him into a short hallway containing the downstairs bathroom and linen closet.

"Yeah dad?" Peter called out from the living room at the front of the house.

Crap. He wouldn't be alone after all. It was three o'clock and having somehow forgotten his fifteen year tenure as a responsible parent, his dream of self-induced solitude was quickly becoming just that, a dream.

"Yeah Peter, what?"

There was a moment of silence before Peter appeared in the living room's arched entry.

"Huh?" Peter responded.

"Didn't you just call me?" James questioned.

"No, I was answering you."

"Well, I just walked in the door. I didn't call you."

"Oh," Peter responded, sure that he'd heard someone call his name.

"Where's your sister?"

"At Uncle Mike's. Remember? We're supposed to be spending the night over there tonight?"

"That is tonight, isn't it?" James vaguely recalled his conversation with Rebecca's brother in law earlier in the week. Though James hated Rebecca's sister, her husband wasn't such a bad guy. He just had poor taste in women. His kids on the other hand were monsters. He had two boys about Peter's age and a young girl about six months older than Emily. Every so often, all the kids would get together and spend the night at one or the other's house. Tonight it was Mike's turn to referee the late night wrestling match.

James never had understood the term "sleep over", since most of the night, sleep was the farthest thing from occurring...for anyone in the house.

"When's your mother getting back?"

"I don't know. She left a note in the kitchen telling you to bring me to Uncle Mike's when you got home."

Just what James had figured. Rest would have to wait but, at least it wouldn't have to be cancelled all together. With the kids gone for the night and Rebecca likely out on the town for the evening, he'd have the house all to himself. Just a fifteen minute drive across town and he'd be free to erase the unwanted memories of the less than pleasurable day by whatever means necessary.

"Dad I need to show you this book," Peter spoke excitedly.

"Can you show me in the truck?" James responded with little interest.

"Sure, I guess," Peter answered, dejected by his father's uncharacteristically dismissive attitude.

"Then go put your stuff in the truck and I'll be out in a minute. And make sure you put the trash out while you're waiting."

Peter just stared, confused by his father's peculiar demeanor but before having a chance to question the cause behind the old man's sullen mood, James turned his back and disappeared into the bathroom.

*****

The truck was filled with the aroma of cheeseburgers and French fries. Peter had sensed that something was wrong. Usually his father showed nothing but enthusiasm for anything his kids wanted to show him but this time, when Peter had brought up the strange book, his father had only brushed the topic aside and retreated to the bathroom to delve into the latest issue of Popular Mechanics.

Even stranger was the presence of the fast food wrappers scattered about the truck's interior. His father never ate fast food but judging by the mess, it seemed that he'd recently abandoned his healthy habit and chosen to devour what appeared to be at least three cheeseburgers, a large fry and half of a large Coke.

This strange behavior, and his father's apparent bad mood, had led to a completely silent trip thus far but Peter couldn't take it anymore. He had to tell his father about the book and all the strange things Geoffrey had been doing lately. He had to know where the book had come from and whether his crazy idea, that it was in some way linked to Geoffrey's behavior, was in fact that...crazy.

"Dad, remember that book I mentioned?" Peter tested his father's mood before delving into the strange events of the past two days.

"Oh yeah, that's right. You wanted to tell me about some book or something."

"Yeah I--"

"Listen, back there at the house. I didn't mean to blow you off like that. I've just had a tough day," James tried to explain himself to his son.

"That's all right. I didn't mean to bother you."

"No, you didn't bother me. You know you could never bother me," James said with a grin as he lightly punched his son's shoulder. "You go ahead and tell me about this book of yours."

"Well," Peter started, retrieving the book from his bag and placing it on his lap.

"Whoa, that's a big book."

"Yeah, Geoffrey found it yesterday in the school library."

"Then how'd you get it?"

He couldn't tell his father that he'd stolen it. All his life Peter had heard his father preach about integrity and the evils of crimes against society; theft being one of them.

"He let me borrow it," Peter lied, making a mental note to confess the sin to Father Lester this Sunday. "Anyway, I think this book has some sort of curse or something on it."

"A curse huh?" James played along with his son's imagination.

"No, dad. I'm being serious. Ever since Geoffrey

found this thing he's been acting really strange."

"Strange how?"

"Well, yesterday I found him in the cafeteria talking to his backpack. I'm pretty sure this book was in it at the time."

"While talking to a bag is rather odd, there's no crime in it."

"What about assault then? Assault's a crime, right?"

"Who assaulted whom?"

"Geoffrey. He went and decked a kid in gym class yesterday. Remember, I told you last night at dinner?"

"From what I recall of the conversation, it sounded like the other kid was asking for it," James condoned Geoffrey's behavior, much to his son's dismay.

"But I thought you said fighting was bad...a sin," Peter questioned confused.

"I did say that but do you know what an even greater sin is?"

Peter devoted all attention to the lesson he was about to receive.

"Not fighting."

"Huh?"

"Sure, hurting someone else is bad but it's even worse if you don't stand up for yourself and let them hurt you. I'm guessing that Geoffrey was just tired of being pushed around and finally decided to stand up for himself."

Peter was confused by his father's sudden reversal on the whole hitting thing. "But you don't understand. This kid is huge. He's on the football team. There is no way that Geoffrey would even dream of taking him on."

"But he did."

"No, he didn't."

"He didn't?"

Now James was confused.

"No, I think it was the book."

"So you're saying that a book...that book...decked a kid in gym class."

"No, not the book itself. The..." He wasn't sure how to explain what he was talking about.

"Do you feel all right?" James jokingly questioned with a smile.

"Yes, I'm fine," Peter answered in a serious tone, erasing the smile from his father's face. "Listen. I think the book has some sort of control over Geoffrey, like it hypnotized him or something. During SSR he--"

"SSR?"

"Silent Sustained Reading but that doesn't matter. During the entire class, Geoffrey was frantically writing in this book."

"And?"

"The book is blank dad."

"But you just said he was writing in it.

"Yeah, he was but now it's blank."

"So maybe he didn't write in it."

"Dad I watched him. I've never seen anyone write that fast before. And the pages...it was as if the book was..." he decided to refrain from mentioning the glowing paper. He probably already seemed crazy enough by mentioning his far-fetched theory of possessed literature. He didn't need to nullify all credibility to his story.

"The book was what?" James asked.

"Look." Peter grabbed hold of the top cover and opened the book to a point about a third of the way in.

"Doesn't look blank to me," his father commented, sneaking a peek at the book before turning the truck onto his brother-in-law's street.

He was right. The pages weren't blank. Peter flipped through the book. Where white paper had once resided there was now line after line of elegantly written text.

"Looks like poetry," James commented looking over at his son. "When did you get into poetry?"

"No. This wasn't here earlier. I've gone through this entire book over and over again. Nothing was written. I'm sure of it."

James issued his son a concerned look.

"Honestly. I'm not crazy. It was blank."

"I'm sure it was," James agreed with his son, though wondering what might be wrong.

"Great, now you think I'm crazy."

"No, I don't think you're crazy. You wear a medium right?"

"Huh," Peter responded confused by the odd question.

"For the straight jacket. I'll send the men in white over around six, maybe seven so I can be sure that you've eaten. We're gonna fix you right up son. Everything will be all right," he joked as he pulled to the curb in front of Uncle Mike's house.

"Ha, ha. Funny dad."

James smiled.

"Seriously though. There is something strange about this book. I was hoping you could take a look at it. Maybe find out where it came from or even who might have written it...now that it has some sort of story."

"Poems, not stories. Stories only describe. Poems make you feel."

"Dad, I don't need a lesson in literature."

"Sorry."

"Can you take a look at it?"

"Sure I'll take a look but I can't promise anything."

"Thanks."

Their conversation was abruptly ended as a light rapping against the passenger side window summoned their attention. Standing on the curb, beside the truck, were Bobby and Joseph Weintrotter.

"I've gotta go," Peter turned to his father.

"I know...the pressures of childhood. So much playing to do and so little time," James teased.

"I know," Peter agreed with his own exasperated sigh.

"Have fun tonight and behave yourself."

Peter opened the door and, grabbing his bag, jump from the vehicle to join his cousins.

"Hey Peter," James called out through the open passenger side window.

"Yeah dad."

"Don't read any evil books tonight."

"Funny. Just take a look at it for me."

"Don't worry, I will," James agreed and with that pulled away from the curb.

THIRTY

Having allowed nearly half an hour to pass before lifting himself from a memory induced pit of despair, brought on by the glass door, Parker now found himself standing where grass met dirt and the openness of the side yard met the dense woods to the North. Shadows danced across a narrow path, deterred only by the occasional glimmer of the sun's rays as they took turns poking holes in the densely woven canopy above.

"Pathetic," he commented on his own irrational fears.

For three months he'd been attempting the short journey to his wife's gravesite and for three months he'd done nothing but fail.

The burial service had been the last time that he'd been able to work up the courage to lay eyes on the painful stone. It was courage he had attributed to nothing more than the continued state of shock brought on by the news of Amanda's untimely death. Since that time, shock had been replaced by depression and depression by guilt.

A good husband would want to visit his wife. A good husband would still have countless memories and thoughts to share, even if the conversations could never be more than one sided. At least that was how he thought things should be. Deep down though, he didn't want to visit that macabre patch of land, for he knew that the strength required to move him from his current position, to the clearing at the other end of the path, would ultimately fail him, as it had so many times before. Even if he did manage to complete the journey, he feared his ability to fend off the intrusive shadows through which he must pass. They would surely poke and prod at his mind, toying with his emotions and threatening to leave a fear born blankness in his eyes, which Amanda would surely find offensive.

For the first month after her death, he'd been able to go no further than Veracini Two's north steps. By month two his nerves had taken him as far as the spot at which he now stood, just thirty-five feet from those familiar stairs.

Parker peered down the first fifty feet of the winding path, wondering if this time he'd even make it to that first, sharp bend. A week ago, with Jack Daniels by his side, he'd managed a surprisingly swift journey, almost a hundred feet past that point, before his temporary wall of strength had crumbled, allowing a wave of fear to wash them both back toward the house and into an alcohol induced vacation from reality.

Obviously lacking the strength Parker so desperately needed, Jack remained at home this time. Today the captain stood by Parker's side with a full belly of courage and a fierce grin of confidence.

With a quick swig, the two entered the shadows between life and death.

*****

Just as Parker's passion for literature burned deep within, so did alcoholism. Some of his oldest memories involved his worthless father and his frequent, alcohol induced rages; rages that had usually placed his mother on the receiving end of a verbal onslaught of profanity and hate, which often resulted in an open handed blow to the face.

"You always slap a woman with an open hand. It is ungentlemanly-like to use a closed fist. That's reserved for everyone else," Mr. Veracini had instructed then seven year old Parker at the conclusion of one of his tirades.

Even then he understood the erroneous nature of his father's twisted lesson. He didn't believe that any act, which involved his loving mother lying in a bloody heap on the kitchen floor, had any place in the world.

By age ten his father had taught him another important lesson in the ways of being, "gentlemanly-like". While a closed fist was considered excessive and uncalled for, the use of an unopened bottle of Kentucky Redeye was apparently an acceptable substitute.

The bottle had refused to break upon contact with his mother's forehead and while a full bottle was far more devastating a weapon than one which had been previously drained, he was thankful that it had remained intact. He knew that the loss of that prized liquid would have sent his father into a realm in which rules ceased to exist and where his mother's life would have surely found its end.

Spared a visit from the hands of death, his mother had spent seven nights in Atlanta General with a severely fractured skull. His father had spent the next eight years in Ravenswood Prison, before falling victim to the likes of a man who had apparently never been schooled in the ways of "the gentlemen".

Parker had sworn to himself that he would not end up like his father; that he would never drink and would never harm a single soul. He was one for two.

By the age of fifteen he'd built up such a remarkable tolerance that, even given his lesser stature, he could and had gone up against some of the area's best tequila shooters. By eighteen he'd acquired his first DUI and had been well on his way to adding a second.

Keeping his problem hidden from the world had been

little trouble. Though free of her abusive husband, his mother had grown so accustom to the presence of alcohol in the house that her son's possession of the liquid demon had done little to faze her. And since Parker's grades were at an all-time high, she'd seen no reason to interfere.

Not only had his grades miraculously improved during his influenced years, he'd also become a highly popular figure throughout the school, not to mention a fairly good athlete and a valued asset to the school paper. And though thrilled with his social advancements, these continued successes had only managed to compound the growing problem. With each new achievement came an even deeper desire for the substance that he'd deemed as his source of strength...his spinach.

By freshman year of college though, everything had changed. The ready availability of alcohol had finally brought Parker's hidden issue to light as his once stable life and elaborate façade began crumbling down around him.

Though unaware at the time, Amanda had been the angel sent down to rescue him from his self-destructive path. Sharing the same major, they'd met as project partners in business ethics class, a title both had agreed reeked of contradiction. Also in common were their past, fatherly troubles. His had shown him no love, while hers had shared too much.

These common troubles had acted as an instant bond, making each a source of comfort for the other when life and school overwhelmed. And even though this instant connection had started them out on a track of mere friendship, over time, they'd found themselves spending increasingly more time by one another's sides.

Action and comedy films turned into romances and dramas. Informal dinners gradually became formal. And evenings spent in the rec. room, shooting pool and watching television, became evenings spent in one another's dorms, innocently embraced in a peaceful slumber.

The innocence restored to Amanda, through years of childhood therapy, had been a long touted trophy of hers; a trophy that had attracted many suitors, all asserting the same false promises and fictitious claims of love. However, none had laid claim to the prize. That long kept innocence had made September sixth of their sophomore year a landmark in both of their lives. It had been a night of romance, a night of passion. More importantly, it had been the night on which Amanda had finally been able to place her troubled past behind her.

For Parker, it had been a wakeup call. He'd allowed someone into the deepest recesses of his heart. His father had blown full steam past the point of no return and it had shown on his mother's face. Amanda didn't deserve to be treated as his mother had been for so many years and he didn't want to be just another man, haunting her dreams at night. So, with Amanda's support, Parker had chosen to leave school for the remainder of the semester and began the program that would eventually lead him to a life of sobriety and a level of happiness he had never before known to exist.

*****

Unfortunately, life has a way of changing and instead of his angelic wife by his side, Parker now walked hand in hand with a fuzzy bearded pirate, slowly navigating a narrow plank toward a not too distant grave.

Parker froze in his tracks. The Captain urged him on but his feet remained cemented to the patch of ground where dirt again met grass. The unobstructed sun poured down on him from its descending position to the West.

At the center of the clearing, overlooking Silver Lake, a band of red rose bushes surrounded a ring of white just fifteen feet away. An unusually wet season had ensured the flowers continued beauty, though Parker was still surprised to see their impeccable condition, having provided them no attention since their planting.

Amanda's headstone stood tall at the center of the colorful rings, its large, polished, granite body glimmering under the amber rays of the setting sun.

Desperately seeking the additional strength needed to continue on, Parker turned to the captain, only to catch a glimpse of the once eager pirate now fleeing in terror.

Instantly, the mind intruding shadows he'd earlier feared began their invasive probing, allowing anxiety and grief to wash over him as he watched the swaying flowers beckoning him nearer.

Sensing Amanda's disappointment, he remained frozen near the edge of the clearing as the flower manipulating breeze gradually grew to a swirling wind, tossing the first of the season's fallen vegetation high into the air.

Unbothered by the suddenly active forest, Parker continued to focus on the self-forbidden stone. He wanted to approach it, or at least he thought he did, but each time he attempted to lift his foot from its earth bound position, some unseen force passively denied his progress.

Taking another swig from the bottle, in hopes that his absconded friend might return, Parker attempted yet another advance. However, instead of moving closer to the blooming rings of loss, he wound up take two retreating steps back toward the unnervingly distance house.

The swirling foliage gradually began to thicken as increasingly more of the forest's ground cover violently leapt into the air, forming a moving wall of color which encompassed the outer perimeter of the small clearing. The crystal blue lake to the West, quickly faded from view, as did Parker's escape route to his rear.

Overwhelmed by emotion, Parker dropped to his knees, still clutching the nearly empty bottle as the vortex of energetic foliage instantly ceased, raining its leafy contents down around him.

With his free hand over his face, Parker wept.

THIRTY-ONE

Though not a big drinker as of late, alcohol wasn't exactly a stranger to James' system. He'd done his fair share of tequila shots in college and awoken many a morning with only hazy memories of the prior evening's wild antics. It had been years since he'd intoxicated his system to excess but given the day that he was having, not to mention the many preceding months, the idea of a spirit induced blackout seemed deeply appealing.

Unlocking the bottom right cabinet of his Mahogany desk, James withdrew a new bottle of Scotch and a small tumbler. At times, he'd used the loosening effects of his favorite drink to aid in the creation of his many stories. Normally a bottle, once opened, would last for at least a month, maybe even two if nursed carefully along but seeing as writer's block hadn't paid its once frequent visits in some time, the unopened bottle had remained in his desk for what he figured had been at least a six month stretch. That was about to end though. He wasn't about to let this bottle go unattended any longer. By morning he planned to have the entire thing in either his gut or the toilet.

He had to let go. His tight control over every aspect of

his life had apparently been nothing but a waste of time. He couldn't control the world around him. He wasn't even sure he wanted to control himself anymore. Everything he once cherished was falling apart and all he wanted was a night of no cares. No publishers. No wife or family. No responsibility. Just himself and his new, bottled best friend.

Leaning back in his chair, James downed the first glass with such ease that even the most hard core frat brother would've been proud.

"One down, a whole night to go," he spoke aloud to the bottle as he held it in the air before him.

On the desk sat the book which had been at the center of Peter's earlier rant.

"Cursed book," James chuckled as he refilled his glass.

He'd had no intention of examining the book any further than its front cover but the fact that it had been found in the school library puzzled him. A book this size and of this dated construction, typically had no place in a modern, school library. It looked as though it was better suited for a museum.

He rubbed his finger over the book's title, confirming his initial guess that the letters, forming the morbid heading, had been somehow burned into the leather cover. The book's creator had shown great care in carefully forming each successive letter but had failed to perfectly align each one with the next, giving the blackened words a shaky appearance across the top half of the book. Another detail that caught his attention was the large, steel buttons fastening the leather "X" to the cover. This was not typical construction for a book of modern time. No company would spend the money to mass produce a novel of this quality without surely expecting to lose their ass in doing so. Just looking at the thing, James's speculated a price tag far exceeding a hundred dollars, if sold new in the modern marketplace.

Finished with his initial examination, James once again

lifted the amber liquid to his lips, though this time only emptying half of its contents before returning to the fascinating piece of literary history before him.

Opening the front cover, he wasn't surprised to find the book's initial few pages blank. This book had apparently been someone's own private creation. There would be no copyright date or publisher's name anywhere. What was odd though, was that, as he continued to flip through the pages, searching for the poetry he'd earlier seen, he continued to find only blank paper. No poems, no story, not even a stray line or dot to indicate that anyone had ever even thought of using the book to house their innermost thoughts or ideas.

Peter had claimed that the book was blank and had seemed genuinely shocked upon discovering its poetic contents. Now James was equally as shocked by its lack thereof.

Halting what had turned into frantic page flipping, James downed the remainder of the glass and, filling it once more, emptied that as well.

Though the idea that a book could be cursed was ridiculous, it did seem to possess a few peculiarities. Maybe the ink is only visible in certain types of light, James thought to himself before deeming that idea silly, considering the books age. In modern times, with companies such as Crayola hard at work creating what some would consider magic inks, anything was possible. But obviously this book had not been created in a lab by some crazy scientist, attempting to perfect his formula for disappearing, reappearing ink. It had been created long ago, in a time when chemical concoctions were more likely to be passed off as miracle elixirs, than as cool toys for juvenile entertainment.

Based on the book's overall appearance, James could only conclude that someone had cared very deeply for it at some point, which made it's sudden lack of contents only that much more confusing.

"James," a soft voice whispered.

James looked up from the book, expecting to see someone standing in the doorway but the door remained closed. That's odd, he thought to himself as he reached for the bottle and began pouring himself another drink.

"James Madison," the voice spoke again.

"Who's there?"

No answer.

"Probably just that bitch, home from her sexual escapades," James spoke aloud, expecting Rebecca to become offended and burst into the room, revealing herself as the name calling prankster. But the door remained shut.

James downed what had now become a glass of liquid courage and, unlocking the top drawer of his desk, removed the loaded revolver he kept tucked away in case of an emergency. Popping open the revolving chambers, he confirmed six ready shots before closing the gun again and slowly making his way toward the door, listening for any sign of the person hiding just beyond the office walls.

He wanted them to make a noise, just a minute shift that tell could confirm their exact location before he chanced bursting through the door, turning the wrong direction and therefore inadvertently setting himself up for a knife or a bullet to the back.

Gun in hand, careful not to make a sound, James took hold of the shiny brass knob and on the silent count of three yanked the door open and jumped out into the hall.

Shit, he thought as he looked toward the stairway. There was no one there.

Fearing his back already at the center of the intruder's crosshairs, he quickly spun toward the bathroom at the other end of the hall.

Again, nothing.

Returning his aim toward its initial target, James slowly crept toward the stairway leading to the foyer below. A floor board creaked beneath his feet, bringing him to a halt as he feared his position unmasked by the noisy, wood floor.

"James," the voice spoke again, this time to his back.

James swung around again and would have sent a barrage of bullets straight through the bathroom door if it hadn't been for the gun's safety being engaged. Taking a deep breath he disengaged the safety and slowly returned to the portion of hallway just outside his office door.

There's no way someone could've been so quiet as to slip by him and into the room without him noticing, James thought to himself.

As he approached the open doorway he contemplated just rounding the corner and opening fire but dismissed that line of thinking when he considered how it would look when the police showed up to investigate a Swiss cheese desk and computer screen suspected of breaking and entering. Instead, he slowly peeked around the doorframe and examined the room in which, only a minute ago, he'd been comfortably seated.

Just as the hallway had been, the room was empty.

"James, we need to talk."

James stared disbelievingly at the book on his desk. Though it remained motionless and open, just as he'd left it, it also appeared to be the source of the mysterious voice.

Given the impossibility of such an occurrence, he quickly scanned the gap between the desk and floor, half expecting the intruder's exposed feet to lend some credibility to the peculiar situation.

The space was clear.

Convinced that he was alone, James returned his attention to the open book and then to the already half empty bottle beside it. Had he really drank that much already? he thought to himself as he sensed the first signs of a rapidly approaching buzz.

Behind him, the door slowly swung shut as James Madison curiously advanced toward the book.

THIRTY-TWO

"I will be having the Beef au Poivre," Francesco Savaree informed the tux adorned waiter standing dutifully at his side.

"Very good sir," the waiter acknowledged before turning to Rebecca. "And for the young lady?"

"She will be having the Chicken la Madeleine," Francesco took it upon himself to order for his date.

"Excellent choice sir," the waiter made mental note of the orders before collecting the menus and leaving the two lovers to one another's company.

That was what Rebecca loved most about Francesco. He wasn't afraid to take charge of a situation. She had no idea what he'd just ordered but she had faith in his judgment and knew that, whatever it was, she was going to love it. James had never taken the initiative of ordering for her, not even during their initial courting period and after sixteen years of marriage, there was little hope that he would suddenly start now.

James Madison was a simple man with a very short resume when it came to a life of excitement and adventure. Not to mention, he was probably the most introverted person Rebecca had ever met. Over the years, his self-invoked separation from the world had grown tiresome. She wanted to go out. She wanted to experience all that the world had to offer. James, on the other hand, wanted nothing more than to spend every waking moment of his existence at his desk where he could create his own world into which only he could escape and where the rigors of reality had no place.

It wasn't like she blamed her husband for his unique personality. That's just who he was. It was who he'd always been and when they'd first met, back in their early twenties, it had been what she'd loved most about him. He'd seemed strange and a bit mysterious. He'd seemed exciting in the sense that he cared very little about what the world thought. If he disliked a part of his world, he would simply pick up a pen and change it. His power of creation was almost God like to her at first and every time he wrote something new, she'd insisted on being the first to read it. But now...now he just seemed pathetic; locking himself in his office for hours upon hours, sometimes skipping meals to create the fantasies that no one wanted to read anymore...including her.

She no longer insisted on being the first to read his work. Hell, most of the time he didn't even tell her what he was working on or that he'd even completed a new project. Often times, she discovered the release of a new book in the same manner as the rest of the nation...by catching a glimpse of it on the shelves at the local bookstore or on Kindle's latest releases list.

It wasn't that she didn't still love her husband, because somewhere, beneath all the recent anger and bitter disgust, she was sure that that initial spark, which had ignited their love so long ago, still glowed bright. Unfortunately, it was probably all that was left. The kindling, which had fed their romance for so many years, had long since burnt out and the odds of finding more fuel, to feed the dwindling flame, looked hopelessly grim.

"Darling, you look sad," Francesco remarked on the

sullen expression plaguing his companion's face.

Rebecca looked up, realizing that she'd been staring at her wine glass for quite some time.

"No, I'm fine," Rebecca lied.

"Have I told you how breathtaking you look this evening?"

"Francesco, I think we're past the sappy pickup lines," Rebecca blushed.

"Pickup lines are for boys. Men speak only truth."

It was that which Rebecca needed most; a man with confidence and not the confidence of a man so removed from society that he felt empowered to sustain his existence from within his own, internal world. She needed the confidence of a man who not only lived in the real world but who dominated it. Francesco was just that and more.

A successful business man, he'd come to America a little over ten years ago from a little town in France, whose name she could neither remember nor likely pronounce. He'd come with a dream and in a few short years, had made that dream come true. His chain of personal fitness clubs had grown dramatically, setting up shop in numerous major cities throughout the country and making national headlines by rapidly posing a substantial threat to some of his larger competitors.

Those competing chains had, in fact, on numerous occasions, offered to buy out Francesco's company but seeing that his success had already brought with it substantial wealth, he'd cared very little about adding the offered pocket change to his enormous pockets. Besides, he wasn't in the business of fitness for the cash. His beliefs were his only true driving force. Francesco believed that God had given human-beings the potential to do something great with their bodies. He believed very strongly that that gift had not been a mistake and that, when bestowed a gift of such divine origins, one should embrace and cherish it.

Francesco had nurtured that gift to its fullest potential and it showed. With a chest nearly twice the width of her shoulders and a set of biceps as big around as her head, the man was a giant, though gentle beyond belief.

Rebecca had never considered herself the shallow type, chasing after a man for his looks but she couldn't deny her body's primal urges and every time she laid eyes on her loving hulk, she couldn't help but grow moist at the thought of what that finely tuned machine could do to her.

"You're wanting sex again, no?" Francesco interpreted Rebecca's exploratory gaze.

"What? No. I was just...I am a lady and we don't think about such matters," Rebecca poorly recovered.

"I do not mind. Sex is like a fine French pastry."

Huh?

"You stare at it. You crave it. But you do not touch."

Rebecca had no idea what he was talking about but continued staring into his eyes with nothing but fascinated interest, as she became pleasantly lost within his romantic accent.

"You wait. You wait until the moment is right and when it seems you have waited until you can wait no longer, only then do you allow the soft creamy pastry past your lips."

She wasn't sure what pastry's had to do with good old fashion lust but what she did know was that, based on the sudden tingle between her legs, she'd never wanted a cannoli more that she did at that very moment.

"I'm leaving my husband," Rebecca blurted out before even realizing that she'd been contemplating the statement.

"What?" Francesco appeared puzzled by the news.

She *had* wanted to wait until later, when they were alone and nestled in one another's arms beneath the covers of his grand, four poster bed but all night the news had been burning in her mind. Apparently, her brain couldn't take the excitement any longer and had allowed her lips a chance to relieve the building pressure.

"Why?"

"Why? So we can be together, that's why." She was shocked at his reaction. She'd anticipated his shared excitement. She'd never felt before what she felt with Francesco.

"Please, rethink this decision."

"Rethink my decision? I tell you that I'm leaving my husband for you and you tell me to rethink my decision? I thought you loved me. I thought you wanted to be with me. I thought you said that we were perfect together."

"I did...for now," he spoke softly.

"For now!?" Rebecca shouted, showing no regard for the volume of her own voice as she drew curious stares from other patrons as well as the wait staff. "What do you mean for now!?"

"Please, you are making a scene," Francesco attempted to calm his enraged date. "I did not mean it like that."

"Oh, what did you mean to say, that I'm the perfect little whore to slut it up with for the time being!?"

"Rebecca, please," Francesco pleaded for her to calm down.

"Please what? Please suck your cock a few more times before you trade me in on a younger, fresher model."

Gasps from surrounding onlookers caused Francesco to partially conceal his face in his hand.

"Oh no, don't hide that pretty face of yours. Your next lay might come from one of these other slutty wives."

Rebecca scanned the room, taking in dozens of scornful scowls from fellow women and amused grins from their husbands.

"Ok, let's go outside," Francesco started to get up.

"No. You know what? I'm not going anywhere with you anymore. You stay right here and finish your crappy French delicacies. You can start with this glass of wine." She grabbed her glass of untouched white zinfandel but instead of acting in a stereo typical manner by splashing the drink across her offender's face, she opted to send not only the liquid but the glass along with it.

Francesco instantly threw up his guard, blocking the glass projectile with his right forearm but was unable to shield himself from the dampening effects of the sparkling wine.

Rebecca didn't wait to see his reaction to the assault. She didn't care how angry or not angry he got. She just wanted to leave as she pushed past the stunned doorman.

As if anticipating the woman's rapid departure, the manager must have ordered the valet service to retrieve her car as quickly as possible because, before she could even hand the kid at the podium her ticket, her convertible glided up alongside the canopied curb.

Rebecca stormed toward the car, tossing her ticket at the exiting teenager and lowering herself in behind the wheel.

Throwing her purse in passenger's seat she glanced back at the nineteen year old kid who'd retrieve the car and now stood beside his coworker at the valet podium.

"You wanna be a real man?" Rebecca teased the boy with a seductive smile.

"Excuse me ma'am?"

"Do you wanna fuck?" Rebecca dropped the seductive game for a more direct approach.

The kid just looked at his coworker and then at the manager and with a shrug, removed his red jacket and hopped into the car as the sound of squealing tires filled the night.

THIRTY-THREE

The Cadillac's engine purred as Rebecca yanked the wheel, making a skidding entrance into the quiet neighborhood. The teenager's firm grip on the dash suggested fear but the smile across his face made it clear that he was having the time of his life. A wild journey along the streets of Carson wasn't the only ride Rebecca intended on giving her new companion. Based on the boy's rough, frat boy appearance, she was sure that he had plenty of experience when it came to the bedroom. She was also well aware that no nineteen year old girl could possible know half of the tricks a woman of her age had acquired. He'd accepted her invitation for a quick fling. She intended on retaining his services all night.

Jerking the wheel again, Rebecca slid the car into the driveway with stuntman like precision, bringing the performance vehicle to a sudden halt beside James's pickup.

"Whoa," the teen released the breath that he'd probably been holding since their wild escapade had begun, back in the restaurant parking lot.

"You liked that?" Rebecca continued the seduction of her prey.

"Lady, I don't even know no guys who can drive like that."

"Well, I can assure you that I'm no guy."

The teen looked down as Rebecca took hold of his left hand and placing it on her exposed thigh, slowly guided it up her dress.

Rebecca smiled, suddenly tossing the boy's hand aside as she yanked up on the emergency brake and opened her door.

The teen followed suit, getting out beside the pickup. "Hey who's truck?"

"Oh that's my husband's," Rebecca answered nonchalantly as she pushed a button on her key, locking the doors and returning the retracted roof to its protective position.

"Your husband?" the kid questioned nervously.

"Yeah, he always did have a thing for simplicity. But don't worry about him. He's out of town on business and won't be back for days," she lied. "How 'bout a drink?" she offered as she made her way toward the front door, her young suitor following close behind.

"I'm not twenty-one."

Rebecca stopped at the door. "Listen. Some would say that what I'm about to do to you could border on illegal so I don't really think that one little drink is going to hurt."

"Ok."

Fumbling with the keys she unlocked the door and showed him in. She didn't need to liquor the boy up to get his clothes off. She was sure that would be a simple task at this point. The drink was more for her benefit. She knew James was home and though he had recently become aware of her unfaithful activities she'd never before shown the guts to actually bring one of her play toys home, especially with her own husband in the house.

She wasn't sure how he'd react. A part of her hoped that he'd become enraged; that he'd show the intruding male to the door, preferably with a broken nose or arm. It would be nice to see that he still cared, at least on some level but she didn't have her hopes up. He was probably pent up in his office and wouldn't even bother to come out, even if the noises across the hall did grow so loud as to draw his attention. He just didn't seem to care much about anything anymore. That had been evident when he'd informed her of his knowledge concerning her infidelities. He'd never confronted her. He'd never demanded that she stop. He just went on with his life as if nothing was wrong and she went on with hers knowing that everything was.

"Nice house," the kid eyed the extravagant foyer. "What does your husband do?"

"Do you really want to discuss my husband's career right now?" Rebecca responded, somewhat put off by the inappropriate question.

"Yes!" an animated voice carried down the stairs.

"Who was that?" the boy asked startled.

"What the hell is he doing now?"

"Who?"

"Ah...my brother. He's been staying with us lately. Don't worry about him though. He doesn't care what I do," she continued the lie.

"Your brother doesn't care that you bring home strange men while your husband's out of town?"

"No," Rebecca answered as she moved toward the stairs, staring up at the landing above. Forgetting the drinks, she began ascending the oak steps.

The boy followed.

"He's a big sports fan, my brother is. He's probably just watching football or something," she attempted to explain away the sudden, joyful cry.

"But its Friday night."

Rebecca paid no attention to his correction as she continued up the stairs, bringing James's closed, office door into view.

"Which way is the bedroom?" the boy impatiently questioned.

"Shh," Rebecca admonished as she approached the closed door, placing her ear to the wood. As she listened she could have sworn that she heard James quietly talking, as if someone else was in the room with him but before she had time to confirm her belief, the door swung inward, almost taking her off her feet as she stumbled forward and into a scruffy, disheveled version of her husband. He was no longer wearing his typical buttoned up shirt, neatly tucked into his jeans. Instead, only what appeared to be a freshly stained wife beater covered his top half, his excessive chest hair overflowing from the opening around his neck.

"Hey honey," James greeted his wife with a quick peck on the cheek.

She didn't need to ask what was wrong with him. His breath and the nearly empty bottle of scotch in his right hand was answer enough. She hadn't seen him this wasted since New Year's Eve when, In an attempt to one up everyone involved in the peculiar birthmark conversation that night, he'd chosen to reveal his mottled testicles by resting them upon the coffee table for all to see.

"What the hell are you doing?" Rebecca quietly scolded her husband.

"Having a little drink," James answered cheerfully.

"I would say that there's nothing little about it," she responded, waiving her hand in front of her face as to dispense of the foul stench emitted from his liquor saturated tongue.

"Hey, who's this strapping young lad?" James turned to the now petrified juvenile.

If the boy hadn't been frozen in fear, he probably would've already been out the front door and halfway home but, immobilized by anxiety, he remained stuck in the hall.

"Here to fuck the wife, huh?"

"Ah...ah...no sir," the kid struggled to come up with an explanation for his presence.

"Oh, it's ok, James moved into the hallway, throwing his arm around the young lad. "You think you're the first?" he asked the boy with a smile. "Then again, this is the first time she's opted to bring one home for my approval but you're most definitely not the first to take a ride on the whorebag express."

"Fuck off," Rebecca defended herself.

"Listen," James whispered in the kid's ears. "It's been a while since the little miss and I have...well...you know. You think you could stop back by my office and give me the play-by-play when you're through? I need some new images to jerk it too, you know, to help me get to sleep tonight."

"God you're disgusting," Rebecca grabbed hold of her young stud, freeing him from James's offensive presence.

"Listen, I don't think this--," the boy attempted to announce his departure.

"Shut up." Rebecca silenced him. "Listen," she turned to James who wobbled from one side to the other, as if the hall were adrift on turbulent waters. "I don't know what it is that you think you're doing in there or who you think you're talking too but--"

"Oh, that's my new friend William. Say hello Will," James waived at the open book on his desk.

"Talking to your own character's now are we?"

"Oh, I didn't create him," James slurred. "He's much too entertaining to be one of my creations.

"Well, at least for once we agree."

"Hey I--," the kid again attempted to interject.

"You heard the lady. Plug your hole or else she might not let you plug hers."

"Jesus!" Rebecca responded to his over the top vulgarity. "How about you just go back in there with William or whoever and finish your little conversation."

"You know what? That's a superb idea," James agreed,

raising his bottle for a toast, then placing it to his lips, only to realize its bottom had run dry. "Would you look at that?" James stared through the distorted glass at his company.

Rebecca grabbed hold of her husband's shoulder and guided him into the room, closing the door behind him.

"I'm back ol' buddy! You miss me!?"

"I--,"

The boy hardly had a chance to form the first syllable of his protest before he himself was guided toward a doorway.

"Do you really wanna to go home or are we gonna fuck?" Rebecca asked in a frustrated tone.

Taking his silence as a desire to stick around, she opened the door to the master bedroom and shoved her acquired plaything into the room, slamming the door shut behind them.

THIRTY-FOUR

A half hour of self-pity on the floor of the darkening woods had erased all desire to conclude his illusive quest. Unable to even look in the direction of his wife's grave for fear that, this time, he would be unable to compose himself, Parker had gotten to his feet and hastily scampered for the house.

The confrontation with his deepest fear, in conjunction with the vortex of leaves, brought on by his once trusted friend, had been more than his fragile mind could bear. For forty-five minutes, while a hot deluge of water cascaded over him, Parker carefully attempted to reassemble the shattered fragments that had once been his nerves.

Showered and as centered as he could manage, Parker returned to the kitchen where he'd abandoned the hallucination inducing pirate. The captain stood on the counter, empty and smiling, as if nothing had happened. Parker grabbed the pirate by the neck and resolutely delivered him to his grave beside an empty bag of Doritos and a half eaten Twinkie.

In yet another display of inner strength, Parker declared his two deceitful, alcoholic companions banished from the house...for the night at least.

A glass of peach-cranberry juice took the buccaneers place at his side, joined by a double-decker sandwich of bologna, pepperoni and salami; a concoction he liked to refer to as the mystery meat club.

With his betrayers banned, Parker could now concentrate on the one remaining, nondestructive vice in his life...reading. Over the years, reading had provided Parker with much of the wisdom he'd needed to succeed. It had inspired and polished his writing. It had helped educate him about life and the world around him. Now Parker hoped that literary insight would grant him the knowledge that would allow him to understand why he was allowed to remain in this tormenting world, while his other half rested peacefully in a place beyond the comprehension of man.

Parker halted the assembly of the mystery meat club. He'd never before contemplated his own death and though he hadn't actually wished for a visit from the Reaper himself, this new low in his depression frightened him. He didn't feel suicidal, though he couldn't be sure, since he'd never before teetered on that ledge. He figured the true test would come momentarily in the study, where the cabinet of decorative weaponry would seem a macabre toy chest to anyone with suicidal tendencies.

Clearing this new worry from his mind, Parker placed the final piece of meat on the sandwich and capped it off with a third slice of wheat bread. After cleaning the counter and providing the discarded captain with a fresh layer of waste to keep him warm, he picked up the small plate and glass of juice and headed for the doorway that would lead him to the South staircase.

The North staircase hadn't seen use since Amanda's body had taken up residence just beyond the trees to that side of the house. Besides his occasional tests of courage, Parker had neglected that side of the house altogether, using neither its stairs, nor any of its doorways to pass from one room to the next. This selective route of travel, however, had proven very minimal an inconvenience, since the glass dwelling had been designed with symmetry in mind. If a route of travel existed on one side of the house, its twin resided on the other. At least that was the rule in effect for the outer cube.

*****

At first glance, Veracini Two appeared to be nothing more than a large glass cube in the woods. In actuality though, it had been constructed as two; one cube inside of the other. The outer cube provided all points of entry to the house while also acting as the first line of defense against the sun's destructive rays and the noises of nature's more violent moments. The inner cube acted as the living space of the structure, with a modest twenty-three hundred square feet of combined floor space split between the two stories. The dual cube construction allowed for a generous eight feet of space between the inner and outer walls. This encompassing hallway provided the only route of travel throughout the house.

Parker, going with the "nature is the décor" mindset of Patrick Henstridge, had requested that the only doorways in and out of the living room and kitchen, which shared the first level floor space, be placed at each of the house's four corners, providing two doorways to each of the divided rooms.

"That's brilliant, Mr. Veracini," Patrick exclaimed at first mention of the idea.

"That seems very inconvenient to me," Amanda quickly chimed in, slowing the growth of her husband's expanding head. Amanda, senior vice president of a company she'd helped create, regarded herself as a fairly intelligent person, though Patrick's and the newly proclaimed architect's bizarre idea continued to elude her.

"Less support," Patrick reemphasized, as if this new

tidbit of information did anything to untangle the illusive concept. "Less support means more glass; larger, grander sheets that could rival those of skyscrapers."

Parker's head slowly returned to its normal diameter as he realized his responsibility for supplying the source of Patrick's new found excitement.

"The inner cube...," Patrick continued, "...requires much more framing and less glass, as to allow for the tremendous weight of the second story. Less glass means more of an obstructed view from within. By pushing the doorways to the outer corners, it requires you to spend more time in the outer corridor and hence, one step closer to nature."

Parker began to feel as though Patrick was not the renowned architect he'd been touted as but instead an insane witch doctor and he was the doctor's very own shrunken head. He'd thought that the idea had been creative but after hearing the excited man's mantra of insanity, he began questioning his own mental wellbeing.

"I love it," Amanda excitedly responded, either the idea finally sinking in or insanity claiming yet another victim.

*****

Parker exited the kitchen at the southeast corner of the inner cube. Nature's dark, oak sentinels stood silent watch over the land beyond the outer walls. Though his presence within Veracini Two was much like that of a fish in a decorative tank, Parker had never given much thought to the possibility of onlookers, spying in on him from beyond the tree lined property. The closest neighbor lived nearly eight miles away and it had been at least six months since a visitor had made the long trek, up the densely wooded driveway, with the exception of the unwelcome bearer of bad news three months earlier.

He glanced at the cracked, south door as he passed.

xaleR

Parker grinned at the backwards and fractured engraving, though more in a state of powerless self-pity, than amusement. The word from this perspective seemed much like his life, cracked and out of order.

All of a sudden, movement diverted his attention from the fractured etching, to the towering oak guardians just thirty feet away. Quickly his grin was replaced by the same fear he was sure had plagued his face during his earlier travels into the north woods.

Parker moved closer to the outer, glass wall, peering out at the tall oaks as a slowly drifting cloud joined in blocking the moonlight from the shadowy land. A small, yet prominent bulge, protruded from the closest of the relatively straight trunks. Parker moved closer to the glass and, balancing the juice on the plate beside the mystery club, he reached for the door knob, turning it until the metal latch slowly disengaged from the frame.

You've seen enough horror films to know not to open the door, an inner voice demanded that he reconsider his current course of action. As the latch again engaged the door frame, the small deformity jumped, as if startled by the almost inaudible click. Its movement was followed by the formation of two, catlike eyes, peering at the house. Parker jumped back, skillfully balancing the delicately perched juice.

"Shit!" he exclaimed, turning his attention to the teetering glass as he removed it from the already crowded plate.

Apparently satisfied with its received reaction, the mysterious figure nimbly leapt from its vertical perch and retreated into the shadowy woods.

"There you go Parker, afraid of a fucking cat now."

Deep down though, he wasn't sure what the creature had been and before he could contemplate any further, he found himself ascending the southerly staircase at an accelerated pace.

As if the inner shell of the house offered any more safety than the outer, Parker paused just inside the doorless loft entry, the forgotten grin again returning to his face.

"You jackass," he addressed himself, realizing that he was no safer in his new location than he had been just inches from the outer, glass wall.

Given the obviously, fragile construction of Veracini Two, the glass comprising the outer cube had been reinforced with the same shatter proof films found on many homes under the constant threat of hurricanes. While not bullet proof, the glass could withstand the assault of a blunt instrument, such as a rock or even a hammer. So, short of driving a car through the house, no one could get in or out without passing through one of two securely locked doors.

Dismissing the woodland visitor, Parker proceeded toward the center of the fifteen foot wide loft where a statue of a nude man and woman stood entwined in a twisted pose of balance and passion. At this point in the house Parker had a decision to make. Straight ahead stood the doorway to the neglected north staircase and to his right the elaborately decorated entry to the only bedroom and bathroom within the residence.

Parker turned left, toward the westerly facing, lake view side of the house, where a four foot wide walkway lay before him. The walkway connected the loft space on which he currently stood, to another lofted space, which terminated at the far west wall of the inner cube. Parker had asked for this design personally. He'd always loved the idea of a lofted study and a narrow walkway, leading to an isolated span where he could sit and relax while delving into his latest assignments. As with the rest of the house, this space was entirely open to viewing from inside and out, but its single point of entry and the illusion of floating high above everything, allowed the space a feeling of privacy, more so than any other room in the house.

At the center of this lofted space stood Mike, a tattered, brown leather chair, named after the salesman who'd sold it to Parker and Amanda nearly fifteen years ago. It had been the first pieces of furniture he and Amanda had ever bought together and in honor of that landmark moment in their relationship, they'd informed Michael Fitzpatrick, the perplexed salesman, that his name would forever grace the beautiful piece of furniture.

After a decade and a half, in no way did the worn out piece of furniture fit in with its accompanying décor but Parker had never felt as comfortable in a chair as he felt in Mike. So, when Amanda had argued to get rid of the tattered leather beast, Parker had stood his ground and won. Now the chair shared floor space with only four other fixtures.

An elegant, round end table stood beside the chair, both facing a wide, stone fireplace rising up from the floor below. To the left of Mike, at the far end of the loft, stood a large bookcase, filled with numerous titles both renowned and obscure. And, to his right, towered another set of expansive shelves—these displayed behind a glimmering set of glass doors. Within the display case, perched delicately upon small, hand carved pedestals, was Parker's extensive collection of fire arms.

Some modern weaponry shared the brightly lit space, though the majority of the collection was composed of antiques. Parker owned at least one gun used in each war that the United States had ever been involved in since its days of British rule. The oldest of the collection was a worn, black powder musket, dating back to the revolutionary war and a soldier named Samuel Keens who'd been struck down in the third line at the battle of Lexington.

Parker wasn't sure if many of the older guns still worked, since ammunition for them had been long since obsolete and the risk of damage to the delicate weapons or himself was far too great. The newer of the pieces however, worked with the finest precision. He'd used the 45 magnum, 9mm and laser scope rifle on many occasions at the shooting range, becoming impressively proficient with each but his interests had always lied more with his admiration for the history of the pieces, rather than their functionality. So the weapons remained, for the most part, safely behind glass.

Placing his juice on the small end table beside him, Parker lowered himself into his cushiony, leather throne. *Beyond* was the title of his current assignment. He'd read and reviewed a couple of this author's previous works and knew from experience that, this too would likely prove a painful read.

"I would rather throw myself from this loft than finish this book," he'd once complained to Amanda.

"You're over exaggerating again," she'd responded, taking the book to read for herself.

By page thirty, Parker had found himself poised to play catcher to a woman determined to practice her swan dive in an environment deficient of water.

A lack of storytelling ability was the main problem with each of this author's previous literary attempts but it was the one word titles which Parker could never seem to get past. This author had never used more than one word when naming his books. He probably saw it as a clever attempt at the dramatic. Parker just found it simple and uncreative. So when he'd learned of his latest assignment, he hadn't been surprised to see the new book, *Beyond*, joining such catchy titles as *Slice* and *Betrayal*.

"Parker," a gentle breeze whispered as it wafted across his left ear.

Parker jumped from his chair, knocking the book to the floor. He spun in place searching for the source of the vocal breeze, half expecting to find the peeping cat clinging to the stone lovers or even the back of his chair.

He was alone.

"Just a lingering prank from the good old captain," he reassured himself.

Retrieving the book from the floor, he returned to the comfort of his favorite chair. Skipping the copyright page, the dedication to some woman he could only assume to be the author's wife and a quick letter to the reader, Parker read the first line of the anticipated, mind numbing book.

The dream I had that night was only the first in a long series of life changing events.

"Of course it was jackass." The stereotypical dream is probably the most overused tool of foreshadowing in the history of literature. "It's not like it hasn't been done to death," Parker criticized aloud, his immediate, negative response hinting at the sure to be brutal review to follow.

He thought he'd been hard on James Madison with his scathing review of *The Doorway to My Own Hell*, but he could already tell that the words used to describe this book would be far less merciful than any he'd ever used before.

An audible pop, then crackle pulled his attention from the printed words. Though he continued to hold the book before his face, blocking his forward gaze, he noticed a soft, orange glow emanating from around its edges. Another crackle snapped in the open room. Parker lowered the book, bringing the lit fireplace into view. A fire hadn't burned there since the previous winter and he'd had no intention of lighting one that evening, yet somehow, the large flames licked at their stone enclosure. Removing a small remote from the end table, he extinguished the propane fed flames before returning his attention to *Beyond*.

A blood moon hung low in the night sky, the quiet town awash in its imposing glow.

A click again pulled his attention away from the tedious

assignment, followed by the audible puff of gas as it ignited within the concealed space.

"I like it on," a soft, whispering voice floated through the room, affecting Parker in the same manner as a brisk wind might on a cold New England morning. This time Parker did not jump to his feet. The familiar voice fused him to the cushion, the book now clutched nervously in his hands.

A moment passed. The apparently desired flames continued to lick at their grey, stone wall prison. Parker sat motionless, his mind questioning the reality of what he'd just heard.

The room remained silent, except for the occasional crackling of flames. A cool bead of sweat slowly grew on Parkers brow, migrating south along the crease of his nose, the salty ball of moisture dispersing along the corner of his lips as another prepared for its southward journey. However, Parker's attention was immediately drawn away from this second, moist traveler, by a new and foreign sensation.

Thin, string like objects began slowly brushing along his left ear. Closely cropped hair, neatly buzzed on all sides, made this peculiar sensation impossible, yet the feeling persisted. The strings seeming to dance back and forth, playfully batting at his ear.

Increasing terror demanded he not look, even while human curiosity slowly pulled his gaze toward the source of the odd sensation. Even before his head could complete the partial rotation, Amanda appeared in the corner of his gaze, her face only an inch from his and wearing a broad angelic smile.

"Jesus Christ!" he exclaimed as he jolted away from the impossible guest.

The book sailed from Parker's hands, sliding across the floor, between the loft's railings and fell with a soft thud to the wood floors below. As if mimicking the book's rapid retreat, Parker flipped over the chair's armrest, falling to the floor, luckily one story higher than the discarded novel.

In a frantic, backwards crab-walk, Parker scurried about five feet further from the chair before freezing once again. His eyes remained locked on his beloved, dead wife, only she did not appear dead. In fact, if anything, she looked years younger. He would've guessed late twenties. The grotesque injuries sustained from the accident three months earlier, were no longer visible and his favorite, white lace teddy adorned her lush, toned body.

"No fucking way," he addressed the impossible vision.

He would've blinked if he'd thought that it would do any good but something inside told him that this was not a hallucination.

"You're dead," he finally addressed the resurrected woman.

"I'm sorry I left you," Amanda spoke as she rose from her slightly slouched position beside the chair.

The light, emanating from the wall fixtures behind her, outlined the woman's thin figure through the sheer fabric of the provocative outfit. The short cut fabric, trimmed with a feathery ring of fur, fell just inches below her hips, allowing a hint of her feminine treasure to remain visible to Parker from his partially inclined position on the floor.

Until that moment, the thought of sex had been the farthest thing from his mind since the night before his wife's life, and the life of the six month old child within her, had perished beneath the frame of the nineteen-ninety-eight Ford Explorer.

The memory of that tragic night instantly triggered another realization about his astonishingly resurrected wife. Amanda did not appear pregnant. At six months, she hadn't been excessively large but the presence of the life growing within her had been noticeably apparent.

Amanda began slowly moving toward her terrified husband. Parker would have moved away but, with the railing only another three or four feet behind him and the catwalk to the other loft blocked by his slowly advancing spouse, he knew he had nowhere to run. Besides, something inside was compelling him to stay. It eagerly welcomed the return of his old life, even if under such impossible circumstances.

With only a couple of feet between he and his wife, Parker suddenly began to feel at ease. The peculiarity of the situation began to diminish and if it weren't for the nagging truth in the back of his mind, he would've thought that she'd never even been gone.

Love and desire filled Amanda's eyes as she positioned herself over her newly relaxed husband. Parker shifted slightly, not in response to the uncomfortable hardness of the floor beneath him but in an attempt to adjust his rapidly changing, physiology.

"I came back," Amanda spoke softly as she lowered her self down upon her husband, placing both of her hands on his t-shirt covered chest.

Parker submitted to the woman's dominant position, drawing his elbows toward his body and lowering his back to the floor.

"I saw how miserable you were and demanded to come back. I couldn't stand to watch you suffer any longer. I wouldn't. From now on, I will be right here to fulfill your every desire."

He wasn't sure when it had happened but he could feel the elastic waistband of his cotton pajama pants confining his knees to the limits of their stretchy, fabric waistband.

"Every desire," Amanda reemphasized as she lowered herself onto his rigidly awaiting partner.

Parker ran his hands up his wife's thighs and under the teddy, grasping her hips and gently guiding her velvety sanctuary up and down upon his animated limb. All fear and confusion was rapidly diminished with each fluid movement. No further words were spoken, only the soft moans and deep breaths shared between them. Parker tilted his head back, closing his eyes as his lower body joined in his wife's orgasmic rhythm. The pleasure was unlike any he'd ever felt before.

He'd once read, in a copy of Cosmo, that a woman's toes will curl at the peak of pleasure, so it was no surprise when he discovered the same to be true for men.

Parker could feel his wife's delicate hands firmly planted upon his broad chest as she continued her ride. But as the overwhelming sensation of climactic pleasure slowly faded, a new, more disturbing awareness took its place.

His head still back and eyes closed, he sensed something cool and slick slowly encompassing his neck. The foreign object completed one loop and had just began its second trip around when Parker opened his eyes to Amanda's bloody, half missing face hovering above his. Her tongue flowed from her mouth like a long rope being draw from a bottomless sack and lay in a moist, knotted heap upon his chest as its forked tip began tightening around his throat.

Parker shot up, clawing at the looping intruder. With a firm grip, he ripped the terrifying object away from his neck and threw it to the ground. The snake hissed as it quickly retreated into the nearby brush.

Parker sat stunned for a moment, searching for the sexually deceitful apparition. All that lay before him, were the tall trees of the dense forest and his wife's headstone only twenty feet away.

Shifting, Parker felt a cool, hard object graze his right hand. Beside him lay the nearly drained bottle of Captain Morgan. One last glaze of fluid lined the bottom of the bottle as it lay on its side. He quickly snatched up the glass container, emptying its soothing contents onto his tongue.

With the captain bled dry, Parker stumbled to his feet and without hesitation, scurried for the house.

THIRTY-FIVE

"What a fucking pussy," the book scoffed at James's return to the office.

"What?" James questioned, puzzled by the book's harsh ridicule.

"What kind of man just loafs about while some other bloke puts it to his old lady? And in his own house nonetheless."

"Look, you don't understand."

"Oh, I think I do."

"Listen. Rebecca and I are through," James continued, slurring his defense. "I think it's fairly clear that she no longer wants anything to do with me. There's no fixing what's occurred. It's over."

"It's only over because you let it be. Only a spineless twerp would allow himself to be walked upon by a tart like her."

"Fuck you William!"

"You hear that?"

"Here what?"

"Listen."

James listened and at first didn't hear a thing but as more time went by, noises began to arise from across the hall. Soft moans slowly grew into loud, pleasure-full cries of passion, both male and female. James closed his eyes and cringed in disgust.

"See, it does bother you. I'll bet she hasn't made sounds like that with you in ages. Can you even remember the last time you were the cause of such ecstasy?"

"Shut up."

"I'll bet she's loving every moment of it; every touch of his young, toned body as it pounds against her flesh; every exotic sensation arising from his invasive masculinity."

"I said shut up."

James unwillingly continued to take in the book's provoking banter as well as the pornographic soundtrack emanating from across the hall.

"There's no guilt over there...only pleasure. What's to make her feel guilty when all she can think about is the river of sexuality flooding her loins? You were right. She doesn't want you anymore. She has a new stud in the stable and based on what I can hear, the stallion is giving her the ride of her life."

"Shut up!" James suddenly cried out. "Shut up. Please. Shut up. I can't...I mean..."

"Then what are you going to do about it my boy?"

"I...I don't know."

"You can't allow this abhorrent act to continue."

Eyes shut and hands firmly planted over both of his ears, James attempted to turn off the adverse reality unfolding around him.

"You're the man of this house," William asserted. "This is your castle and across the hall, your wife is engaged in a treasonous affair with that impostor. He cannot be allowed to get away with such a violation. You must reclaim your house. You must take back that which is yours and dispatch of those who have treaded upon you. Eliminate the source of your pain, James."

"Eliminate?"

"Yesss," the book encouraged. "Show them that you

are in charge. Show them that they have violated the sanctity of your home, your life, your marriage. Make...them...pay."

"You're right," James suddenly understood. "I can't let them get away with this."

A cry of ecstasy, from both parties, bellowed from across the hall, bringing a cringe of emotional pain to James's sweat soaked face once again.

"I'll do it," James firmly declared as pain gave way to rage.

"That's my boy," William contentedly whispered. "Now, take back that which is yours."

"Mine," James growled as he yanked the office door open.

Without the insulating benefit of the second door, Rebecca's peak of ecstasy wrenched at his heart. William was right. This was his house and that was his wife. He couldn't let them get away with this. Someone had to pay.

Without even testing the lock, James reared back and with all his might, struck the door with his right foot. The frame around the latch exploded as the door swung violently inward, lodging the interior knob in the drywall of the abutting wall.

Rebecca screamed as her stud jumped from the bed in surprise, either unaware of his nudity or too frightened to care. Rebecca, on the other hand, scrambled to cover herself as she watched her husband looming in the doorway.

"What the Fuck James!?"

"Dude I--" the kid attempted to speak but immediately fell silent at the evil glare issued by the fuming husband.

"Get the fuck out of here!" Rebecca ordered, but James unwaveringly continued his advance until he was standing right beside the kingsize bed. He didn't say a word. He just glared.

"This is why it's over! You're out of your fucking mind! You always have been. It just took me this long to figure it out."

Leisurely, James raised his hand and, placing one finger to his lips, shushed his nagging wife.

Rebecca complied, not so much in response to her husband's disturbingly simple command but more so as a reaction to the troubling glare permeating from deep behind his eyes. Though he was staring right at her, it was as if he wasn't there, as if he was lost within his own mind and no longer in control of his actions.

Lowering his hand, James smiled as he gradually opened the top drawer of the nightstand.

"What are you going to do, James?" Rebecca traded anger for fear.

"Listen mister...I..."

James turned toward the nightstand and, unzipping his pants, began pissing in the open drawer.

"That's just fucking great," Rebecca's fear gave way to disgust as she watched the steady yellow stream soak the inside of the thousand dollar piece of furniture.

James just tilted his head back, enjoying the relief he'd brought to his body.

"You people are fucking nuts!" the shocked kid exclaimed as he grabbed his jeans from the floor and, opting to leave the remainder of his clothing behind, darted from the room, dressed only in sweat.

Shaking it a couple of times, James placed himself back inside of his pants and without a word, returned to his office, locking the door behind him.

THIRTY-SIX

"Wait," Rebecca cried to her retreating lover, chasing after him in only a bed sheet.

By that point the teen had managed to slip into his jeans and was quickly scurrying from the house, toward the street.

"I said wait a minute. I want to apologize for--"

Stopping in his retreat, "I don't know what's wrong with you people but it's fucked up," the boy asserted.

Rebecca just stood, shocked by the sudden outburst.

"I don't know whose worse, urine boy up there or his slut wife who brings home strange men to fuck, while her husband drinks himself to death."

"Now wait just a God damn minute! A few minutes ago you and your prick had no problem taking full advantage of the opportunity you were given."

"Yeah well...*then* I just though you guys were a little weird or maybe swingers or something. Now I know that you're both fucking psychotic."

The kid brushed her hand from his shoulder and continued to walk away, his bare feet slapping the cool, concrete with every step.

"Well just wait a minute and I'll give you a ride. We

can go to a hotel or maybe--"

"Crazy bitch," the boy muttered as he disappeared around the neighbor's hedges.

"Fuck you then!" Rebecca screamed before turning back toward the house, looking up at James's office window.

James stood between the parted curtains, watching as she and the departed youth ended their brief affair.

"Son of a bitch," she huffed as she secured her sheet and marched back toward the house.

THIRTY-SEVEN

"Honey, what happened to the television?" Uncle Mike called to his wife from the living-room couch.

"What?" Aunt Mary responded in a frustrated tone.

Considering the less than appetizing aroma wafting from the kitchen, not to mention the occasional, unladylike outbursts emanating from his aunt's direction, Peter assumed that dinner wasn't exactly going as planned. That was one reason he'd chosen to avoid the kitchen for the past hour.

"The T.V.. What's wrong with it?" Uncle Mike repeated, this time in a much louder tone as to be heard over the again alert, smoke detectors.

"I'm a little busy at the moment. I don't think you need the T.V. that bad," the increasingly annoyed voice boomed back from the kitchen.

"But the game is on tonight," Uncle Mike whined as if he were just another one of the kids currently terrorizing the household.

"I got you!" Joseph yelled as he whizzed by Peter's chair.

"No, you didn't!" Bobby screamed back over his shoulder as he ducked into a nearby bedroom.

Peter watched in fascination as the action just continued to unfold in this familiar, yet strange setting. Shortly after arriving, he'd claimed to have a headache and taken up a position on the large, Lazy Boy recliner in the corner of the living room. In actuality though, he felt fine, physically at least.

Mentally on the other hand, he was a wreck. He couldn't get his mind off of the book. Was he really going crazy? Could a book really be responsible for such a bizarre series of events? Everything he'd learned in his fifteen years of life and every law of reality screamed as to the impossibility of the ludicrous theory but the explanation that, Geoffrey had just finally had enough, wasn't much better.

His problem with Steven was understandable and maybe he had reached his breaking point with the bully but what then was the explanation for his issues with his best friend and what really had happened between Steven and Dexter back at school?

The quandary of the past days odd events was beginning to take its toll on Peter's head, lending a bit of truth to his previously fictitious claims of ailment. He needed to relax. If there was any legitimate mystery to the odd book, his father would solve it. The old man was brilliant. He hadn't attended an Ivy League school. He hadn't even graduated at the top of his class but something about the way his father carried himself and his mere presence at times, told Peter that he was the progeny of greatness and that someday, if he worked hard, he too could emulate such remarkable grandeur.

"Did you hear me?" Uncle Mike called from the couch again.

"Yes, damn it! I heard you!" Aunt Mary cried back, this time from the kitchen's doorway. "What would you like me to do about it, fly you to Boston so you can watch your precious White Sox play their silly game?"

"Red Sox honey. The White Sox are from Chicago."

262

Aunt Mary just returned his corrective comment with a thousand word glare, none of which seemed pleasant.

Peter was glad the television was out. He hadn't been completely sure how he was going to handle his aunt and uncle's discovery of the disturbing events which had occurred at his school earlier in the day. He'd planned on telling them that he and his father had already discussed the troubling situation, knowing full and well that he would then be facing even further discipline when his parents found out about yet another lie but he couldn't risk his father's distraction from what was truly important at the moment...the book.

"When the guys were out there replacing the siding today, they accidentally cut a wire to the dish but don't worry, I called the satellite company and they will be out sometime tomorrow to fix it, all right?" Aunt Mary comforted her traumatized husband.

"But, what about the game tonight?"

"I guess you'll just have to miss this one honey."

Aunt Mary's calming tone oozed of false remorse for her husband's loss.

"But--"

Before his uncle could continue his childlike protest, the rhythmic screeching of the smoke detectors once again filled the house, calling Aunt Mary away, uttering yet another barrage of frustrated expletives.

"Ahh! Fire!" Bobby screamed, darting through the living room once again.

"We're all gonna die!" Joseph added to the commotion, following closely behind his brother.

Uncle Mike just continued flipping through the hundreds of snow filled channels, as if hoping by some miracle that the severed wire would either repair itself or no longer be needed in the delivery of his precious game.

"Fire is the least deadly thing to worry about in this house, Pete," Uncle Mike addressed his silent nephew while nodding in the direction of the kitchen.

"I heard that!" Aunt Mary snapped back, silencing the smoke detector once again.

Peter just listened and smiled, unsure what to say. He wasn't used to an environment filled with such hostility and sarcastic bickering. His parents loved one another deeply and had, for as long as he could remember, never directed one negative comment toward one another.

"Uncle Mike?"

"Yeah, Pete."

"Can I use your computer?"

THIRTY-EIGHT

"What the fuck's wrong with you!?" Rebecca screamed as she pounded on the office door.

James remained at the window, following the half-naked man down the street, around the corner and out of sight.

"That was hardly what I had in mind," William spoke.

"What was I supposed to do, kill him?" James slurred his speech.

"Who the fuck are you talking to!?" Rebecca continued her assault on the door.

James just looked at the rattling barrier between him and his wife.

"You know, deep down I always thought you were a bit of an asshole but now...now I know that you're just a fucking lunatic! It's over! You can just drop dead for all I care!" And with a final strike of the door, Rebecca retreated back across the hall, slamming the bedroom door behind her.

James remained silent, staring at the once again, calm doorway.

"Do you remember what I told you, James?" William took advantage of the returned calm. "Do you remember my offer?"

James turned to the book.

"For years you have taken the abuse of others. For years you have been forced to live under the oppressive finger of a society intent on crushing your every hope, your every dream. How would you like to take back control of your life, reclaim your fate?"

James, intrigued, slowly approached the open book.

"You don't have to stand idly by as your family, your career, your life crumbles down around you. But you must be willing to listen to what I say. You must be willing to do all that is necessary to reclaim that which is rightfully yours. Can you do this, James? Can you once again seize control of your destiny?

James nodded as he continued to stare blankly at the book.

"Good," William responded to his subject's cooperation with eerie glee. "First you must eliminate those who stand in your way; those whose very existence has brought nothing but pain and misery to your life."

"Eliminate," James agreed in a monotone response.

"Do you have a name?" William asked.

James nodded.

"Then write it down my boy. Take your revenge and free yourself of this ongoing agony. Free yourself of the pain and sorrow gnawing at your soul. Pen the bastard's demise."

A broad smile grew upon James's face as the pages of the book slowly turned, revealing a clean sheet of paper and an antique feather quill.

Lifting the old pen from the page, James scribbled the name of his victim.

THIRTY-NINE

Though put off by Rebecca's restaurant explosion, Francesco was determined to not let it put a damper on his evening. Following the outburst, he'd risen from his seat and, tapping his knife against his wine glass, brought the conversations of shocked onlookers to a pause.

"Excuse me," he spoke. "I just want to apologize for that horrendous display and for disrupting the evening you fine people were enjoying. And, as a sign of my deepest regret, everyone's meals are on me tonight."

As he'd expected the entire restaurant fell into a state of silent shock. Fanaciellies wasn't exactly the cheapest restaurant in the city, a fact of which he was well aware given his frequent visits to the upscale establishment. But, as much as the evening was going to cost him, Francesco knew that it paled in comparison to the positive press this gesture was sure to garner. The local media would sing his praises and inform the world that he was the kindest, most generous man alive, when in actually he cared very little if his romantic turmoil was a hindrance upon anyone else's lives.

Aside from his quest for positive P.R., Francesco was doing nothing more than fishing; the pricy meals acting as his bait and the unattached women, scattered about the restaurant, his prey.

It wasn't the first time he'd deployed such a flashy technique and as with each previous attempt, in no time, he found himself reeling in a trophy catch, perfect for mounting.

Following a brief courting over dinner, Francesco very publicly covered the bill before ushering his lovely new prize out to his awaiting Aston Martin and eventually to his estate.

Built half in and half on top of a solid granite hill at the foot of the Sierra Mountains, there was no other house in the valley that could rival Palais-De-Savaree's unique atmosphere. On numerous occasions, Francesco had allowed the house to be photographed by several architectural magazines, including industry staple, Architectural Digest but other than in the case of those select few strangers, it was considered a great privilege to even be allowed near the extravagant abode.

The home contained three levels, two of which resided within the strategically hollowed out hillside, while the top floor, containing the bedroom and a large, partially screened lanai, sat at the peak of the granite formation.

It had taken nearly five years to obtain the proper permitting and another two to find the correct team of architects and contractors to pull off such a daring structural feat but when it was completed, Palais-De-Savaree was a breathtaking example of just what America could offer and why he'd chosen to come to this great land.

"This is the guest level," Francesco informed twenty-four year old Samantha Flowers as they reached the top of the first, granite staircase and stood within the massive hallway of the second floor.

Samantha's mouth remained agape at the continued beauty before her eyes. She'd never seen a house of such grandeur before. The walls of the hallway were lined with rustic timbers, giving the second floor a much more authentic western feel than the beautifully elegant marble décor of the first. The floor had been left in its original stone state with intricate lines cut into its surface to resemble laid stone tiles and the ceiling overhead had been cut away into a graceful arch of polished stone and covered in a massive, hand painted mural, depicting cowboys on horseback and Indians in hurried pursuit of wild buffalo.

"You like the painting?" Francesco asked as he sensed his guest's skyward gaze.

"It's beautiful."

"Why thank you but as much as I would like to, I cannot take credit myself. It was painted by a local artist by the name of Philip Prescott. I saw some of his work on display one time and just knew that I had to retain his services.

"Well if you ask me, it was the right decision. Are those cows?"

"Those are buffalo my dear," Francesco politely corrected the woman, while attempting to conceal his growing frustration over yet another in a series of ridiculous questions and comments.

"Wow. Like the wings right?"

Francesco didn't respond. The silky dress clinging to her slender frame was his only interest. It was the type of dress that many women attempt to wear but that only a select few can successfully pull off. Samantha was one of those few and he couldn't wait to find out just how beautiful the dress looked crumpled up on his bedroom floor.

"After you my dear," he motioned to a spiral staircase at the far end of the hall.

Staring up as she climbed the first few steps, Samantha attempted to see the top of the solid stone stairwell but the winding steps continued to inhibit her view and after what seemed a nearly twenty foot climb, the two emerged from the peak of the hill, into the moonlit master bedroom, overlooking the city below.

There was little doubt that Samantha had been in awe of the house up to that point but given the woman's new expression of overwhelmed appreciation, Francesco knew that he would have no problem sealing this deal.

"This is absolutely amazing," Samantha announced as she approached the exterior glass wall overlooking the city below.

Every wall of the upper level was made of glass, allowing no obstructions to the three hundred and sixty degree view of the high desert landscape. The bedroom was massive, though minimally decorated, allowing a clean and open feeling. The only furniture within the immense space was a large four poster bed at its center, a set of giant armoires along the westerly wall and a series of nude sculptures strategically positioned atop pedestals throughout the room, each with their own lighting to accentuate their curvilinear forms.

"Can I get you a drink?" Francesco offered as he moved toward the open doorway to the adjoining lanai.

"A rum and coke would be good," Samantha answered, continuing to indulge in the lavish surroundings.

"How about some Champaign?" Francesco rebutted, with no intention of breaking out the Dom Perignon for such an easy conquest but still feeling that he at least owed the girl a touch of class before having his fun.

"That would be perfect," Samantha accepted in a flirtatious voice.

Easy as cake, he thought to himself, wondering if he'd gotten one of the many American expressions he'd learned correct before disappearing behind a frosted, glass-cube wall.

Beyond the expansive alter of drinker's delight, the sparkling lights of the city below, twinkled under a vale of moonlit darkness. Kneeling, Francesco removed one of the numerous bottles of Champaign, all organized by brand, year and price, from the extensive wine cooler and gently plucked two long stem glasses from the sparkling, crystal display overhead.

Rustling in the other room drew his attention as he uncorked the bottle and made his way back toward the bedroom. He knew what the noises were. It wasn't the first time he'd heard such commotion while in the process of retrieving drinks, so it wasn't a surprise when he reentered the bedroom to the sight of the young woman seductively embracing one of the four, massive bedposts, her dress hanging haphazardly from the outstretched arm of a nearby statue.

She was a wild one, Francesco thought to himself as he watched the woman run her thigh along the dark mahogany pole. Disregarding the bottle of wine and two glasses, Francesco released his grip. The sound of shattering glass filled the room but only momentarily as he approached the bed and with a show of forceful passion, tossed the temptress down upon the lush, pillowy surface.

Samantha playfully giggled at the forceful play as she assisted in freeing him first his shirt and then his pants, all the while giving her body over to the passionate kisses and gentle caress of her suitor's muscular physique.

Francesco lightly nibbled at his plaything's ear and with a series of gentle, passionate kisses, slowly moved southward to the nape of her neck. Samantha jumped as a chill overtook her body. Francesco took note of the sensitive location for later exploitation.

Continuing his southerly journey, he gently ran the tip of his tongue over her chest and onto her breast, running ever tightening laps around the beautiful c-cups until applying the slightest of bites to each of the cherry red peaks.

Samantha moaned.

He knew he had her. All he had to do was touch her in just the right way and her sexual future would be forever ruined. No other man could compete with his

271

performance. From that night on, in Samantha Flowers' life, Francesco Savaree would be a legendary name.

As his tongue continued its exploration of the young, taught flesh, he was pleased to find that the woman possessed an inverted belly button. There had always been something about an outwardly inclined naval that turned him off but, free of this mood killing deterrent, he applied a gentle, yet passionate kiss to the inward opening.

Samantha let out another giggle as the touch of his tongue tickled her body.

Wishing not to distract her climactic assent any further, Francesco moved on, approaching the field of play where grass was usually a clear sign of maturity. Samantha on the other hand, though old enough by legal standards, obviously remained young at heart, as the playing field was perfectly groomed. Only a thin strip of hair remained in tack, acting as the perfect guide, drawing him in for a mutually desired landing. Veering off course at the last moment though, to the playfully disappointed whine of his partner, Francesco instead made his way to the woman's inner thigh, where he went to work on leaving a sign of his presence.

Samantha arched her back as Francesco found yet another sensitive location on her perfect body.

Sensing she was ready, he abruptly stopped and grabbing her hips, flipped her onto her stomach, draping himself across her body.

Samantha seemed to have no problem with this sudden change of position as she shifted her weight to her knees and lifted her lower half into the air, leaving her face nestled against the soft, down pillow while the sensation of Francesco's manhood slowly slipped inside her.

He'd been right about her assumed, perfect form. There wasn't one flaw on this one, inside or out. Her exterior beauty was breathtaking and interiorly she had complete control over her sexual palace. Holding the beauty's hips, he repeatedly drew her close, then, guided her retreat as he thoroughly explored the recesses of her femininity.

Forfeiting the muffling qualities of the pillow, Samantha lifted her head and filled the room with a beautiful song of pleasure.

A few more strokes and she would be done but he had no intention of stopping there. Over the years he'd developed amazing self-control and though his body craved the explosive release of his loins, he continued to delay the encounter's climactic end. This girl was amazing and though the world was filled with many more like her, he wanted to enjoy her company for as long as possible. Not only did he want to become a legend in her mind, he wanted to be her God.

Samantha's back arched and her inner walls tightened as she reached climax.

Francesco just grinned at the gratifying reaction but did not stop. He wanted more and undoubtedly, so did she.

Her body's first climactic response complete, Samantha turned her head, peering up at her lover from the corner of her eye as if to say, "Please. Give me more". But that wasn't all her expression said.

As her eyes met his and his body continued to fulfill her every desire, Francesco watched as Samantha's vision abruptly turned skyward, fear quickly replacing pleasure.

Continuing his probing motions, Francesco watched as a long stream of clear, glistening slime fell from overhead, striking Samantha's shoulder blades and running into the small of her back.

What the hell, he thought as he turned his attention to the ceiling overhead.

"L'oh mon dieu."

Hanging over the bed, claws buried deep within the wooden ceiling, was definitive proof as to the existence of hell.

Samantha screamed.

FORTY

William Thurston Grave was a renowned British author, turned serial killer in the late eighteen hundreds. Nicknamed, 'The Grave', by history, Grave was a pre-curser to and is thought to have influenced the most infamous of serial killers, Jack the Ripper.

It had taken Peter a few minutes and some patient wading through countless, homemade horror sites before his search for Tales From "The Grave" had brought him to the site on the screen before him.

Scrolling down he read on.

Though often compared to the Ripper, unlike old Jack, the world had quickly learned the truth about William Grave. On September 6th, 1882, the body of the reclusive sociopath had been discovered, face down, on the street below his Claremont Street flat. According to reports, not one person had witnessed the author's demise but based on the evidence recovered from his bedroom (three stories up) in conjunction with the contents of the large book still held firmly in his grasp at the time of his discovery, police had quickly confirmed Grave as the killer who'd struck terror into the hearts and minds of the women of England for the past year and a half.

"Come on. Get off the computer," Bobby wined as he wandered into the den.

Joseph followed in close pursuit.

"I'll be done soon," Peter sighed impatiently, bothered by the sudden interruption.

"At least look at something cool," Joseph asserted as he muscled his way in on the keyboard, quickly replacing Peter's page with the image of a nude woman, spread eagle on a bearskin rug with 'click here' providing the only censorship evident on the site.

"Hey, I was reading something," Peter protested his sudden eviction as Bobby pushed in on his other side, taking over control of the keyboard from his brother.

"That's my girlfriend," Joseph claimed proudly, eyeing the luscious plaything on the screen.

"No, this is your girlfriend," Bobby clarified as his fingers flew across the keyboard, displaying what appeared to be a transvestite site with a full screen image of a man in drag and wearing a pair of crotchless panties.

"I'm not even gonna ask how you know about this site."

"Please!" Peter shouted, taking back control of the computer from his two childish cousins. "I was trying to read something."

"Sorrrry! Come on Joseph. Maybe we can look up your girlfriend's number on our computer and give her...I mean him a call."

"That's not my girlfriend," Joseph wined, giving into his brother's torment as the two exited the room.

Free of his two, moronic cousins and more than a little disgusted by the image before him, Peter quickly grabbed hold of the mouse and navigated back to the story of William Grave. Scanning the following paragraph he skipped past the police theories and brief history of the killings. He cared about only one thing...the book.

After struggling to pry the large book from the author's fingers, police had been shocked to find detailed accounts of each of the Grave murders neatly contained within its pages. Not just journal entries, containing the victim's names and methods of death, but full blown stories with beginnings, middles and ends. Nearly three quarters of the book had been filled at the time of discovery, the last entry having been that of Emily Hallows, who's naked and defiled body had been found in a heap on the dead man's bedroom floor.

Scanning further.

With the Ripper killings arising only six short years later, Grave's sick rampage had been all but forgotten until 1896 when a woman by the name of Margaret Howser had been placed in the custody of Meadow View Mental Institution on London's West End after insisting that a book--claiming to be the living spirit of William Thurston Grave--had instructed her to kill her estranged husband and his new lady friend by means of brutal decapitation.

"Holy shit," Peter, shocked, blurted at the screen, quickly placing a hand to his mouth. He'd be spending a lot of time in the booth this Sunday.

Many more accounts of a possessed book, claiming to be William Grave, arose over the next hundred years; the last one being that of a Plymouth, Massachusetts resident who, in 2003, was shot and killed by police when a standard traffic stop had turned into a full blown shoot out at the discovery of the man's dismembered wife, in a duffle bag in the trunk.

Though the people involved and the details of their atrocious crimes have always differed from one story to the next, two aspects of each account have always remained the same; the book and the trail of death following in its wake.

Below is the image of a replica book, recreated from detailed police reports and witness accounts.

Almost forgetting how to use the mouse, his nerves so rattled by what he'd read, Peter finally managed to get his finger to stay on the wheel and frantically scrolled down, where the image of Geoffrey's mysterious book appeared on the screen.

"Holy shit!"

FORTY-ONE

Snakes had never been a real problem for Parker. Even now, after the close encounter with his dead wife's dreaded tongue snake, he possessed no fear of the slithering creatures. Dreams however, were quickly climbing to the top of his phobia list, natural or black out induced. This wasn't the first time Amanda had appeared in one of his dreams. Twice, since the accident, his mind had reconstructed what he believed to be a reasonably accurate representation of the events which had left him widowed. Both occurrences had taken place in the first two weeks following his wife's death. Since then, only one dream had involved his late wife. Unfortunately, the recurrence of that dream had become an almost nightly event.

Amanda was always standing just out of arms reach as he struggled to reach her but no matter how close he got, the illusive apparition would always move farther away until eventually fading from sight, replaced by a hazy mist. He knew what the images meant. Even without a background in psychology, Parker could see the obvious meaning behind the brief visions. Denied the opportunity to say goodbye, his mind longed for the chance to bring closure to the devastating experience; closure which had been denied to him by the intoxicated Madison Karlofski and her rundown Ford Explorer.

Since his old friend 'the Captain' had assisted in the fabrication of the disturbingly realistic, slumber time visitor, Parker felt that he and Mr. Morgan should probably spend some time apart. Instead, Parker pulled an unopened bottle of Jack from the cabinet and, forgoing a glass, exited the living room into the eight foot wide, outer hall.

The house possessed limited exterior lighting, as to lessen its modern infringement on the brilliant night sky. On this night however, outdoor lighting wasn't necessary. Though not quite full, the moon's large, circular body shone down upon the earth, illuminating those portions of the forest far beyond the tree lined perimeter of the property.

Upon exiting the living room, Parker turned right, toward the West side of the house and away from the stairs that would return him to the lofted location of the fictitious, yet all too real encounter.

Normally, during times of high stress or even after the occurrence of a nightmare of less extreme intensity, Parker would sit in his big leather chair and read his current assignment or just a chapter from a long list of favorites he kept on the nearby bookshelf. He knew though, that if he sat in that chair, no amount of concentration could prevent him from succumbing to the fear of what might come up behind him. He was sure that it would be some time before he could again fully enjoy his favorite spot in the house. For now, his second favorite would have to do.

The West side of the house overlooked a serene lake at the bottom of a steep incline. The house's position at the peak of that incline allowed for an unobstructed view of the lake and the peaceful world beyond. As with the rest of Veracini Two, the house's position on the land it occupied was also unique in that twenty feet of its lake view side overhung the rocky slope, supported by numerous, reinforced concrete pillars, each dressed in a stone façade.

Even given the amazing vantage point provided by the westerly facing hall, it still managed to claim only third in Parker's list of favorite locations; its claim to second stolen by the hidden balcony beneath its floor.

The secret balcony was unlike that of its typical counterparts. There were no sliding, or French doors leading to the exterior floor space. In fact, this balcony couldn't even be seen from any part of the two story glass palace. The only access to the isolated spot, lie beneath Parker's feet, evident only by the eighth of an inch gap outlining the narrow trap door but cleverly concealed between the seams of the wooden floorboards.

Bottle of Jack in his left hand, Parker bent over, grasping the door's small, recessed handle and with little effort, lifted the hinged, horizontal doorway up and away from him before carefully descending the eight narrow steps that led to the five foot by ten foot balcony beneath Veracini Two. The balcony was supported by only the stairs and a narrow column at each of its four corners. Minimal furnishings adorned the small space; two, thickly padded, wicker chairs, each with their own miniature end table beside them. Parker took a seat in the chair to the right of the blind staircase, placing the now open bottle in his lap.

The magnificent view from the front hall was dwarfed by the balcony's unique, open air location. Fifteen feet behind him, the steep slope concluded its accent into the underside of the house. Just beneath the balcony the slope was already ten feet lower in elevation and growing increasingly steeper before gradually flattening into a heavily wooded buffer surrounding the lake.

Lacking the same passion for literature as Parker, this had been Amanda's favorite spot in the house. They'd spent countless hours in those two chairs, just gazing out onto the vast beauty of the world and many more enjoying the physical beauty of each other.

Parker shuddered, the dream's disturbingly sexual imagery still running freely through his mind. More than the endlessly uncoiling tongue, he was disturbed by the image of his wife's shredded and bloodied face, the result of the high speed vehicle and the course pavement beneath it.

*****

The uncommon heat, combined with the very thought of the long drive ahead, had induced an urgent craving for brain freeze in a very pregnant Amanda Veracini. Since the bank resided next door to the king of all convenience stores, Amanda had felt no need to return to the sweltering car just to move it thirty feet to the adjoining lot.

The sixth month chapter of Dr. Phillis's book, Phillis Knows Pregnancy, had stated:

Walking is one of the most beneficial exercises in which an expecting mother can partake.

Amanda had agreed completely. Sit-ups were defiantly out of the question at that point.

Parker too had been reading Dr. Phillis' book and much to his nature, had offered a counter opinion.

"Sex...I think sex is the most beneficial exercise you can do," He'd told Amanda upon completion of the chapter.

"If that's the most beneficial exercise, then I should be losing weight instead of gaining it."

"I guess you're not getting enough then," he'd stated with a smile while locking the bedroom door.

The horny, nineteen year old boy Amanda had fallen in love with had diminished over the years, giving way to the wiser more passionate man Parker had become. Amanda's pregnancy though, had been the surprising catalyst in allowing that repressed teenager back into their lives.

Determined to use know-it-all Phillis' "expert" advice, Amanda passed through a narrow gap in the row of hedges which divided the two businesses. Unfortunately in doing so, her left foot caught an exposed root, sending her stumbling into the convenience store's parking lot and into the path of an oncoming Explorer.

The impact of the already slow moving vehicle, though enough to knock her down, did little harm, apart from a scratch or two where her belly saving hands had struck the pavement. It was the stunned driver's reaction to the accident, that proved fatal blow.

Miss. Karlofski punched the gas, striking Amanda in the face with the front bumper and forcing her beneath the accelerating vehicle. With her figure not as dainty as it had been only six months earlier, Amanda's left leg and loose clothing managed to entwine with the car's undercarriage, dragging her through the parking lot and onto the busy street.

For three quarters of a mile, the heat of the car and the coarse asphalt joined in burning and tearing at Amanda's flesh until the jolt of a deep pothole finally shook her free and into the path of horrified motorists.

A flower delivery truck, avoiding the quickly approaching obstacle, swerved to his left, striking a Honda Civic and sending it into oncoming traffic where it and a Taurus met with an explosive storm of glass and metal.

Screeching tires and raining auto parts continued their assault on the busy roadway as Amanda's lifeless body finally come to rest in the center of the westbound lanes.

The man in the flower truck, though shaken, was the first to Amanda's side and the first to vomit at the sight of the mangled woman's, half missing face.

*****

The recalled memory of Amanda's tragic fate,

combined with the general disregard for human life displayed by Miss. Karlofski, enraged Parker.

Holding jack by the neck, he flung the nearly full bottle across the balcony. The ensuing eruption of glass and booze sparkled in the moonlight, as did the single tear slowly descending Parker's reddened face.

FORTY-TWO

Though in what he considered to be relatively good shape, Peter struggled to catch his breath as he frantically rounded the corner into the kitchen, nearly crashing into the table on which Aunt Mary had just placed the burnt remains of a fleshy object they were apparently calling chicken that night.

"Whoa there Pete!" Uncle Mike addressed the sudden arrival of his nephew with a surprised grin. "Excited about dinner are ya?"

Peter didn't answer, still trying to regain the breath that had been stolen by the menacing image on the computer and his brief sprint through the house.

"You probably should've saved your energy for the sprint to the bathroom later," Uncle Mike jokingly whispered in Peter's ear before noticing the 'I heard that scowl' on his wife's face. He lowered his head in shame and took a seat in front of the dead bird.

"Come one Peter. Take a seat. It's dinner time," Aunt Mary instructed as she retrieved a bowl of corn from the microwave.

"May I use the phone?" Peter huffed, finally managing to articulate the question that his mind had been yearning to ask since leaping from the computer chair.

"Why don't you wait until after dinner. Now it's time to eat," Aunt Mary instructed as she placed a spoon in the corn and set the bowl on the table.

"But I need to use it now. Please."

Taken aback by the urgency of their nephew's plea, both Aunt Mary and Uncle Mike just stared at Peter.

"What's for dinner mom!?" Joseph yelled as he entered the kitchen, still wearing the headphones to his iPod. "Mmm, Meatloaf."

"That's not meatloaf dill-hole. Its pot-roast," Bobby corrected, slugging his brother in the back.

"Ouch!"

"Boys, sit!" Aunt Mary ordered.

"Peter, why do you need to use the phone at this very moment?" Uncle Mike returned the focus to Peter's urgent, communication needs.

"Wow, dinner smells great Aunt Mary," Emily, as always, kissed her aunt's ass as she and their youngest cousin politely took their seats at the table.

"Common Peter. Take a seat. The phone's not going anywhere," Aunt Mary instructed, disregarding her husband's question.

"But I need to use the phone."

"Take your seat I said," Aunt Mary now ordered, obviously vexed by Peter's sudden and uncharacteristic defiance.

Uncle Mike immediately turned his attention away from the conflict and onto the food. Typical of his nature, he wasn't about challenge his wife, especially now that she'd used the 'angry voice'.

Completely ignoring his Aunt's order, Peter plucked the cordless from the wall and immediately began dialing.

"You put that phone down right now!"

Joseph and Bobby looked at one another in shock. They'd never seen their mother yell at anyone other than them, especially not their goody-two-shoes, older cousin.

Completing the number to his house, Peter held the receiver to his ear, ignoring the fact that his Aunt had just lifted herself out of her chair at the other end of the table.

Busy.

Hanging up, he dialed again.

"Peter! You put that phone down this instant or--!"

Peter just held up one finger instructing his aunt that she'd have to wait to finish her threat.

"Oh no you did not," Aunt Mary fumed.

Joseph and Bobby continued to watch the escalating conflict with mouths agape while their father, continuing the practice of self-preservation, proceeded filling his plate with the offerings before him.

Busy again.

Who's on the phone and what happened to the call waiting? Peter wondered to himself before placing the phone back on its base.

"Good, now get your butt over here and take a seat."

Peter heard his Aunt's order but, pondering how he was going to warn his father, continued to ignore her commands.

Email.

If his dad was home, he was most likely working at his computer.

Peter quickly turned and exited the kitchen with as much speed as with which he'd entered.

"Peter, get back here!"

He had to get to the computer and his dad's email as quickly as possible, even if it did mean his first ever punishment at the hands of his enraged Aunt.

He should've never left the book with him in the first place. If the article was correct and the book, in some impossible way, did house the spirit of a century old killer, he had to make sure that his dad got as far away from it as possible. He only hoped that he wasn't too late.

Darting through the doorway to the den, Peter leapt for the computer chair, rolling across the floor to the keyboard.   Quickly signing into his Gmail account he typed a brief email that would've made Mrs. Gloucester, his English teacher, cringe.

Dad. Book evil. Don't ask question. Just get rid.

Hitting send, he hoped that his father would understand the message and do as instructed.   Then he began to worry. What if his father doesn't get the message in time?

Maybe he could get his uncle to drive him home, he contemplated but quickly dismissed the idea recalling the scene in the kitchen.

Luckily, he wouldn't have to test the waters any further with his Aunt and Uncle as a return email quickly appeared on the screen.

Peter clicked.

What? Peter I told you. The book is not evil. It is just a book. Now forget about the book and go have fun.

He wasn't going to listen, Peter worried.   Maybe if he directed him to the online article he'd understand.

Peter quickly began another message.

See linked article and please, get rid of the book.

Linking the web address he clicked send and moments later was surprised to see yet another email in the received folder.

Peter, I already saw that article and I assure you, there's nothing to worry about. I promise, if anything out of the ordinary happens, I'll get rid of the book. Ok? Now please, trust me and quit worrying about the book. I'll see you in the morning. Love you.

It was possible that his dad had already seen the article.

It was fairly easy to find online and he probably should've assumed that his father would've already learned all that he needed to know about the book by now but even so, Peter couldn't help but worry. He loved his dad and, as impossible as it sounded, he didn't want anything to happen to him but he knew that he could take his father at his word and was confident that he'd get rid of the book if anything odd did occur.

Closing the email Peter let out a deep sigh of relief.

"Peter, I don't know what's gotten into you tonight but--"

"Coming Aunt Mary," Peter interrupted, swiveling in the chair before getting up and slipping past the confused woman on his way back to the kitchen.

*****

Peter, I already saw that article and I assure you, there's nothing to worry about. I promise, if anything out of the ordinary happens, I'll get rid of the book. Ok? Now please, trust me and quit worrying about the book. I'll see you in the morning. Love you.

The brief email remained on the screen as the mouse casually navigated its way over to the send button, instantly folding the message up into a tiny envelope and sending it on its way through the postal-service of the digital age.

"I can't just sit over there and pretend like nothing happened!" Rebecca suddenly burst through the office door, surprised by the empty office chair behind the desk. "James?"

Quickly scanning the room, Rebecca's anger gave way to confusion. She could have sworn that she'd heard the muffled continuation of his delusional conversation with that stupid book only minutes ago.

Now, only the book remained in the room, motionless and as silent as ever beside the keyboard.

"Where the fuck did that drunk idiot go now?" Rebecca

sighed as she exited the room, slamming the door behind her.

FORTY-THREE

On any other night, the fact that he was seeing two centerlines would've probably been enough to convince James that he shouldn't be driving but with his judgment clouded by the river of scotch coursing through his veins, the inebriated writer drove on.

Nearly an hour had passed since James's last recallable memory involving Rebecca's heated exchange with the fleeing, half naked teenager below his office window. He could remember taking great pleasure in watching the couple issue their departing insults and vaguely recalled Rebecca, shortly after, attempting to break down the office door in a fit of rage but that was it. The remainder of the nine o'clock hour was a complete blur.

Though initially unaware of his intoxicated mind's apparent desire to drive, he'd quickly come to as the Tacoma's engine sprang to life.

For the first five minutes of the law breaking journey, James hadn't even known where he intended on going but with each meandering turn, he vaguely began to recall a conversation between he and Peter's book, now resting in the passenger's seat beside him. And though unable to recall exactly what the topic of the delusional conversation had been, James was aware of one thing. Whatever unseen force had coaxed his less than capable body behind the wheel, was now guiding him ever closer to Francesco Savaree's hillside manor.

Francesco's extravagant house was widely known in the area. It had been in all the papers when the permits had been granted to create the elaborate underground dwelling. Many had predicted that the house would collapse in on itself with the first tremor to shake the hill from which it had been carved.

Since those predictions, only two minor earthquakes had affected the area, the extent of their damage consisting of only minor bumps and bruises, some damaged household items and one broken hip, belonging to an elderly woman who'd toppled from the crapper and into the bathtub where paramedics had found her six hours later.

Francesco's house had survived unscathed and with the amount of money the man had invested in creating the unique dwelling, James had no doubt that the cavernous mansion would remain a tool in Francesco's marriage shattering arsenal for quite some time.

As if the distraction of his body's impairment and his mind's inability to focus on the road ahead weren't enough to make him a mobile threat, the cell phone, nestled in the center console, suddenly sprang to life, giving the Baha Men even more undeserved play time.

"Hello," James picked up the phone.

"Where the hell are you!?" Rebecca yelled on the other end of the line.

"Oh, hey honey."

"Don't hey honey me. You know you're drunk right?"

"Of course. Never been drunker."

"Then what the fuck are you doing driving around town?"

"Just wanted to show William around this fine city of ours."

"Who the fuck is William?" Rebecca asked confused.

"You know, I introduced you two back at the house. I believe it was just before you ran off to fuck that kindergartner."

"Screw you."

"You know honey, I respect your dedication, even against such deterring odds," James took on a serious tone.

"What? What the hell are you talking about?"

"I mean, there are so many people in the world. The odds of fucking each and every one of them are...well...impossible would be my best guess but you just continue to plug along."

"You know what James, I'm glad you're out showing 'William' around town."

"There you go," James smiled.

"Maybe you two can make the trek up to the lake as well. You know, drive William by the old cabin...maybe hit the casinos. Oh, I know, maybe you could even take one of those sharp, mountain turns a bit too wide and oops."

"Now honey bunny, that's not very nice. Besides, the lake is in the complete, opposite direction. Francesco's expecting me any minute now," he lied.

"Bullshit."

"All right, you got me. He's not actually expecting to see me but I'm sure as hell expecting to see him."

"What are you talking about? What are you planning to do?"

"Oh nothing. I just thought the three of us could sit down, share a cup of coffee, you know, chit chat for a while. I've been dying to ask him how he does it."

"Does what?"

"Gets a fringed bitch like yourself so hot and bothered. You know, guy talk. So maybe the next time you and I are in bed together my dick won't get frost bite and fall off."

"The next time we're in bed together?" Rebecca laughed. "I wouldn't touch you again if my life depended on it."

"How about Francesco's life then?"

"Is that a threat? What do you really think you're gonna do? He'd crush you."

"Then I guess it's a good thing I have William here."

"What, is your imaginary friend gonna to kick his ass?" Rebecca chuckled as she found amusement in her husband's delusion.

"Oh, wait a minute honey. I think I have to go. Talk to you later sweetie."

"James wait--"

James ended the call as he looked up at the flashing red and blue lights in his rearview mirror. This new set of lights, combined with the already dominant neon, illuminating the main strip, was breathtaking. With every luminous shift in color, everything from street signs to the occasional homeless person seemed to take on a new artistic quality.

"You in the truck, pull over," a voice boomed.

James quickly searched the cab of the truck for the source of the new voice, ending on the book. "Friend of yours?"

William gave no response.

"Pull the truck over, now!" the amplified voice ordered again.

This time James complied with the unseen voice and brought the truck to a stop.

"You just stay quiet and let me handle this," James instructed the book.

A moment later a bright light appeared alongside his window. Attempting to find the correct button on the door, James began to roll down, then roll back up each of the other three windows before finding the correct one, revealing the patiently waiting officer on the other side.

"Evening officer, what seems to be the problem," he struggled to maintain his composure.

"Sir, are you aware that I've been trying to pull you over for nearly a mile now?"

"Why, no sir. I must not have seen you back there. I was on the phone with the wife. You know how that can be."

"No sir, I'm afraid I don't and the use of a cell phone while driving is illegal within the city limits."

"Is it really?" James questioned with a bit too much interest, as he rested his elbow on the door and his chin on his open palm.

"Get a hold of yourself," William spoke up.

"Shut up," James ordered the book. "Let me handle this."

"Excuse me?"

"Oh no, not you officer."

The deputy quickly scanned the interior of the truck with his flashlight but found no one else to which the drunken man could have been referring.

"Sir have you been drinking tonight?"

"Drinking? Me? Of course not. Never touch the stuff. Why would you ask such a ridiculous question?" James poorly defended himself.

"Well let's start with your parking job," the officer responded while glancing down at his feet.

James leaned over the door, looking down at the ground. Beneath the truck, lit by the officer's light, was a bed of freshly planted, fall colored plants and flowers in preparation for the Nevada Day celebration a little over a month and a half away.

"I thought they only planted those in the center divider," James pondered aloud as he scanned his surroundings.

Instead of parking along the right-hand curb, as law required, he'd somehow managed to park his truck atop the divider in the center of the city's main drag.

"Well, at least I'm straight," he joked to the less than amused lawman.

"Sir, step out of the vehicle."

"Of course officer, just after I--"

Before James could finish his sentence, a stream of vomit erupted from his mouth, covering the cab, himself and the officer's polished shoes in one-hundred-proof regurgitation.

FORTY-FOUR

"Fucking idiot," Rebecca huffed, slamming the phone down. "What the fuck does he think he's doing driving around town in his condition? He's gonna get himself killed."

Before, the thought of James's death would've been an instant reason for tears but now, not even a drop of moisture welled within Rebecca's hate filled eyes. It was truly over. They'd been fools to think that they could ride out their differences and live their own lives while sustaining a stable home for their children. And after tonight's dysfunctional drama, she was sure that they'd never be able to look at one another without issuing at least some form of hateful comment, even if in the presence of Emily and Peter.

The more Rebecca thought about it, she was glad that James had chosen to explore the town. It wasn't that she necessarily wished death upon her husband but if death were to rear its head a bit early, she didn't feel that it would necessarily be a heartbreaking event. Sure, she'd play the distraught widow for Peter and Emily's sake but deep down she knew that his passing could only be a blessing. No longer would she have to deal with his reclusive, self-obsessing bullshit. No longer would she be hindered by his continued failures in life and career. She'd finally be free to see and be with anyone she wanted, without the apparent spying of a jealous spouse.

The kids would surely be devastated but she'd be there for them. She could raise them on her own. Though, not worth much in life, James was surely worth a fortune in death. With the cabin now sold, the bank account had a bit of extra padding and with the million dollar life policies they'd both taken out only two years ago, she'd be able to hire the best therapists for her kids.

But who was she kidding? She'd never had that much luck. In a few hours, after the crazy bastard sideswiped a few cars and ran over a few cats, he'd surely come stumbling in the door. He'd probably even try climbing into bed with her, insisting that she help a man in need or even try to start the process himself, until she awoke to the boldly intrusive act already in progress. Nothing was going to kill James Madison. Even death wanted nothing to do with him.

On the other hand, could he have been serious about paying Francesco a visit? No, she thought to herself. He'd seen Francesco. The man was a beast. He was huge. There was no way that James would even consider confronting him.

He wasn't exactly thinking clearly though. Maybe he was on his way over there. What if he *did* get in? What if he *did* find Francesco? It was all but guaranteed that he wouldn't make it out of that house alive but then the police would come asking questions about why her husband had been there in the first place. They'd undoubtedly link Francesco to her through gym records. It would surely come out that the two had been having an affair. She couldn't have that.

She was a well-respected member of the community. She'd spent years taking part in the local, political scene. She'd attended numerous legislative gatherings and had once even dined with the Governor himself. She couldn't afford to let a skeleton like that escape from the closet. She had to call Francesco. She had to warn him of her husband's planned arrival. She had to make sure that he didn't call the police or do anything stupid.

Rebecca hurried to the phone and without missing a beat, began dialing. The phone rang...and rang and rang and rang. The man hated answering machines. He'd claimed that they were an, "impersonal devise, creating just another way for people to monitor and distance themselves from one another". Now she understood the true reason why a machine had no place in the man's home. An answering machine, to a man of his promiscuity, was like a ticking time-bomb, packed full of explosive evidence about his affairs, just waiting to be triggered by a snooping, sexual liaison.

Rebecca hung up the phone and immediately dialed his cell. Again the phone just rang. He'd even disabled the message service on his cell, a bit of information she hadn't been aware of. As much of a pig as he was, the man was efficient. She should have seen it earlier. No man with that body and his money would or could settle for just one woman; not when hundreds were lined up at his door for a chance to touch greatness. But, as much as she hated him for his selfish use of women, her loins continued to burn with desire. He was amazing. Far superior to anything James had ever dreamt of being in bed. The man was a god; in control of his world and skillfully able to maintain his flock with that thunderbolt between his legs.

Rebecca dialed again.

FORTY-FIVE

Whether it had been the explosive regurgitation or simply the sobering effects of his first ever arrest, James had once again, at least partially, regained his ability to decipher between reality and the fictitious fog through which he'd been wandering the last few hours.

While his judgment had somewhat improved since taking up residence in the sheriff department's basement, his motor skills hadn't yet reclaimed full control from the bottled puppeteer. A fact of which he'd been made well aware of by his many failed attempts to sit on the cell's wall mounted benches.

"What have I done?" he contemplated, giving up his quest for the elevated seat in exchange for the cool, concrete floor. He'd never even contemplated drinking and driving in the past. Hell, he was even a local member of Dad's Against Drunk Driving; at least until news of the night's little escapade reached the charter members' ears. He hated drunk drivers, not only for their irresponsibility and utter disregard for those around them but because it had been a drunk driver who'd stolen most of his family from him.

The man had been on his way home from a Super bowl

party and, thinking that he'd taken the correct onramp, had inadvertently wound up on the wrong side of interstate fifty five, meeting his mother's car head on in what the news had described as one of the most horrific accidents to ever befall the great state of Illinois. His mother's accident had spurred a spike in M.A.D.D. and D.A.D.D. memberships and had generated hundreds of thousands of dollars in donations to the two groups, as well as a fund established in his name. But no matter what action had been taken post-accident and no matter how much money had been donated, it still hadn't returned his family. His life, as he'd known it, had ended that night and from that point on he'd vowed never to be the man responsible for devastating another person's family.

The ceiling overhead began to spin as the scotch launched yet another wave of attacks on his senses. Closing his eyes, James refocused his mind, slowing the room's movements and returning the overhead structure to a standstill.

What were his children going to think when they found out what their father had done? Especially Peter, after suffering through many lectures about the dangers of alcohol and the irresponsibility of those who choose to drive while under its influence.

"Quit your moping," a voice filled the quiet space.

James turned his head, expecting to see a guard at the cell door or his attorney, whose answering service he'd left an urgent message with hours ago. Instead, resting on top of the low bench, on which he'd earlier intended to sit, was the book.

"Fuck off," James dismissed his imaginary companion, returning his attention to the ceiling overhead.

"Fuck off? Now is that any way to greet an old friend?"

"You're not an old friend, hell, you're not even real. Just a figment of my imagination, brought on by bad judgment and cheap scotch."

"If I'm not real, then why are you still talking to me?"

"Because an insanity plea may be my only hope at this point."

"Well, I regret then to inform you that, you are not crazy."

"Thanks for the vote of confidence but I really think I may be, you know, since I'm lying in a jail cell, charged with a D.U.I. and having a conversation with a figment of my imagination."

"Things could be worse."

"Really?" James turned to the book in shock. "Please, tell me, what could be any worse than this?"

"You could be in this alone."

"Great. That really helps. Hey, maybe we can be cellmates in prison, you know, we could start a gang or something...Hell's Novels."

"I can help you James."

"I think you've helped me enough. What I need right now is to get some rest so I can sober up to a point where I'm no longer seeing talking books."

"And then what? Then what will you do? You can't just go home and resume your life with your *loving* wife can you? Of course not, because she's too busy prancing around town fucking every age group but the elderly right now.

"Shut up," James quietly commanded.

"And what about your career? Didn't your publisher recently terminate you? And, seeing as you fired the only other person in the world who gave two shits about you, I don't see losing yourself in your work to be a viable option either."

"I said shut up!" James shouted.

"Quiet down in there," a guard at the end of the long hallway ordered before returning to his newspaper.

James fell silent as did William. But, unable to stop his mind's constant questioning, James quickly broke the peaceful lull.

"Who's the other?" he questioned quietly.

"Excuse me," William asked.

"You said there were only two people in this world who still cared about me. Who's the other?"

"Me, James. That is why I am here. I want to help you. I want to return your life to you. I want to bring back all which you have thrown away. With my help, you could be on top once again."

"How? Even if you were real, how could you possibly help me?" James questioned curiously as he sat up confronting the closed book with an intent stare.

"By eliminating those who stand in your way."

"Ah we're back to the psycho book routine again."

"Take a look at this, James."

"Take a look at what?" he questioned, glancing around the room until finally noticing a newspaper lying only inches from his outstretched feet. "It's the New York World Journal," James read the paper's title aloud.

"It's Sunday's Journal," William clarified.

"But today's only Friday. How...?"

James picked up the paper in awe of the impossible date.

"Wasn't something very important supposed to appear in this weekend's edition?" William hinted.

He was right. The review of *The Doorway to My Own Hell* was supposed to appear in this issue. Brandon had somehow gotten Parker Veracini, a man known in the past to make or break writer's careers, to write his latest review on the book. It had been a risky move but given the already plummeting path of his career, they'd both figured that the judgmental columnist's criticisms couldn't hurt. Maybe the man would love the book, touting its genius and in effect, spurring a renewed interest in his work.

Maybe the fact that his publisher had chosen to release him from his contract *didn't* matter. Dozens of new publishers would surely be pounding at his door with new deals. And with Brandon's now apparent, genius handling of the deal, he would be on top of the industry once again.

Excited to read what Mr. Veracini had written, James frantically tore through the pages. "Life, Sports, Politics," James called as he thumbed past each section. "Ah, Arts," he announced ripping the section from the paper and discarding the body of the publication to the floor.

Skimming through the six page sea of content, Parker's name finally appeared at the top of a long review. The picture beside the name was not an encouraging first sign. Along with his typical, scathing remarks or gleeful praise, Mr. Veracini also liked to hint at the review's subsequent tone by placing one of many emotionally descriptive self-portraits right beside the opening paragraph. For this review Parker's head was cocked slightly to one side with his eyes rolled back in their sockets. The only thing missing from the disheartening photo was a noose around his neck.

"Maybe it's a misprint," James hoped aloud as he read the first line.

'The Doorway to My Own Hell'--never have I read a book with a more appropriate title.

This wasn't good, James thought, choosing to skip the ridiculing remarks that followed and find the final review score at the end of the piece.

"One bookmarks out of five!?" James exclaimed.

"Shut the hell up in there!" the guard yelled back once again.

"That can't be right," he continued, undeterred by the officer's command as he scanned the last paragraph.

In short, do not purchase this book. Don't even borrow it from a misguided friend or from one of those now illusive palaces of culture my generation once called a library. In fact, if you are out, in search of that ever elusive masterpiece, and you happen to come upon this pile of...well...you know, stop where you are, slowly turn around and run as fast as you can in the opposite direction. The effects of this travesty aren't yet fully understood...

"Travesty?" James objected. "Who the fuck does this guy think he is?"

"I can fix it James. I can make it all better."

"What are you going to do, buy up every copy in print and burn them? Because that's about the only thing that can salvage my career at this point."

"There are other options my boy. There are other means by which to deal with this defamatory prick."

James listened carefully as the consuming blankness, which had earlier inspired his unlawful road trip, once again took control.

"Who is he to criticize your work?" William continued. "Mr. High and mighty in his lush, New York office. Mr. Knows everything about 'quality' literature. How could he possibly know anything about writing when all he does is criticize those whose work he probably finds threatening to his own?"

James nodded in deadpanned agreement.

"You James, you are the true artist here. You should be the one telling him what quality is. You should be the one with the fortune and fame. Something needs to be done James. Someone needs to set that arrogant bastard straight."

James remained silent.

"Write it my boy. Show that miserable prick what a true writer can do. Reclaim your dignity and make that rancid puke eat each and every sordid word."

The book slowly began to open, once again revealing the awaiting, pre-dipped quill.

Obediently, James's plucked the pen from the page

"Yesss," William hissed as his puppet, once again, contributed his malevolent tale.

FORTY-SIX

At what point is a person considered suicidal? Parker wondered as he stared at the Bic razor held firmly in his grasp. Did the mere consideration of such a question already qualify him for such categorization?

Though intrigued by the unusual query, Parker knew without a doubt that a continued desire for life still burned deep within him. Its evident glow had only been temporarily masked by the tragic events of recent months and with enough time, the pain of Amanda's death would surely fade, replaced by the heart-warming memories of their many years together.

At least that was what Parker hoped his future held. Days like the emotionally destructive one he'd been having were beginning to take their toll on his youthful, yet aging face.

For years he'd fielded compliments from friends, family and even the occasional stranger, who, when told his age, would often gasp at the seemingly inflated number. Bright blue eyes, dark Mediterranean skin and thick black hair had always aided in his age defying appearance but in the last month or so, it seemed that more-and-more telltale grey was starting to creep in. On top of that, pencil thin lines were beginning to appear at the corners of his eyes and mouth, adding years to his previously unblemished face.

As Parker stared at his aging reflection, the hot steam of the shower to his back, launched another attack on the oversized sheet of reflective glass, requiring him to wipe away a face sized circle in the condensation before continuing his disheartening examination.

"So, old man, just another night of you and me," Parker addressed the mimicking image.

With the way that his mind had been playing tricks on him since giving control over to the captain, he wouldn't have been the least bit surprised if the reflection before him had suddenly began talking on its own, no longer needing the guiding lips of its reality based counterpart. But as much as he fully anticipated the realization of such an illusion, the reality based portion of his brain continued to maintain control, leaving the reflective image to continue its mimicking ways.

With the dampening fog imposing its control once again, Parker turned away from the glistening mirror, discarding the question invoking razor in exchange for an electric toothbrush and tube of Colgate.

Parker flipped open the toothpaste tube but stopped short of applying the glimmering blue gel to the brush's awaiting bristles as an unfamiliar tingle drew his attention to his bare feet and the black, shag bathmat which lay beneath them.

Nothing unusual occupied the space; only the familiar mat and Jack soaked clothing piled on the floor beside him. And since the sensation had diminished with his redirected attention, Parker returned his concentration to the awaiting brush and curl of toothpaste already hanging from the threaded tip of its pliable container.

He'd never cared much for the taste of the cleansing substance. As far back as his memory served, he could remember doing everything in his power to avoid the minty gel, often brushing his teeth with only water; that was of course until his father had discover what he'd been doing and in response, had force-fed him an entire tube of Pepsodent as punishment.

From that point on he'd been a Colgate, Crest or Arm and Hammer man...anything but Pepsodent. The very sight of the brand on store shelves often caused an uncontrollable urge to gag, leading Parker to purchase sometimes a year's worth of toothpaste at a time, as to limit his needed trips to that menacing aisle.

Lightly coating only the tips of the bristles in the tormenting blue substance, he hesitantly applied the toothbrush to his teeth. But this time, it wasn't the grotesque chemical concoction which caused Parker to quickly withdraw the battery powered apparatus.

Startled by the return of the odd sensation against his feet, Parker again turned his attention toward the floor.

"What the--," he addressed the peculiar sight with a toothpaste induced mumble.

The bathmat, which had remained understandably dormant, suddenly began to take on the appearance of a mutated Chia Pet, taking advantage of the shower induced moisture in the air as it wrapped its stringy, fabric fingers between Parker's toes and around his feet.

Panicked and off balance, Parker stumbled back, striking the toilet bowl with his knee and collapsing to the damp marble floor as the tangled mass continued its enveloping journey Northward.

With each tug at the undeterred menace, Parker grew increasingly panicked, his heart pounding against his ribcage.

As the mat reached the middle of his calves the recalled images of the dream based tongue-snake suddenly returned to mind, causing Parker to wish for nothing more than to wake up on the forest floor, his legs tangled in a mass of low lying vines. But, no matter how hard he wished, reality did not falter.

With the first of its thousands of fibers reaching his left

kneecap, the mat, without cause, stopped.

An abrupt squeak stole Parker's attention away from the suddenly dormant knot as the sound of the shower's cascading water fell instantly silent, giving way to a broken and unsteady pattern of strained breathing.

Already troubled enough by the unexplainable attack launched by the floor bound accessory, Parker wasn't about to stick around to find out who or what was the cause of such an erratic respiratory pattern.

Determined to be anywhere but where he lay, Parker, hindered by his clinging captor, began sliding himself across the bathroom floor in search of the temporary freedom offered by the nearby doorway. But, as he began his awkward journey and without warning, the frosted glass door, concealing the uninvited bather, swung violently outward, striking the adjacent wall and showering the room in tiny shards of frosted debris.

Parker fell to his back, shielding his eyes from the sparkling explosion. Though his new position limited his line of sight toward the recessed shower, it didn't inhibit his view of the strip of silky white fabric peeking around the corner, dancing in the impossible breeze being generated from within the damp, enclosed space.

He knew that fabric. He'd paid a hefty sum having it transformed into a sexy, yet elegant dress. It had been a dress intended for a formal engagement and had been custom tailored to flow from the stunning body of the beautiful angel who'd graced his life for the past twenty years.

The last time Parker had seen the chic dress he'd watched as it and its angel were slowly lowered into the ground, coming to rest six feet beneath the forest floor.

Consumed by his memories, Parker remained frozen, unable to flee from the impossible reality unfolding behind the shower's concealing wall.

The heavy breathing fell silent and the gusty wind which had lifted the flowing fabric into view, slowly retreated, withdrawing the dress with it.

Is it gone? Parker wondered, propping himself up on his left elbow for a better view.

Still unable to see clearly, he slid himself farther to his left, taking the corner of the impeding wall out of focus and revealing the now empty shower.

Panicked by the unseen visitor's sudden absence, Parker quickly scanned his surroundings but found nothing. He didn't have an explanation for what was happening and he wasn't sure that he wanted one. Nothing his mind could come up with could comfort his frantically racing heart. No logical reasoning could be concocted to justify such a peculiar chain of events. He'd hoped for this encounter, like earlier, to all be some sort of twisted dream but given his ongoing presence in this perverse reality, all he could hope for now was a chance to free himself from the tangled mesh clinging to his feet and get as far away from Veracini Two as possible.

Grabbing hold of the knotted, black fabric, he began tugging at his captor, jerking his legs from side to side but continued to make no progress with the clinging mat. The harder he pulled on the stubborn accessory, it seemed the tighter its grip became, until both of his feet began to grow numb from their lack of oxygen enriched blood.

Frustrated by what seemed to be a losing battle, Parker began violently tearing at the mat, finally ripping a small portions of its extended fingers away from his legs but with each woven digit he managed to tear free, two more took it place.

He wasn't going to get free like this. He needed a knife, which meant traversing the steep staircase, down to the first floor kitchen. Impossible? No. But, aware of the spreading numbness, consuming his lower appendages, he knew there was no time to waste. He had to get free quickly, before the mat decided to spread again, subjecting more of his body to the limb deadening sensation.

Propping himself up on two hands, Parker prepared to

scoot himself backwards, through the doorway and into the upstairs loft but instantly ceased all preparations as a single bead of water fell from overhead, striking the top of his firmly planted right hand.

He stared at the glistening spec for a moment, watching as it slowly traversed the veiny ridges along the back of his hand before maneuvering between his knuckles and disappearing between two outstretched fingers.

Lifting his gaze, Parker hoped to encounter a small patch of moisture clinging to the room's lofty ceiling but instead came face to face with the bloody vision of his dress wearing angel.

Under a vale of silence, Amanda had somehow managed to position herself only inches from his back, leaning over him with what appeared to be a twisted smile, though he couldn't be too sure, given that half of the dead woman's lower lip had been torn completely off in the accident. The remainder of the corpse's face looked as though it had been repeatedly scraped across a cheese grater, its dangling strips of moist flesh swaying from side to side as they hung low over Parker's head.

Startled by the Amanda-thing's sudden presence, Parker didn't know what to do. Running was definitely out of the question and given that his body seemed to be ignoring every command his brain issued, it seemed that remaining frozen in shock was his only option.

Even if his body *had* broken free of its icy trance, he probably wouldn't have had time to react anyway as Amanda abruptly swung her arm toward him, shoving three of her bony fingers deep into his throat. Using his upper pallet as a handle, she dragged her husband the remaining five feet toward the bathroom door before heaving him into the upstairs loft.

Sliding across the hardwood floor, Parker suddenly felt a sharp pain in his left shoulder as he struck the tall podium displaying the ornate statue of the twisted lovers. The sculpture sprang to life. It's erotic couple swaying and tilting in a seductive dance atop the stone pillar.

Anticipating the newly animated couple's immanent plummet, Parker quickly assumed the fetal position, throwing his arms over his head in an attempt to avoid the skull crushing blow of the falling lovers. But, when a few second had passed and the excruciating trauma of the plummeting stone didn't come, he returned his arms to his chest and glancing up, watched as the couple somehow danced their way to a standstill, maintaining their balance even though three inches of their footing hung ominously over the chiseled ledge.

"Where are you going sweetheart?" a gurgling voice called out.

Parker turned his attention away from the statue above, to the Amanda-thing, now standing in the bedroom doorway. He'd once enjoyed the sight of his beautiful wife standing in that very place as she seductively enticed him to enter. This time there was nothing she could've said or done to reverse his current direction.

Finding his body now more willing to cooperate, he followed the life preserving commands of his mind as he carefully slid himself away from the pedestal and toward the narrow walkway to his back.

Amanda continued her advance, slowly and awkwardly, like every zombie in every Hollywood movie ever made, as if there were some sort of zombie code adhered to by the living dead, which dictated their appearance and actions.

As Parker reached the narrow walkway that would lead him to the site of the now prophetic dream, Amanda too bumped the pedestal. The couple resumed their dance, this time pirouetting from the edge. Somersaulting toward the floor, the statue snagged the dead woman's dress, tearing the loose, wet fabric from her body and leaving her in nothing but the conservative panties in which she'd been buried.

With the sudden removal of the dress, even more grotesque wounds became evident.

Parker again froze.

He hadn't noticed it in the bathroom, which wasn't all that surprising given that his vision had been all but consumed by the blue grey skin of the Amanda-things tugging forearm. But now, observing from a much farther vantage point, it was all to clear. The nearly third trimester child, once growing within the woman's lower abdomen, was gone; missing from that dormant, gestational womb and leaving behind an empty void of guts and gore which slowly ran over the fleshy ledge outlined by the blood stained panties.

Though mystified by this sudden, disturbing discovery, the sight of Parker's missing son only temporarily slowed his retreat.

As the woman stepped onto the walkway, only ten feet from where he lay, Parker continued his hurried retreat, again bumping into the loft's limited décor. This time his beloved chair hindered his escape, though threatened no direct physical harm, as had the now shattered couple.

Maneuvering around the chair, Parker continued in reverse until he found himself backed up against the large glass wall between he and the lake facing, outer hall.

A glimmer of reflected light suddenly drew the trapped man's attention away from the advancing abomination. The silver finish of his most recent addition to the cabinet of weaponry gleamed under the influence of its florescent lighting as if to say, "Parker, let me help you".

Parker started toward the beckoning weapon but as he did, the Amanda-thing, disregarding all zombie code, bounded toward him with an eerily vicious cry.

Never having a chance at the cabinet, all Parker could do was close his eyes and cower as he felt his body lifted into the air by the remarkably powerful corpse.

The Amanda-thing's left hand clung tightly around his neck, restricting his airway as she drew his face in close and like a dog, checking for a scent, began sniffing at his left ear, slowly making her way down his neck to the base of his shoulder. As if jealously smelling the life within him, the decaying creature began to hiss and thrust Parker away, still grasping his now reddened neck.

Restricted mobility and a dwindling supply of oxygen began to limit Parker's senses, though not enough to dull the spine chilling screech that suddenly erupted from the Amanda-thing's mouth.

With her free hand, Amanda violently snatched her husband's testicles, squeezing them between her skeletal digits. The pain was excruciating. If he'd had the ability, Parker would've dropped to the floor and remained there for weeks but, given that he was at the mercy of the creature's suspending grasp, his body instead began teetering on the verge of blackout.

The Amanda-thing continued its violent, physical examination of her lightly clothed victims, slowly twisting them from side to side.

Parker moaned, causing the resurrected woman to tilt her head, as if curiously analyzing the resulting pain inflicted by her exploration.

The numbing results of shock began to envelope Parker's body but not before the piercing pain of torn flesh replaced his guttural cramping.

Releasing yet another shrill squeal, the Amanda-thing tore her husband's testicles from his body, leaving his remaining skin and intact member to hang exposed without the dignity of clothing.

Drawing Parker close once again, Amanda shifted her emaciated body and heaved her husband through the tall glass wall, sending him plummeting fifteen feet to the hardwood floor of the hallway below.

FORTY-SEVEN

Turning onto High View Terrace, Rebecca wondered what Francesco's reaction would be to her unannounced arrival at his gate, especially after the incident in the restaurant earlier that evening. For nearly three hours she'd attempted to get him on the phone but as midnight came and went, she'd begun to grow concerned.

Francesco's life was the most structured she'd ever seen. Each day his alarm clock went off at precisely five-ten, a number he was very fond off since he claimed to hold a record with the International Weightlifting Federation by hoisting exactly that figure onto his massive shoulders. He had the trophy to prove it in his gym but she didn't need any cheap, gold statue to back his claim. Just one look at the guy was all the proof needed.

Francesco never deviated from the schedule. He brushed his teeth at five fifteen, sat down with the paper and a protein shake at five twenty, and was always in the gym at precisely six o'clock for a six thirty opening.

His evenings, though varied by social engagements, also contained the same regimented structure. The man never ate dinner after six o'clock, citing the body's ability to better digest a meal early in the evening when it was still active and not winding down for its required seven hour sleep, which began promptly at ten-ten every night, no matter what social or sexual encounter presented itself.

At first Rebecca had found such a scheduled lifestyle strange and a bit sad. He was a grown man, living his life as if he were still a child under the restrictive rules of drill-sergeant parents but over time she'd gotten used to the man's regimented existence and eventually had even come to understand and respect it. When you've dedicated your entire life to your career as Francesco had and your career is based solely on how you look, it's important that you maintain your physique to the best of your ability, fending off the withering effects of time.

Unsure whether Francesco had just been avoiding her call or if James had actually been crazy enough to show up at the trainer's house, Rebecca stopped her car at the front gate.

"That's ridiculous," she spoke aloud at the thought of James enacting revenge on the giant man. Francesco had to be avoiding her calls she thought as she lowered the driver's side window.

In conjunction with an obviously brilliant and original design, the multimillion dollar homestead had been equipped with the latest in home monitoring and surveillance technology. Hundreds of cameras covered every square inch of the property. Most remained hidden; concealed within unimposing objects, such as artificial tree knots, realistic enough to fool even the best dendrologists.

Though much of the security system remained a guarded secret, there was nothing secretive about the ominous set of cameras guarding the front gate. Two, large, industrial cameras stood on top of the wall, one to either side of the decorative, wrought-iron gates with a third, smaller camera built into the call box just beside the main entrance. She was sure that she was being monitored by all three cameras as well as any other unknown electronic devises Francesco had chosen to keep secret from her.

She didn't need to press a button or honk the horn to make her presence known. The driveway, on which she'd parked, contained dozens of weight sensors which would alert the mansion's inhabitant to any activity taking place outside his gate. From the moment that the Cadillac's first tire had left the public roadway, Francesco had been alerted and, by now, was most likely staring at her image on one of a dozen monitors, contemplating whether or not to let her in.

At least a minute passed and the gates remained closed. Knowing that he hated to be bothered by the intrusive intercom but determined to see him and apologize for the scene earlier that evening, she pressed the red button on the box just beyond her window.

"Francesco, it's me. Let me in. I want to talk," she spoke into the camera, then released the button.

No response.

"Listen I just need to talk to you. I'm sorry about the restaurant. I over reacted."

Still no answer.

"I mean, I shouldn't have expected you to dedicate your entire existence to me and me alone, hell I'm the one still married here. I know it was unfair and I just want you to know that I'm ok not being the only one right now. I just hope that over time, when you're ready, you'll want to settle down and maybe then we could start a life together."

The speaker remained silent. If he was watching, she knew that he could hear her. Why wasn't he answering? She'd just giving him permission to sleep around, as long as he continued to allowing her into his life and his bed. Isn't that a guy's ultimate dream, she thought to herself.

"Damn it Francesco, I know you can hear me," she pressed the button again, instantly wishing she'd controlled her anger before speaking. She wanted to get into the house, not give him reason to call for the police to come drag her away.

Another minute of unanswered silence told her all she needed to know. Apparently she'd been erased from the rotation. Her little outburst that evening had been enough to change his feelings. He'd moved on. But she wasn't about to be shoved aside without at least one last confrontation. He was going to have to make his final decision and tell her to her face.

She was sexy damn it. Though much older than the bimbos he was probably used to bedding, she knew that she had one thing on her side...experience. She could do things in bed that those younger, less experienced sluts had never even dreamt of doing and when she met him face to face and reminded him of those sexual qualifications, she was sure that her placement in the rotation would be instantly restored. In fact, she would most likely wind up spending the night, performing such acts even though the timing went completely against the man's strict schedule.

Determined to get inside, Rebecca backed the car away from the gate and pulled alongside the curb of the tight cul-de-sac. She had to get inside but, staring at the ominous wall, wondered how.

FORTY-EIGHT

Though happy to have survived what had probably been the worst looking swan dive in history, he was even more thrilled that the plummet had been made while already unconscious. Whether he'd been fully awake or not, his last horrific memory was that of the Amanda-thing's bony fingers wrapped firmly around his neck. He had no idea what had transpired after that. He didn't want to know. Staring up at the shattered remains of the inner cube wall above, the only thing Parker cared about now was that his resurrected spouse was gone.

Attempting to prop himself up and scan his surroundings, Parker could feel the tiny bits of broken glass beneath him, cutting and slicing at his skin. It was a feeling that, any other time, would have probably drawn his full attention but this time, all he could think about was the searing pain suddenly arising from his lower half.

Overwhelmed by pain, Parker fell back to the floor, lodging more glass into his already bloodied skin. But he didn't care. The piercing agony pulsing in his groin was unlike anything he'd ever experienced before. Unable to recall what had happened to cause such discomfort, Parker quickly began searching the area with his hands while keeping his eyes closed and jaw clenched as every movement made the burning sensation doubly worse.

Fearing the worst he was pleased to find his manhood still in tack. It felt a bit wet, likely from blood but it was there nonetheless. But as he continued only a couple of inches further south, his fingers unexpectedly slid into the bloody remains of an injury that no man should ever sustain.

The pain instantly tripled. Panic over his missing anatomy overruling the fire emanating from that region, Parker frantically began exploring the damage, hoping that maybe the mental map of his body was wrong and that his hands were mistakenly exploring an open wound on his thigh or even his lower abdomen instead.

Still unable to locate the other half of his pride and undeterred by the pain, Parker shot up, visually confirming what his fingers had already told him. They were gone. Instantly he cupped both of his hands over the area, wanting to scream but somehow managing to hold it in as the vocal reaction to his wounds instead found escape in a river of free flowing tears.

He didn't know what to do. He didn't know how he was going to get away. Hell, he didn't even know if the hell-spawn that had done this to him was still in the house. What he *did* know though, was that he had to get as far away from Veracini Two as possible. His life, along with the remainder of his pride, depended on it.

Looking behind him, the silver Mercedes seemed to scream "this way", but the keys for the car were still in his pants and those were in a pile on the bathroom floor. Not only was he dead set against ever returning to the rebirthing room of the demonic corpse, he was also sure that, in his current pain besieged state, he wouldn't even make it half way up the stairs before blacking out once again and tumbling back toward the hall below...probably breaking his neck in the process this time. No, the car could not save him.

319

Frantically searching for another answer to his dilemma the wet slap of a falling object against the hallway floor pulled his attention to two small orbs coming to a rest only ten feet in front of him. Having not been permitted to make the initial leap with their owner, Parker's boys had finally taken the plunge, striking the glass littered floor with a form flattening splat.

Terror again overwhelming every emotion in his pain riddled body, Parker slowly turned his gaze skyward, spotting the Amanda-thing standing in the empty frame of the shattered loft window.

Panicked by the visual confirmation of his ongoing nightmare, Parker quickly scooted himself toward his mangled jewels. With little interest in the pancaked twins however, Parker instead reached for the nearby handle of the trap door and with one quick heave, hoisted the door out of its horizontal frame and immediately began lowering himself through the narrow opening to the concealed balcony below.

His legs still impeded by the persistently clinging bathmat, Parker attempted to acquire adequate footing on the undersized treads of the ladder-like-staircase but just as before, the impeding presence of the tangled web of cotton fibers proved too much of an obstacle, causing him to slip through the opening, his back and head striking every step of the painful fall.

With nothing to grab onto, to slow his rapid decent, Parker's feet struck the balcony floor with a loud snap, shoving his right tibia through his skin, the mat and into the open air.

With no ability to compensate for his awkward and painful landing, Parker stumbled forward, striking the balcony railing and somersaulting over the edge to the jagged slope below.

During his head over heels tumble down the steep incline, Parker was surprised to find his mind focused more on his inner thoughts than the brutal pain of the jagged stones as they tore at his flesh and took turns snapping his ribs. At one point during the what seemed an endless tumble, he even found himself counting the rotations as he cart-wheeled toward the lake below.

As the slope gradually leveled out, Parker tumbled past the first of the tall trees standing guard over the dark waters of Silver Lake but came to a bone shattering stop as he struck a three foot wide oak only twenty feet from the water's edge.

With both of his arms and legs broken, along with countless other internal and external wounds, Parker remained motionless at the massive tree's base, listening to the nighttime insects recite his requiem.

Surprisingly though, at a time when death should have been a more than welcome companion, Parker found himself already attempting to work out his next move in a desperate attempt to cling to life. He knew it was a losing battle, and still, the drive to survive remained. For the first time in three months, he felt a purpose in life. He understood the weakness of self-pity and was ready to continue the life he'd abandoned. He had been so busy sulking over what he'd lost that he'd lost sight of the things he still had. If he did get out of this situation alive, he was going to make a promise to himself. No longer would he view the world in such a negative light. No longer would he shut out those who still loved him and never again would he be so arrogant as to insist on building a house so close to such a steep cliff.

A limb snapped in a nearby tree. Parker shifted his eyes from side to side, searching for the source of the noise. He half expected to see the naked woman crouched on one of the massive limbs above. Instead, his gaze fell upon a set of small white lights, high up in the foliage of a tree just ten feet away. The lights remained motionless for a moment and then blinking, quickly darted from tree to tree, stopping again just fifteen feet to his left before again continuing its erratic acrobatics from branch to branch.

Parker followed the lights as much as his limited movement would allow and as he watched, the chilling eyes began taking on a more reflective, cat like nature.

The small, woodland spy returned to the forefront of his thoughts. The memory of the dreamt eyes both soothed and frightened Parker. He hoped he was watching the acrobatic stunts of an overactive feline, though his instincts told him otherwise. Nothing about the night thus far had been normal or as easily explainable as a wild cat and he knew better than to think that anything had changed.

The eyes darted to the tree against which he lay. Parker tilted his head back, straining for a view of the mysterious creature overhead. As he did a sharp pain ran the length of his spine but, given the excessive pain already present throughout his body, he found this additional discomfort easily tolerable.

As he continued to watch the single pair of eyes, he realized that they were growing larger, not because the creature possessing them was growing in size but because whatever it was, it had already begun a slow decent toward him.

The shadows of the forest continued to conceal the identity of the mysterious visitor until a single beam of light, managing to penetrate the thick canopy overhead, suddenly illuminated the creature in an eerie glow of moonlit haze.

Terror, unlike any he had experienced to that point, overwhelmed the remainder of Parker's fragile mind. The catlike eyes did not belong to a wild animal of any breed or species known to man. Instead, clinging to the bark with all four limbs, drool glistening on the tips of its snarling, pointed teeth, was his six month old, unborn son.

Parker closed his eyes and wept as the beast child released a bone chilling screech before plummeting toward its defenseless father below.

FORTY-NINE

"Now isn't that a pathetic sight," Brandon announced his presence as he rounded the corner to find James sprawled out across the cell bench.

"Hey buddy, I think someone's here to see you," an unfamiliar voice aided in awakening James.

James opened his eyes to the sight of a bearded, grizzly man sitting on top of the bench opposite him. He jumped to his feet, surprised by the unexpected cellmate.

"Who are you?"

"Meathead," the man extended his hand.

"Meathead?"

"Yeah, nice to meet you."

James ignored the man's offered hand.

"You might want to shake his hand James. Just in case I decide to not post your bail," Brandon reestablished his unnoticed presence.

James turned, surprised to see his ex-agent standing beside an officer who looked no older than the kid he'd chased out of his house earlier that evening.

"How did...?"

"You got two minutes," the child in uniform established the time limit before returning to his post.

"Your attorney told his office to call me. Apparently I'm not the only one that you've pissed off lately. They said something about unpaid fees. I don't know, nor do I care."

"But how did you get here so fast? I thought you were in Frisco?" James joined Brandon at the bars, leaving Meathead and his massive paw un-greeted.

"I was but I thought that I might be able to talk some sense into you. My plane got in a few hours ago. I was going to come to your house tomorrow but...", gesturing at James's current predicament.

"Yeah, I don't think I'd have been there," James sheepishly grinned.

"What the hell were you thinking?" Brandon sternly questioned.

"You know what? I don't know what I've been thinking. I've had so much to drink tonight that I think I've even been hallucinating a bit."

Just then James remembered the book.

"Hallucinating about what?"

James quickly turned back to the bench. The book and newspaper were gone. He quickly scanned the surrounding floor and then the bench on which Meathead was sitting. He tossed James a playful waive.

"What are you looking for," Brandon questioned.

"Nothing," James spoke, knowing how crazy his explanation would sound if he gave voice to the words in his head. "You're getting me out of here, right?"

"I don't know. I wouldn't want to spoil Meathead's fun."

Meathead just grinned and bowed his head in a show of bashful innocence.

"Why should I bail you out anyway?"

"Because I'm such a likable guy," James joked.

"I don't think this is the time for jokes, James. You've been charged with a D.U.I. Granted, this is your first...this is your first, right?"

James nodded.

"Even so, you're still in a world of shit here, James. You could do some time. It's unlikely but it's still a remote possibility, not to mention that they've already suspended your license and impounded your truck."

"I know. I...I don't know what--"

"I need to hear you say it," Brandon cut in.

"Say what?"

"I think you know."

"I'm sorry?" James guessed.

"And..."

"And...I shouldn't have treated you the way that I did."

"And..."

"And you're not fired."

"Well, we'll discuss that another time but I want to hear you say it first."

James thought for a moment before issuing the statement he was sure his old friend was waiting to hear. "I'm an asshole and a self-centered prick who doesn't deserve a friend like you."

"Close enough," Brandon smiled. "Officer."

A wave of relief washed over James. So far this had been the worst night of his life and he wanted nothing more than to go home and sleep the remainder of it away, without the eerily watchful gaze of King-Kong beside him.

"Yes," the guard spoke as he retook his position beside Brandon.

"I would like to post this man's bail."

"Hey, what about me?" Meathead growled his disappointment.

"What did he do?"

"I believe he was found on his neighbor's ranch with one of the sheep," the guard answered disgustedly.

All three looked at Meathead. Meathead just returned their judgmental stares with an embarrassed grin.

"No, this one will do," Brandon pointed at James. "Sorry Meat."

Meathead just shrugged his shoulders as the guard opened the cell door and let James out.

"Thanks man," James hugged Brandon.

"That's enough," Brandon patted James on the back before breaking the embrace. "I'm supposed to be mad at you, not turned on by you right now."

Any other time, such a statement would've bothered James but since the man had just prevented him from becoming molested livestock, he didn't care what Brandon said.

"This way," the guard ordered, trying to sound as authoritative as his boyish youth would allow.

Followed closely by the guard, James began his journey toward renewed freedom as Brandon took one last look at Meathead who just returned his intrigued gaze with an air-born kiss. Brandon just raised an eyebrow and shook his head as he followed the two departing men.

FIFTY

After nearly fifteen minutes of pacing back and forth along the wall lined perimeter of Francesco's property, Rebecca had decided that there was no way she was getting into the fortified domicile without an invitation. True to his perfectionist nature, Francesco had removed every boulder and tree within ten feet of the wall, eliminating nature's helping hand in her unauthorized entry.

Defeated, Rebecca had returned to her parked car and spent the next ten minutes just staring at the locked gate and towering wall.

"There must be a way in", she spoke aloud to herself.

Then, as if triggered by the statement, a thought popped into her head, followed by a smile.

Turning the key to the ignition, she placed the car in drive and slowly inched toward the wall, gently driving the Cadillac up over the curb to within inches of the impeding barrier. She placed the car in park and, grinning again, stepped out of the vehicle, removed her shoes and climbed onto the car's hood.

With the additional height provided by the sixty-thousand dollar ladder, Rebecca was able to pull herself up and over the previously thought to be un-scalable obstacle.

"Shit!" she exclaimed as she slid down the other side, scraping her elbow during the decent.

It was worth it though. During her contemplative walk along the property wall, she'd thought hard about how she would convince Francesco to even consider giving her a second chance. She couldn't just walk right up to the front door and ring the bell. He was most likely asleep or already intent on not letting her in, since he hadn't answered her calls, not to mention she'd just violated his trust by jumping a wall which had obviously been designed to prohibit such activity from occurring. No, she couldn't approach this situation in such a direct manor.

The way she saw it, there was really only one good reason why the man should even consider taking her back. Francesco was a perfect specimen. He could have any woman he wanted but she knew that she'd satisfied him in ways no other woman ever could. She was sure that there was a special weakness in his loins for her company. All she had to do was exploit that weakness and she'd be back in play once again.

With the front door off limits, she began to climb the steep, rocky slope of the hill, turned house. Though the mountainous terrain was nowhere near extreme enough to require specialized climbing equipment, Rebecca did wish that she'd at least worn sneakers instead of the heels she currently relied on to protect her delicate feet.

As she pulled herself up, onto a large, granite outcropping, the top of the third floor bedroom came into view. That was her goal. She was sure all doors to the upper level were closed and locked but the covered lanai had only been constructed with three encompassing walls. The forth had been left open to the grand view of the majestic sierra's jutting up from the West in their timeless quest to reach the heavens. All she had to do was slip into the enormous enclosure, undress and make herself at home within the warm waters of the extravagant pool. When Francesco awoke to the calling splashes of a naked vixen, she was sure that he'd forget all about his strict sleep schedule and her earlier, embarrassing behavior and instantly take to the water to accept her apology.

She couldn't wait to watch as the man tossed back the covers, revealing nature's eighth wonder as he strutted toward her, his body illuminated by the bright moonlight pouring through the bedroom's glass walls.

The pool had been the first place in the house in which they'd made love. It had also been the best. She was going to remind him of that and remind him that, without her, he could never expect anything better than mediocre.

Sliding down the side of the large granite rock she sped up her assent toward the house. She couldn't wait to surprise him. She couldn't wait to remind him of what he'd almost thrown away. She couldn't wait to--

Rounding the last of the large outcroppings, the third floor bedroom came into clear view. Rebecca froze in her tracks, staring at the glass walls. Usually spotless, free of all streaks and imperfections, as Francesco demanded from his help, many of the large panes currently displayed long trails of splattered residue.

Rebecca approached the wall slowly, attempting to see inside but having difficulty as the closer she got, the more obvious the obstructing substance became.

"What the hell?" she spoke softly as she stepped up onto the one foot ledge surrounding the top floor and ran her hand over the window. Whatever the substance was it was on the inside of the glass. Moving to her right, the moonlight shone through the glass from the adjoining wall, illuminating the dark fluid and revealing its crimson quality.

Subconsciously she knew what it was but it wasn't until she spotted the room's lone inhabitant that her mind became fully aware of the scene she'd stumbled upon.

At the center of the room stood the massive four poster bed, to which she'd been bound on more than one occasion. Only now, the white, down bedding, in which she and her lover had so frequently become entangled, was stained in the same deep red that had been used to redecorate the walls. Even more troubling than the dirtied linens though, was the source of their grotesque pigmentation.

"Jesus Chr--," Rebecca's shock was cut short by a sudden urge to vomit.

Stuck upon one of the tall, spiraling posters, was the body of a naked girl but it wasn't the fact that the girl looked like a skewered piece of meat, ready for a summer barbecue that sent Rebecca's stomach churning. As if aroused by his sick act of mutilation, whoever had done this heinous act had sat the girl atop the tall wooden pole and, with a disturbing interest in phallic symbolism, had slid the body down the widening post until its pointed tip had pierced her skull.

Rebecca turned away in disgust.

Who the hell would do such a thing? she thought to herself and then realized that she hadn't seen Francesco in the room. Only he would be strong enough to lift a girl into such a position. No, she thought. He was as gentle as they come. There's no way he could've done this. Then, a peculiar sight caught her eye.

Back, toward the tall outcropping, to the right of which she'd just passed, appeared to be someone standing motionless, gazing up at the moon overhead.

"Francesco?" Rebecca called out quietly, sure he hadn't heard her and unsure now whether she really wanted him to.

Avoiding another look at the violated girl, Rebecca stepped down from the ledge and slowly moved toward the moonlit figure. As she drew closer, careful not to make a sound, she could make out the naked man's large upper torso and huge biceps, raised to his sides as if flexing his might to the sleeping city below.

It had to be Francesco. She was sure of it. But what was he doing and why was he naked? she wondered.

Something inside told her to run; run and never look back. Maybe he wouldn't see her. Maybe he wouldn't care that she'd discovered the brutal scene within his bedroom. Curiosity overruling logic however, she inched closer.

"Francesco?" she called out again.

He remained motionless, frozen in his pose of dominating might.

"What are you doing? What happened?" she questioned as she drew to within only fifteen feet of the shadowy figure, the details of his body obscured by the moon's backlighting presence.

As she approached, she noticed something odd about his stance. As if unable to maintain his balance on top of the large rock himself, it appeared that he'd wedged a portion of a broken tree branch between his lower back and the rock beneath his feet. Even more peculiar, were the two sticks positioned between his waist and raised arms, seemingly holding them in their, now apparent, limp, flexing posture.

"Francesco," Rebecca announced her presence one last time as she rounded the large boulder and gasped at the moonlit corpse standing before her. Francesco's upper torso had been shredded by what appeared to be hundreds of claw marks, while his lower abdomen struggled to contain the remainder of the man's intestines, which oozed over the rock's edge, forming a shimmering, tangled pile in the dirt beside her feet.

Though the sight of such brutal savagery was enough to renew her stomach's previous urge to purge itself of any and all contents, Rebecca fought to maintain control but finally lost the battle as she noticed Francesco's severed manhood shoved deep inside his mouth. One of his testicles hung exposed from its sack, slowly rolling back and forth across his chin under the manipulating influence of the night's gentle breeze.

FIFTY-ONE

"So you're gonna be all right?" Brandon questioned James through the lowered, passenger side window of his Lexus.

"Yeah, I think so. I just need some sleep to forget about this whole night."

"Well, don't forget too much. You still have to go before the judge," Brandon reminded. "After that we'll figure out how to handle this situation."

"Does that mean you're my agent again?"

"No. It means I'm your friend. We'll discuss the agent thing after your hearing. In the meantime get some rest and I'll try to convince your attorney that you're really not such a bad guy, even if it means settling your bill."

"I don't want you to spend any more money on me."

"Oh don't worry, I'll get it all back through increased representation fees and a newly instated problem client surcharge," Brandon joked with a smile.

"Fair enough."

"Take it easy James and get some rest, you look like shit." And with that Brandon drove off.

God I'm a prick, James recalled the way that he'd treated Brandon the other morning. Brandon was one of the only people left in the world not looking to destroy his career or life. He'd always been a good friend and continued to be to this very day.

Turning toward the house James had never been so glad to be home. All he could think about was going upstairs and crashing on the couch in his office. And though he was well aware of the alcohol and jail cell stench permeating his clothing and breath, a shower now would mean less time for sleep and at this point, sleep was the only thing that mattered.

Extracting keys from his pocket James unlocked the deadbolt to the front door and entered the house. All the lights were off, leading him to assume that Rebecca had long since gone to bed and, remaining true to character, could have cared less if her husband stumbled through the foyer or tripped over one of the kids discarded toys due to the pitch black atmosphere looming throughout the home. Finding the switch, James illuminated the entry, spoiling Rebecca's probable hopes.

She hadn't been his first choice of people to call for bail. In fact, she hadn't even made it into the top five. He knew how that conversation would've gone.

"You're where?" she would've crowed just before admonishing him with, "Well it serves you right you drunk piece of shit."

He didn't crave anymore abuse. He'd dealt himself enough already, so he'd called his lawyer instead, forgetting about the unpaid balance from his failed lawsuit against the tabloids who'd help initiate the rapid deterioration of his career.

Making his way up the stairs, James did his best to make his footsteps light, as not to disturb the witch sleeping only a couple doors down. Halfway up the wooden steps, he even made it a point to remove his shoes and climbed the rest of the way in just his socks. The last thing he needed was to wake Rebecca and get her going again on what a waste of life he was and the other ten million insults she could surely think up if given the opportunity.

Reaching the upper landing, James turned toward the sanctuary of his office but out of the corner of his eye saw something that momentarily distracted him from his mission for sleep. Across the hall, where the wife from hell should've been sleeping, stood a wide open bedroom door.

She never sleeps with the door open, he thought to himself.

Approaching the door he peeked inside to find an empty bed.

"Rebecca?"

The adjoining master bath and closet also stood empty.

"Rebecca, are you home?" he called out, again received no response. "God, who is she out screwing now?" he dismissed his wife's absence as he crossed the hall and locked himself behind the isolating walls of his favorite room in the house.

Looking at his desk, he was glad to see that the book Peter had asked him to look at was no longer there. He thought he'd remembered bringing it with him for his little joy ride but with blackness where recent memories should have been, he couldn't be sure.

The cops must still have it, he thought as he unbuttoned his shirt. For all he cared they could keep it. He never wanted to see the strange book again. Not that his lack of self-control could be blamed on the inanimate object but just the fact that he'd spent half the night talking to the peculiar piece of literature gave him the creeps. Never before had he lost control of himself so much as to hold a conversation with a person who wasn't really there, let alone a person whose spirit resided in a century old novel. As far as he was concerned, all books were off limits until this whole mess was behind him.

Removing his shirt James tossed the foul smelling garment over his writing chair and pick up the television remote from his desk.

Maybe he'd made the news.

With a static click, the flatscreen on the dresser came to life.

"...The driver apparently lost control when the bus was hit by a strong crosswind while making its way along Interstate three-ninety-five through Washoe Valley. None of the passengers were seriously hurt in the accident and the driver sustained only minor injuries," the anchorman read the teleprompter as if this bit of news rivaled that of the ten car pileup, which had claimed the lives of six people along the same stretch of road only a month earlier.

James hated the news, they were always trying to over sensationalize everything. He understood why. Each network wanted to boast that their newscast was the best and to be the best they had to have the ratings to back it. Unfortunately the public cares very little about the good in the world and only wants to see the mayhem and carnage happening to their fellow man. So, when the bad news is scarce, potentially bad stories must be exaggerated to make them sound as if, from that one, minor incident, a chain of events might have been set into motion that could, one day, destroyed the world as we know it.

James smiled at the ridiculous report as he unbuttoned his pants. If he had made the news, what would they've said about his little incident tonight?

"Local author James Madison was arrested on drunk driving charges this evening after narrowly avoiding a collision with a bus full of nuns on their way to cure sick lepers at a nearby children's orphanage," James imagined the anchor's telling of the story.

"This just in," the news man continued in his serious tone.

James slipped one leg out of his pants and then the other.

"We are receiving word that Parker Veracini, renowned writer and columnist for the New York World Journal was found dead at his vacation home in Cannon Massachusetts earlier this evening."

James ceased his undressing and holding his pants in one hand, listened intently to the previously disregarded news man.

"Police aren't releasing any details about his death at this time but we are being told that Mr. Veracini's mother had discovered the body and that homicide has not yet been ruled out."

"Oh isn't that just horrible?" a voice spoke from the desk to James' back.

James spun around to find the book lying face up on the desk.

"What the hell?" he yelped as he stumbled backwards.

"Well it's nice to see you again too, Mr. Madison. Can you believe it? Found by his poor mother. We hadn't thought of that angle."

"What?"

"James, you look a bit tense. Are you alright? Do you need another drink?" the book teased.

"You're not real," James mumbled.

"Are we going to go through this again? I'm real, you're real. I'm the only one who cares about you. I'm here to help, yada-yada-yada," William droned.

"No, you're a hallucination, brought on by the lingering effects of too much scotch."

"Well, you look sober to me, so I don't think that's the best explanation."

"The police took you. You're at the station right now."

"In a big, plastic, evidence bag, right? Yes, well I don't care much for humidity and I was getting a bit of a crick in my spine so I thought I'd stop back here and see how you were doing. Maybe we can write a few more tales together. The other ones went so well."

"Other ones?" James asked.

"Sure. Don't you remember? Of course you remember Parker."

James glanced at the television. The news anchors were really drawing this report out. Now they were rehashing the story about Mr. Veracini's wife and the fatal hit and run which had claimed her and her unborn child's life only a few, short months ago.

"What about Francesco? Surely you remember Francesco. If you ask me, that story was a work of sheer genius. Your best piece to date."

"What do you mean Francesco? That was just a story. That wasn't real," James attempted to convince himself.

"Like Mr. Veracini there? I suppose that's not real either," William taunted.

James looked at the television again. "Coincidence."

"Coincidence? Well, I guess we'll see how much of a coincidence it is when the police read the story about Francesco and then find his mutilated remains exactly as you described them."

"What?"

"Come here James. I want to show you something," the book spoke as it slowly opened to reveal page after page of hand written scribble.

James approached the book, watching as each page slowly turned.

"What? What is this supposed to be?"

"These are your tales, your stories; the evidence that will see you hanged my friend."

"Bullshit. That looks nothing like my writing."

"Well, you were a bit drunk at the time," William explained as the words began shifting on the page, straightening into neat rows and legible letters. "Is that better?"

James stood stunned. The writing on the page was now identical to the dozens of first drafts he kept in the bottom drawer of the desk. The book wasn't joking. The police could easily match the writing.

"Oh, and I almost forgot," William spoke proudly as the page turned again.

On the last page of Francesco's story, about half way down in large looping letters, was signed...

James Madison

It was true. Everything the book had told him earlier that evening was coming back to him. He had signed it and the book had made his words a reality. As impossible as it sounded, there was no denying the report on the news. He was sure Parker had died the very way he'd described and when the police finally pieced together the clues about the apparent bodies at Francesco's house, they'd surely come asking about Parker's death as well. His life was over.

"It will be all right," William sensed the tension in his author. "With my help, we can keep you out of jail. We can stop them from sending you to the gallows. Hell, together we could destroy all who stand in our way. What do you say old friend? Shall we get started?"

The familiar quill appeared just below James's signature. James stared at the pen, contemplating the offer.

"You and me, James. No one can touch us."

"No," James mumbled.

"Excuse me?"

"I said no."

"I don't think you've thought this one through James. You don't exactly have a choice here. If you want to remain a free man you will have to write your own survival. Those who oppose you will have to be eliminated. So I ask again. Are you with me?"

"Fuck you," James spat at the book as he lifted his head in his first real moment of clarity since taking that first, influential drink hours ago.

"That is not the answer I hoped to hear Mr. Madison. Let me tell you-"

"No, let me tell you," James confidently interrupted.

"I'm taking back my life. No more complaints. No more woe is me."

"Well that's good to hear my boy but--"

"Shut up," James commanded.

William obeyed.

"No more self pity and most importantly, no more talking books."

Hoisting the book into the air James flung it into the nearby fireplace.

"You have no idea what you have just done. I offered you the world," the book began rambling in a hostile tone.

James ignored William's threats as he circled the desk and retrieved a small remote from the top drawer.

"It's not that easy James."

"I'll show you just how easy it is," James firmly addressed the discarded book as he pushed a button and watched as the gas fireplace sprang to life

The book remained silent as its paper body quickly succumbed to the hungry flames. Not even a scream or plea for mercy escaped the brick enclosure; only the satisfying crackle of the fire as it graciously consumed its provided meal.

FIFTY-TWO

With the horrific images of Francesco's body and that of his shish kabobed date seared into her mind's eye, Rebecca flung open the Cadillac's door and frantically dove inside, eager to escape from the place to which she'd before been so fervent to arrive.

Fumbling with her purse, Rebecca dug for her keys. Never before had she witnessed a sight so ghastly as to invoke an unwilling urge to vomit but on that hill she'd done just that...twice...before frantically retreating from the horrific scene.

Stumbling down the rocky terrain she'd remarkably managed to avoid breaking her ankles, though the same could not be said for the heels of her Louboutins . She was only glad that she hadn't needed to rescale the massive wall to free herself from the blood tarnished property. Thankfully, more concerned with intruders getting onto the property than keeping visitors from getting out, Francesco had installed a manual over ride button just inside the gated entrance that had allowed her, with the simple touch of a button, to flee from her gruesome discovery and back toward the perceived safety of her vehicle.

Hearing the jingle of metal as her fingers rooted around the bottom of the bag, Rebecca let out a sigh and, retrieving the cluttered ring of keys, started the car.

"Hello Rebecca."

Startled by the sudden, unexpected voice, Rebecca jumped, swinging her frantic gaze in the direction of the self-announced company. Even more shocking than the mysterious voice however, was that, where she'd expected to find the person responsible for the nearby crime scene, there rested a book instead.

Rebecca stared at the unfamiliar book, puzzled by its presence in the passenger seat beside her and then began scanning the outer perimeter of the car, looking for the prankster responsible for this humorless joke.

The night seemed quiet. She hadn't seen or heard anybody else out there with her, though the lifeless bodies above seemed to suggest otherwise.

Confident that no one else currently shared her nearby surroundings, she returned her attention to the book.

"Mrs. Madison, we need to talk."

FIFTY-THREE

He *had* thought that the experience of being arrested, processed and locked away in the county jail for half of the night had done a fairly decent job of sobering his system but as he stood before the fireplace, watching the final scrap of the psychotic book's cover shrivel into an unrecognizable, blackened mass of ash, he began to reconsider the normalcy of his condition. He *had* had a lot to drink. He must still be drunk. That was the only logical explanation for his continued belief in the existence of a talking book. Not crazy, just drunk. Nothing that a little sleep couldn't fix.

Opting to leave the fireplace burning, just in case, James plucked the sheep skin blanket from the back of the couch and with a relaxed sigh, lower his body onto the pillowy, suede furnishing.

This was going to be a record, he thought, as he considered the time it would take for sleep to arrive; come to whisk him off to a land of care free make-believe. It was a land in which dreams of talking books and cold jail cells were just that...dreams; a land in which reality gave way to the control of his mind and not a bottle of scotch; a land from which he knew he would return by morning, rejuvenated, refreshed and eager to put the past twenty-four hours behind him.

The crashing of glass somewhere downstairs however caused his eyes to spring open, chasing away the harbinger of clouds and slumber time fantasies.

James sat up, listening for further indication that his sought after R.E.M. state had not been the cause of the unexplainable noise.

The house remained quiet, except for the crackling of the fireplace as it continued to consume the remains of its recent meal. Reaching for the remote, James silence the satisfied flames and continued to listen as he thought he heard footsteps slowly making their way up the stairs.

"Two o'clock?" he read the display of the nearby alarm clock.

What the hell is she doing coming home at two in the morning? If Rebecca was out at two in the morning, as opposed to being comfortably asleep in her own king size bed, there were only two possible explanations: one, she was currently enjoying yet another ride on an unexplored piece of man meat or; two, she'd just completed her ride and was fast asleep in whatever loser's bed she'd seduced her way into. Either way she was hardly the type to drag herself back out, into the night, just so she could return home to share a house with a man she clearly despised.

Moving toward the door James listened even closer as the footsteps made their way to the upper landing and then paused, as if the intruder were attempting to decide which direction offered the most profitable merchandise. With only a couple of rooms to the right and five to the left the decision was apparently an easy one.

If this was a thief though, he sure wasn't trying very hard to mask his presence. With the blatant smashing of what James assumed was a window to gain entry and the nonchalant manor in which the burglar was marching about the house, it almost seemed as if he assumed that no one was home; an understandable assumption given that both vehicles were currently either on missions of infidelity or being held for ransom by the city impound yard.

Utilizing whatever trace remainder of alcohol still coursed through his veins, along with a strong desire to not be made a victim, James repressed his fear, returned to his desk and withdrew the gun he had earlier pulled when faced with the presence of the mouthy book.

Seeming to take forever in their journey, James continued to listen to the approaching footsteps while at the same time picking up on another, stranger set of noises accompanying the intruder's casual stride. With each strike of the man's shoe against the hall floor, he'd have sworn that he also heard a set of accompanying clicks, as well as a heavier than usual breathing pattern. He didn't have much time to analyze the curious, audible accompaniments though as the noises ceased with the stranger's stalled progress just outside the office door.

James's heart raced. He'd never shot a man before, only cardboard cutouts made up to look like men. Over the years he'd touted himself as an expert marksmen but now, he was unsure if he could actually bring himself to pull the trigger in a time when his acquired skills were needed most.

As James contemplated his ability to take a life, the brass doorknob began to jiggle. The intruder was clearly outside the door.

With surprisingly little thought, James grabbed hold of the rattling knob and yanked the door open, hoping to catch the intruder off guard and unprepared to defend himself but as he swung the gun into the hall, only darkness greeted the weapon.

Scanning the hall back and forth James began to regret his snap decision, expecting a bullet to explore the inner recesses of his skull at any moment but the hall remained silent. No gunshot broke the silence and no retreating footsteps signaled the intruder's sudden departure. The man, for all practical purposes, had vanished.

Stunned by the intruder's peculiar absence, James stepped out further from the safety of his office and listened again for the distinct, telltale footsteps of the felon's presence.

The house remained silent.

"Rebecca?" he nervously called out, sure his violent opening of the door had already given his position away to whomever shared his surroundings.

As if in response to his call, a long, drawn out scraping noise suddenly consumed the stairwell, joined by the sounds of shattering glass and tearing paper.

Again, acting on instinct over logic, James rushed to the top of the stairs, ready, he hoped, to open fire but again found only darkness awaiting him.

The stair treads were littered with bits of shattered glass and busted family portraits, once proudly displayed along the descending wall but now replaced by a faintly lit trail of three, long gashes in the wallpapered drywall.

Cautiously scanning the foyer below, James began a slow descent, running his left hand along the path of destruction while his right dutifully maintained the gun's drawn and ready posture.

Taking a closer look at the marks in the wall, James began to wonder just what this guy could have possibly brought with him as his weapon of choice. The gouges were far too thick to have been made by a set of razors or knives, besides, a blade wouldn't have left behind such a jagged and uneven mark. Nor would it have made the cracking and crumbling noises James had rushed to investigate. No, these marks looked more like those of a garden cultivator than finely sharpened cutlery. In fact he was almost positive that, if he went out to the shed and retrieved the small, forked gardening tool, its prongs would probably line up perfectly with the newly created markings.

Figuring out the exact identity of the intruder's weapon

however, was the least of his worries. With how quickly the man moved, James figured that he could've entered the house with nothing more than a dull pencil and still have been just as lethal.

A breaking dish drew James's attention toward the kitchen as he reached the bottom of the stairs. Though numerous routes existed, which would lead him to the intruder's newly declared whereabouts, James wasted no time in deciding and almost immediately turned left. This guy was fast and he couldn't afford to take the long way around.

Slipping around the corner, into the family room, James ducked behind the end of the large entertainment center, peeking out twice before quickly maneuvering himself toward the center of the room and into a squatting position behind the leather sofa.

Resting his now trembling hands on the back of the two-piece sectional, he painted the kitchen's arched doorway with the muzzle of the gun. Since the kitchen resided at the back of the house it didn't bear the influence of the street lights outside and therefore remained almost entirely dark. It's only source of illumination was that of the soft blue glow generated by the clocks on both the microwave and the stove but neither were strong enough for James to discern between what could've been either a room full of shadowy furniture or very possibly a whole team of awaiting assailants. Either way, he had to make a move. Even if the shadowy figures were to suddenly spring to life, what was he to do, remain cowering behind the couch all night, waiting for the stranger to finally get bored and open fire? Though he'd carefully concealed much of his body behind the large sofa, he was sure that the plush furnishing would do little to slow an irate bullet, let alone stop it.

With reckless abandon, James jumped up from his hideout and charged the awaiting shadows, ready to fire at the first one to show any signs of movement but all remained still and James quickly found himself standing in the middle of a room with numerous hiding spots and multiple entrances. He felt like a sitting duck in the open and quickly ducked between the island and the refrigerator, limiting the intruder's possible lines of sight.

Now what? James thought to himself. He had no idea where the man had gone. At this point he could've ducked into another room and easily been following James' hasty advance throughout the house. He could appear at any minute from the direction in which James himself had just come.

James turned back toward the family room, the glow of the streetlights aiding in his confirmation as to the room's abandoned status.

His heart was racing faster than he'd ever felt it before. Either the blood pumping machine was preparing to burst from the confines of his chest or he was rapidly nearing the threshold between common fear and a massive coronary.

Closing his eyes for a moment James took a deep breath, attempting to slow his adrenaline's frenetic influence over his body but as the stranger had already proven, he was in control of the situation. As the sound of the kitchen's only outside access loudly slammed shut, James jumped to his feet, shocked that the man had been able to slip back into the room and, only ten feet away, exit the house.

James rushed around the island, his heartbeat keeping pace with his rapid footsteps. Reaching for the door knob James reconsidered his haste. Maybe the man had only slammed the door to throw his pursuer off guard. Maybe the man was waiting from a position to James's rear, preparing to sink whatever weapon he'd used in the stairwell into the persistent homeowner's head. Either way James' best bet was to get out of the house. In the house his options for escape were limited and hiding places for the intruder plentiful. Outside he stood a better chance of getting the man into the open and maybe getting a shot off before he could duck around a corner and into another game of hide-and-seek.

Before James knew it, he was standing on the walkway, which connected the driveway to the side of the house and staring back at the doorway through which he'd just passed but had little recollection of doing so.

Movement in the corner of his vision quickly shifted his attention from the kitchen door, toward the rear of the house, where he could have sworn that he'd seen something swiftly slip around the corner and into the backyard.

James contemplated heading in the opposite direction, going back inside to call the police or running to a neighbor's house to do the same but after his less than pleasant experience with the law that evening, he preferred to continue his pursuit and handle this matter with his own form of justice.

Previously unsure whether he'd be able to open fire on another human being or not, he was beginning to actually take some pleasure in the thought. This person had violated his home. The son-of-a-bitch had taken it upon himself to enter another person's house and for what? The man's carelessness suggested the home invasion skills of an amateur at best. He wasn't there to clean the house out. He probably only wanted a few pieces of jewelry and any money he could find laying around; crap that he could pawn to supply him with enough cash to get him through his next meth fix or crack or whatever addiction was probably driving his actions.

The thought that the man was probably a coke head or a meth addict both calmed and worried James even more. If he was lucky, the moron would be so strung out that his reaction time would be slowed, placing James one up on his competition. On the other hand, the intruder had already demonstrated lightning fast speed and stealthy maneuverability, not to mention the brutal strength it would have taken to create such destruction over nearly ten feet of drywall. If this man was a drug addict, out for the means to his next fix, he most likely had not yet come down from his current bender and was probably operating under the complete control of the manipulative drug.

Peeking around the corner, James reconsidered his quick dismissal of police assistance but scanning the deserted yard he noticed the door to the shed open ever so slightly. With a six foot, wooden fence surrounding the property and no exposed cross members to propel himself up and over, it was possible that the man had just ducked into the shed in hopes of hiding out until his pursuer tired of the chase and returned to the house to call the cops. At that point he'd probably emerge from his hideout, slipping away unnoticed and unpunished for his unlawful actions. No, James wasn't about to let that happen.

Scanning the yard one last time James darted across the freshly mowed grass and, careful not to bump the shed, took up position on the windowless side of the small structure. Thinking about his planned attack, James contemplated whether he should order the guy to toss out his weapon and reveal himself or just kick door in and open fire. With the amount of metal and gasoline stored in the shed though, logic told him that the first of the two was the more intelligent approach to the situation. He could easily open fire and only wind up hitting himself with an unlucky ricochet or even worse, blow himself to bits as the bullet tore through one of the small, fuel filled containers.

Remaining true to his already irrational behavior however, James spun around the corner and kicked the door inward, ready to fire but stopped as the violently swinging door struck the rack of tools suspended on the abutting wall, causing the mass of landscaping equipment to slip from its brackets and plummet to the floor with a series of loud bangs and crashes. Startled by his recklessly created destruction, James leapt back, out of the way of the falling tools and into the yard.

His off balance retreat and the uneven surface probably would have sent him flailing to the ground if it hadn't been for the bulky, upright obstruction which had prevented his fall.

A low growl emanated behind him as James froze in place, still staring at the heap of tools as the last garden trowel leapt onto the pile. A warm breath beat against his exposed back, its downward flow suggesting its creator's lofty height and powerful lungs.

Unsure of exactly who or what was standing behind him, James slowly tightened his grip on the gun but as he spun around to take the shot, he was met with the powerful blow of a large, leathery fist to the face. Knocked completely off balance, James stumbled back, striking the side of the shed with a loud crack and falling to the ground, dazed by the unexpected blow.

As the world slowed its battery induced rotation and James rediscovered the still functioning motor skills in his neck, he lifted his vision toward his assailant and as he did, became filled with joy at the realization that he'd somehow managed to maintain his grip on the firearm; not for the purpose of shooting the mammoth beast before him but for use in extinguishing his own life before his repulsive assailant could get the chance to.

Standing before him, erect but with a slight hunch, was the hairy, baboon like creature he'd created for the brutal assassination of Francesco Savaree earlier that evening. He couldn't explain how it had come to be that the fictitious creature was now standing before him but there was no denying what he saw. Everything he had described in his story was clearly present on the creature, from its massive hands with protruding, dagger like claws, to the burning hatred permeating from its deeply recessed eyes. He knew there was no way to kill the abomination. He'd created it to take down a man twice his size.

Placing the gun to his temple, James closed his eyes.

"Forgive me Lord."

The gun let out a quiet click, causing James's eyes to burst open...just in time to witness the demonic beast release a deafening yowl toward the heavens, before pouncing on its prey.

FIFTY-FOUR

Signing her name to the bottom of the page, Rebecca let out a small chuckle. She'd never felt so good in her life. The abusive treatment she'd recently unleashed on James's psyche paled in comparison to the joy she found in conjuring the man's fictional death.

Outside of book reports and research papers from her educational past, she'd never before sat down and written anything of substance in her life. She'd always thought it a difficult task and had always looked on in wonder as James gave life to character after character in one story after another but now, now she began to wonder what the big deal was. Pick up the pen and just write. The book had been right.

Though she would never admit her temporary mental breakdown to anyone else, for some reason, at that moment, a talking book made perfect sense. She was sure that the voice was only that of a very vocal inner dialogue, brought on by her all too recent encounter with the horrific corpse still watching over her from the hill above but at that moment, she didn't care. Whatever the cause of the phantom voice, there was no denying that it had been right. James had killed Francesco. It had to be true.

He'd said so himself that he'd been on his way over to the man's house earlier that evening and then, had never returned home from his drunken expedition.

She wasn't sure how such a minuscule man like James could manage to take down such a perfect physical specimen such as Francesco but he had and he'd done so in the most brutal way imaginable.

Yes, it was definitely him. The man's relocated genitalia...Rebecca shuddered at the thought...had not been a product of drunken rage. It had been a clear sign. Francesco had intruded on the sacred bonds of marriage so James had attacked the very tool used in such an intrusion.

Closing the book, Rebecca returned it to the seat beside her, contemplating what she should do next. She couldn't just go home. While she had enjoyed creating the story immensely, she had no faith in the voice's claim that anything she wrote would instantaneously "come to pass" as the book had put it. Most likely James was sitting at home at that very moment, awaiting his wife's return so that she too could pay for her sins. She definitely could not go home. However, she couldn't necessarily go to the police either. What was she going to say, that she just broke into her ex-lovers house and found his body and that of his tramp bed buddy. They'd think she did it.

"Just another scorned lover enacting revenge on the man who'd betrayed her," is what the prosecutor would say and the jury would believe it. Hell, there had been dozens of witnesses who could testify to her angry outburst at the restaurant that evening.

The police were definitely out of the question. She had to get away. She had to go somewhere else, at least for the night while she contemplated just how she was going to handle this delicate situation.

"Ma'am," a muffled voice called out beside her, followed by two, quick taps against the driver's side window.

Startled, Rebecca turned toward the unexpected voice to find a police officer standing beside the car. Raising her hand, she attempted to shield her eyes from the intrusive beam of light as the officer examined her face and then the contents of her vehicle.

"Ma'am, could you roll down your window please?"

Rebecca complied and with the touch of a button watched the glass shield between them slowly retreat into the door.

"Good evening miss. May I ask what you're doing here tonight?"

"What do you mean?" Rebecca stalled, not quite sure what she should say.

"Well, for starters, let's talk about why your car is parked on the grass and not the street where it belongs?"

"You know officer that's a really funny story. You see-_"

"Why don't you tell him," William chimed in for the first time since enticing her to write the story.

"Shut up," she responded, turning to the book.

"Excuse me," the officer reacted with surprise.

"Oh, no, not you officer. I would never tell you to shut up."

"Ok, then how about that explanation."

"The explanation...yeah," she continued to stall, giving him the quick once over.

Though not usually attracted to heavier set men, she was surprised to find that the patiently waiting officer wasn't all that unattractive. He was no Francesco but he was definitely a huge step up from James. She contemplated avoiding the explanation all together, in exchange for a quick sexual favor or two in the backseat of his cruiser but quickly talked herself out of it as he returned the light to her face.

"Today ma'am,"

"Ok, I'm not going to lie to you officer."

"Well, I appreciate that."

She couldn't believe what she was about to do but what else was there? She couldn't just feed him some bullshit story and then just drive off like nothing had happened. Sooner or later someone would find the bodies. He'd most likely already run her plates and reported her presence at the scene. Once she was found, there would be no way to deny the crime. The truth was her only way out, no matter how risky.

"You see officer; I had to pull my car up to the wall here..." She motioned toward the wall, "...so that I could climb over it."

"So you broke into this house?" the officer responded, surprised by the woman's honesty.

"No...well...not exactly. I had to talk with someone," Rebecca further explained.

"So you know Mr. Savaree?" the officer asked.

"I'm his girlfriend...well...ex-girlfriend I guess."

"So you're telling me that you drove all the way up here, in the middle of the night and broke into your ex-boyfriend's house just so you two could talk?"

"That's right. I know it sounds a bit weird.

"Just a bit," the officer agreed. "So what did you guys talk about?"

"That's just it. When I got here he was dead."

"Get out of the car miss," the officer ordered as he took a step back and drew his gun.

"What?"

"Get out of the car with your hand up, now," he commanded for a second time.

"No you don't understand. I didn't--"

"Now!" the officer barked.

"Oh, oh," William mocked.

Rebecca turned to the book with a sneer as she reached for the handle and opened the door.

"Nice and slow," the officer spoke nervously.

As Rebecca stepped out into the cool night air she was puzzled by the officers widening eyes as he glanced down at her hand.   Suddenly she noticed a definite weight difference between her right hand and her left.

"Drop it now!" the officer shouted.

Following his gaze, Rebecca looked down at her right hand, shocked to find a shiny, revolver clenched tightly in her grasp.

"No," she addressed the spooked officer in shock as she lifted her hands in a calming manner but before she could even get her hands above her waist, two rounds erupted from the officer's weapon, passing through her mid torso and punching two holes in the leather upholstery to either side of the book.

Dropping the gun, Rebecca stared in shock at her wounds as her lacy, white blouse slowly forfeited its innocent hue.

"Suspect down.   I need an ambulance out here immediately," the officer shouted into his radio.

She wanted to ask the officer "why" but even as the words began to form in her mind the light from the moon overhead slowly began to fade.

Leaning against the car for support, Rebecca slumped to the ground.

FIFTY-FIVE

"Give it," Joseph wined as he reached for the Nintendo DS currently under his brother's hoarding command.

"No, It's still my turn," Bobby insisted.

"It is not. You died already. Now it's my turn to play."

Peter watched from the back seat of the minivan as his two, younger cousins went at each other over the silly handheld device. Uncle Mike and Aunt Mary sat in the front seats, never once turning their heads to survey the conflict and only occasionally issuing a "Come on you two," in a poor attempt at defusing the escalating situation.

Emily sat beside her older brother, either oblivious to the conflict taking place or too intent on sharing her dolls with their youngest cousin, Sarah, who was only six month older than her.

"It's my turn," Joseph grabbed hold of the game only to have his hand swatted away by his brother. "Ouch!"

"It's your turn when I'm done," Bobby explained in a condescending tone.

"Oh yeah and when will that be?"

"I don't know, how long do the batteries last?"

"Asshole," Joseph responded, obviously aware that he'd just managed to cross the seemingly invisible line as his and his brother's eyes widened and Sarah looked up from the dolls.

Before Joseph could even manage to form an apology, Aunt Mary was already turned, glaring at both of her sons.

"We don't use that kind of language. You hear me?" she blasted her children.

It's about time, Peter thought to himself but, based on his aunt's expression, dared not speak.

"I don't know what's wrong with you boys that you can't manage to get along for one simple car ride but I am getting sick and tired of your behavior...both of you. And if you two don't shape up we're...we're... Your father is going to stop the car right here and you two can walk the rest of the way."

"Oh no, a whole two blocks," Bobby whispered loudly as he gave his brother a nudge.

Joseph new better than to smile, laugh or show any reaction at all to the humor of his brother's poorly timed joke. Bobby quickly understood his brother's silence as he returned his attention to the beet red face glaring back at him from the front seat.

"Turn the game off," she ordered.

"But mom it's my turn," Joseph whined again.

The glare shifted to him.

He returned to silence.

"Better yet, I think its Peter's turn. Why don't you let him have a try?" Aunt Mary glanced in her nephew's direction. "Peter, do you want a turn?"

"Ah...no thank you, Aunt Mary," Peter responded, not interested in taking any part, other than as an observer of the chaotic situation.

"How about you girls, do you want to play?"

"Mom, they can't play, they'll break it," Joseph interjected.

"Yeah and they're girls," Bobby added.

"No thank you," both girls spoke up, their attention having already returned to the dolls.

"Thank you very much though, Aunt Mary," Emily sugar coated her response.

Peter had the feeling that his little sister knew exactly what she was doing. Intrigued by her strategically formed response, he glanced in the girl's direction, eager to read the expression on her face but never once did she look up to admire the effects of her excessive politeness. Like a pro, she continued to play.

Peter smiled.

"Why can't you two be more like your sister and cousins?" Aunt Mary questioned her sons.

"What, gay?" Bobby whispered again, apparently having not learned from his last bad joke.

"We're going to have a little talk after we drop your cousins off," Aunt Mary issued her own, loud whisper in Bobby's direction.

"Ooh, you're in trouble," Joseph taunted his brother.

"Don't get too cocky young man," she turned her attention on her other son. "You'll be there too."

Both kids fell silent and Aunt Mary returned her sight to the road ahead. Uncle Mike remained silent throughout the conflict, which didn't surprise Peter. Aunt Mary had always been the disciplinarian of the family. Uncle Mike had established himself as the fun parent. He always wanted to be involved in whatever his kids were doing and at times even got into a bit of trouble himself but no matter how much or how often he got scolded by the true head of the household, he never changed.

Peter loved Uncle Mike for this reason. If there were ever to be a definition created for what constitutes a "fun uncle", Uncle Mike would be the best candidate for the illustrative photo to go along side it.

As if unaware of the battle that had just taken place beside him, Uncle Mike casually turned on his blinker and slowly made the turn onto Peter and Emily's street. He apparently didn't want to draw any attention to himself from his other half, so he maintained a steady speed along the road, avoiding drawing his wife's typical, nagging complaint that he was driving too fast. It also helped his speed that a garbage truck was currently making its rounds through the neighborhood.

Slowing as he approached the truck, Uncle Mike peeked around the large vehicle before slowly passing, waving at the garbage-man as he emptied the contents of a trash can into the truck's open back end. The sanitation worker nodded and they continued on their way.

Peter couldn't wait to get home. Between his cousins' incessant fighting and his Aunt's apparent, pent up hostility, he just wanted to return to life as part of a normal, down to earth family.

Besides his desire to escape the madness of his relatives, he couldn't wait to talk to his father. He'd spent most of the night thinking about the strange book and, while everything he'd learned in his first fifteen years of life spoke against the possibility of such a book, he couldn't help but feel that maybe there was some truth to what he'd read in that disturbing, online article. Maybe the soul of William Grave did posses the aged piece of literature. Maybe it did harbor not only the ability to deliver death to all who possess it but the desire to do so as well. Whatever the book was or wherever it had come from, all Peter cared about now was that his father get rid of it, before something bad could happen.

"Oh my god," aunt Mary suddenly mumbled from the front seat.

Peter looked up.

Three marked police cruisers and two unmarked vehicles occupied and blocked the driveway to their house, their uniformed drivers and passengers pacing back and forth across the yard and in and out of the house, while another man diligently applied a barrier of crime scene tape around a fence post, connecting it to the mailbox and then to the lamp post on the front corner of the lawn.

Aware that whatever had happened could not be good,

Peter felt his heart sink and as he turned to his sister he watched as a single tear, slowly traverse the young girl's delicate face.

*****

"Did you see that, Chuck?" Larry asked as he climbed back into the passenger side of the garbage truck.

"See what?" Chuck responded, having no clue as to what his partner was referring to.

"There are still some good people in the world, despite what you apparently think," Larry continued the conversation in which they had earlier been involved.

"What are you talking about?" Chuck asked confused as he put the truck in gear and continued forward, past the string of houses who had neglected to place their trash out for pickup.

"That guy in the minivan. I don't know him. In fact, I don't think I've ever even seen him in this neighborhood before."

"And?" Chuck remained confused.

"And, even though I don't know him he still has enough kindness in his heart to smile and wave at a complete stranger.

"Maybe he likes you."

"Well, maybe he does," Larry played along with the homosexual insinuation. "Either way, he's still a kind and polite person; you know, one of those so called mythical creatures you say no longer exists."

"Just because someone waives at you doesn't make them a good person."

"Oh yeah, then what does?"

"Maybe he just had a muscle spasm," Chuck answered, avoiding the question.

"Muscle spasm," Larry quietly repeated with disgust at his friend's constant negativity.

"Oh look, maybe you two can hook up," Chuck

indicated as he watched the minivan slow to a stop at one of the houses on their route.

"Oh my god," Larry spoke as he looked up and took notice of the apparent crime scene ahead. "What the hell happened?"

They both watched as the Caravan's passengers poured out onto the sidewalk, apparently also stunned by the unexpected scene before them.

"Oh I hope they don't live there," Larry spoke as he watched the people get out of the van and slowly make their way toward the house, only to get intercepted by a plain clothed officer.

"No, they don't live there. Everybody gets out of their cars and wanders onto a crime scene when they just happen to stumble across one. The cops love shit like that," Chuck responded in a patronizing tone.

"I hope everyone's all right," Larry ignored his partner's comment as Chuck slowed the truck in front of the neighboring house.

Hopping from the cab, Larry retrieved the two large cans at the end of the driveway and deposited their contents into the back of the truck before walking to retrieve the can sitting in front of the police occupied dwelling.

Chuck continued to watch the police activity as he slowly rolled forward, following his partner up the street and watching as Larry lifted the lid from the lone container and tossed it onto the ground. But instead of lifting the can up and depositing its contents into the truck, Larry suddenly waived for his partner to join him in examining whatever it was that had captured his attention.

"What the hell," Chuck huffed as he set the truck in park and hopped down from the cab. "This better be good," he warned as he approached his trash fixated friend. "This street is my turn to drive and your turn to toss. I don't like getting out of the truck when I don't have to," he continued to complain as he joined Larry beside the can. "What?"

Larry didn't say a word. He just continued to stare at the open can.

Looking into the can as well, Chuck was less than impressed by what he saw. It was filled with the same black trash bags as the hundreds of other cans they'd already picked up that morning. The only thing that made this one any different was the large, old book resting on top of the pile.

"Congratulations. You found a book. Now all you have to do is learn to read."

"But look at it. Have you ever seen a book like that before?" Larry questioned, still fascinated by the can's peculiar inhabitant.

"Two covers, some paper in-between...yep that's a strange one all right. Quit wasting time and toss it in the back."

"No!" a woman's cry grabbed both men's attention.

Larry looked up from the can and Chuck again turned toward the house. Both watched as the woman from the minivan fell to her knees, her husband standing beside her with his hand on her back. Three of the children stood frozen, apparently stunned or not understanding the news they'd just received. The oldest of the boys quickly wiped his eyes before proceeding to comfort what appeared to be his sister as she threw herself around his leg and buried her face in his hip.

"Excuse me," one of the officers called out from the front porch.

Chuck and Larry turned to see a uniformed man making his way across the front lawn.

"Yeah, guys. I'm sorry but you're going to have to leave this one here. There was a bit of an accident last night and this can might contain some evidence," the officer explained as he approached the two men.

"Oh, no problem officer. Sorry," Larry issued an apology.

"Since when do 'accidents' involve the trash?" Chuck quietly mumbled.

The officer just glanced at Chuck and then returned his focus to Larry's apology.

"Thanks a lot for your cooperation guys. Have a nice day," he spoke as he removed a roll of crime scene tape from his belt and began including the can in the investigation.

"Oh, no problem officer. Is there anything I can do to help, maybe suck your dick or something?" Chuck mocked his friend's politeness as the two made their way back to the truck.

"Screw you man. Something bad apparently happened and the police have enough to deal with without us getting in their way."

"They're just wasting their time. I can already tell you what happened?"

"Oh yeah, go ahead Sherlock."

"Ok, the wife comes home from work last night, finds her husband in bed with some bimbo half her age and twice as attractive. She loses it, retrieves the butcher knife from the kitchen and hacks the prick and his ho to bits."

"Nice."

"Then, seeing that she's just gotten blood all over her five thousand dollar dress, she decides that she just can't go on anymore and turns the knife on herself. She probably hid the bodies in the bottom of that trashcan."

"Before or after she killed herself over a ruined dress?"

"You know, I don't think I want your company in the cab anymore. Your negative attitude is a real downer," Chuck responded.

"My negative attitude?" Larry questioned surprised. "No problem. I'll ride on the back."

"Three more days until vacation," Chuck spoke aloud as he rounded the front of the truck and climbed inside. Checking the mirror he watched as Larry hopped up onto the truck.

"Chuck," a voice called from the other side of the cab.

Chuck turned, expecting to see Larry suddenly standing at the passenger side door but, glancing at the mirror again, he could see Larry still holding firmly onto the truck's side handle, waiting for the vehicle to pull away.

"Chuck," the voice whispered again.

Chuck glanced down at the passenger seat to find the book they'd just seen in the trash, now resting beside him. Letting out a sigh he looked over at the mirror again. "What, are you trying to get us both arrested?" he shouted toward the partially open passenger window.

"What?" Larry shouted back.

"Never mind," Chuck muttered as he glanced down at the book again. "You got such a hard-on for the thing you can have it."

Setting the truck in gear the engine roared as the massive vehicle pulled away.

"Not like the book killed anyone."

FOOK

Only once before had a pair of eyes been so beautiful. It had been six years, three months and eleven days since he remembered first staring into a set of eyes as breathtaking and mesmerizing as the sleepy pair into which he currently stared. Now that original pair was probably tightly shut in the other bedroom, having given up on their husband's timely return.

As another flash of lightening illuminated the powder-blue nursery, followed by yet another newborn startling boom, Bill rechecked his math as his son began to once again express his fear of the unknown taking place beyond his bedroom windows.

"Six years...three months...and...no...twelve days," Bill quietly corrected his previous calculation, recalling the leap year that he'd previously overlooked.

As if intrigued by the still new sound of his father's voice, little Oliver Nesbit temporarily ceased his terrified rant to shoot his father a puzzled look.

"You think Daddy's strange?" Bill questioned his son with a grin.

The perplexed look on Oliver's face deepened.

"Daddy's a silly one isn't he? Well, you just wait. You'll see how silly Daddy can be, because Daddy has no clue what he's doing. No, he doesn't."

Welcomed silence filled the room as the two just stared at one another, silently agreeing that neither one of them had any clue about what the future held, but at the same time seeming to believe that, no matter what, everything was going to be okay.

Another boom rattled the colorfully decorated room, replacing silence with the more familiar wails of the four day old in his arms.

"Yeah, I know. I've never been a big fan of this either," Bill continued to comfort his son. "I guess Florida's the wrong place for us both."

*****

"So where we going?"

Bill jumped at the sound of his wife's voice as he entered the dimly lit bedroom; the only source of illumination coming from the faint green glow of the indicator light on the baby monitor beside the bed.

"Huh?" he question, his temporary fear apparently inhibiting his ability to hear the question.

"Florida's not the place for you two. So, where are we moving?"

"I forgot about that thing," Bill smiled as he glanced at the monitor beside the bed.

"What else did you hear?"

"Besides a musical recital of the alphabet?...followed by a brief, yet informative synopsis of American history, capped off by our national anthem in what I can only describe as the worst Eddie Vedder impersonation I've ever heard...I didn't hear anything."

"You heard all that?", Bill grinned sheepishly as he made his way across the room, removing his t-shirt.

"You think he'll stay down this time?"

"If I can get even an hour of sleep before the next round, I can declare victory."

"I'll take the next one."

"No, it's my night. I'm gonna have to get used to this, so what good would it do to admit defeat on the very first night. Besides, I have no intention of showing such chivalry on your nights, so we don't need to be setting a precedent now."

"Fair enough," Jennifer welcomed her husband to bed with a kiss as he slowly slid under the covers beside her. "Maybe I can do something else to make your night a bit more enjoyable," she offered, her hand slowly tracing the faint outline of what used to be a solid six pack, now beginning to show signs of an eventual keg if diet and exercise continue to be omitted from their lives.

She hadn't married him for his looks but she couldn't complain. Though it embarrassed him to admit it, Bill had been a pageant child from the age of three when his mother had entered him in a local county fair pageant in Ohio. Having easily taken the title of Little Mister Hamilton County, Bill and his mother had been invited to take part in the state pageant a month later in which he'd once again come out on top and claimed the title of Little Mister Ohio. The only thing that had ended his domination of cuteness and stopped him from claiming the national title, was what his mother frequently recalled as "a breathtakingly impeccable, red headed, blue eyed bundle of sugar that must have been created by none other than God himself."

"Jonathan Mitchell Walker was his name," Mrs. Nesbit had often recalled whenever the conversation managed to wander down the path of her son's breathtaking good looks, which had been quite often. "It wasn't fair. That little thing was the most stunning creature I've ever laid eyes on," she'd continue, seeming to forget that her son was often in the room during such conversations.

Bill didn't mind though. He'd seen photos. He'd seen the miniature tuxedo that he'd worn when he'd claimed the state title, then once more when he'd suffered defeat at the hands of Little Mister Texas. He knew that his mother had been proud of him, even if he hadn't brought home the national trophy. Or, maybe she'd been proud of herself for creating such a breathtaking, human specimen. Either way, the thought of his mother and her silly, yet touching admiration for beauty always brought a smile to his face. She'd have been thrilled to see her new grandson. Though adopted and of no blood relation to her, Mrs. Nesbit would have surely thought young Oliver the most beautiful creature to ever grace God's earth.

Sensing his distraction as he showed no response to her hand stealthily slipping inside the waistband of his pajama pants, Jennifer paused in her seductive massage. "Are you okay?"

"What?" Bill reemerged from his memories to the realization of what was taking place just beneath the covers. "Yeah, yeah I'm fine."

"What were you thinking about?"

"Nothing...I mean...it was just my mother."

Quickly, Jennifer let go of her toy, withdrawing her hand from beneath the covers to a less erotic position on the pillow beside her head.

"No! Oh God no! That...that...well...that sounded horrible."

"No, this is good," Jennifer reversed her previous decision as she returned her hand to her husband's chest and once-again, began to caress her way south. "It's always good to learn new things about one another...even when it's disturbing. If thinking about your mother is what you need then who am I to judge," she continued, trying as hard as she could to hold back the grin, fighting to break free at the corners of her lips.

With each word Bill grew more at ease. Jennifer always did have a way of turning an awkward situation into a laughable moment.

As her fingertips again broke the loose seal posed by her husband's plaid pajama pants, she purred, "You know, I never told you this, but just as I'm about to finish I often think of my father and the sensual way he used to—"

"—Okay..." Bill quickly interjected, putting an abrupt end to his wife's sick sense of humor as he yanked her hand from his pants, his uncomfortable reaction finally drawing the laughter that had previously been dying to erupt from her quivering lips.

Having accomplished her goal, Jennifer attempted to rebottle the humor as she slid even closer to her squeamish husband, who's hand was now firmly planted over his eyes, a broad, tight lipped smile doing little to contain the uncomfortable chuckles pouring out of him. A sensual kiss quickly brought back the moment of passion and Bill's hand slowly slid away, returning that original set of breathtaking eyes to his field of vision.

Another loud boom seemed to throw itself at the roof as concern replaced love and drew both of their attention to the monitor. The speaker remained silent, the audible absence reaffirmed by the lack of flashing lights along the top of the tiny white receiver.

Both remained silent for a moment, listening for the faint sounds of a shifting child and the telltale signs of an impending cry. The monitor echoed their silence.

"That was a close one," Jennifer whispered as she continued her lip's migration to her husband's neck.

"I know. You almost had to get up."

"Me? What happened to getting used to this and not wanting to set a precedence?"

"You and I both know that women are the more nurturing of the sexes. I think it would be best if you handled the nightly duties from now on. You know, so I can get more rest."

"Oh, you think so, huh? Well, I was trying to see to it that neither of us got any slee—"

"What was that?" Bill again hit pause on the adult fun.

"What?" Listening for a moment. "I don't hear anything."

Bill continued to listen intently, sure that he'd heard something. Again the monitor confirmed silence in Oliver's room.

"Listen, I really want you right now, so you better quit delaying this and take care of business or I might just have to do it myself."

She knew how hollow that threat sounded. One of Bill's favorite things was to watch as she explored her femininity, usually bringing herself right to the brink of

371

climax before he'd jump in and claim responsibility for the eruption of pleasure exploding within.

Bill showed little interest in the erotic threat, however; a look of concern and intense concentration dominated his serious face as he continued to listen to the faint patter of raindrops striking the skylight overhead. "Are you sure we're doing the right thing?" he suddenly broke his long silence with a recently common question that confirmed she was on her own.

"I've told you a hundred times, yes. Besides, it's a little late now," Jennifer responded, trying to be as comforting as she could, knowing how worried Bill had been about his new role as a father, but at the same time a bit annoyed at the thought of having the same conversation yet again.

She loved children, she always had. The youngest in a family of eight kids, Jennifer thrived on family and the sounds of chaos and family interaction. Every job she'd had since the age of fifteen had involved some form of child care; from babysitting for the Johnsons back home in Jacksonville; to working in a daycare all through high school; right up to college where she obtained her masters in education at Florida State. There was no doubt in her mind that she was ready to be a mother. Bill on the other hand hadn't been so sure.

It wasn't that he didn't like children, but growing up an only child in a house where his father was often out of town on business and his mother a bit on the over protective side, he'd never really had what most would consider a typical childhood. He'd had very few friends since his mother had always thought the neighborhood youth far too corrupting for her little angel. The only interaction he'd ever really gotten as a child had come from relatives and family friends at least thirty years his senior; so it was understandable that he'd never really seen himself as a father, a fact which he'd been very forthcoming about as soon as they'd both realized the seriousness of their relationship. But, he loved his wife and knowing how much being a mother meant to her, the two had decided to try for a family almost as soon as they'd been married. Unfortunately, the Lord had formulated a different plan for them and after nearly a year of unsuccessful attempts, they'd sought out the help of Doctor Huller who'd informed them that children, at least in the traditional sense, would never be an option. For some reason, which they still struggled to understand, Jennifer's ovaries were incapable of producing eggs and, therefore; would never be able to produce the genetic material needed to generate life.

Understandably, they'd been devastated by the news; Jennifer from of the loss of her only real dream in life and Bill from having to watch the woman he loved suffer such devastating news. For the next year, either out of denial or just a stubborn refusal to accept what they both knew deep down to be the truth, they'd continued to try and a year later, they'd remained childless. That year of refusing to accept reality, however; hadn't been a complete loss. It had allowed them to grow closer to one another. It had acted as a form of therapy and somehow had made the thought of not having children, though not ideal, somehow okay. It was at that point that they'd began to consider adoption and eighteen months and one unwanted teen pregnancy later, Oliver had entered their lives.

"You're going to be a wonderful father," Jennifer continued to reassure her worried husband.

"But how do you know? I hardly knew my dad. For all intents and purposes I didn't have a father at all. What makes you think that I can take care of a child? How do you know that I won't leave Oliver in the backseat of the car instead on dropping him off at daycare on my way to work? How do you know that I won't back over him with the lawn mower one day?"

"Really?" Jennifer responded, caught a bit off guard by his gruesome examples of bad parenting.

"What if I—"

"—Listen, you're going to be a wonderful father. You know how I know? Because you're a wonderful, loving husband who's taken care of me every second of our relationship and Oliver is blessed to have someone like you to call his dad."

He was still terrified, but somehow hearing those words of loving encouragement was exactly what he needed. At that moment, convinced by Jennifer's reassurance, Bill really did believe that everything was going to be alright.

"Now, forget about being a father for a moment and think more about being my husband," Jennifer renewed her attempts to bring pleasure to what had become a very heavy moment by gracefully sliding her right leg across Bill's lower torso and coming to rest face to face in a straddled position on top of her husband's excited partner.

Forgetting all worries, at least for the moment, Bill reached up, grabbing the back of Jennifer's head, and pulled her in for a passionate kiss. Like gasoline on an open flame, the touch of Bill's lips caused an explosion in her loins as Jennifer began undulating against her desired playmate, undeterred by the pair of lace panties and thick pajama pants currently obstructing maximum pleasure. It was a barrier that stood little chance of keeping them apart and like second nature, within seconds Jennifer managed to free her partner from his cotton prison and slip him past the lacy guard standing watch outside the palace walls.

"Boom!" another thunderous crash exploded from the night sky.

"What was that?" Bill once again allowed himself to be removed from the moment of ecstasy.

"It's just thunder," Jennifer continued her undulating dance as she attempted to keep her husband's attention focused on the task at hand.

"No, I know I heard something this time," he insisted, removing Jennifer from his lap and sliding off the bed to his feet.

"What did you hear?" Jennifer, frustrated, watched as he fixed his pants and quickly made his way to the doorway, disappearing into the hall.

He wasn't sure what he'd heard but he knew that it wasn't just thunder. Driven by adrenaline, Bill made his way along the dark hallway, the absence of light doing little to prevent him from making his way toward his son's bedroom. The nursery door was shut, just as he'd left it, Oliver's name proudly displayed on the plaque created by Jennifer's oldest sister and given to them during the baby shower two weeks earlier.

Bill placed his ear to the door, fearful that his worried imagination had created the sound and that he was about to burst into his son's room unnecessarily. The room seemed quiet and then there was a faint thud.

"Bill, there's a noise in Oliver's room!" Jennifer cried from the bedroom.

That was all he needed to reaffirm his suspicions. Quickly, Bill burst through the door, no longer worried about waking his sleeping son. The room was just as he'd left it. The fluffy white clouds, painted across the bright blue walls, seemed to dance around the room as always; their soothing presence topped only by the abundance of stuffed animals innocently resting upon the shelf lined wall beside the dresser and changing table. At the far end of the room stood Oliver's crib, the very same crib in which he'd spent his first years of life, nearly thirty-six years earlier. In it rested the colorful, Loony-Tunes bumper they'd picked out to prevent young Oliver from hurting himself on the wooden rails. Above it dangled the matching, animated mobile to provide sleep inducing comfort, and beside it stood a man, dressed in black, who was leaning over the low rail with a stuffed bunny in hand, suffocating the young child who had been innocently trying to sleep.

"Hey!" Bill yelled as he charged his son's assailant, struggling to pull the man away from the crib.

Seemingly undeterred by his discovery, the man continued to hold the soft pink bunny over the child's face, struggling to stand his ground as the angry father delivered blow after blow to his ribs and head. In the meantime, beneath the large stuffed animal, the young child's little legs seemed to slow in their struggle, the lack of oxygen finally taking its toll on the infant's failing lungs.

Panicked by the noises she'd heard, Jennifer appeared in her son's doorway to find the strange man standing over her son and her husband doing all he could to free him from the stranger's murderous grip. She screamed.

The distraction of the blood curdling scream seemed to momentarily startle the mysterious assailant, allowing Bill to finally pull him away from the crib and knock him to the floor with a swift right hook. With the intruder temporarily separated from his son, Bill turned back to the crib but Oliver was gone. Only the plain white onesie he'd been wearing remained in his place.

Quickly the assailant got to his feet and scrambled for freedom, knocking Jennifer to the floor as he scurried toward the front door before Bill could even process the impossible disappearance of his son.

More concerned with her son's well being than the man who'd attacked him, Jennifer got to her feet and ran to her husband's side, baffled by the empty crib.

"Where is he?" she cried.

"I don't know! He was just here!"

Just then, the unmistakable sounds of a terrified infant echoed from across the house. Both Bill and Jennifer turned simultaneously and ran from the room, following the new, yet familiar cries of their son.

The end of the hall opened up into the large livingroom. The front door stood wide opened; the unwelcome visitor having apparently exited through it only moments earlier, and on the floor, in the center of the room, lay terrified little Oliver, naked but unharmed, screaming for the comfort of his horrified and bewildered parents.

"I'll call the police," Bill declared, frozen by confusion as Jennifer rushed to comfort their son.

Want more?

Visit:
AuthorBrianDrinkwater.com
for an extended preview and more

ABOUT THE AUTHOR

Brian Drinkwater is an American horror/suspense writer with a knack for mind bending stories of a darker nature. His first book, *Book of "The Grave"*, was released in 2013 with his follow up, *FOOK,* being release one year later.

Born in Southern California, but raised on Massachusetts' South Shore, Brian has been writing since he was a small child, often testing the boundaries of his school assignments by writing fictitious stories in place of daunting reports. He even invented an English poet his senior year of high-school in order to bypass the school's rule of 'no self written yearbook quotes'. Readers now know this poet as William Grave.

Though never a big reader, as odd as that may sound, Brian did grow up a fan of Dean Koontz, so it's no surprise that his writing style mimics that of the renowned author, with multiple storylines cohesively coming together by story's end. And with a knack for creating vivid characters with dynamic personalities, as a reader you'll find yourself rooting for, and sometimes against, the people who make up his imaginary world. But don't get too attached, because standard rules don't always apply, and not everyone makes it out alive.

Brian lives in Southwest Florida with his wife and son.